Knockout F

Hardcore Hardboiled

AND

Thuglit

"So good, it's almost dangerous."
—*Crimespree*

"So hard-boiled, the shell is still on."
—**bn.com**

"Solid . . . will appeal to those with a taste for explicit violence."
—*Publishers Weekly*

"A showcase of new and exciting talent."
—**Charlie Stella**, author of *Shakedown*

"Thuglit has become one of only a small handful of must-read sites for devotees of dark, tough, mean crime fiction."
—**Charles Ardai** (Richard Aleas), Edgar- and Shamus-nominated author of *Little Girl Lost*

"You have to look hard to find two consecutive pages that don't deal with sex or violence, but why would you want to? If you're man enough, you'll love this book. If you're not, give it to your girlfriend. If she accepts it and enjoys it, never turn your back on her."
—**Otto Penzler**

Also by Todd Robinson

Hardcore Hardboiled

Published by Kensington Publishing Corporation

sex, thugs, and rock & roll

EDITED BY TODD ROBINSON

INTRODUCTION BY SARAH WEINMAN

KENSINGTON BOOKS
http://www.kensingtonbooks.com

KENSINGTON BOOKS are published by

Kensington Publishing Corp.
119 West 40th Street
New York, NY 10018

All Kensington titles, imprints, and distributed lines are available at special quantity discounts for bulk purchases for sales promotion, premiums, fund-raising, educational, or institutional use.

Special book excerpts or customized printings can also be created to fit specific needs. For details, write or phone the office of the Kensington Special Sales Manager: Kensington Publishing Corp., 119 West 40th Street, New York, NY 10018. Attn. Special Sales Department. Phone: 1-800-221-2647.

ISBN-13: 978-0-7582-2267-1
ISBN-10: 0-7582-2267-X

First Kensington Trade Paperback Printing: June 2009
10 9 8 7 6 5 4 3 2 1

Printed in the United States of America

CONTENTS

Introduction

Sarah Weinman

It's a strange time to be a writer of short mystery fiction. On the one hand, print magazine outlets have dwindled to the point where longtime stalwarts *Ellery Queen* and *Alfred Hitchcock* are still just about the only places to get paid a decent wage. On the other hand, thanks to Akashic's "City Noir" series and upstart small presses like Busted Flush Press and Bleak House Books, the anthology market is so glutted that I pity anyone judging the short story category for the Edgar Awards.

But if you're a writer and your voice and style doesn't fit EQMM or AHMM's guidelines, if you don't have an in with specific editors or if you're still not known enough to be picked up by one of the themed anthologies sponsored by the major crime writing associations, where do you go?

For the last few years, the answer is online.

It took a while for that answer to gain any sort of traction. Like any new medium, the Web was greeted within publishing circles and by would-be authors with skepticism and scorn, and often for good reason: poor presentation, questionable editing, and seeming instability. Many heralded early players like *Blue Murder*, *HandHeldCrime*, and *Plots with Guns* no longer exist; others have severely curtailed activity or dropped fiction altogether. For those that remain, creating their own distinct presence, adopting strict editorial guidelines and producing quality fiction, what still remains a sticking point is the lack of cash—the equivalent of a couple of high-priced beers if the writer's lucky.

So why go online?

Several reasons. First, it gives undiscovered writers a wonderful opportunity to get their unique voices heard and distributed to, potentially, a bigger audience than a tiny print magazine that goes out of print after a month. Second, because of the dwindling print markets, more publishing professionals are looking to the Web for talent and quality. I can name example after example: Scott Wolven, whose stories have almost exclusively been published online, has been included in six consecutive editions of the *Best American Short Stories,* published a collection of short stories with Scribner, and has a novel in the works with Otto Penzler's imprint at Harcourt. Allan Guthrie, who went from publishing his first story online to three-book deals with Harcourt and the Scottish publisher Polygon. Ray Banks, following Guthrie's trajectory almost note-for-note; and Dave White, moving from critical acclaim for his Jackson Donne short stories to similar acclaim for his Jackson Donne novels published by Three Rivers Press.

The Web has become a haven of experimentation and risk—of stories that don't quite fit a particular mold. It's inspired a new wave of noir and allowed younger writers to have their voices heard, and there's no better example of this than *Thuglit.* From the moment Todd Robinson launched this online magazine in late 2005, I've been impressed with the caliber of stories, the quality of prose, and the gut-wrenching emotions that pulsate on the virtual page. No wonder *Thuglit* made the jump to print format, mixing all manner of dark doings originally published online with original stories by the brightest (or is that blackest?) stars of contemporary noir like Wolven, Guthrie, Joe R. Lansdale, Jason Starr, and Marcus Sakey.

The big guns may be the draw to entice readers to open this anthology's pages, but the reprints—from Jónas Knútsson's knucklebuster tale of a Budapest brawler to Justin Porter's depiction of Mexico City at its seediest to Patricia Abbott's sly twist on noir conventions—are the meat of *Sex, Thugs, and Rock & Roll,* dripping so much blood and guts and marrow that it's impossible to read this book in more than a single sitting. Be prepared to be shattered, shell-shocked, and bruised as *Thuglit*'s emissaries continue to write wrongs that are very, very right.

A Message from Big Daddy Thug

Welcome to the second collection of the best crime fiction culled from the depths of Thuglit.com and some of the best literary purveyors of mayhem and attitude on the planet.

Sex . . .

We got femmes fatales, lying Lotharios, and some Mexican porno comics, to name a few elements of the horizontal chicken dance we got going on between these covers.

Thugs . . .

Open any page. There's bound to be one there. Hell, we even got a couple of bisexual ass-kicking Vikings on a Crusade.

No. Don't read it again. That's what I said.

Rock & Roll . . .

Shee-yit, brothers and sisters . . . we *are* Rock & Roll. These stories are the guitar-slingin', drum-kit-kickin', bass-amp-exploding riders on the storm of pulp fiction.

Testify!!!!!

Where else you gonna find psychotic street gangs, jailhouse lunatics, brawlers, psychopaths, pimps, hookers, and PIs all in one place? And in case you think you've seen it all, we still got those kooky Vikings.

Who else is going to give it to you, if not *Thuglit*?

You're welcome.

—TODD ROBINSON (BIG DADDY THUG)

Double Down

Jason Starr

I needed the six horse to win the fourth race at Belmont in a big way, but as the horses went around the far turn I knew it wasn't happening. The six made the lead but he was all out and another horse, the nine, was flying on the outside. In mid-stretch the nine hooked the six, but the six dug in—just to extend my torture a little longer—and they went neck and neck past the sixteenth pole.

"Hold him off, you cocksucker!" I yelled. "Get up, you fucking son of a bitch!"

Naturally, I was wasting my breath. Seventy yards to the wire, the six hit quicksand and the nine drew off to win by an open length.

I went back into the grandstand, cursing, ripping tickets. The six was my big play of the day. I bet my lungs on it—five hundred win and another six hundred in exactas and triples. Yeah, I hit a couple cover exactas on the nine-six, but what would that get me, a hundred and change? Big whoopy shit.

I rode the escalator to the second floor, went to the saloon, and ordered a J.D. straight up. I downed it in one gulp and asked for a refill. A guy sat next to me. He was my age, early forties, had a big gut and thinning gray hair. He was in an expensive suit and was wearing a Rolex. But he had a wannabe way about him. Maybe he was rich, maybe he wasn't, but he wanted everybody to think he was.

He ordered a gin and tonic, then said to me, "How you doin'?"

At the racetrack when somebody asks you how you're doing they're not inquiring about your health.

"How do you think I'm doing?" I said, figuring I'd let the fact that I was at the bar downing J.D.'s at two in the afternoon on a bright sunny day do the talking.

"Had the six in the last, huh?" he asked.

"Tell me how he fuckin' loses that race," I said, getting aggravated all over again. "I mean, okay, the nine was good. But with the fractions he got, what, half in forty-seven and change? He should've won by open lengths."

"Maybe he was a little green?"

"Green? Come on, give me a fuckin' break. It was, what, his fourth time out? Mark my words, that horse'll never win a fuckin' race, not at this track anyway. Maybe if they ship him up to fuckin' Finger Lakes or some shit track he'll break his maiden."

My heart was racing and my face was burning up. I felt the way people probably felt before they had heart attacks.

"Well, thank God there's five more races to get 'em back, right?"

"Not for me. I came here to be the six horse."

"And I came here to talk to you."

During our conversation so far, I'd been looking away and at my glass mostly, but now I looked at the guy in the suit and said, "And who do you think you're talking to?"

"Your name's Jimmy Guarino, right?"

He got my name right, but I said, "Who the fuck're you?"

I'd been doing PI and protection work for eleven years, three on my own. I hadn't made a lot of friends along the way and I never knew when somebody's life I'd fucked up would show up looking for payback.

"DiMarco," he said, extending his hand. "Andy DiMarco."

I didn't shake his hand, just asked, "The fuck do you want?"

"Big Mikey said I could find you here."

Big Mikey was a good guy, a bookie/loanshark from Staten Island. He grew up in my neighborhood—Brooklyn, Bay Ridge—and when I was a teenager I went out with his sister for a while.

"Sorry about that," I said, feeling bad for treating him like shit. I smiled, trying to make nice, and said, "I hope you're not looking for a hot tip, 'cause I'm telling you right now, you came to the wrong guy."

"I'm not looking for any tips, I'm looking for a good PI, and Big Mikey said you're one of the best."

"I always do what I'm hired to do if that's what you mean by good."

"I was interested in hiring you to do a job."

"What kind of job?"

He took a sip of his drink, swallowed hard, then said, "I think my wife's fucking somebody."

He sounded a little choked up, like it was hard for him to talk about it. I almost felt sorry for him.

"Take it from me," I said, "guy's been divorced three times. If you think she's fucking somebody, she is."

"Yeah, well, I want to know for sure."

"Yeah, well, I'm telling you for sure."

He glared at me, then said, "I want the fuckin' evidence."

They always wanted evidence. I guess seeing was better than believing, or at least it made it easier to walk out the door.

But I didn't know why I was giving this guy marriage counseling. Cheating spouses were my easiest cases, how I made most of my money. I liked them because they were fast and uncomplicated. When spouses cheated, they were so lost and inlove that they got careless: writing incriminating e-mails, making long phone calls, doing public displays of affection. It was almost like they were begging to get caught, to get out of their shitty marriages. So I just took the pictures, got paid, and everybody was happy.

"If you want evidence, I'll get you evidence," I said.

"Thank you," he said. "What do you take up front?"

I usually took five hundred as a retainer, but I took another glance at the well-pressed suit, the gleaming Rolex, and decided to roll the dice.

"A thousand," I said.

"No problem," he said.

Fuck, should've asked for two. Talk about nothing going my way.

He opened his wallet and took out a money clip. He peeled off ten hundreds from the wad and handed them to me.

I pocketed the money, then asked, "So why do you think she's cheating?"

"She's acting funny," he said. "Been acting funny for a year, wanna know the truth."

"Funny?" I asked. "What's funny?"

"She doesn't tell me where she's been, sometimes I can't get her on the phone, shit like that. I swear to God, I don't know how many times she's told me her cell phone wasn't working or she couldn't get service. Shit like that."

"Who do you think the other guy is?"

"Got no fuckin' clue, that's why I'm hiring you."

I asked for the usual—his address and phone numbers, his wife's work address, the time she left for work in the morning, the time she usually came, et cetera.

"And I'll need a picture," I said.

He opened his briefcase, took out a photo, and handed it to

me. I suddenly understood why he was so worried. Some guys came to me, worried their wives were cheating on them, and then I'd see a picture of the old cow and think, *What's your problem? You should be thanking God she's fucking cheating on you.* But Debbie DiMarco was a total knockout—wavy blond hair, dark tan, and somebody had paid good money for that rack.

"Good-looking woman," I said.

"Don't get any ideas," he said seriously, like he really thought I wanted to bang his wife. I did want to bang her, but still.

"Take it easy," I said. "It's a compliment. You have great taste."

I looked at the picture again, thinking, *There's no way in hell this broad ain't cheating on this guy.*

"Sorry," he said, calming down. "I just get a little possessive sometimes, I guess. As you can see, she's very beautiful. I was the happiest man in the world when I met her, but now she's making me fuckin' miserable."

Jesus Christ, he wasn't going to cry, was he?

Yes, he was.

He dabbed his eyes with a napkin, then blew his nose into it. People were looking over.

I downed the rest of my drink, then said, "Look, I'm gonna do everything I can to get you what you want, but just get ready because it probably won't be pretty."

He stood up and looked at me, eyes all bloodshot, and shook my hand, squeezing much harder than necessary.

"Thank you, Jimmy," he said. "I'm really counting on you, man."

He finally let go of my hand, and I walked away, letting Mr. Rich Guy pick up the tab.

I probably should've left the track with DiMarco's thousand bucks and considered myself a winner for the day, but when was the last time I did the thing I "should've done"? Instead I went back downstairs and invested about two hundred bucks in triples and pick threes and watched the bets go promptly down the tubes as none of the horses I needed on top hit the board. This time there was no drama, no close calls. I just bet, watched, ripped.

In the next couple of races, I didn't fare much better, dropping another couple hundred. I knew it was happening, that there was no way I was leaving the track a winner, but I stayed and bet the rest of the card. I hit a nice exacta in the seventh race, which built up my stake back to about a thousand, but then I went banzai in the late double and walked out with about two hundred bucks in my wallet.

I knew the smart thing to do was to stop gambling and get right to work on the case, but I got in my car and drove right to Yonkers Raceway. By the fourth race, around nine o'clock, I was back in my car, driving home to Brooklyn, broke and feeling like shit. I knew this wasn't any way to live my life, but I didn't know any other way to live it. I didn't smoke, barely drank, and never did heavy drugs, but I'd been gambling for years, losing my money faster than I earned it. Sometimes I felt like I was falling, except, unlike a dream, I didn't wake up and find out everything was okay. My nightmare went on and on.

In the morning, I woke up and got to work on the car. I had no choice. I would've loved to chase my money at Belmont, but I was broke and had rent and bills to pay. Business had been slow lately and if I hadn't run into DiMarco at the track, I didn't know what I would've done for money.

I lived in a ridiculously small apartment in Brooklyn, above a deli on Avenue M off Flatbush. It was on the second floor of a tenement-style building. There was one room—my combination living room, dining room, and kitchen—and a tiny bathroom. I couldn't meet clients there, so I did most of my business at diners, bars, and racetracks. I had no overheard and

I didn't run ads. My business was all word of mouth and by referral. My only equipment was a laptop, a digital camera, and a gun. I usually left my gun at home, knowing firsthand what kind of trouble those things can get you into.

The DiMarcos lived in Mill Basin. When I got to the house again, I realized how badly I'd fucked up by only asking for a thousand up front. The house was three stories, had to be worth a couple million.

But I already had an idea how I could make that lost money back and then some.

He said his wife went to the gym every day at seven fifteen and, sure enough, at seven fifteen she left the house. Man, she was even better looking in person. She had great legs, like she could've been a model, and looked like she was thirty, tops.

She got in her shiny red Merc and drove to the gym DiMarco said she'd go to on Ralph Avenue. I was in sweatpants and T-shirt and followed her inside. I watched her head towards the women's locker room; then I went to the desk and told them I was thinking about joining and asked for a free day's trial. The guy tried to make me fill out a form and wanted me to go into the office for a sales pitch. I didn't want to let Debbie out of my sight, so I promised the guy I'd listen to his spiel after I worked out. Yeah, like that was gonna happen.

While Debbie used a StairMaster, I was right behind her, using an exercise bike. Let me tell you, it was a nice place to be. She was in great shape and spent about forty-five minutes on that thing. I was pedaling as slow as possible and I was still winded.

She did a half hour running on the treadmill while I did some pull-ups and very slow rowing. After she did about twenty minutes of abs and stretches, her workout ended, thank fucking God. If it went on any longer I probably would've died.

She went into the locker room again, and came out about a

half hour later looking all spruced up and perfect. Meanwhile, I was a sweaty mess because I didn't want to wash up and risk missing her leave the gym.

She got back in her car and I thought she was heading back to her apartment, but she turned down Avenue N and double-parked in front of a dry cleaner's. She came out with the clothing, got back in the car, and then drove to Flatlands Avenue. She pulled into a gas station, filled up, then went inside to pay. Then she got back in the car and drove home.

So far the tailing had been a big bust. I was on DiMarco's tab, but I liked fast cases. I wanted to get my money, ideally today, so I could make it up to Yonkers for the early double.

For all I knew, she was going to stay in her house all day and I would just have to give up and come back tomorrow morning. But after about an hour, she left the house and got back in the car and I followed her onto the Belt Parkway, heading south. She was driving fast, weaving in and out of traffic. A couple of times I thought I lost her.

She exited near Brighton Beach and I figured she was just going to do some shopping or something. But instead she drove into the parking lot of a motel right off the Parkway. Suddenly things were heating up.

She got out of her car and went right to a room. My camera was zoomed in, ready to shoot. The door opened and, as she planted a kiss on the guy's lips, I started snapping pictures, getting at least four good ones before the door closed.

So it had turned out to be an open and shut case after all.

The guy she'd met seemed familiar, and then it clicked—he was the mechanic I'd seen her talking to earlier at the gas station.

I smiled, then said out loud, "Guess she likes to get her tires rotated every once in a while."

It wasn't exactly hard to connect the dots of Debbie Di-

Marco's story. She married a rich guy, got bored, and started screwing the hot young Guido at the gas station.

I took out my cell, about to call Andy DiMarco, when I suddenly had a better idea.

If I gave DiMarco the pics, he'd pay me the balance due—a thousand bucks, plus another hundred for expenses. But I had rent and bills coming up, and the way my luck was going, that eleven hundred bucks wasn't going to last very long. I needed more than eleven hundred bucks and I knew exactly how to get it.

I drove back to the DiMarcos' house and parked right in front. A couple of hours later, the red Merc pulled up into the driveway and Debbie DiMarco got out. As she passed by on her way toward her house, I said, smiling, "Have a nice afternoon, Miss DiMarco?"

She stopped, turned, and looked at me suspiciously.

Before she could say anything, I said, "I'll take that as a yes."

She started to walk away.

"I think you're gonna want to take a look at these," I said.

She looked back slowly and saw me holding up the digital camera. "Who the hell are you?"

I laid it all on the table—told her I was a PI, that her husband had hired me, and that I had pictures of her and the mechanic.

"Let me see them," she said.

She came over, looking at the slide show on the LCD screen.

"Why're you showin' me these?" she finally asked, her voice trembling.

"Because I'm a nice guy?"

"Fuck you."

"Hey, is that a nice way to talk to a guy who might be able to save your marriage, or at least your ass in a divorce settlement?"

"The fuck're you talking about?"

"These are your two choices," I said. "I can give these photos to your husband and he can divorce you like he's going to, or we can go on to plan B."

"What's plan B?"

"I don't give them to your husband. I delete them and you do the right thing and fix your fuckin' marriage."

"And how much is that gonna cost me?"

"Five thousand dollars."

"That's blackmail."

"I like to call it 'a favor.' "

Of course she bit, why wouldn't she? Nothing like making a quick, easy five g's. I felt like I'd just hit the fucking triple.

She got back in her car and I followed her to the nearest Chase bank and she made the withdrawal. Before she gave me the money, she said, "Let me see you delete the pictures."

I deleted them one by one. Satisfied, she gave me the five large.

"Pleasure doing business with you, Miss DiMarco," I said.

The next afternoon at the bar at Belmont, I met Andy DiMarco.

"Got good news for me?" he asked.

"Depends what you mean by good."

I handed him printouts of the photos I'd taken. Before I'd deleted them from the camera, I'd uploaded them onto my laptop. I guess I could've played it straight and told him his wife wasn't cheating on him, but I'd already lost most of the five grand I'd gotten from Debbie DeMarco and I wanted the one-grand balance from Andy DiMarco. In other words, I wanted to soak this thing for all it was worth.

Looking at the photos, DiMarco said, "I can't believe it. I feel like such a fucking idiot. I go into that gas station all the time."

"Hey, it happens to the best of us," I said.

DiMarco gave me the thousand balance and expense money,

which of course I'd jacked up by a few hundred bucks. The first race was going off soon and I couldn't wait to go play it.

DiMarco was saying, "Funny thing is, things were getting better the last couple of days. We've been talking more, spending more time together. It seemed like we were working things out."

He looked like he was about to start crying again. I couldn't take it and said, "Good luck to you," and headed for the betting windows.

A few weeks later, I was in A.C., at The Taj—broke, losing my balls—when I ran into Big Mikey by the slots.

We bullshitted for a while; then I said, "Oh, I meant to tell you, thanks for that client rec."

He looked lost.

"You know," I said, "the guy from Mill Basin with the slut wife?" For a few seconds I couldn't remember his name; then I said, "DiMarco. Remember, last month you put him in touch with me, told him he could find me at the track? I did a job for him, caught his wife with another guy."

Big Mikey's eyes widened.

"What's wrong?" I asked.

"You didn't hear?" he said.

"Hear what?"

"It was in the papers."

"The only paper I've been reading is the fuckin' *Racing Form*."

"Holy shit, you really don't know."

"Know what?"

"Couple weeks ago DiMarco came home from work and shot his wife a bunch of times, then shot himself. It was a fuckin' bloodbath. Sucked too, because he was a big client of mine. He didn't know shit about football, dropped five g's a week like clockwork. And baseball, forget about it. You say you found dirt on his wife?"

I felt sick, knowing if I'd kept my word to Debbie DiMarco she'd probably still be alive.

"Yeah," I said, "a little."

"That's fucked up, but it's kinda funny too. I mean, when you think about it. You okay?"

"Yeah, fine," I said. "I'm just getting the shit kicked out of me on the tables, that's all."

"Join the fuckin' club," he said. "I'm tellin' you, gambling's a lot more fun when you're on the other side of the action."

Big Mikey told me a story about this big hand he'd lost in seven-card stud at Bally's, but I was barely listening. I really needed to bet, to clear my head, and I told him I'd catch him later.

I dropped another few hundred in slots, played a few more losing hands of BJ, got the shit kicked out of me in craps, then walked away in disgust. At least I wasn't thinking about that other thing anymore.

On the way out of the casino, I passed a roulette wheel and put all the chips I had left—about four hundred bucks—on black.

Guess what came in?

The story of my fucking life.

Like Riding a Moped

Jordan Harper

. . . And now, the last bad thing about being so fat: my fingers can't find the bullet holes. They're there, because they brought me down and now there is sticky blood mixing with the sweat all over, but my clumsy hands can't find what kind of holes just got poked into my body. Are they just little puckers in the flesh? Or is it worse than that? Are scoops of me missing?

Somebody will write about this on the Internet. I bet they call the article "Fatty and Clyde," or something like that. Everyone will read it and chuckle. And everyone will look at me and see something else, which is what always happens. That's how Benny got to me when I should have known better. He looked right at me.

Men sit next to me on the Metrolink and talk about women like I'm not even there. I'm just the thing taking up two seats when the train gets crowded. Everyone shifts their body away from me. Nobody looks and nobody points and laughs unless there's a kid. Then the mom can try and shush the little kid and maybe smile an apology and then look away, tell the kid it's not polite to stare. Honest, it's okay when the kid stares. At least it stops me from feeling invisible.

The others, the adults, they look and they just see other things. They picture me sitting at home, a pizza box open in front of me and me eating with the lazy mania of a zombie in a horror movie. They see my chomping jaws and glazed eyes, dipping crusts in ranch dressing, how only one slice lives to make it to the safe haven of the freezer—me eating so much that for the next hour every burp will send a chunk of half-chewed dough back into my mouth, so I have to swallow it again.

Maybe they wonder about my shower, about how I have to lift the three folds of my belly and point the handheld nozzle to try to clean out the gunk that forms there. They wonder how I wash my back, if I own something like the rag on a stick in that *Simpsons* joke.

They imagine the underwear hidden beneath my clothes, both wispy and huge, a negligee knapsack. Maybe they think of the way the panties must smell when I peel them off at the end of the day, like a swamp or a beer left open.

All these things are true.

All these things are true, so when Benny puts his tray across from mine at the Galleria food court, I don't believe him for a second. But he is so pretty, really, like Brad Pitt in *Thelma & Louise*. Later on I'll learn that he's from Springfield, down in the opposite corner of the state, same as Brad. And once he'll even try to tell me that they're cousins. Yeah, right, I'm sure Brad Pitt just has dozens of relatives who work for the St. Louis mob. What kind of cousin, I ask, like your mother's brother or what? And he says, No, I mean *cousin* cousin, like that means something.

But all that comes later. When Benny sits across from me I'm sitting in a corner of the food court with my fried rice and egg rolls, thinking about the store. I want to be a salesgirl.

Mr. Nesbitt laughed when I told him, and said he didn't know what he'd do without me working the computers. The salesgirls—like Amanda, who sits in the middle of the food court eating a salad—don't know half what I do about carats and cuts and clarity, but they look like the kind of woman you want to drape in diamonds. And now I'm replaying the conversation in my head, the way Mr. Nesbitt won't look at me while he laughs at the idea. And then there's Benny staring straight into my eyes and asking if this seat is taken.

So he sits across from me talking and smiling, and I'm trying not to stare at him. The napkin I put over my General Tso's chicken is turning orange from the grease it's drinking, and there's still my crab Rangoon under that napkin. As soon as this gorgeous dip gets up and leaves I'm going to dip it in the General Tso sauce and suck out the cream cheese. But he doesn't leave, and after one lame joke he tells he actually winks at me. I wonder if the girls at Nesbitt's maybe hired this guy or something.

I mean, I've met chubby chasers, and this guy isn't one. Guys like that like to say something about my size right away, to try and make me feel comfortable. Oh God, like how they like a woman with some meat on her bones. Great image, right, like maybe they're planning on cooking me up later.

Most amazing, he's not looking around the room while we talk. Most men, when they end up in a conversation with me in a bar or something, they're always looking around. Maybe they're looking for better options, but mostly, I think, it's because they're afraid someone might see them. A friend told me this joke once, I guess it's a joke men tell to each other:

Why's a fat girl like a moped?

They're a lot of fun to ride, but you wouldn't want your friends to see you on one.

Benny looks right in my eyes. His eyes are clear blue, and I don't see myself reflected in them at all.

He asks if I want to go see a movie after work. I never told him that I worked at the mall. I could have been shopping. This is something I don't think about until later. At the time I can hardly think at all. But later on, it will come back to me and make perfect sense.

Back at the store, Amanda corners me. Her skin is the color of Arizona dirt, and it's stretched so tight you can see three sides of her collarbones. She asks me who I was talking to. Just some guy. Pretty cute, she says back, the way you'd say it to a niece who has not yet admitted to liking boys. Whatever, I say, just like your niece would.

After work, I stop at Lion's Choice and pick up a few roast beef sandwiches and eat them while I drive, barely chewing at all. He's taking me to dinner, and I'll be damned if I'm going to the restaurant hungry. He's not really going to show up, I tell myself as I drive and swallow. There's no way. Maybe he's just into fat chicks, I tell myself. But that doesn't feel right. To a guy like that, a fat chick is like Renee Zellweger clocking in at 130 pounds for that stupid movie.

Maybe he's hogging, I think, and the roast beef lumps in my throat. I read one time about guys who will all set out to pick up the fattest thing they can find, and they all show up someplace and the guy with the biggest girl wins. Wins what, I don't know. Respect? I can see in my head a table full of women like me, all of us knowing what was going on and not a one of us doing a thing about it while the men get drunk and laugh at us. And for the hundredth time I cancel the date in my head and then remind myself that I don't even have this guy's number. So one way or another, my fate, at least for the night, is sealed.

It takes me about three hours to get dressed, an hour of that in the shower, getting everything, shaving my legs, even that patch down by my ankle. I have to hold my breath to reach it. I'm lucky I don't break my neck. Choosing a dress takes longer.

Lane Bryant of course. Black, of course. Black's slimming, you know, so I only look big as a townhouse. I put my makeup on using a mirror and trying not to actually look at myself, which of course is hard. Then I eat a pint of Cherry Garcia standing over the sink thinking he's not going to come and if he does then that might be even worse and that there's something wrong, there must be something wrong but even if there is I don't care because at least that kind of wrong will be something new.

When the doorbell rings, I just about bite through the spoon.

We eat Italian on the Hill, and I get fettuccini with white sauce and laugh at his jokes, which aren't very funny. He tells me he works in contracting, and I ask him what that means, and he fumbles a bit. So we drink more, and I let myself get drunker than I should on a date, because if I don't I'm going to jump out of my skin. Which wouldn't be so bad.

After the dinner, after I refuse to have dessert, just say no, when he asks me if I want to go to his place, I say yes. I breathe in deep, trying to see if my nervous sweat has kicked up any of the smell, but I don't smell anything. And the way Benny smokes, I'd be surprised if he can smell anything at all. So we go to his place in the Central West End and it's done up in that way that looks tasteful but just means that you bought everything at the same store. And I'm looking around and he puts a hand on my shoulders and it's like someone set my insides on puree.

When we make love, he wants to leave the lights on, but I will not let him. He almost glows in the dark.

Lying in bed, the light through his window throws my silhouette against the wall, hiding Benny's completely. He doesn't try to put his arm around me, thank God. He sits up against his headboard and smokes and talks. He lets the name Frank Priest slip, and anybody who reads the paper knows he's like the biggest mob boss in town, and another part of Benny becomes clear. Then he asks me what I do. I tell him I run a computer system at a store in the mall. He asks what kind of store and I tell him, jewelry, and he says, oh, really?

Two nights later he takes me to a bar, and anorexic bitches look at me with hateful eyes like maybe I'm holding Benny hostage. Benny gets up at one point to get us refills and some guy with gelled hair and an upturned collar comes by my table, the muscles in his face slack and his eyes shot. He's trying to talk to me but he's laughing too hard to do it. At another table behind him his friends are tamping down their giggles like children in church.

The guy never gets his line out. Maybe it was about being a moped, I'll never know. Benny comes out of the dark and doubles the guy with a punch in the stomach. Then he gets both hands in the crisp bristles of the guy's hair and slams his head against our table, making my amaretto sour jump. The guy just drops after that. Benny holds his hand out to me, palm up, and says, m'lady. It has little specks of blood on it. I take it in my own and I walk out of that place feeling like I left two hundred pounds sitting on the bar.

That night, after we make love, I tell him I know what it is that he wants. And that it's okay.

Yeah? he asks me.

Yes, I tell him. Just tell me what your plan is, and let's work together to make it better.

It turns out that his plan needs a lot of work. Benny doesn't know much about jewelry stores, or even jewelry. So I tell him about the security room and its own special server, which I can access. I tell him about the loose stone set, and how they keep another box just like it full of cubic zirconium fakes.

He talks about us robbing it together, like Bonnie and Clyde. You could wear a mask, he tells me. And I just look at him. A mask? What kind of mask could I wear?

He wants to blow the safe. He's already got a bomb, he says. He shows it to me, how you just twist these wires onto those connectors and then push down the little plunger and boom! Never thought I'd learn how to set up a bomb. When I tell him that we won't need to blow anything up, that the best stuff sits out in the inventory room so people can look through it, he gets a look on his face like I just took away his lollipop. He spent a lot of money on the bomb, he says. Well, it doesn't go bad, does it? I ask. Just put it in the closet, and maybe we'll need it next time.

Over the next two weeks I lose ten pounds. I don't know if it's all the exercise he's giving me or if maybe I'm not stuffing my face quite so much, but I haven't seen the numbers head south in years. In that scale there's a future where diamond money can buy the gastric bypass, buy new clothes, the kind of clothes they put in the window of the stores at the mall. There's a future where people could see me and Benny at a bar somewhere and not laugh or gape or guess I'm his sister. And we finally come to make a plan that I'm pretty sure will work. When we finally get it all set out and planned, Benny gets out a bottle of champagne and after a toast he pours some of the champagne on me, and licks it off and I don't push him away or wonder how I smell. I just look up at the ceiling and see that other life hanging there, so close I can almost taste it.

The morning of the robbery, we leave from Benny's place, each in our car. Just before we pull out, I get back out and head back inside. Benny gives me a look like, what? I just point to my stomach and roll my eyes and let him paint the picture. It only takes a minute to do what I have to do. Then we're on course.

* * *

None of the salesgirls hanging around the display cases say hello. My card opens the door into the back of the store. I boot up the store server, then buzz the door to the inventory room. Jack, a sweet old guy with a gun on his ankle, lets me in. I boot up the security server, and then wreck it with a few clicks of the mouse. I act confused and ask Jack to check a connection across the room. While he does that, I put a little red sticker on the top of the loose stone case, the one without the fakes in it. Jack comes back and tells me the wires are plugged tight, and I say, well, that probably makes it the motherboard. Let me make a call. I step outside the inventory room and dial Benny's number. He doesn't answer, but he's not supposed to. He's coming from the food court where we first met. He should be here in the time it takes me to take five deep breaths.

He wears a wig and dark glasses, and he steps into the store with his silver pistol pointing right at Amanda's face. With his left hand he grabs her by the hair and yanks her across the counter. That's how skinny she is. And then he's pushing her to the back of the store and one of the other salesgirls starts screaming. Benny pushes past me without even looking and gets Amanda to open the back door and then just pulls open the inventory door, because I zapped the electric lock when I fried the server.

A few seconds later the gunfire starts.

Maybe Jack went for his gun. I don't know. But there are two loud pops and Amanda screams and then Benny is back out, kicking Amanda in front of him, the loose stone case in one hand and the pistol in the other. Right in front of me Amanda falls down and Benny points the gun down and there's a bang and all sorts of stuff slops out of Amanda onto the floor. I would never guess she'd have so much inside her.

Then Benny looks up at me, and even though he's wearing

glasses and a wig I can see him perfectly, and he sees me, like we're both naked in the daylight.

I turn so I don't have to watch the gun barrel raise, or Benny's face when he pulls the trigger. That's why the bullets hit me in the back.

If it had gone according to the plan that both of us knew was a lie, then Benny would have headed out the door next to the Foot Locker across the way, ditched his wig, glasses, and coat in the hall, and put the loose stone case inside the big plastic Gap bag he had tucked inside his pants. He would have gotten in his car and driven to the motel just past Six Flags on I-44. After the police questioning finished, I was supposed to drive there myself.

But first, I would have stopped at his apartment and unhooked Benny's bomb from the front door. I would have put the bomb back into the closet and gotten ready for my new life. But I guess Benny will just have to find it himself. See, Benny never really had me fooled. But he did make me hope.

Damn him for that.

Viddi and the Bucharest Brawler

Jónas Knútsson

For a few blessed hours in the early afternoon, The Palooka Bar is transmogrified into a country club of sorts, a veritable Agora of Socratic discourse where elevated exchange of ideas and sentiments becomes possible before the drudges and working stiffs pour in. By the round table, Viddi, The Cadaver, Rhino, and Hulk the bouncer nursed their Buds, all smiles but each sporting a shiner.

Into The Palooka Bar breezed Mercy Beaucoup, bringing with him spurts of the autumn sun. "What's with Petey the pit bull family reunion?"

"We were gonna roll this guy . . ." jubilated Rhino.

"Just wanted to borrow a few rubles and he wasn't too forthcoming," Viddi hastened to add.

The remembrance brought forth a gentle smile across Hulk's broad face. "We ran out of beer money."

"He beat us to a pulp," Rhino chimed in.

"That should make you happy," Mercy Beaucoup acknowledged.

"Scuzzy's our one-way ticket to the land of plenty," Hulk announced with pride.

"First he lays some rubes on the canvas," extrapolated Rhino in a reverie. "Then he lays the golden eggs, and then Scuzzy lays some bread on us and we lie back and live the good life."

"But, Viddi, you're not allowed within a mile of a boxing ring after—"

"Bah, Burgess Meredith can train him for all I care," retorted Viddi. "Kid's got the stuff. All I'm going to do is sit back, watch the show, and count the cash."

"To Dimitri Sciatscu of Bucharest," toasted The Cadaver.

Rhino raised his beer mug high. "Our gravy train just come in, straight from Bulgaria."

The first sparring session took place after-hours in the deserted Crooked Nose Gym—Mercy Beaucoup having slipped Stinky the janitor a couple of greenbacks, as the only resolution every boxing association in the land, including the GID, KDJ, KDH, UID, KDD, KKK, YDU, GWU and IOU, had ever agreed upon was to bar Viddi from all matches and venues in perpetuity.

"No way am I getting into the ring with that shrimpster," whined Beardy. "I'll be busted for child molestation." In the opposite corner, Scuzzy's pot belly jutted out as he lounged on his stool, his physique offering a scant testament to a predilection for sports, or solid food for that matter.

"It's somebody or nobody, and nobody's out of town," countered Viddi.

"Here, you take the gloves." Beardy brandished Hulk's Popeye boxing gloves at Viddi.

"I slip in there and you lot will be left to the Indians," Viddi warned with a passion. "Think of the green across the Glean."

"What's a Glean?" wondered Rhino.

"Ready, Scuzzy?"

"Ready-steady. Rocking to go. When I get money?"

The longest time took to disentangle Beardy from the ropes and explain to him where and who he was. After Rhino had taken Hulk to the Hoboken Methodist Hospital and The Cadaver discovered he had a limp, Mercy Beaucoup was left with no choice but enter the ring in his mustard Calani pants and shiny Hungarian shoes.

Although Mercy Beaucoup danced like a butterfly, he most assuredly did not sting like a bee. For three minutes that seemed to pass slower than the seasons, Mercy buzzed around the ring, maintaining a steady presence in the corner farthest from Scuzzi, doing the Ali shuffle, gyrating his head, feigning with great flourish, and not once getting within ten feet of his opponent. Anon, Mercy Beaucoup fainted from exhaustion, falling face-first on the post. By this time, Weeping Willy had locked himself in the powder room and Viddi tried unceremoniously to pry the door open with a rusty umbrella in lieu of a crowbar as Dimitri Sciatscu voiced some reservations about the quality of his sparring partners.

At The Palooka Bar, Viddi was late for their meeting with South African trainer Ludwig Van Oizman, a contemporary legend west of Transvaal. Although Oizman had coached some Olympians of note in Jo'burg, he did not command an exorbitant fee in the land of the free, as he was just off the boat after causing a tribal dispute of some acrimony in his homeland. To boot, he met the one requisite no trainer in the Big Apple did: he'd never heard of Viddi.

"Sorry 'bout the delay, guv'nor." Viddi was beaming with even more confidence than usual.

"No harm done. You have my fee, Mr. Golbranson?"

"In what sense?"

"In your pocket. In that sense."

"With the neighborhood going to seed and all . . ." Viddi explained with forbearance.

"We gave you the dosh last night," sighed Rhino.

"You left us ruined, man." After his punishment at the hands of Scuzzy, Beardy found it somewhat difficult to speak.

"Well, I don't have it on me, physically."

Oizman, though not amused, knew the world too well to be angry. "You carrying it metaphysically?"

"You told us the dough might as well be at Fort Knox," wailed Hulk.

"Let's not get into politics."

"Viddi, Viddi, Viddi," singsonged Mercy Beaucoup, glaring at Viddi through the blackness of his eye.

"Rollo was celebrating his last outing as a free man for quite some time. You expect me to treat my own brother to tap water and easy-listening radio under such circumstances?"

Calmly, Oizman stood up and walked away.

"But who's going to train Scuzzy?" bellowed Viddi with indignation as he tried to grab Oizman's shirtsleeve.

"You do it for all I care." Oizman tore himself free with a light middleweight's grace of movement.

"Hey, Jungle Jim there isn't as stupid as he looks," exclaimed Viddi as the boys scowled at him in disappointed silence, reassuring them with the famous Viddi wink.

At the Ring of Fire Gym, Dan Prince had been listening long enough to the out-of-towner with the chapeau Alpin and thick sunglasses sing the praises of his prodigy—much too long, since the man kept tugging at his sleeve to the point of playing a tune to the jangling of Dan Prince's vast array of rings and amulets.

"What title did you say your fighter holds, Mr. Gunnerson?" queried Dan Prince, his patience on the brink of exhaustion.

With caution, Viddi looked around. All it took was one palooka who recognized him and he'd be outward-bound faster than a mermaid out of a tuna factory. "The YMCU."

"How can he be a champion when he's never had a professional fight? In my fifty years in the game I've never heard of such a title."

"It's East European. You'll have people from the former Ukraine stampeding at the gates."

"The Ukraine?" Dan Prince could swear the Bedlamite was trying to play "When the Saints Go Marching In" by yanking hard enough at his sleeve.

"Scuzzy's from Bucharest." Viddi kept rattling the moveable jewelry store on Dan Prince's person.

"And where do you hail from, Mr. Gunnerson?"

"In my day I was a contender in Lilleby, in Norway."

"Professional boxing isn't allowed in Norway."

"I had to go all the way to Finland to beat guys into meatballs."

"Also illegal in Finland."

"It's okay for Norwegians to box there, in the north."

"Mr. Gunnerson, please go away."

"Yumpin' yemeni. Want to project your ham-and-eggers from m'boy, be my guest." Viddi's dramatic exit was somewhat foiled by his missing the door by seven inches as his dark glasses allowed for limited view.

All heads, bare and geared, Alpine and native, turned at the muffled explosion and flurry of strange curses followed by a soft hiss.

"Not again," sighed Dan Prince.

Mambo le Primitif found himself unable to retrieve his

gloved hand from the other side of the sighing boxing bag as he waited for some of the sand to sift out.

"Third bag this week." Babycakes McGee, the trainer, yawned.

"About time he came out," said Dan Prince softly.

"You'll have to fly someone in from Touristown. Word's spreading and no one east of Palookaville would be stupid enough to take him on."

An angelic smile lit up Dan Prince's face like all the votive candles at St. Peter's, a portent he was about to make or save money. "Oh, Mr. Gunnerson. Wait . . ."

Joe, the owner, was none too happy to see the Katzenjammer Kids saunter into The Palooka Bar like an invading horde. To date, he had profited little from his acquaintance with Knold and Tot, the grandsons of the infamous Torsten "The Hooch" Jones—who spent the last fifty years of his life in Sing Sing after killing off a whole Elks Lodge in the Catskills with a batch of homemade brew labeled The Tallahassee Twister. Knold and Tot tried to slide inconspicuously towards the bar, no mean feat for the identical albino twins, Knold limping on his left leg and Tot on his right.

"I'm still in court because of that Elderberry Nectar."

"Vintage stuff that. Chap had a defective immune system." Tot did not take kindly to ingrates casting aspersions on their skills at the family trade.

"Check this out," whispered Knold, affecting a conspiratorial glance.

"We call it 'the Alabama Mama,' " hummed Tot softly but proudly.

With stealth, Knold opened his Tasmanian Devil bomber jacket, revealing a plain quart bottle. "Scentless as a Methodist altar. Go on the town and the missus won't smell a thing."

"And you can tipple all you want while you do the racing

forms at work," added Tot. "It'll sell like tutti-frutti ice cream in hell."

"I'm still using your 'Hiroshima Hummer' for pest control," objected Joe.

"Keep it as a free sample," offered Knold. "The rubes'll be crying out for more."

"Dying for more, most likely," retorted Joe.

"Just keep it away from heat. It's got a kick," warned Knold.

Joe offered neither remonstration nor resistance as Knold thrust the bottle into his arms, seeing he was out of paint remover.

At the round table, Scuzzy and Mercy Beaucoup had waited for over an hour, the match slated to start at any minute.

"Why no one let Viddo near boxing square?" wondered Scuzzy.

"He gets kind of . . . involved," explained Mercy Beaucoup. "Say, want another Bud, Scuzzy?"

An inexpertly wrapped package under his arm, Viddi dashed in with a lot of Golbranson determination and the boys flocked over.

"Did you get the belt?" asked Beardy, shooting Viddi a glance harder than an algebra test.

"A slight snag. Had to make one myself."

"Told you we shouldn't hock our Babe Ruth cards," wailed Rhino

"With Rollo going on the lam, was I supposed to say goodbye to my own flesh and blood for who knows how long, the constabulary on his heels, without giving him a proper send-off? Am I not my brother's keeper?"

"But the cops always pick him up at Barbie's," objected Shadow.

"Got to get cracking." Viddi turned away from Shadow abruptly.

Beardy took Shadow aside and placed his index finger over

his shoulder. "Take it easy on Viddi. Rollo was an ace safe-cracker before he devoted himself to the potato juice. Could've amounted to something."

"Word is this Mambo dude's been pulverizing boxing bags," injected Joe.

"What is 'pulverize'?" queried Scuzzy.

"Two of his sparring partners are sucking eggs in Hoboken." Joe looked Scuzzy in the eye as he spoke.

"Not to fret. Like Joe Louis, I see something." Viddi pointed to his eye as he gave Joe the famous Viddi wink. "Scuzzy'll take him to the woodshed."

"Man, ten minutes to showtime," exclaimed Hulk.

At this, the boys darted out. Viddi ran straight into Joe, tearing the bottle of Alabama Mama from his grasp. "Thanks for the water, Joe."

"Hold on a dadgum—"

"I'm on the beam." Viddi was out the door before Joe could utter another syllable.

With Viddi sunglassed and chapeau'd proudly by his side, Scuzzy strode into The Banana Ballroom with his newfound YMCU championship belt, which consisted of a weightlifter's belt sprinkled with glitter and adorned with tenuously glued-on Diet Pepsi tabs, antique French postcards of questionable taste, fifty-cent imitation Red Army medals, and, inexplicably, Elvis Presley and ABBA cards hooked on with safety pins.

"*. . . making his professional debut from the People's Independent Democracy of Saal-Am-A-Bu, Mambo le Primitif,*" clamored Morty Buffet, the ring announcer. "*In the opposite corner, the YMCU supermiddleweight champion of the world, the uncontested, undefeated, unmolested Bucharest Brawler Dimitri 'Scuzzy' Sciatscu.*"

"Viddi, what exactly does a cutman do?" queried Beardy.

"Moral support, mostly. Hotter than hell in August here,"

added Viddi, taking a swig from the bottle generously supplied by Joe.

"Where's helmet? I'm Olympic boxer," complained Scuzzy.

"Welcome to the U.S. of A., land of the hard-asses," snapped Beardy.

"Yeah, this ain't Ruministan, bub," explicated Hulk.

Going nose-to-nose, Viddi crouched in front of Scuzzy, looking his protégé square in the eye. "First, do a bit of the Ali shuffle, then take a few on the kisser to lull him into complacency."

"Who is Ali? What is complacency?"

"Next give him a Reykjavik roundhouse, coupled with a haymaker."

"What is haymaker?"

"Then some love taps, *eine kleine Schubster*. You with me?"

"No."

"Before the bell tolls, go south of the border when the cyclops is winking at the rubes."

"No border. No have green card."

"Seconds out," bellowed Referee Thorndigger.

Referee Emil Thorndigger, tough as nails, old as the hills of Kilimanjaro, and brooker of no nonsense, motioned the two warriors forward to face off. As he stepped between the two fighters, Thorndigger found himself facing a smiling Viddi. "Get back to your corner."

With his one eye, Thorndigger glared at each boxer as hard as a Quaker at a brewery. "Your show, not mine, so don't make me rain on your parade. Keep it clean and defend yourselves at all times. May your God be with you." As the bell chimed the first round, Mambo cannonballed out of his corner with all the fury of hell, whereas Scuzzy lumbered to the center of the ring as if taking out the garbage against his will. Within three seconds, the Bucharest Brawler was splayed across the canvas. Bopping up and down, Viddi held on to the ropes, shouting lofty encouragements to his fighter. "Get up, you bum. We got the farm riding on you here." At the count of nine, Scuzzy stood up, uncoiling languidly as Mambo gazed in awe upon the rising Lazarus and Thorndigger tried to ascertain whether the fighter was in a coma or simply not overly interested in the matter at hand.

"You okay?"

"Okeydoke, let's hit a road," replied Scuzzy.

For the rest of the round, Mambo kept Scuzzy at the end of his left jab but did not commit to a power punch as the Bucharest Brawler's eyes were clear as a Quaker's rap sheet. Little did Mambo look forward to sampling Scuzzy's punches if his fists proved as hard as his jaw. At the bell, Scuzzy dribbled down onto his stool, more exhausted than injured.

"Where's the cutman?" roared Viddi.

"I'm the cutman," drawled Beardy, brandishing the corkscrew on his Swiss Army knife.

"He'll never walk again," some ringside wisenheimer cracked.

"Cut his eyelid," commanded Viddi.

"But no hit in eye," remonstrated Scuzzy.

As he announced his new strategy, Viddi poured liberally from the bottle of Alabama Mama down Scuzzy's throat. "Okay, you gotta gimp the geezer. Go whorehouse on him. Then go roughhouse. Go whorehouse again, then go to town on him with the world and his wife watching."

"I go to town with wife?"

"Go old school on him."

"We go to school?"

"Remember what Abe Lincoln said," injected Beardy. "We shall fight them bitches. We shall never surrender."

"You have to Jones him. Then give him a kisser-upper. Throw in a little Archie Moore. Once you're done Mongoosing, use love taps."

"I bring no taps."

"And try catching him with a Hail Mary. Then it's bedtime for Bonzo."

"I pray?"

Referee Thorndigger caught a faint but mysterious whiff as he passed Scuzzy's corner. "You whooping it up between rounds?"

After all the Alabama Mama, Scuzzy plodded out of his corner wobblier than he went in. This time, Mambo came out with a straight right, catching the YMCU champion flush. The primitive one went southpaw, laying thunderous right hooks on Scuzzy, snapping his neck back each time. Not to a cheering corner did the Bucharest Brawler return.

"I said left, left, left," crowed Viddi. "How difficult is that for a Communist to understand?"

"I go left, left all the time and he hit me."

"No, no, to *my* left. First you Obi-Wan Kenobi the bum, then go south on him when sourpuss isn't giving you a gander—and throw in a little thumb for good measure," exclaimed Viddi before darting to the middle of the ring.

Viddi stood himself in front of Referee Thorndigger, halting the popular march of Pixie the card girl to the bitter disappointment of the whole auditorium. "I wish to file an objection. On deep background," added Viddi as the crowd remonstrated with abandon.

"Get back to your corner before I DQ your drunken heinie," thundered Referee Thorndigger.

"I'm claiming unfair distraction in breach of the letter and spirit of the Queensberry Rules and the Tammany Hall Regulations of Fistic Fighting."

"Stop your yappin' and get back to your corner, pronto."

"The ringading's shaking her tush at my guy much more than she's sashaying for the house fighter. That's dirty pool."

"Never mind her tush. Get out of my ring."

Distraught, Pixie returned to her seat only to find Mercy

Beaucoup firmly in place between Trixie and Lulu claiming to be a model scout from *Nouvelle Vouge.*

"Why you piss off referee, Viddo?" For the first time, Scuzzy seemed to be taking an interest in the proceedings as Rhino spilled more Alabama Mama down his gob.

"Psychological warfare, my friend. Boxing's a battle of minds," quoth Viddi, pointing to his forehead as he liberated the bottle from Rhino and partook of it unstintingly.

For the last three rounds, Mambo le Primitif had pounded his opponent with every fiber in his body and then some. Yet he had never witnessed boxing tactics as exhibited in this match and grown more and more apprehensive, mindful of stories of boxers from strange lands resorting to hemlocked gloves and breathing garlic into their adversary's eyes.

As Mambo paused for the briefest of flashes to appraise Scuzzy's Lithuanian defense pose, popular at the Prussian Kriegsakademie in 1805, the Bucharest Brawler appeared to melt down into the canvas before emerging again with a nuclear left uppercut, leaving Mambo suspended in air for a twinkling. Once landed, Mambo—who had never tasted the canvas—adopted the peekaboo stance while Scuzzy proceeded to pummel him into the corner.

Before he could scarcely walk, Viddi's grandmother Amma Hia (who upon a time spent her entire lottery winnings on stock in the Hindenburg) taught him the Nordic adage, "You can't fool the country pumpkin." He was not raised to be taken in by such threadbare shenanigans just as his careful study of the manly art of self-defense was about to bear fruit. Immune to the transparent posturing of Mambo and his handlers, Viddi shot to the ringside table. "I demand this travesty be paused for deliberations."

Bert Yulson, the New York boxing commissioner, thought he recognized the rather obstreperous gentleman with the funny hat from somewhere.

"My fighter's shoelace is practically undone and the referee ain't doing a blessed thing about it," complained Viddi.

"I don't see anything wrong with his shoelace." Mr. Yulson was as calm as Bournemouth in winter.

"It's coming apart any minute. That bum's playing possum, just waiting for my guy to slip on his own shoelace."

Mambo had yet to respond to the last three overhead rights from Scuzzy as the crowd clamored for the fight to be stopped when Viddi, seeing through their pathetic ruse, jumped over the ropes as Referee Thorndigger was just about to step in.

"I demand my guy be allowed to tie his shoelace," roared Viddi as every soul in the auditorium rose in protest to his intervention.

"Are you out of what passes for your mind?" growled Referee Thorndigger in disbelief.

"But I make Mambo kaput," objected Scuzzy.

A ruckus broke out, the scope of which was unheard of in the annals of the noble art of self-defense. The ensuing melee lasted almost fifteen minutes, with the crowd in attendance throwing everything not bolted to the floor into the ring while Viddi argued with Referee Thorndigger and Referee Thorndigger argued with the boxing commission and the boxing commission argued with Viddi whether Scuzzy should be disqualified for Viddi's stepping in as Viddi tugged at Referee Thorndigger's sleeve expounding the letter and spirit of the Queensberry rules and those of the Ukrainian Athletic Association to which the U.S. was a signatory member since the 1896 Athens Olympics while Beardy emptied the last dregs of Alabama Mama, no longer having to share the murderous mead with Viddi.

Before starting the fight once again, Referee Thorndigger gave Scuzzy a long, harder-than-granite look and grumbled, "Whatever you're paying this guy, it's too much." Without further ado Scuzzy resumed his biffing of Mambo.

"Too bad Mambo doesn't have the presence of mind to employ the same tactic I did," Mercy Beaucoup muttered rather loudly, already making quite an impression on the ring girls.

"You fought the Hungarian?" squeaked Pixie. "What happened?" echoed Trixie.

"All I say is, good thing it was stopped," answered Mercy Beaucoup, his shiner lending credence to the grandeur of his statement.

"Ooooo," cooed Pixie and Trixie in saucy unison.

As the bell rang for the last time, Mambo was held up by his tribal dignity alone while Referee Thorndigger's scowl betrayed his concern.

Alas, the last of the Alabama Mama had somewhat diminished Viddi's and Beardy's professional acumen. "Stop the bleeding," commanded Viddi, stepping with force on Scuzzy's toe. As the boxer howled like a Steppenwolf, desperate to extricate his foot from under his trainer's heel, Viddi rose to the occasion. "Hurry up. Can't you see he's in pain?"

Beardy, wasting no time, missed the miniscule drop of blood on the champion's nostril by an inch with his Q-Tip, sinking it right into Scuzzy's left eye.

As the buzzing pain shot through bone and marrow, Scuzzy rocketed off his stool, oblivious to Viddi's foot on his own, plummeting facefirst onto the canvas.

"You okay, comrade?" inqueried Viddi, snarling at Beardy before Scuzzy could answer. "You broke his beak, you muttonhead." Viddi brandished the empty Alabama Mama bottle at his cutman-in-training. "You KO'd our guy, you dumb beatnik. Gimme that smelling salt."

"Eh, strictly speaking . . ." Beardy looked around, furtively.

"We have but one recourse," slurred Viddi, pointing to Scuzzy's snoot.

"Is always this way?" Prompted by some avatistic sense of caution, Scuzzy covered his nose with his glove.

In the opposite corner, Referee Thorndigger took a hurried

peek at Mambo's mangled face and shook his head as the sullen cornermen administered to the scars of defeat covering his proud visage.

"No two ways about it. We're seeing this thing through." Viddi grabbed Scuzzy's nose with both hands. "One day you'll thank me for this," reassured Viddi as he began realigning Scuzzy's nozzle.

"What's up with Scooter?" asked Referee Thorndigger as Scuzzy tried desperately to extricate his nose from Viddi's grasp.

"He's just excited to be in America." Viddi's response was drowned by the cracking of Scuzzy's nose.

With the blood from his cleft schnozzle spouting profusely all over the canvas, the Bucharest Brawler sprinted in wild pursuit of Viddi around the ring, peppering him with expletives seldom heard even in the roughest nautical haunts of the Rumanian capital.

Before Thorndigger waved the match off, Mambo had long left the ring, pronouncing his professional integrity compromised.

A postfight medical examination of YMCU champion Dimitri Sciatscu, the Bucharest Brawler, revealed the most formidable amount of illegal substances found in any athlete in recorded history—absinthe, tequila, Norwegian wormwood liquor, PCP, peyote juice, lighter fluid, motor oil, juniper sapling juice, nitroglycerine, liberal doses of Danish Jolly Cola, barnyard cocaine, Grand Marnier, Old Spice, and six substances yet to be identified. The Katzenjammer Twins contemplated instituting legal proceedings against the New York State Boxing Commission for divulging the secret ingredients of their new concoction, patent pending in Uruguay and all three Baltic States.

Dimitri Sciatscu was never seen or heard from in the United States of America again. Rumor has it he became a gymnastics instructor in his native village of Timisobiurest and left for a holiday resort in southeastern Bulgaria every time a local boxing match was announced.

Wallace Beerbauer, head of security at The Banana Ballroom, was issued strict orders to shoot Viddi on sight should he ever show his face within a ten-block radius of the establishment.

Thus ended the only match in boxing history where a fighter was disqualified for attempting to strangle his own trainer in the middle of the ring with a championship belt that has yet to be claimed by anyone in the muddled world of leather and glory.

A Flood of Mexican Porn Star Tits

Justin Porter

When Dad paid for art school, they never said anything about career possibilities. Not for a fine arts degree at least. Although, if they had, I'm sure it wouldn't have included drawing a giant Mexican force-feeding his giant cock to a drawing of a chick with giant tits.

Maybe I should explain.

I had to run away to Mexico. Drug charge, too pretty for jail, blah, blah. I'm far from my father's hard-knocks upbringing.

"I brought myself up with these two hands. I fought tooth and fucking nail, every day, for the shit you take for granted!"

Whatever, Dad. It all amounts to having to draw cartoon rape and giant cock. For pesos no less.

It sucks.

Well, not for me directly, but for this one drawing I'm doing? Well, all I can say is I hope this girl's colon is double-jointed.

When I got caught with some drugs—to be specific: two hundred vics, 150 percs, a shitload of reds, and a handful of whites (or at least what looked like whites), half kilo of smack, bundled and ready to go, and a half pound of weed—I got caught with a dealer friend of mine's entire inventory. Noah's ark for the drug addict. I know it sounds unbelievable, but it's actually pretty simple.

"Hey, can I leave this here for a couple days?"

"Sure, man."

Just like that, I'm fucked. Well, there might be more to it than that, but you get the picture.

So now I'm in Mexico City. Drawing giant Mexican cock. Which is great. Hey, fuck you. At least I'm making money off my artisticness, or something.

Now, I don't know what the stereotype is for the great people of Mexico. The Irish and the Asians are supposed to be tiny. Black people are rumored to be huge—it's part of the reason I fled to Mexico. In jail I'm sure I would have ended life as a condom.

So, what's the common misconception? Because most of the Mexican women I've seen are pretty small. If all the guys down here are walking around with that shit hanging between their legs, then I just feel bad.

Inadequate, but bad.

So I got arrested, somebody was looking for the drug dealer, but they found me. It didn't help my case that I had looked in the bag, and by looked I mean rifled through it and taken two of fucking everything. What a great weekend. I mean, I don't remember shit, but it must have been great.

I threw a huge party. I invited everybody. I parceled out the contents of the bag.

I did not, however, invite *la policia.* Somebody else must have.

"No, Officer, I am not a drug 'dealer.' I gave all those drugs away for free! They weren't even mine!"

Nope. Nope, I'm drawing Mexican cock and violent rape cartoons and living in Mexico City.

* * *

When I got down here, I had no prospects. So with that and a pocket of money (courtesy of Dad), I ended up in a bar.

Crossing the border wasn't a problem. My court date wasn't for a few months and Dad's attorney convinced everyone I wasn't a flight risk. He was there when Dad sent me off. In fact we both got envelopes. His was fatter by far, and he echoed my father's sentiments with a grunt of assent.

"I don't ever want to see you again, you hear?" Dad held my eyes while the lawyer grunted and looked into his envelope. Asshole.

"Okay, Dad," I said, and my heart was in it. I mean, Dad never wanted to see me again. I'd been praying for that most of my life. Also, we both know what prison would be like, better heartbreak than ass-rape.

So this was a good thing. Let's just hope ass-fucking isn't a national sport in Mexico the way I heard it was in jail. Word to the wise—if you're ever thinking about doing something that could land you in prison? Watch *Oz* . . . seriously, 'cause if that shit's even half true, fuck that. *Oz* is about the worst concept on earth. It's a soap opera for dudes . . . Wait, I'm not finished . . . mostly *about* dudes, and heavily involving penetration of either meat or knife variety.

Either way, no, thanks.

So I got in the car and did what I was told to do. I drove and never looked back.

Hey, you know what the hardest part of drawing a big dick is? Not the head itself, that's easy—it's the fucking veins. They're a pain in the ass. You need them to wrap correctly and make it look cylindrical. I fuck up more veins on dicks than anything else. A pussy is east to draw—it's either a vertical line with a bunch of short strokes for hair, or it's a vertical oval filled with something. Easy. Give me pussy any day over dick. Even as an artist I'm straight.

Dammit, I got off track again. Any time you catch me talking about dick instead of telling the story, just remind me. Occupational hazard and all.

So I drove until I got about halfway there, which took about a week. I would have been quicker, but the Percocet I was popping to combat the anxiety and the homesickness made it hard to drive. In between the puffs of sluggish thought, I remembered something about switching cars, because of something . . . It came to me almost a day too late that Dad was planning on reporting his car stolen. Fuck. So I switched the car and used the money Dad gave me for the purpose of buying another. But, fucked if I am, I spent a little of that money on good drugs, so the car I could afford was a little shittier than the one Dad probably intended.

So me and my vintage—fuck you, it's not just another word for old—VW Bug made it across the border in one piece. The first thing I noticed? Mexico is fucking hot, and ugly, and seriously? The square whores I could do without. Anyhow, I ain't writing a travelogue or review and if this is whetting your appetite to come here? All I can say is, leave your scruples, sense of personal hygiene in your other pair of pants and get your shots.

I found my way into a bar, got a beer, and sat down. *Now* what the fuck was I gonna do?

"Those're great veins, *mang.*"

"Thanks, *mang*. And Eduardo? Don't talk like a stupid Mexican, okay?"

I was sitting at my desk working on a panel for yet another comic book—*Los Vaqueros con Los Chorizos Largos*, or something like that. What it amounted to was drawing another big cock in a long line of big cocks. The difference here was that it was the only thing in the panel. I had to pay close attention to what it looked like, so I was shading in the veins.

Eduardo was a colorist. He was responsible for the lovely flesh tone with purple tints that would soon fully define my cock. The one I was drawing, that is. Eduardo went to a good university here, and while he is a Mexican coloring pictures of dicks, he's certainly not dumb.

"Okay, *carnal.* Damn *ese'* pardong thee fock outta me ang sheet."

I sighed and went back to shading veins.

That first day I got here, I was drinking in the bar, which happens to be around the corner. I still go there. Anyhow, I was drinking. After the third beer, I was a little drunk (painkillers—fuck you, I'm not a lightweight) and doodling on the napkin in front of me.

I'd almost completed the drawing. In this case, a likeness of this pretty Mexican girl I'd seen in the street, walking to the bar with these incredibly bouncy unconfined tits. Unreal, miniskirted ass. Unbelievable. So I was sitting there putting the shading around the tits to give them some erect nipples . . . well, you know I can't resist improving on reality. They call it artistic license.

But a voice woke me up out of the place where I go when I'm drawing. It's that place where I can see the hands on the clock just spinning by in fast-forward and my insides get quiet and painful. Like I'm bleeding directly onto the page. Doesn't matter if I'm putting together my portfolio for art school or drawing a picture of a chick with huge knockers, it's there.

I looked up and saw this guy sitting next to me, ogling the drawing.

He started asking me questions about the drawing, asking me if I could always draw shit like this. What, tits? Yeah, I can almost always draw tits. In between the broken bits of language overlap between us, I figured out that his cousin worked at this place where they needed artists to draw shit like this. He called them *las historias*, told me he was gonna bring his *primo* by the bar tomorrow. He was gonna give me some *trabajo*—drawing titties.

I got up to leave and put some American *dinero* on the bar in front of me (See? My Spanish is gettin' better already) and walked out the door. I left the napkin with the naked chick on it on the bar. By the time my conversation with the guy was over, she was sporting a sombrero and leading a burro on a rope. Just your everyday naked *vaquera*. Big ten-gallon titties and sombrero.

By *la semana proxima* I was working in this little office, making pesos.

The first letter I received was directly after I had this huge argument with my boss. That beaner's got no sense of humor whatsoever, or imagination. How the fuck's he expect me not to go crazy without a little variety? He checks over all the finished art boards for the books before they go to the writers, who, incidentally, have gotta be even more bored than me. . . . I mean, Christ, how many times can you write "*devora me otra vez*," really?

So I happened to draw a few of the girls in my drawings with smaller tits than normal. I just wanted to inject a little variety, a little realism in with everything else. Shit, maybe some of the guys buying these things don't like enormous titties? Right? Maybe? No. They *all* like enormous titties . . . and for some reason every guy in the audience likes to see a huge cock too. Someday someone is going to, how you say, 'splain this to me. Why the fuck does it matter to a bunch of straight, male porn freaks how big the guys' cocks are?

So I got hauled into my boss's office where he spent the better part of a half hour ripping me a new asshole about how he wanted huge tits and huge cocks—no kidding—he actually said the people want huge cocks . . . *Mi gente quiere culo grande y la carne aun mas grande.*

Oye, Jefe? Tu gente, maricon son. Serio . . . Buncha faggots.

I was at my desk afterwards, fuming about the exchange and redrawing the art boards so that they could get to the writers and then to the press because they were due today. I was giving every girl a rack so big that you could nickname her cleavage Silicon Valley and every man a schlong large enough that they's gonna have to register it with the local police department, when this envelope landed on my desk and Eduardo's words drifted over the divide between the desks like some kind of ugly-voiced whorish siren.

"*Oye*, Buddy-Love, there's some mail for you."

I don't know why he calls me that.

It was addressed to the name I use down here, for bills, payroll, rent, yadda, etc. What's that? No, I'm not gonna fucking tell you. Anyway, there was this, I guess, fan letter in there, it was all in Spanish, and there were these awful drawings all over the letter, in the margins and along the top, breaking the text up. It was these stick figures with these huge circles, which I guess were supposed to be tits . . . somewhere underneath the little lines that were supposed to be arms. All I could think of was Juan at the local bar, telling me when "I find the *pendejos* who draw all that shit on the bathroom walls, I'm gonna *matalo,* cut off their *huevos* and whatnot."

Hey, Juan, I think I found their art teacher.

So the text was a little hard to read, looked like a third grader did it. It was so badly misspelled and there were these creepy little misshapen hearts all over the place, dotting the *I*s and replacing some of the *O*s. Like some kind of perverted, malevolent and prepubescent lesbian-retard wrote me a letter. I checked the front for the return address and saw it was from La Penitenciaria de la Ciudad de Mexico. What the fuck?

I managed to pass the next several weeks without pissing off *El Gusano Grande*, my boss. Eduardo and I passed the time talking about art in these oddly hushed tones . . . we might have been the only actual educated people in the place. Discussing actual art in here was like discussing multiplication tables at a George Bush address.

While we sat there, I got the next letter. So far, it had been six weeks since the first, and six letters. One a week. Each had gotten weirder. I asked Eduardo to look at them and tell me what this person could possibly be talking about. I found out the following things.

Thing number won: The letters espoused their love to the recipient. Me. Eww.

Thing number tu: The sender was obsessed with me—he somehow figured out which comics were mine and read every one.

Thing number fwee: "My" little porno comics made *los noches solidades y tristes*—those lonely nights—so much easier to bear.

Thing number kwatro: La Pencitenciaria de la Ciudad de Mexico was a men's prison.

The following week was memorable for three reasons. The first was that my boss was on vacation in Caracas with his wife. I'm sure he had no earthly idea why his wife insisted on hiring a personal valet assistant for the trip. I just hoped Manuel was smarter than the guy who was signing his paychecks. The second reason was that because my boss was gone, I got to fuck off all I wanted. I drew small titties all week. The third reason was that I got another letter that really crossed the line. It's not that I was ignoring the letters, it's just that I decided to drop them into a drawer under some unfinished sketches under some crap, and then not think about them at all.

But when this week's installment of Male Prison Pen Pals in Love arrived, I got a truly fucked-up little nugget. The mystery and revulsion was delivered in two parts.

Eduardo was sitting right there when I opened the letter. It was oddly colored, and once more written on paper that looked like it had been torn from a marble notebook. You know, one of those composition books? But the color was off and it smelled funny. Some of the paper was normal looking, but huge portions of it looked like something had been spilled on it. Like the guy who wrote it was eating or drinking something at the time. Eduardo's theory was that it was tea or beer or something. . . .

"*Carnal*, that shit looks like beer," Eduardo espoused with certainty.

"How could this possibly be beer? *He's in fucking jail!*"

"*Oye, homes*, don't get all fuckin' aggro with me."

"Eduardo, please, cut the shit for five seconds . . . this is freaking me out."

"All right, relax, let me think for a minute. So it's no beer? Could be tea."

The image of a hardened criminal sitting in his cell drinking tea, one pinkie finger extended and writing me love letters, was pretty terrifying.

"What about coffee?"

"Too dark."

"Soda?"

"Same thing . . . and it doesn't explain the smell."

"Shit, I don't know. Anyway, who fucking cares? He's in jail."

"Yeah," I said, not comforted by the fact much. "Sure."

"Just hope he doesn't get out. You seem to have one hardcore faggot after you."

"What makes you think he's hardcore?"

"He's a fag who writes letters covered in little hearts, maybe drinks tea, and he's in a Mexican prison—and as long as you keep getting these, it means he's staying alive. That's one badass *maricon.*"

Point.

Later that night, I was home after a short visit to the bar and a tequila-pounding session. The nice thing here is that you can buy painkillers over the counter that you would need scrips for in the States, so lucky me, I had alcohol and painkillers.

I got home and was flipping through some of my drawings and some of the other magazines that the place puts out. Some of the more conventional ones. I started to get my own personal motors running and, as I have been wont to do, since being here and unable to meet women, I rubbed one out. As I was getting up to clean off, I noticed a smell that was really familiar. I walked around for a bit, smelling my hand, trying to figure out where it was familiar from. I mean, not like it's the first time I've done the five-knuckle shuffle, but it was different. Closer somehow. Then I remembered the letter. I went to my bag and got it out. I brought it up to my face and caught a big whiff—way too similar to what I was smelling just moments ago. And vomited all over the letter and the kitchen floor.

"Eduardo, he fucking came on the letter!"

"You mean, the letter came, right?"

I forced a little more patience into my voice before answering. Eduardo was smart, and he was educated but this wasn't his *lengua primera* we were speaking, out of respect for my *blancito* ass, no less.

"No, he ejaculated all over the letter," I said, suppressing the gorge rising in my throat.

"Ewww."

"Yeah."

We both looked up at a voice that came from the entrance to my cubicle.

"E'cue me, can I talk to you for a momento?" my boss's wife said, looking at me.

Eduardo looked at her, looked at me, pursed his lips, and got the fuck out of there. I toyed with the idea of calling out, "Take me with you."

"*Que tu hace*, Gloria? *Gonyo*, you're gonna get me fucking fired."

"*Que tu hace*? Fuck joo, *pendejo*. Joo said joo was gonna call me."

"What's the matter, Gloria? Get bored with the valet?"

She pouted and sat down, going for hurt and vulnerable and just succeeding in looking cunty and swollen. . . . Works for me.

I'd fucked my boss's wife last month. Yeah, I know I didn't mention this earlier. I don't really remember it too well. A bunch of us went out to the bar after work, and my boss showed up with his wife and driver in tow, trying for a folksy "get to know you" with his employees. It worked like a solar-powered flashlight.

He started drinking immediately, got a cheer when he bought us all a round. I was thinking of making a statement and not drinking it, but fuck—a free drink's a free drink. So we all got kinda sloshed, but then he started arguing with his wife and she ended up shrieking, throwing a drink into his face, and bursting into tears. I hear communication is key to a healthy relationship, so maybe that wasn't such a big deal. But then he stood up, said, "*Puta*!" nice and loud, and stormed out, stopping long enough to grab his driver by the arm and split. Leaving wifey to find her own way home or not.

She continued to drink and we all tried to deal with it in our own way. Most everybody else ignored her, but I ended up talking to her—and then taking her home. I think. The next morning I woke on the floor next to the bed, with the pattern of the molding at the base of the wall embossed in my cheek. Further inspection revealed that my face stank and my dick hurt. I popped my first herpes sore a month later.

Puta.

By the pointed looks whenever she came by the office and by the way she was looking at me now, I guess I fucked her.

"You gave me herpes, Gloria."

"No. I no 'ave, wha' chou say, 'erpez."

The only woman I've ever come across that could make the word *herpes* sound sexy.

"Well, maybe not, but you should get checked. Because I have it and you're the only one I've fucked recently."

"Chou lie. Chou 'ave beeng fauckinngg deez Tijuana whoooars."

"No, I haven't. . . ." This was bullshit. I didn't know *whore* had that many *R*s.

"Chou dong care sheet forrr mee. *Bastardo!*" she said, and stormed sobbing from my cubicle. By the time she was three feet away, it was a full-on siren wail that didn't seem to require breathing, since it never stopped all the way to the elevator. I followed her half of the way. I don't know what I was thinking, just trying to get her to shut the fuck up before somebody got theories. But when she stormed into the elevators and gave me the finger as the door closed, I gave up and turned to go back to me desk. Only to see my boss staring at me from the open door of his office.

That afternoon, at five, I packed the stuff from my desk that was mine into a shoulder bag, swept everything else into the trash, and got ready to go. I walked out, passed by Eduardo's desk, and gave him the finger on the way out. I don't think he saw me. I decided to hit the bar on the way back, just to take the edge off. I was still flipping out a little from the scene in the office, what with it looking like I had made my boss's wife cry. Not a great career move. I couldn't even put that on a résumé should I get fired.

I sat down at the bar and the bartender nodded to me, the height of familiarity for him, and I ordered a beer and a shot. After that, I started to think maybe things weren't that bad. After the second round, things started to seem downright okay. I had a good job, never mind that I hated it . . . tons of people around the world hate their jobs, right? I had a place to live. So did (what seemed like) half the *cucarachas* in Mexico. But it had a roof, didn't it? I ordered a third beer and shot, and at the end of that I was the luckiest motherfucker in the world. I was like a cat—nine lives and feet that no matter which way I was thrown stayed beneath me. Everything was great.

I paid up, tipped well, and left the bar. As I tottered to and fro on the way home, I had the sudden urge to sing, so I did. I warbled the whitest, most off-key version of "Guantanamera" ever to defile the empty uncaring streets of Mexico City. I turned down alley and street, side and back, before I learned that I was lost. You see, I hated the place. So the year that I had spent there, I literally spent walking only to work, the bar, the *taqueria*, and back. Tacos there suck, by the way.

There was no exploration and no deviating from this formula. When a place simultaneously makes you want to vomit and scares the shit out of you, it tends to happen.

When it was definite that I was lost, I turned around and figured out that I wasn't completely alone. There were some guys behind me enjoying the night air too. . . . Excellent. I'd just ask them for directions. So I called out:

"*Buenos noches, caballeros, ayuda me, por favor, con los direciones. No se ir a mi apartamento.*"

They didn't say anything, just kept walking closer to me, and that's about when I started to get scared. I started to back away but they just got closer. The beer goggles kept me from really gauging their distance to me until one of them sank his fist into my gut, and I stupidly thought to myself: *Yup, they're too close*. I was dragged, gagging for air, into a nearby alleyway, where I guess the beat-down of the century was supposed to take place. I got hit a second time and one of the guys kicked me on the way down, where one guy, the linguist of the group, leaned down and said:

"Stay the fuck away from Gloria, *maricon*."

I would have laughed if I could have gotten air. Gloria was fat, ugly, and I had already drunk-fucked her once for which I was given the parting gift of a lifelong STD—plus the bonus for playing, a gang beating. I really could have laughed, but it would just have dissolved into tears. Luckily, I was spared having to think about this. They started the beating in earnest.

But just as soon as it began it seemed like it was over. I looked up for my aggressors and saw somebody taking out of all of them. I saw steel flash in the streetlamp and this short, stocky guy was alternating between kicking, punching, and slamming what looked like an ice pick into anything soft enough. Sheer aggression won the day. Pretty soon, the two that were able were running away; the rest looked like they were either dead or wished they were. Then strong arms were lifting me to my feet and a shoulder snugged itself under mine. I was slowly half dragged, half carried home, where I was tucked into bed like I wished my father had, and I passed out gratefully.

When I woke up the next morning, my legs, arms, head, and torso each resonated with pain like the brass tubes on a pipe organ. I could hear somebody puttering around in the front of the apartment near the front door and living room. I lay there for a minute, trying to put together exactly what happened. I remembered the beating. I remembered being helped home by that guy, who during the moment was just a shadow. So with Captain fuckin' Nemo playing, like, an aria or something on my body I got up and walked out into the other room.

And nearly shit myself.

What could only have been my benefactor from last night was standing in the kitchen wielding a frying pan like an ex-con version of Martha Stewart. Okay, fine . . . you know what I mean, an ex*er*-con Martha Stewart. Whatever. That's not the point. The point is that he was wearing this little dandelion-yellow apron that he had to have brought with him. And, yup—that's all he was fucking wearing. Plus he was flexing his butt cheeks in time with the Enrique Iglesias track pumping on the stereo.

Oooookay.

He turned around and looked at me and I felt naked. I mean, more naked. Fuck. Anyway, he was looking at me in approval.

"*Me gusta tus huevos, y pinga.*"

"What!"

"Do you want some brekfas'? I said."

I stared.

"Are you the guy who saved my ass last night out there?"

"*Sí.*"

"And you brought me back here?"

"*Sí.*"

"How did you know where I lived?"

He ignored this one and put a plate with eggs and beans on the table and gestured at it with his hand. Not knowing what else to do, I sat down and started eating. All fuckin' around aside, it was really good. The cross-dressing, Mexican ex-con Martha Stewart had a gift. He stared at me with a disturbing fondness and ruffled my hair and touched my cheek before turning around to go back to the kitchen counter to fetch a carafe of orange juice.

I sat there eating, the place on my cheek feeling hot and violated. He returned, putting a handful of pills on the table for me, I suppose—three of which were white and recognizable as generic Vicodin, the rest were little and blue. Those I didn't recognize.

"For dee paing and dee possible infection, *que no*?"

I swept up the pills, swallowed them down with OJ, and kept eating. It was about the best fucking meal I'd had since I got here. You know, for Mexico? The Mexican food sucks mammoth shit. But this guy could fucking burn, man. It was righteous. He could cook and he could fight.

Then I remembered the butt-flexing in time with ol' Enrique "I'm so straight I'm queer" Iglesias and my blood ran cold. I looked up at him, he still had his back to me and he was dancing around. He was the ugliest motherfucker I'd ever seen. He was all lumpy and his ass looked like two pit bulls fighting in a sack and one has managed to claw halfway free and the other's dead. He was covered in bad tattoos—knives, *la Virgin de Guadalupe*, prayerful hands on one arm, but there was a razor blade pressed between the fingers. Nice.

At no time during this ridiculous exchange did I stop and say, "Wait a fucking minute. Cut. Hold the phone." I gotta put that up to shock . . . or maybe I was hypnotized by the butt-flexing. But this was outta hand. My brain was having a rough time connecting Tammy Faye Bakker over there and the display I had witnessed the previous night with those hired thugs. I was officially having a hard time with this. So when he put down a plate of *chicharron* to go with the eggs and beans and everything else, I figured freaking out could wait until after breakfast. But then I saw him sit across from me with what looked like a salad. I had to ask.

"Dude, you just made all this good food. What's with the salad?"

"I watching my figure, I want to look cute."

Well, that's when I snapped.

"Are you fucking kidding me? You look like a Sailor Jerry ad, for fuck's sake!"

Then I witnessed what must truly be the most disturbing thing ever. Somebody who looked like a cross between RuPaul, Carlos Mencia, and Ron Jeremy . . . pouting.

Fucking pouting, for Christ's sake.

"Look, man, I'm sorry about that. I'm just a little on edge."

The pout faded, replaced by ice-cold eyes and a stone-hard thousand-yard stare. My nuts shrank up inside me and lodged in my throat like an extra set of tonsils. Desperately, I tried a different tack.

"The food's really good. Thanks, really. I don't think my mother or last girlfriend could cook like this. Where'd you learn?"

"*En la carcel.*"

"*La carcel*, what's that? Like a cooking school here or something?"

"In jyail."

Jyaii, jyail, what the fuck was jyail? Then I looked at him again a little closer. Oh, fuck, he meant *jail*!

I just stared at him stupidly, trying to figure out what the fuck I was gonna do, when he held up a finger and flounced happily over to a bag in the corner and got some papers out of it. He came back to the table and shoved my breakfast out of the way, from which I had just rescued my coffee cup before it all went crashing to the floor. He stared at the mess in confusion from his little "Fag-Hulk smash" moment but soon recovered and pointed at the papers in front of me triumphantly.

I looked down and saw one of the comic books I had recently worked on. The *Chorizo Largo* one, and then under that I saw this handwritten letter that looked really familiar . . .

there were some *I*s dotted with hearts and . . . oh, sweet blue-blistering fuck. I had found my secret admirer.

"I jor beegeest fang, I love jew," he said, his eyes gone all wet.

"Yeah, well, I ain't so fond of them myself, but whatever." What the hell had this got to do with the Jews? Or fangs?

"Que?"

"The Jews, they're okay, I guess." Me, still not getting it.

"No, I love joo."

"Oh . . ." Oh, he meant "you." Oh, fuck.

He started moving toward me. I looked down in horror to see that his apron was tenting, rapidly transitioning from pup to four-person. Oh God, I'd rather the beat-down in the alley-way. This sucked, I came all this way to avoid prison and a convict was gonna fuck me anyway.

Then this cat did something that I really didn't expect, not that I was sitting at home one day expecting a tattoo-covered Mexican convict with an identity crisis and a love of cartoon porn to save my life and then fall in love with me, but you know what I mean. I was revising my position by the nanosecond. Back on track now, he grabbed my hand and led me back to the bedroom.

"Look, man. Can we talk about this, please? This really isn't my thing. What do you want? An autograph? Money? What!" Desperately trying to bargain my way out of it. All he did was grunt and pull harder.

When we got into my bedroom he pulled a knife out from Christ knows where (and believe me, the options were limited and nothing nice). He showed it to me and said, his voice thick with what could only be excitement: "Jew, jew don' go no place."

Then he got on the bed on all fours and arched his back like an overaffectionate house cat. My "weird" threshold was gaining by the minute.

"I wan' jew to fock me."

"Wha?"

"Fock me."

Oh no. . . .

"Joo betta, o' I keel jew."

My mind rather inappropriately muttered: *Yeah, joo an' 'itler*, tambien. "I'm not gay!"

"*Yo no soy un maricon. Yo soy una princessa, una chiquita bonita.*"

"Uhhh . . ."

"*YO SOY UNA PRINCESSA*!" he says, slamming the hand holding the knife into my mattress repeatedly like a homicidal little girl. This was bad.

"I ga' jew dee leetle blue peels. Dee Biagara."

I was getting better with the accent. Biagara = Viagra. Shit. "So, jew fuck. I mean, you said those were for pain!"

"*Sí*, it aches so bad, *señor, por favor, ayuda me, con mi dolor*! *Ayuda me, capitan*!" he said, wiggling his hips.

So I had to make some quick decisions. Clearly, we could establish that he was crazy, could kill me, and probably would kill me. He also thought he was a pretty princess and he wanted me to fuck him. Or he was gonna kill me. Well, at least it wasn't me getting plugged. I picked up the comic book, one of mine, and held it up at arm's length so that I was looking at it, and not him. Then I reached down with my other hand and unzipped. Time to save my life. This was gonna be awful.

"*Un momento, caballero.*" I heard a thump and saw a little jar of off-brand Vaseline.

Okay . . . deep breath. Don't puke. Don't puke.

I found myself thinking of the little Mexican chick with the breasts—the first naked girl I drew in Mexico.

When I was ready, I could tell he really had slipped me a shitload of Viagra. He looked over his shoulder and disappointment was plain in his eyes.

"*Un pocito pequeño. Pero,* it will do."
"*Hey, fuck you!*"
"*Sí, ahora.*"
So I did, God help me.

After it was over and I tamped down my sense of nausea, he rolled over and said, "*Oye,* my turn now. Fleep over."

Have I mentioned I *hate* Mexico City?

Markers

Albert Tucher

"You're going to owe me big time," Diana said.

"I already owe you," said Detective Tillotson. "By the time you collect on all my markers, you'll be retired. Or I will."

He walked her down the corridor, past a series of open doors. Even blindfolded, she would have known she was in a hospital. Each room sent that disinfectant-and-dirty-diaper odor out to meet them. He stopped by the only closed door and took a photograph from his breast pocket.

"This is all he had on him. No ID. We haven't matched his fingerprints to anything yet."

He turned the photo around to show her. "Can you do this with your hair?"

"Sure. But the nose is a problem. Maybe I had it done, but most nose jobs go the other way. Smaller, not bigger."

"He won't be able to tell," said Tillotson. "Only one eye is open, and the docs think his optic nerve is damaged. He'll only see your coloring and your general shape. Close enough."

She made a face. "Somebody did a job on him."

"Get ready. It's not pretty."

She went back down the hall to the unisex visitors' bathroom. Diana watched herself in the mirror as she tied her dark blond hair at the back of her neck. Her regular clients preferred her hair long and loose, but it didn't matter. This job was still hooking—being what a man wanted her to be.

She didn't mind this man, as cops went. He had called on her for help several times. It was tactful of Tillotson to pretend that he owed her, but when a cop asked, she didn't consider saying no. He could make it impossible for her to work.

She found him where she had left him. "Why am I doing this?"

"He's not talking. Maybe you can get something out of him."

"Talking I don't mind. Just be around in case he gets physical."

"He won't. Believe me, he can't."

He looked at his watch. "The docs say five minutes."

She opened the door and entered the room. Tillotson swung the door closed behind her, but he left an inch of space for listening.

The man wouldn't have passed for human anywhere but in a hospital bed. If she had seen him shrink-wrapped in a supermarket, she would have complained to the meat manager.

She knew which eye wouldn't open. Someone had worked the entire left side of his face into a bulging purple mass. The right side looked better, but only in comparison. The eye was bruised, but it probably had some leeway to open.

He looked asleep. She hoped that he was. It would make things easier for him, and Tillotson might excuse her from her task.

Yeah, right, she thought.

She made herself take the man's hand.

His right eye flickered. The lids parted painfully. She felt a stinging behind her own eyes.

Tears. When had she cried last? She blinked several times and told herself to concentrate on the job.

His weakness wouldn't allow him to turn his head. She leaned over to let him see her. His swollen and shredded lips moved, and something raspy happened in his throat. Diana looked around the room. On a wheeled cart sat a water bottle. A bent plastic straw stuck out of its lid. She tried to free her right hand, but he gripped it with surprising strength. Unwilling to wrestle with him, she stretched and just reached the straw with two fingers of her left hand. She rested the bottle on the bed, changed her grip, and gently inserted the straw between his lips.

She watched to make sure that he didn't drown himself, but he lacked the strength to take that much water. She pulled the bottle away, waited for him to swallow, and gave him the straw again.

He lay still. Diana thought she had lost him to exhaustion, but then he spoke in a thread of a voice. "I knew you would come."

She thought about saying something vague but decided to keep quiet. Her voice might spoil the illusion.

"It was worth it. I'd do it again. Whatever it takes."

Diana thought she understood. She fought the urge to pull her hand away. She had to make sure she was right.

"I can do anything, knowing you'll be there," he said. "I knew you didn't mean those things you said. I knew you would love me sooner or later."

This time she did jerk her hand away from him. She turned and ran for the door. It opened to meet her, and Tillotson caught her before she collided with him.

"Whoa," he said. "What happened? Did you get anything?"

She nodded and paused to calm herself.

"I got enough," she said.

He gave her a skeptical look.

"What I wish you would do," she said, "is go in there and lean on his chest until he stops breathing. Save the world a lot of trouble."

In three years this was the first time she had shocked him.

"But what I think you'll do is go through the local restraining orders and see if anybody is missing a stalker. That woman in the picture you have is getting a breather. From him. And I have a feeling it's not going to last. And you're probably going to end up arresting her father, or her boyfriend, or her brother, while he walks."

Tillotson nodded toward the room. "Sounds like you know something about this kind of thing."

"I picked up a stalker a while back. Occupational hazard. No matter what I did, he just took it as a test that he had to pass. Pass enough of them, and we would live happily ever after. The problem was, if he saw me with anybody else, it took him about a tenth of a second to go all psycho on me."

"Is he still a problem?"

"No," said Diana. "Not for a couple of years."

She met Tillotson's eyes. "Since then I have another client who gets freebies for as long as he wants them."

"I didn't hear that."

She shrugged.

"Thanks for coming out," he said.

She left him alone with his problem.

Two days later she opened the *Newark Star-Ledger*. She was about to skip to the Olympic news from Barcelona, when she noticed a story about a man who had died in Morristown Memorial Hospital. The man had a name now, but it meant nothing to her. The doctors suspected a blood clot resulting from injuries that he had suffered in a severe beating. They would have to conduct an autopsy.

Police were questioning a young woman and her two brothers.

She called Tillotson at his office. He was in. He sounded as if he wanted to be somewhere else.

"They're not talking," he said. "At all. Not many suspects are that smart."

In other words, she thought, *I can keep hoping*.

"I owe you," he said.

"Not this time."

Bullets and Fire

Joe R. Landsale

I had hit the little girl pretty hard, knocking her out and maybe breaking something, messing her nose up for sure. But for me, it was worth it.

I sat at the table in the bar and smelled the sour beer and watched some drunks dance in the thin blue light from behind the bar. I was sitting with Juan and Billy, and Juan said to me, "You see our reasoning. You gonna get in with us, you got to show what you got. And fighting a guy, that shows you're some kind of tough, but hitting a girl like that . . . her what? Twelve or thirteen? Way you smoked her, now that shows you don't give a damn. That you ain't gonna back up. If we say what needs to be done, you'll just do it. That's the way you get in with us, bro."

"Yeah," Billy said, "it makes you tough to fight a guy, brave maybe. But to hit someone like that you don't know, just someone we pick on the street and to savage her up like that? My man, that's where the real stones is, 'cause it goes against . . . What is it I'm looking for here, Juan?"

"What Mommy and Daddy taught?" Juan said.

"Shit," Billy said, "my daddy hit me so much, I thought that was how you started and ended the day."

"Hell," Juan said. "I don't know. You guys want some more beers?"

I sat there and thought about what I had done. Just got out of the car when they told me, and there was this young girl on the sidewalk, a backpack on. I could still see how she looked at me. I was just going to hit her once, you know? To knock her out, a good blow behind the ear. Nothing too savage, and then I got to thinking, *These guys are going to take me in, they want to see something good*. I did what had to be done. I beat her up pretty good and then I took her wallet. I started to take the backpack, but I couldn't figure on there being anything in there that I'd want. But she had a little wallet that was on a wrist strap. She ought not to have been wearing it like that, where it could be seen. Someone should have told her better.

Juan came back with some beers and a bowl of peanuts and we sat and drank some beer and ate the peanuts. I like peanuts.

I touched my shirt and felt something wet. I started to wipe it, but then realized it was sticky. The girl's blood. I wiped it on my pants. It was dark in there and you couldn't see much of anything.

I watched some more couples get up and start dancing to the music on the jukebox, moving around in that blue light to a Smokey Robinson tune. My dad had always liked that song, about seconding and emotion. Billy said, "You know, even being a black man myself, I don't like it when they play that old nigger music. How about you, Tray, you like that old nigger shit?"

I did, and I didn't lie about it. "Yeah, I like soul fine. I like it a lot."

Billy shook his head. "I don't know. It's all kind of mellow and shit. I like a nigger can talk some shit, you know? Rap it out."

"All sounds like a hammer beating on tin to me," I said. "This stuff, it's got some meat to it, cooked up good. Plenty of steak, not just a bunch of fucking sizzle."

"He told you," Juan said. "One nigger to another. He told you good."

"Yeah, well, I guess nothing says we got to like the same stuff, but that's all Uncle Tom jive shit to me. A little too educated, not street enough."

I remembered what my brother Tim said to me once, "Don't let these neighborhood losers talk you down. Education hasn't got a color. Money, it's all green—and education, it gets you the money. It gets you something better than a long list of stickups and stolen money. You got to have pride, brother. Real pride. Like Daddy had."

Daddy had worked some shit-ass jobs to help us make it. Mama died when we were young, fell down some stairs drunk. Broke her neck. Daddy, he didn't want us to end up drinking and fighting and getting ourselves in trouble the same way. He tried to raise us right, told us to get an education. That's what Tim had done, got an education. He'd gone straight, done good. I loved Tim. He was a proud man. Well . . . *boy*, really. He wasn't much older than me. Twenty-two when it was all over for him. When I thought of him, what I thought of as a proud man, I hated that he was gone.

Me, tonight, I wasn't so proud. I'd beat that girl good and taken her little pink wallet from the pocket of her dress. A pink wallet that when you opened it and folded it out had some pictures, some odds and ends, and five dollars.

"So, you guys, to get in with the gang, you do something like you had me do tonight?" I said.

I knew the answer to that, but I was just making conversation.

"Yeah, well, we did one together," Juan said. "He was Mexican and almost as dark-skinned as me, and that's pretty damn dark." All I could see of him really was his teeth in the blue light from behind the bar. He said, "We did a guy, me and Billy. Did him good."

"So you do a guy, and then you have me do a girl, and you tell me that's the way to do it? What about the rest of the gang? Any of them do like I did?"

"Sometimes, something like it," Billy said. "We had one boy who loved dogs, we had him shoot his own dog. Pet it on the head and open its mouth and stick a gun in there and shoot him. Shot came out that dog's ass, ain't kidding you. Went through that dog's ass and through a wall in the guy's house and knocked a lamp over."

"I think the bullet went in there and hit the end table," Juan said. "I think the table jarred and the lamp fell off."

"Whatever," Billy said. "You know what? That guy, he don't stay in the gang long. He shoots himself. Found him dead, lying over his dog's grave. That's no shit. Can you imagine that, getting that way with a dog? You got your gang, and your family . . . and everything else? That's just everything else, and that includes dogs or the fucking kitty."

"So I beat up a girl and this guy shot a dog, and you guys did a guy, so now we're all equal? That the way it works?"

Juan shook his head. "Well, you got to do something to get in, but we did something big, and that made us kind of lieutenants. You, you're just like a private. But you're in, man. You're in."

"Mostly," Billy said.

"The gang, they still got to have a look at you, and our main man, he's got to give you the okay."

"So what did you do?" I said. "I've heard around, but I was wondering I could get it from you."

Juan sipped his beer. "Sure," he said.

Billy said, "Way we did the guy was the thing."

"We may be small town, baby," Juan said, "one hundred thousand on the pop sign, but we got our turf and we got our ways, and we did that boy good."

"He was young, maybe about your age," Billy said. "Age we are now. He worked at a little corner grocery, was a grocery boy."

"What grocery?" I said.

"One around the corner, just a half block from here," Billy said. "Or *was* around the corner. Ain't no more. There's a big burn spot where it used to be."

Billy and Juan laughed and put their fists together.

"You mean the Clement Grocery?" I said.

"That's it," Billy said. "Guess it was, let me see . . . how long we been in the gang, Juan?"

"Three years come October," Juan said.

"I know the place," I said. "Course, I'm pretty new here now, but I used to live here when I was younger, so I know the place. I didn't live far from here."

"Yeah?" Billy said. "Where?"

"I don't remember exactly, but not far from the grocery. I used to go there. I don't remember where I lived, though, not exactly. Not far from here, though."

"You ain't that old. You remember the grocery, you got to remember where you lived," Billy said.

"I could probably find the place, just don't remember the street number. You took me around, I could find it. But, man, I don't give a shit. This thing you did with the grocery boy. Tell me about that."

"We should have left that grocery and the kid alone," Juan said. "It was a good place to get stuff quick, and now we got to go way around just to buy some Cokes. But, man, what we did, it was tough. We was gonna be in the gang, you see? And the Headmaster—which is what he calls himself—ain't that something? Headmaster? Anyway, he says we got to do something on the witchy side, so we went and got a hammer and nails. When we got there, the kid was working in the store and the place was empty. Just goddamn perfect."

"Perfect," Billy said.

"So we got hold of the kid and while Billy held him under the arms, I got my knee on his foot and got a big ole nail I had brought. And with the hammer, I drove it right through his foot and nailed him to the floor."

"He screamed so loud I thought we was caught for sure," Billy said. "But nobody come running. They must have not heard him, or knew it was best to pretend they didn't."

"Fucker kicked me with his other leg, two, three times and I just hammered the shit out of his leg. Billy couldn't hold him anymore, and he fell over. Then I kicked him a bit and he quit struggling, but he was plenty alive."

"That's what makes what happened next choice," Billy said. "We put some boxes of popcorn on him and then we set fire to the place."

"You forget I nailed his other foot to the floor."

"That's right," Billy said. "You did."

"He was so weak from the kicking we had given him, and all the blood that had filled up his shoe, was running out over the top of it, he didn't know I was doing what I was doing until the nail went in."

"He really screamed that time," Billy said.

Juan nodded. "That's when we got the popcorn, bunch of other stuff, and started the fire. We ran out of there and across the street and in the alley. We could hear that kid screaming across the street, but nobody came. A light went on in a couple windows of buildings where people lived upstairs, but nobody came."

"Fire took quick," Billy said. "We were so close—and if I'm lying, I'm dying—we could hear that popcorn popping and him still screaming. And then we saw the flames licking out of the open doorway. Then we saw the kid. He got his feet free, probably tore the nails right through them, and he was crawling out the door. He was all on fire, looked like that Fantastic Four guy. What's his name, The Flame?"

"The Human Torch," Juan said. "Don't you know nothing?"

"Yeah, him," Billy said. "Anyway, he didn't crawl far before that fire got him. Then we finally did hear some sirens, and we got out of there."

"Last look I got of that kid, he wasn't nothing but a fucking charcoal stick," Juan said.

"That's what got us in the gang," Billy said. "And the Headmaster, he said it was a righteous piece of witchiness, and we was in, big time. You sweating, man?"

I nodded. "A little. I got a cold coming on."

"Well, don't give it to me," Juan said. "I can't stand no cold right now. I hate those things, so stay back some."

"This Headmaster, he got a name?" I asked.

"Everyone calls him Slick when they don't call him Headmaster," Billy said. "Shit, I don't even know what his real name is, or even if he's got one. He's maybe nearly twenty-six, twenty-seven years old. It don't matter none to you, though. You done done your thing to get in, and we're witnesses."

"Once you're in," Juan said, "no one much fucks with you. It's like a license to do what you want. Even the cops are afraid of us. They know we find out who they are and where they live, we might give them or their little straight families a visit."

"Gang is the only way to live around here," Billy said. "Get what you want, feel protected, you got to have the gang, 'cause without it . . . man, you're just on your own."

"Yeah," I said. "I know what that's like, being on my own. So I'm in. I've done my deed and I'm proud of it, and I want in."

* * *

We went out of there and around the corner and walked a few blocks to where the gang had their headquarters. I thought about the streets and how dark they were and figured that fast as the streetlights got repaired, someone shot them out. Maybe the city was never going to repair them again. Maybe they'd had enough.

Dad told me once that if people don't care about where they live, the way they act, people they associate with, they get lost in the dark, can't find their way back 'cause there's no light left.

I had taken a pretty good step into the shadows tonight.

There was an old burnt-out building at the end of the block. We went past that, turned right, and there was this old bowling alley. The sign for METRO BOWLING was still there, but there was nothing metro about the place. The outside smelled like urine and there was some cracked glass framed in the doorway. When we got to the door, Juan beat on the frame with his fist. After a moment the door opened slightly, and a young white woman with long black hair showed her face. Juan said something I wasn't listening for, and then we were inside. The girl turned and walked away. I saw she had an automatic in her hand, just hanging there like it was some kind of jewelry. Juan gave her a slap on the ass. She didn't even seem to notice.

The place stank. You could hear music in the back. Hardcore rap and some good old-school hip-hop going, all of it kind of running together. There were quite a few people in there. The floors where the bowling alley had been were still being used for bowling. Gang members, most of them dressed so you knew they were in a gang, flying their freak flags, were rolling balls down the wooden pathways, knocking down pins. The little pin machine was working just fine and it picked up the pins and carried them away and reset them. The alleys were no longer shiny and there were little nicks in the wood here and there and splinters stuck up in places as if the floor was offering toothpicks.

In front of the bowling alleys were racks for shoes, but there weren't any shoes in them. Some of the gang members were wearing bowling shoes, some weren't. The clack and clatter of the balls as the machine puked them up and slammed them together made my ears hurt. Over near the far wall, a big black guy had this Asian girl shoved up against the wall so that both her palms were on it, her ass to him. Her pants were down and so were his. What they were doing wouldn't pass for bowling, though balls were involved.

"That there is B.G. He's slamming him some nook," Billy said.

"I kind of figured that's what was going on," I said.

We went past them, around a corner, and into a back room. There was a desk there, and a guy that looked older than the others was sitting behind the table with a big bottle of Jack Daniel's in front of him. He was a white guy with some other blood in him, maybe black, maybe all kinds of things, and he was looking at me with the coldest black eyes I've ever seen. They looked like the twin barrels of shotguns. He grinned at Billy and Juan, showing me some grillwork on his teeth that was silver and shiny and had what looked like diamonds in them. For all I knew they were paste or glass.

On his right side was a young white girl who wasn't bad looking except for a long scar on her cheek. On her right hand side was a guy who looked as if he might like to eat me and spit me out. On Grillwork's left was a husky-looking Hispanic guy with eyes so narrow they looked like slits.

"So, you got a wayward soldier," Grillwork said.

"That's right. We known him now a couple weeks, and he's been wanting in. Talking to us, walking around with us some. He did some righteous business tonight," Juan said.

"No shit," Grillwork said. "What'd he do?"

Billy told him and Grillwork nodded like he had just been told I had invented time travel.

"That's good," Grillwork said. "That's real good. So you wanting in, huh?"

I nodded. "Yeah, I want in. I thought I was in. I did what was asked."

"Well, that's a beginning," Grillwork said. "You showed some stones doing something like that."

I didn't think it had taken that much in the way of stones. She was a kid, something a high wind could knock over.

"Sit the fuck down, man," Grillwork said. "What's your name?"

I sat in the chair in front of the table and told him my name.

"What you want in for?" Grillwork asked.

"I don't have a family. It's tough to make it in this town. Jobs bore me."

"All right, all right." Grillwork nodded. "You got to understand some things. You come in, you got to stay in. You want to get out . . . well, you get out all right, but all the way and pretty goddamn final. Not pretty final. Final. Savvy?"

I nodded.

"You get in, we got work of our own, but it's different. You do stuff that makes money by taking other people's money. We sell some chemicals, man. Got our own lab."

"Meth?" I said.

"Oh yeah. Now and again, we deal in some weed and some pussy, but mostly we got the meth. You pick dough up on the side? That's yours, but not by selling chemicals, man. The mind mixer business, that's all ours. I find you dipping your dick into that, you'll wind up in a ditch with flies on your face. Got me?"

I nodded again.

"You can't run your own string of whores, lessen' you hook

up with some gal will pull the train for the club, then go out there and lube some johns. You got that understood?"

"I do."

"All right. The things on the side, you can do what you want to the citizens, you know? I don't care you rob them or rape them or whatever, but you get caught and dragged downtown, not a thing we can do. But there is this. Cops on our turf—which is about twelve blocks, almost square, 'cause it's got an old park in it that fucks up the square thing, makes it like a square with an addition—"

"Who gives a shit?" the girl next to him said. "Just tell him what you're gonna tell him."

Grillwork looked at her, and she looked back. Her eyes were pretty damn cold too.

He looked back at me, said, "Those twelve blocks, the park, that's ours. But these cops, they pretty much leave us alone. 'Cause when they don't, we got a way of not liking it, a way of tracking them down. It's been done, man."

I nodded.

Juan was chewing gum now, and I could hear him popping it. I felt something cold against the back of my neck and turned. Juan had a nine poking against my neck as he was grinning and chewing his gum.

"That there," Grillwork said, "that was in case you didn't have all the right answers. Like maybe you wanted to argue a point."

"No argument," I said, turning back to face Grillwork. "I take it you're the one called Headmaster, since you're the one laying out the ground rules."

Juan took the nine out of my neck.

"No. You don't talk to Headmaster about this shit. I'm one of his lieutenants. You can call me Hummy."

"All right," I said. It was a curious name, some nickname, and I wondered about it, but didn't really care enough to ask.

"You frisked him?" Hummy said to Juan and Billy.

"Earlier tonight," Juan said. "He ain't packing nothing but a dick and balls."

"All right," Hummy said. "Let me ask."

I didn't know what that meant, and I didn't ask who he wanted to ask or what he wanted to ask them about. I found the best thing was just to be quiet and everyone filled things in for themselves. You said too much, then you gave them room for varied interpretation. You didn't say anything, they usually filled it up with what they wanted.

Hummy got up and went away. He was gone for a good while. When he came back, he jerked a thumb towards the door he had gone through. We went through it, along a narrow hall by a bathroom with an open door where a guy that was maybe three hundred pounds sat on a sagging toilet and made noises like he was trying to pass a water buffalo, antlers and all. The hallway was full of stink.

"Close the fucking door," Juan said as we went by. "God-*damn* Rhino. Who wants to smell that shit, or see you delivering it? Close the fucking door."

Rhino didn't reach out and close the door, and we just kept going along the hallway. At the end of the hall was another door. This one was a thick door that looked as if it had been added recently. Billy knocked, and a voice said, "Come in." We went inside.

It was a big stinking room and it was full of weapons. All kinds of things. I saw an AK-47 and some automatic pistols, small and large. There were also machetes and gas cans all over the place. Some net bags were hanging from the ceiling. In the bags were some human heads that were the source of the smell. They were jacking with me, trying to see what I was made of, how scared I was.

Way I felt, scared was not on the agenda. I was way past

scared and had leveled out into a steady feeling of numbness. My body was numb, my mind was numb, my soul was numb. The world to me was nothing more than one big numb ball of grief.

I could cope with it because of the sensei I'd had when I moved away from here, some years back. I had enjoyed the training so much, I almost didn't move back. It almost made me mellow.

Almost.

But I had the demon inside, and I had left sensei and what he had taught me. I wasn't trying to use martial arts to learn to live my life without violence, with confidence and harmony, way he taught me. I wanted to use it to hurt someone, the thing I wasn't supposed to do. I had learned nothing that really mattered from my sensei and I knew it and it made me feel a little ill.

There was a guy in the back, and I took him for the Headmaster, way he carried himself. There were some guys with him. Juan and Billy left me looking at the heads in the bags, and went over to the guy and talked with him. I could hear them whispering, looking back at me from time to time, so I knew I was the subject.

This went on for a while, so I looked around and saw all the guns and the ammunition; all the representatives of power. Straight people, they tell you they like guns because they like to shoot targets. But it's the power, man. That's what it is and all it is. It's the big dick spurting lead cum all over the place. You can call it our rights or you can call it target practice or you can call it personal protection, but it's about power. I wanted power, and I wanted a gun just like everyone else. Martial arts, Shen Chuan, it gave me power—but a gun, that was the ultimate power.

I put that all out of my mind as the crowd back there broke off and I got a really good look at the guy they were surrounding. He was a little blond guy with a burr haircut and he came strutting around one of the racks of weapons. He was covered in weapons himself, holsters filled with automatics all over him. His eyes darted from side to side. He was as paranoid as a staked goat at a Fourth of July picnic. And like the goat, just because he was paranoid didn't mean they weren't out to get him.

"You're the Headmaster," I said.

"They call me that," he said, and he didn't offer me his hand when I offered mine. I put my hand away, feeling as if I had offered him a cold fish. He looked me up and down. He was short, but he was broad and had legs like tree trunks. They were supported on little feet in little black boots with silver tips. With those things, he could kick a cockroach to death in a corner of the room.

"I got word you done some things," he said.

"You mean the girl?" I said.

"I mean the girl. You hit her good?"

"Yeah. I broke her little nose."

"That shows you got some grit. I'm not saying it takes anything to beat up a little girl, but I'm telling you it takes balls to do it."

I had already heard this from his guys, but I didn't say anything.

"We need guys like you, can follow orders, do what needs to be done."

I said, "Okay."

"Those heads you're looking at," Headmaster said, "they strayed. They started trying to hustle their own business—*our* drug business—when their piece was enough. They wanted more. They wanted to sell a little pussy on the side. The pussy is in the river. These guys . . . well . . . you see what's left of them."

"Run a pretty tight ship," I said.

Headmaster laughed. "That I do. What we got to do, man, is we still got some things to try with you."

"Try with me?"

"Yeah," Headmaster said. "Come back here."

There was another room beyond this one and I let the Headmaster lead me back there. When he did, his guys followed me in. Juan hit me a hard one behind the head and made my sight go black. Then my vision jumped back with white dots in it, and I staggered a little. Then someone I didn't see kicked me up under the butt from behind and got me in the balls.

I swung out and hit someone, and then the Headmaster was on me, slamming one in my stomach. I guess instinct took over, because I kicked him in the groin and stepped forward, popped my palm against the side of his head, and he went down.

I whirled then, tried to hit another guy with a jab, but he slipped it and I caught one under the belly. I jammed an elbow into the back of his neck as he stooped, and he grunted. Then I slapped my hands over his ears and he screamed and turned away. I kicked out at Billy's knee, and he screamed. I hit Juan in the throat, and as he dropped, I smelled shit on the air.

I hit another one of the guys with a knee to the inside of his leg, and that dropped him. I poked my fingers in another guy's eyes, not enough to blind him, but enough to make him less interested in kicking my butt.

And then the Headmaster yelled, "That's it, that's enough."

He got up holding his nuts with one hand, grinning at me, holding his other hand up in a stop motion.

"All right," he said. "All right, you got what it takes."

I wiped blood off my mouth.

"We got to see you can take it same as dish it out . . . and man, you can dish it out. Can you teach that chop socky to the rest of us?"

"So this was a test?" I said.

"Big time," Headmaster said. Then he frowned and looked at Juan. "Man, you shit your pants?"

Juan nodded.

"Go get some fresh drawers," Headmaster said. "Damn, Juan, he didn't hit you in the belly."

"When you get hit hard, throat, any kind of place," I said, "you're carrying a load, you'll drop it."

"Ain't that something?" Headmaster said. "I've seen and smelled them do it when they're shot, but I didn't know about the hitting. That's some shit you got there."

"No," I said. "It's Juan that's got the shit."

Everyone, except Juan, who was waddling out of the room, laughed.

I got respect when everyone in the bowling alley heard about how I had fought. Truth was though, had they fought back a little more persistent, martial arts training or not, I would have been toast. They weren't willing enough. Me, I thought I was in for it. Like maybe I was just a test for them, way the girl was supposed to be for me, so I was fighting back big time. Them, they were just testing. I was glad they quit when they did, 'cause I felt like my balls were trying to crawl out of my asshole from that kick I got.

Anyway, I was in.

So, I guess a week went by, and I was doing some little things, like I had to break a guy's leg to get some money that was owed for something or another the gang had going. I didn't know what. I didn't ask. I didn't care. I just stomped the side of his knee with my foot. It cracked like a fruit jar tossed on the sidewalk and he gave up the money. He was ready to give anything up. I asked him to suck my dick and lick my nuts, he'd have done it. Anything to keep me from breaking his other knee.

Another week, and they gave me permission to go in the gun

room, 'cause you had to have one of the main guys open it with a key, and you had to have permission to go in. They took me in there—Headmaster, Billy, and Juan. They gave me a gun, or rather they told me to pick anything I wanted. I picked an automatic pistol out of the pile and I pulled an AK-47 off the rack. I got some ammunition, clips for the AK and automatic. I should have got more clips, but I was nervous. I ended up with an extra load for the AK-47, one for the automatic.

"You're gonna need that shit," Headmaster said, "things we got going. We got a little gang on the other side, bunch of spicks—"

"Hey," Juan said.

"Not our spicks," Headmaster said, and then he looked right at Juan. "And thing is, I don't care to please you anyway, beaner. I'm the man here, and that makes you the boy. You got me, you fucking pepper gut?"

Juan made a face that looked as if he had just been handed a dead rat to eat. He had been using that kind of talk all along, but it caught him funny going right at him and mad like that.

Headmaster leaned forward till his nose was almost on Juan's. "I said, you got me?"

Juan nodded. "Sure, man. I got you. No hard feelings."

"If there is, you'll live with them," Headmaster said. He turned to me then, said, "We're gonna have to cut down on them spicks from out and away. I thought you ought to get your shot to get some blood in, you know? Something serious. Not poking some little girl in the nose or breaking a leg. Something serious."

"All right," I said. "What's the plan?"

"We're gonna get you and Juan and Billy to saddle up, go over there, and take a little cruise by, spread some lead. These guys, they got them a little meth thing going and that's our finance, baby. I don't want them sucking any of our chocolate."

"A drive-by?" I said.

"That's what I said, only more than that, really. We're gonna drive by, and then when they think it's over, we're gonna come back on them."

"They'll be ready," Billy said.

"What about civilians?" I said.

"Hell," Headmaster said, "there ain't no civilians. They're the same as that girl you popped, the shit these guys nailed and burned to get in the gang. There's us and there's them. You pop a few wives, girlfriends, or kids—that's the price of doing business. Price of fucking on turf ain't yours."

"I got you," I said.

Headmaster nodded, said, "You boys get what you need?"

Billy said, "We got guns, and we got these."

He grabbed his loose pants where his balls were, and acted like he was shaking them.

I reluctantly laid the rifle back in the rack, said, "Give me a minute to deliver my last meal," and went out of the gun room and into the little bathroom off to the side. It was cleaner than the big bathroom right next to the lanes. And the big fuck wasn't in there stinking it up. I mean, you wouldn't want to eat off the floor or nothing, but compared to the other one, it was like it had just been sanitized. The other, it never got cleaned, smelled bad, and the toilets all had dark rings inside them. There were boogers on the wall and things written in pen and pencil, blood and snot, and maybe even shit. You went in there, you might step on a needle, a rubber, or find some guy bending a girl over the sink, doing their business, needling enough horse to call it a Clydesdale.

I went in and put the lid down on the toilet and sat there and tried to catch my breath. I was in. I belonged to the gang. It's what I wanted.

I took out the automatic—a nine—and looked at it, felt cold sweat trickle down from my hairline, run along my face, and drip off my chin. I laid the automatic on my knee. I thought about my brother. I thought about my father. My father, he never got over it. Killed himself. Shot himself.

My brother, in that store, his feet nailed to the floor. And those two jackasses having set a fire just so they could be in a club, a gang. Now here I was, having punched a little girl in the face and taken out a guy's knee, about to do some real damage. Of course, my reasons for being here were different. I didn't want to be a member because I respected them, but because I didn't. I hated them. Especially Juan and Billy, and then the head guy. I wanted what my sensei said was useless to have, vengeance.

After my brother was dead and we had moved away, my dad tried to get it together, but couldn't. He put a gun in his mouth and blew his worries asunder. I was mad at him, hated him for a while, but then I got over it because I realized how hard it was to carry on. I was doing the same thing, but in a slightly different manner. Throwing it away. But unlike Dad, it wouldn't just be me and some blood on the living room floor. There were some guys I was gonna flush with me.

If I got out all right, that was good. But I knew this: I was going to make my mark for Dad and for my brother. They were gonna get some blowback on that business they done.

I picked up the automatic and laid it on the sink, lifted the lid, and took a piss. Then I zipped up and washed my face, stuck the automatic in my waistband, and went out of there. When I came back into the gun room, the door still open, Juan looked at me kind of funny, said, "Man, we thought you fell in."

"I was seriously packing," I said.

I picked up the AK-47. I had shot one before. I had learned

a lot about guns from my sensei, the one who told me that guns are about romance and power more than they are about self-defense or constitutional amendments. He also said, "Boys like their toys, the more dangerous and explosive the better."

He said he liked them too, and went to bed at night bothered by it.

I went to bed at night bothered by everything. I didn't see my brother die, but I could imagine how horrible it was. Him crawling and that fire eating at him and that goddamn popcorn popping. And across the way, those two fucks laughing, getting a kick out of it all.

I looked at Headmaster and Juan and Billy, and thought, *These three, they're the main guys I want. I could just do it now.* I could open up and they wouldn't know plums from dog balls. In a moment, it would all be over.

But I didn't want to do that. I wanted more than that, and though I was willing to give what it took to get even, I preferred the opportunity to stay alive. Didn't happen, didn't happen.

I was ready to play either way.

"What now?" I said.

"I'm thinking," Headmaster said, "we should probably arm a couple of the other guys, take them with you. It's best not to take a whole wad. You do that, you're more likely to end up butt-fucking one another. Too many, that's a fucking crowd. A small hit force, that's the way to go."

"You going?" I asked.

The Headmaster looked me as if I had asked if I could stick my finger up his ass and fish for shit.

"No. You're going. You and Juan and Billy, maybe a couple of others. I go when I want and if I want. You aren't questioning my chops, are you?"

"No," I said. "I was just wondering."

"I'll do the wondering for both of us, blood."

"All right," I said.

"Damn right, it's all right. Juan, you go out there and pick you some wham-bang-dangers—two of them—then let's get them fixed with some tools and some lead, and then you guys, I'll lay it out to you. The whole shebang of a plan."

One way, I thought, *one easy way is, I isolate Juan and Billy, take them out*. That would be the good way, the smart way. But it wasn't satisfying to me, not even by a little bit. I imagined Tim squirming with his feet nailed to the floor, screaming, the unbearable heat, the flames licking, him ripping his feet apart to get loose.

While I was doing this, Juan went out of the room. I thought, *Shit, I got to get it together and keep it together. Here I am in my head and outside my head the world is moving on.*

"I'll go with him," I said.

And I was out the door and going down the hall, could see Juan's back as he turned the corner into the room where I had met the guy I thought was the Headmaster. I was almost to the door when I heard Headmaster yell at me.

"Hey, I tell you to go anywhere?"

I didn't look back, said, "What's it matter?"

"It matters 'cause I say so," Headmaster said, in that way of his that lets you know even when it isn't important, he wants you to know he's the swinging dick of the operation.

I looked in the room, and there behind the desk was Hummy, guy I thought originally was the Headmaster, and was probably his replacement. One day, the Headmaster would look south and a bullet would come from the north, probably out of Hummy's gun.

Or that's the way it might have gone over had I not decided to change everyone's plans. I was the fucking fly in the ointment, the crab in the ass. I was gonna mess things up worse than a politician.

Headmaster yelled at me again, told me to stop. I shifted the AK-47 to my left hand and pulled out the automatic and turned and looked at him and Billy, and then I fired. I was a good shot, and I was proud of that, because my first shot caught Headmaster between the eyes. He went down so fast, it was impossible to believe it. Billy—blood and brains from Headmaster splattered across his cheek—tried to pull up the rifle he had in his hand, but I shot him through the heart before he got it lifted. Then I was in the room with Hummy by the time Billy hit the floor.

Juan had already gone through and was at the far door. He had turned, drawn the automatic he had. Now there were guns coming out from under coats, and out of pockets, and from behind the desk. Juan fired twice and the shots slammed into the door frame. I shot at him once, but missed. Then I stuck the pistol in my belt, almost casual-like, switched the AK-47 to my right hand and lifted it firing, bullets going all over the place, crazy-like.

I hit a couple of the guys and one of the girls, and they did a kind of hop and a twist, like they were grooving at a party. There was blood everywhere and people were going down. I felt something hot in my side and I shot Hummy a bunch of times. Then I was walking, just straight out, not thinking about anything but killing, feeling the fire in my side, but not thinking much of it. I walked right through, whipping the weapon left and right, mowing flesh.

As I reached the far open door, I saw they were coming for me—maybe twenty guys, couple of the girls, but there were some holding back. The ones coming had weapons, all handguns, and when they opened up the world went crazy and my ears went deaf, then began to ring. And I don't remember it all, but the bullets cut all around me. One went through my left arm and it hurt like hell. The next thing I knew, it was hanging at my side and I got the AK-47 lifted, pushed up against my hip, and I was rockin' and rollin' and bodies were jumping. I was having a better day than they were. Probably because they couldn't hit an elephant in the ass at ten paces with a tossed bar stool, even spraying. Luckiest motherfucker ever squatted to take a dump over a pair of shoes, 'cause except for that one hit, I was doing good. It was like I was fucking charmed.

I saw my bullets jerk B.G. and Rhino around and take them apart; a lot of the others, they went down too.

I started walking sideways, along the wall, and came to the counter where the shoes used to be given out, slid behind that. I kept firing and their shots kept coming. The wood on the counter jumped and splintered. The shoe racks behind me came apart, and I wasn't hit again. I just kept pushing the AK-47 up against me, firing.

I was almost to the door and could see that the bodies were heaped. And there was that damn Juan, still alive. I pulled the trigger on the AK-47 again, but it was empty. Then I remembered that I had picked up another clip, but couldn't load it with only one hand working. So I dropped the AK-47, pulled the pistol, and fired one shot that didn't hit anyone. I heard the lead bounce off a bowling ball, and then I was at the door. I ran out of there, my arm dangling at my side like a puppet that had lost a string.

It was cool outside for a change and there was a thin rain blowing in my face as I ran. I felt a little dizzy, but for the most part, things were all right. The colors of the night, lit up by distant lights, were mostly shades of black and gray. I was glad there were no streetlights, because I got behind a parked car, dropped behind it, and lay on my belly. I looked under it and down the street at the bowling alley. As I was lying there, I felt the AK-47 clip sticking in my stomach. I lifted up, pulled it out of my belt, and left it on the concrete. I touched my pocket; the extra load for the automatic was gone. It must have fallen out of my pocket. I looked around under the car for it, and then I saw that it was lying in the street between the car and the bowling alley. I hadn't stuck it in good, and it had gotten bumped out. I felt like an idiot.

After a while the door opened a crack, and a head poked out—and then another, and then one other. They looked my direction first, then the other direction. I wondered how many were still in there. I had pretty much wiped out the crop of the gang, scared the shit out of the others. Only thing I hadn't done was blow up their meth lab, which was in a little house down the street from the bowling alley. Some of the gang were there, but, way I felt, they were going to get away. Maybe I'd come back and get them too, just for the hell of it. Kill them all and blow the place up and piss in the ashes.

I kept watching. I saw the heads move, and then the guys were out in the street. Another guy showed, and then a girl. She had long black hair, and I even noted she had a good figure. I thought that was funny; here I am, lying on the ground, people wanting to kill me, one of them that girl, and I'm taking note of her tits and ass.

They all had guns. Handguns. I could see them moving them around in the dark. Altogether, there were five of them. Three of them broke off and went the opposite way, and then the other two—Juan, limping a little, and the girl—started my way. They saw the clip I had dropped, and Juan stopped, bent down, and picked it up.

They looked back for the others, but they had long gone. At least it was just these two who knew which direction I had gone.

It was all I could do to make myself move. The concrete felt good and cool. I lifted up on my hands and knees. When I did,

I could hear the sticky blood that had run out of me make a Velcro sound; it had dried enough to stick me to the cement. I realized then that I hadn't been as charmed as I thought. I had been hit a couple of times, but not anywhere too bad, or so I hoped. I did feel a little light-headed.

I backed up on hands and knees a few paces, then backed into an alley and hoped it wasn't a dead end. It wasn't. I went along it and tried not to breathe too heavy or too loud. I looked up. The sky was just a kind of slick glow. There were no lights where I was, but the city lights licked the sky like that and gave it this gauzy look. I thought of where I had lived when Dad and me moved away from here. There you could see the sky and at night you could hear crickets and frogs and there were tall trees.

I went over a grating. When I did, steam came out of it like devil's breath, and I jumped a little. I went on and around a corner, then started feeling as if someone had opened up a spigot in my heel and the soul of me was running out of it.

I stopped and leaned against the alley wall, moved my shirt back and looked at where I had been hit in the side. I realized it was a bad hit, worse than I thought. The other wounds weren't so bad, but they were all bleeding, and I felt as if there was something tunneling around inside me.

I could hear Juan and that girl coming. I thought about running, but my body wasn't up for it. They knew I was here, and it was a matter of time before they caught up with me. I looked around, saw some garbage cans by some metal stairs. I made my way there and got behind the cans and eased over behind the stairs, watching between the garbage cans as Juan turned the corner, and then the girl.

They spread out, maybe trying to act like movies they'd seen, where the cops search rooms. But this was a big-ass room, this wide spot in the alley. When she went left, Juan came along the wall, then stopped as his arm brushed the bricks. He put out his hand and rubbed the wall. I knew he had found my blood there.

He turned and looked toward the trash cans, and when he did, he saw me between those cans. I knew it. I could tell. I lifted the gun and fired. It hit him and he went down, his pistol skittering across the alley.

Bullets banged around the cans and along the stairs. A light went on somewhere above me, and the girl, panicking, fired at the lit window. I heard glass crash and then someone smartly turned out the light. I stood up and kicked the trash cans over and came out blazing. I fired twice and both shots missed. She fired and hit me in the shoulder—and this one was solid, not just passing through. It knocked me down and I felt as if all the wind was out of me. I couldn't believe how hard I had been hit.

I lay on my back and she came toward me. She was smiling. She had a revolver. She pointed it at me. She straddled me and pulled the trigger. And it clicked empty. She had shot at me in the bowling alley. Maybe one of her shots had hit me, but now she was all used up.

I grinned and lifted the pistol and shot her in between the legs.

She seemed to jump backward, then hit the ground on her back and made a noise like someone trying to squeeze out a silent fart.

I could hardly get up, but I did. I staggered over and looked down at her. She looked young. Not a whole lot older than the girl I had punched.

"Shit," I said.

She quit moving, except for one leg that wiggled a moment, then quit.

I went over to Juan. He was breathing heavy. He had his hands on his belly. I got down on my knees by him.

I said, "That boy, whose feet you nailed to the floor. That was my brother. My father committed suicide over it. I don't like you or any of your gang. I'm glad you hurt bad."

He tried to say something, but he couldn't. All of his air was being used to stay alive.

"I just wanted you to know how much I hate you. You fucked up my life, and this sure fucks up yours. And I got Billy too. And the Headmaster. And a bunch of you fucks. You had a plastic Jesus in your pocket, I'd snap it in half. That's how much I hate you. How you feeling, Juan?"

Juan looked at me, and his mouth came open, like a fish on a dock, hoping for water.

"I could kill you," I said. "Make it stop hurting. But I don't want to."

I stayed there on my knees until blood came out of his mouth and the stink in his pants became too strong for me to take. Then I stood up and looked at him. It was all I could do to stand up. I should have moved on, maybe found a doctor. But I didn't want to miss a second of it.

I watched until he was dead and his eyes were as flat and lifeless as a teddy bear's.

I went away then, moving slow, but moving. I dropped the automatic somewhere. I walked until I came to some lights. Down the way I could hear traffic and see people. People who weren't in gangs. People with lives. People, many of which would live long and die of old age and have families. Stuff I wouldn't know about.

I leaned against a brick wall, under a streetlight. The first I had come to since leaving the bowling alley. I looked up and watched bugs swarm around the light. They didn't know they had short lives and didn't care. They just did what they did and had no thoughts about it.

I grinned at them.

I took the little girl's wallet out of my back pocket and opened it. It had five dollars in it. I looked through it and found her picture, and a picture of her with a man, woman, and little boy. Her family, I figured. I found a little card behind a plastic window that had her address on it. It said: RETURN TO, and then there was the address. I knew that address, the general locale. It wasn't far from where I had lived as a kid, back when Dad owned the store and he and my brother worked there, and I hung out there from time to time. On that day my brother was murdered, set on fire, I had been at a theater down the street, watching a movie. It was a good movie, and now, because of my brother's death, I couldn't think of that movie without feeling a little sick. I couldn't think of it now. I thought about the girl again, and that was almost as bad as thinking about my brother or my father.

I thought about her nose. I hoped she could fix it, or maybe it wasn't broken too badly and would heal all right. I thought about the guy whose knee I had taken out for the lack of payment to the Headmaster. I didn't really care about him. He was in bed with the skunks, so he got stink all over himself before I did anything to him. He had it coming. Maybe he didn't have it coming from me, not really, but he had it coming, and I didn't feel all that bad about him. I didn't feel bad about any of the gang. I just wished I had killed them all.

I read the address in the wallet again. I knew where that was. I started walking.

I went along the backstreets as much as possible. When I got on a main street, people began to pull back from me, seeing all the blood, way my face looked. I saw it myself, reflected in a store window. I looked like a ghost who had seen a ghost. The shock was wearing off. I was really starting to hurt.

I probably didn't have long before the police got me, before people on the street called about this blood-covered guy.

I took a turn at the corner and started walking as fast as I could. I felt as if most of what was left of me was turning to heat and going out the top of my head. I went along until I got to the back alleys; then I darted in and went through them. I remembered these alleys like I had been here yesterday, though it had been a few years. I remembered them well because I had played here. I went down them and along them, and somewhere back behind me I heard sirens, wondered if they were for me.

I finally went down an alley so narrow I had to turn sideways to get through it. It opened up into a fairly well-lit street. I got the girl's wallet out again and looked at the address. I was on the right street. I memorized the number, put the wallet away, and walked along the street until I found the number that fit the one on her little card in the wallet.

A series of stone steps went up to a landing, and there was a door there, above it the number. I climbed up to the top step, and that was about it. I sat down suddenly and leaned back so that my ass was on the stoop and my legs were hanging off on the top step. I could hardly feel that step. My legs seemed to be coming loose of me and sinking into something like quicksand. I had to take a look at them to make sure they were still attached. When I saw that they were, I sort of laughed, because I couldn't feel them. I pulled myself up more with my hands and put my back at an angle against one of the concrete rails that lined the steps on both sides.

I took out the wallet, put both my hands over it, and put the wallet up against my stomach. I tried to put it someplace where blood wouldn't get on it, but there wasn't any place. I realized now that the warm wetness I was feeling in the seat of my pants was blood running down from my wounds and into my underwear. I hated that they would find me like that.

I sat there and thought about my dad and my brother and I thought about what my sensei had said about you can't correct what's done, and if you try, you won't feel any better. He was right. You can't correct what's been done. But I did feel better. I felt bad about the girl, but I felt good about all those dead fucks being dead. I felt real good.

I felt around in my shirt, and my hand was like a catcher's mitt trying to pick up a needle. I finally found my ballpoint and I opened the girl's wallet, which was bloody. I pinched out the little card with her address on it, and wrote the best I could:

I'M SORRY. REALLY, I AM.

I laid the wallet on my knee, got out my own wallet. I had twenty-five dollars in there. I put the money from my wallet in her wallet, along with her five. I turned and looked at the door. I didn't know if I could make it. There was a mailbox by the door, a black metal thing, and I wanted to get up and put the wallet in that, but I didn't know if I could.

I thought about it awhile. Finally, I got some kind of strength and pulled myself up along the concrete railing. When I got up, it was like my legs and feet came back. I made it to the mailbox, opened it, and put her wallet in there with the card I had written on.

Then that was it. I fell down along the wall and lay on my face. I thought about all manner of things. I thought of my brother and my father. But the funny thing was, I began to think about my sensei. I was on the mat and I was moving along the mat. I was practicing in the air. Not traditional kata, because we didn't do that. But I was practicing—punching, kicking, swinging my elbows, jerking up my knees. It felt good, and I could see my sensei out of the corner of my eye. I couldn't make out if he was pleased or angry, but I was glad he was there.

The sirens grew louder.

I thought of bullets and fire, and a deep pit full of darkness. I wished I could see the stars.

Judy's Big Score

Patrick J. Lambe

Judy had every right to be pissed. I wasn't supposed to stop at the bar after I'd cased it; especially not while the owner was there. But I just had to get a look at the loser we were gonna rip off. The other guy she was sleeping with.

She tapped her fingers on the bar, her arms spread out on either side of the beer, eyes narrowed, exaggerating the wrinkles that had started spreading from their corners since the last time I'd seen her—nearly seven years before the call out of nowhere.

"Five bucks," she said.

I knew she'd be mad at me, but I hadn't expected her to actually charge me for a goddamned beer. It was a business expense as far as I was concerned.

A quick glance in both directions showed no patrons within hearing distance, besides my partner, Dell. Tipping the glass towards her, I said, "I didn't get a chance to pick up any cash on the way down."

"Don't look at me, I'm on the dole," Dell said when Judy switched her attention from me to him.

"There's an ATM right behind you." She chin-nodded towards it. "You two idiots forget about it already?"

"Come on, hon, can't you spring for a round?" I said.

"Maybe this wasn't such a good idea," she said, picking up a bar rag from a sink under the cheap Formica bar top. "Maybe we should call it off." She wiped the ring formed by my beer mug.

"Jesus Christ," I said. "I'll pay for the drinks."

Pushing away from the bar, I nearly collided with a guy maneuvering a hand truck behind me. His close-cropped hair was a mix of dark brown and silver. Freshly touched-up tattoos covered the parts of his thick arms exposed by his light-colored T-shirt. One of the tattoos was a Black Flag symbol. Old pop marks could still be seen poking through the fresh coat of ink. Hard to believe punk rock kids were pushing fifty nowadays.

"Can you let me in, hon?" he said, scurrying past me to the part of the bar that swung upward to let people behind it. He had to be Steve, the owner.

Judy worked her way down the end of the bar and lifted the top up to let Steve in with the beer-case-laden hand truck. She was making too much of an effort to ignore me as I went over to the ATM and stuck my card in. I hoped Steve-O didn't pick up on it.

I watched them out of the corner of my eye as I waited for the machine to process my transaction. He effortlessly picked up cases two at a time and set them on the bar, then transferred the bottles one by one into the cooler, rotating the older ones to the top. His arms looked like they were outgrowing the tattoos. I guessed he'd traded in heroin for weight training as his addiction of choice. He certainly wasn't the pushover Judy had made him out to be.

"Something wrong, Judy?" he asked, pausing, looking at her as she brushed past him to service another customer at the other end of the bar.

"We need more Jameson," she said, annoyed.

"What'd I do?" he said, catching a sympathetic look from Dell as she grabbed a near-empty whiskey bottle and poured.

Smiling, I hit my code, authorizing the machine to deduct a dollar fifty for the privilege of taking my money out of it. I guess Stevie boy wasn't used to Judy's moods yet. It'd taken me a while to get used to them myself, when we were together full-time.

A small screen popped up on the ATM, telling me the price for taking money had gone up another fifty cents. Two dollars to take out twenty. Seemed like usury to me, especially since I'd only have thirty-eight dollars left in the account after the transaction.

I guess I shouldn't complain. I'd be getting my money back from the machine tomorrow night, right after Dell and I rolled it out into my pickup truck after the bar closed.

She held a large bag from an art supply store in front of her when I reopened the door to a professional and romantic relationship that had ended nearly seven years ago. I moved aside and let her into my apartment. I'd run out and bought outrageously priced air fresheners from the Indian running the Krausers, hoping they would make a dent in the musty stench my place had accumulated over the years. I wouldn't have bothered with the fresheners under normal circumstances, but when an old flame calls after an absence it never hurts to put up a good front.

Judy wrinkled her nose, but she didn't say anything as she put the bag down next to the front door and took off her coat. The crow's-feet that had begun to gather around her eyes had multiplied and her hair seemed a little faded since the last time I'd seen her. But otherwise she still looked pretty much the same, tight little body, grade-A ass, and an expression that generally had nothing to do with what was going on behind her pretty face.

"Been a while," I said. "Make your big score yet?" I didn't think so, based on the Wal-Mart couture.

It was the reason she'd left. My lack of ambition. We had a nice little routine down. Minimal risk, but the return on the investment wasn't generally more than enough to last us a couple of months, a half year at best. I yessed her to death about pulling off something big: an insurance swindle or confidence scheme that would set us up for life, or at least net us enough capital to start some kind of legitimate business. She finally figured out I hadn't the fortitude to risk hard time for a scheme that big, and she'd moved on.

"I've been out of the game for a while, but I might have something." She took a Corona I'd retrieved from the fridge. I'd given up Corona—bottled beer actually—since the money had become tight. Now it was whatever case of cans was on sale. My new partner and I hadn't done anything significant in nearly six months, but I figured it wouldn't hurt to spring for her favorite brand.

"It'd be good if we could work something out," I said. "I could use some quick cash."

"Heard you got another partner." She sat down on the couch.

"Guy named Dell. He's good, but he lacks your obvious assets."

"We might be able to cut him in too. This job involves some lifting. Two guys should be able to handle it."

"You can count me out if it's your shot at the big times. I'm quite content being a nickel-and-dimer."

Her eyes roamed around the apartment. "That's obvious."

"You know, you still look pretty good, a broad pushing forty," I said.

Judy wasn't one for flattery or idle conversation. Within minutes of finishing her second beer, she was moaning underneath me. Then, a half hour after the awkward act, she lay against me. We talked about mortality and darkening streets, the smell of sex permeating the tent we'd built from the covers over our heads.

We'd gotten our clothes back on and stared at each other over a pot of coffee as we discussed business a half hour after getting out of bed. She'd scored a job as a bartender a couple of years ago. A dive so low they didn't even take credit cards. The owner, Steve, liked the way her ass played under her jeans. She said she let him touch it once in a while to distract him as she took a little out of the till to add to her tip money.

They'd sleep together occasionally, but she didn't respect him. According to her, he was weak in both body and spirit, had less ambition than me. Figured it was time to move on to greener pastures in pursuit of the elusive big score, but she needed a little stake money.

She'd thought about just emptying the cash drawer one night after closing, but Steve was cautious. He'd bring the loot home with him and put it in a safe in his house at night after the bartenders finished counting out the evening receipts. In the morning, he'd deposit money into the bank on his way to work.

Steve had recently decided to bring his place into some semblance of the nineteenth century. He'd made a half-assed arrangement with a fly-by-night company to put an ATM next to the men's room. He couldn't be there the day they installed the thing, so Judy supervised the workmen, showing a little more tits and ass and a little more curiosity about the project than the installers were used to.

Three bolts through the floor held the whole thing in place. Nuts on the other side of the planks secured the bolts. Drop-ceiling panels in the basement hid it all from the public. The downstairs portion of the bar generally only saw weekend use by over-the-hill punk rock bands the owner was still enthusiastic about twenty years after anyone else cared.

An armored car drove by every Thursday morning and put six grand into the thing. Steve usually worked Thursdays, but he had a dental appointment this week for a root canal. Judy would put an Out of Order sign on the machine as soon as it was filled—to ensure we would get our maximum return. Then she'd leave the back door open at the end of her shift and we could use the hand truck in the storage room to wheel the machine into my pickup truck. After that, we could take our own sweet time breaking into it up in Dell's parents' garage.

I had to say I was impressed. Judy might not have gotten her big score, but she'd made huge strides in her criminal repertoire. I'd done all of the significant planning during our time together. She'd served as eye candy and the bait on the end of the hook.

"What's in the bag?" I asked just before she left.

She held it open. "I knew you'd ask." I guess she knew me better than practically anyone. "Some picture frames for my apartment."

"Do you know how to hang pictures?" I asked.

"Sure, you just stick these into the wall and put the wire through it." She pulled out a small packet of hangers from the bottom of the bag.

Laughing, I said, "You can't just stick them in by hand. You need a hammer or something." Maybe her planning skills hadn't advanced as far as I though they had.

"Are you sure? The guy at the store didn't say anything."

I grabbed a hammer from a drawer in the kitchen, and placed it in the bag she held open. "I'm sure. Just get the hammer back to me before we pull this job. It might come in handy."

My partner and I stopped in on a Monday, their slowest night of the week, and checked things out. An alley ran along the back of the bar, between the rear of the place and a bail bonds office. Plenty of room to pull my pickup to the back door.

Dell was a little too distracted trying to burn an outline of Judy's figure into the gray matter of his brain as she bent over the coolers retrieving beer. I wished he could have concentrated a little more on the casing, but I wasn't too worried. It didn't look like we'd be running into any trouble.

The front of the place was typical of the corner bars fast disappearing across America. A row of booths on the left side, the bar and stools on the right as you walked in off the street, a pool table in front of a jukebox toward the rear of the joint.

Judy sent me down the stairs at the back when the bar was slow. I'd have liked for Dell to come down with me, but he said he had to use the bathroom. I stood on a chair under the place where I thought the ATM would be, lifted up the ceiling tiles, looking for the bolts with a pocket flashlight. The setup was exactly like Judy said it would be. Just three bolts anchoring our cash in place.

A selection of ratchet heads downstairs, unplug the phone line and electric upstairs, a quick boost up into my pickup truck, a three-way split, and, if everything worked out right, we'd each be two grand richer. Not exactly Judy's elusive big score, but enough to get her started on it.

Dell and Judy leaned across the bar from each other, talking, their foreheads almost touching when I came back up the stairs. Dell jerked away guiltily when he saw my reflection in the bar mirror behind him. He didn't have to worry. I'd gotten used to it years ago, hadn't ever let it bother me. Judy was naturally flirtatious, a quality that had opened up many doors when we'd worked together as a team.

Still, I was a little pissed. We were supposed to be checking the place out, and here he was goofing off. I didn't say anything to him as we left. Dell was only twenty-two years old. I tend to make exceptions for youth.

I work at UPS every Christmas season as a temporary driver. I'm actually surprised that I'm pretty good at it. They ask me to stay on permanently every year, but I turn them down without an explanation. It'd be a little awkward telling them I only worked there two or three months a year so I can have something to show Uncle Sam during tax time.

Dell was assigned as my helper three years ago. He was giving community college a shot, and figured he could pick up some extra cash working through the break. He was a blond-haired kid with a lopsided smile the women on the route went crazy for. One of the secretaries who worked at an architectural firm on our route once told me she had fantasies about Dell, dressed in the cutoff summer version of the uniform, bending her over the desk.

Caught him trying to stuff a case of iPods in his uniform one day when I had to go back to check something on the truck.

I'd thought about turning him in. This had been a steady gig for me for years, and I could get in a lot of trouble if stuff disappeared from my truck. We talked it out, and I turned his natural larcenous instincts to our advantage. His way with the ladies opened some doors, but not as many as Judy's way with the men.

"You used to hit that?" Dell asked, rolling the windshield halfway down before it jumped the tracks holding it in the door well. I'd have to unscrew the side panel and work it back in place before the next time it rained.

"Back in the day."

"I wasn't trying anything on her back there. Just being friendly." The guy had been riding in the passenger seat of my truck for three years now, and he still broke the window every time he touched it.

"Doesn't really matter to me. We're mostly business partners."

He stopped struggling with the window, said, "She still looks pretty good for an older chick. I'd definitely throw her the hammer."

"You've got a big heart."

"So, you think we'll get two grand each out of this?"

"That's what Judy says."

"I don't mean to complain. I mean, I could use the cash. But it seems like a lot of work for two grand each."

I looked over at him as I took a right turn. "We'll be in and out in, like, ten minutes, tops."

"Two grand doesn't go that far these days. I think we're in a recession or something. Maybe we should start thinking of the future. 'Specially you. You're not getting any younger."

I pulled the truck outside his parents' house. "You're sure your parents are gonna be away Thursday night?"

"I'm dropping them at the airport in the morning. They'll be gone till next Tuesday." He let himself out of the truck, wedged a pen between the window and the frame holding it in place.

"Forget about it. I'll fix it with a screwdriver later."

He put his pen back in his pocket. "If we made a big score you wouldn't have to worry about fixing your window every week."

"Let's concentrate on this one job before we start planning on knocking over the mint."

The bolts had come out easy, a couple of quick turns with the ratchet. I eased the washers off and pushed them up through the holes in the floor. Then I put the ceiling tile back in place and climbed up the back stairs to help Dell move the machine.

It was lighter than either of us imagined it would be. Still, we threw a heavy strap around it anyway. We were almost out the back door when Dell stopped the hand truck, pushed it so it stood upright. "Did you hear that?" he asked.

We both stood still. I listened for half a minute. "I don't hear anything."

Dell put his fingers to his lips and walked through a door separating the bar from the kitchen. I followed. "It came from in there." He pointed to a walk-in freezer.

Opening the heavy metal door, he walked in. I heard him say, "Shit." Then I followed him in. He moved off to the side to let me past him. Steve lay on his back, blood from the back of his head freezing up on the insulated floor. "Holy shit," I said bending down to get a closer look. Then I heard the door to the walk-in close behind me.

There was a little sliver of Plexiglas about eye level that I could see through. Dell struggled with the hand truck for a second; then he put it down and turned around. I couldn't hear anything going on outside the freezer, but it looked to me like someone had called him from his back. He smiled for a second; then the back of his head exploded over the face of the ATM.

Judy threw a pistol at Dell's feet, put another one, the one she shot him with, on the bar. She went over to the phone next to the cash register and dialed three digits. I watched her lips move as she talked to the 911 dispatcher on the other end of the line. She turned away when she caught me eyeballing her through the glass. I doubt the shame on her face was what she really felt.

There was an extension in the freezer. I picked it up and listened in on her conversation. She'd surprised two men robbing the bar she owned with her husband. One of them she'd locked in the freezer. The other one had pulled a gun on her, and she'd shot him with the pistol her husband kept behind the bar for security.

I bent down and looked at Steve. Fresh pop marks had

frozen over on his arm. The hammer I'd loaned Judy lay on the side of his head, covered in gore. Judy's ability to plan had come a long way since we were jungled up together. She'd really thought this one out, probably getting her man so nodded out, his oversized muscles wouldn't do him any good once she started on him with the hammer.

She hung up the phone, turned a bar stool around, and stared at me, holding the dead receiver in my hand. If this were a cartoon, her eyes would have turned into dollar signs as she counted up the insurance money dancing behind her expressionless face.

Part of me, a very small part, was happy she'd finally made her big score.

Killing Billy Blain

D. T. Kelly

I stared out the window of the restaurant into the grayness of a Chicago January morning. The streets were clear of snow, but the sidewalks were dusted white and the curbs caked with black slush. I finished my coffee and motioned the waitress. "This is my last job." She didn't look at either of us as she refilled my cup. We waited for her to leave.

Frank took a bite of toast. "You told me that already."

"Well, I'm making sure you heard me." I creamed my coffee. "Eighteen years of this job is enough."

"I understand. Most people burn out after five." Frank took his cigarette from the table edge and took a drag, blowing the bluish cloud towards the ceiling.

"This job eats at your soul." I took another drink. "It's nothing but negativity day in and day out."

"Billy, I said I understand, quit preachin'."

"Sorry, Frank. I've just hit the point where I can't take it anymore. So, who is it this time?"

"Right." The cigarette dangled from the corner of his mouth as he spoke. I've always wondered how smokers could do that without losing the cigarette. Frank slid a manila envelope across the table. "We'd like you to get it done this afternoon."

I put the envelope next to me. "You sure he's going to be home?"

"Yeah. Larry Spanos is sitting on him."

"Right. You sure Lar isn't banging that little broad of his in the backseat again?"

"Jonny Moon is with him."

"That's comforting. He's probably jerking off in the front seat." I shook my head. "Jonny Moon. Did that sick fuck ever tell you what he used to do when he worked in a sandwich joint?"

"I can't say that he did," Frank said, mildly interested.

"Well, he's someone I won't miss." I took a bite of bagel. "Fuckin' guy."

"So, this afternoon, right?" Frank pinched his cigarette between his fingers and dropped the carcass to the floor.

"No problem, Frank. It's a done deal."

"I can't say we're not going to miss you." Frank lit another cigarette and took a drag. "You're one of the most reliable guys I have."

"Oh, let's not get sentimental," I said, popping the last piece of bagel into my mouth. "I tell you what, I'll let you pick up the tab this time."

"I always pick up the tab." He smiled. "It's my job."

I finished my coffee and stood up. "Take it easy, Frank." We shook hands and I left.

When I got home I opened the envelope and took out its contents. I skimmed the papers and stopped at the picture. He was a small, portly man with more hair on his face than on his head. He had squinty eyes, reminded me of a mole. I tossed the picture onto the table and went to my filing cabinet. My gun cleaning kit was in the top drawer.

After cleaning and loading my Beretta, I slipped it to my inside coat pocket. I found that holsters are clumsy and bulky. Either one could get you killed.

I picked up the picture and studied it again. Mole Man wasn't looking happy. He wouldn't be happy when I got there either.

It was snowing lightly when I parked my Ford pickup two houses down from the apartment complex. Normal protocol would be to park at least a block away to ensure not being seen before the deed was done. I was too tired for protocol.

I spotted Larry's Impala parked on the opposite side of the street with a full view of the apartment's only door. *I'll be damned, Larry is doing his job.*

Larry rolled the window down as I approached. "Hey, you're late."

"Fuck you."

"Touchy, ain't he, Moony? You'd think this was the old man's last job or somethin'."

"I don't need this shit. Just tell me, is there anything I need to know?" I saw Jonny Moon slumped in the passenger side of the car. I couldn't tell if he was sleeping or drunk.

"New, you mean?" Larry wasn't smart.

"Yes, is there anything new?" I clarified, "New since this morning?"

"Nah. Moony and I have been sitting here since six a.m. No one has come in or gone out."

Next to him, Moony mumbled something I could not make out.

"Oh, right." Larry turned back to me. "The little fat fuck came out to get his mail about an hour ago. He wasn't even dressed, came out in boxers and a robe hanging off his shoulders. Moony here got wood from it, right, Moon?" He gave Jonny a backhanded slap in the arm. Moony grunted.

"Whatever," I said, turned, and started walking away.

"Hey, you want us to come with you?" Larry called out loudly. "To back you up?"

I stopped and turned back toward the car. I'd rather have gouged my eyes out with a rusted straight razor than work with these guys more than I had to. "No, thanks."

"You sure? It being your last day and all. Hey, maybe Moony and I can do it for you? Whaddya say, aye, Moony? You up for it?"

I could not hear Moon, but I'm sure he grunted. "No, really. I got it."

"Okay, then."

Moon mumbled again, and again I had to wait for Larry. The first thing I would do when I got to Florida was to see a doctor about my hearing.

"Hey, Moony wants to know if we can split."

"What?"

"You know, jet. Scram. Leave. This is a simple job anyway."

"Jesus Christ." I spun my head around in disgust. I noticed movement in the bushes next to the car. Moon spoke up, like he knew I saw something.

"Hey, man, chill. I was just fuckin' with you. It's your last day, I couldn't let you go without a good fuckin' from Moony."

Larry laughed.

Moon continued. "Hey, word has it you're goin' to Florida, that true?"

"Yeah," Larry added. "You're going to go give it to Minnie up the ass, aren't ya?" Larry laughed, Moony grinned slightly.

"I'm glad to be getting away from you morons. Is your mind ever out of the gutter?"

"Not us, man," Larry said, turning his head for approval from Moony. "We think about sex all the time, ain't that right, Moony?"

"Damn skippy." Moony turned his greasy head. "Hey, whatever happened to the tall brunette you were banging?"

"None of your fucking business," I said.

"Aw, c'mon, you're leaving anyway." Moony took a cigar out of the glove box and bit the plastic wrapper off. "I won't hurt her, just want to bang her for a while."

"She's at least twice your age." I had had enough and started walking away.

Larry called out after me, "Aw, hey, c'mon, he's just fucking with you, right, Moony?"

"I'd rather be fucking her," Moony retorted. They both laughed again. I crossed the street towards the apartment complex. I pretended not to notice the petite woman scurry from the bushes to Larry's car.

The apartment complex was a simple layout, four units on the first floor, four units up top, stairs at both sides. It sat sideways on the property, opening up to a duplicate layout across a small courtyard. I pulled the papers out of my back pocket. I was looking for apartment 2-D. I saw the numbers on the door closest to me, 1-D. This was going to be easier than I thought. I studied the door marked 2-D. This one was different than the rest in that it was missing its screen door. Even better, one less barrier to get through.

I slipped the papers into my coat pocket with my gun and walked carefully up the sides of the metal stairs to make as little noise as possible. Age still had nothing on my agility. It was snowing harder now, turning into a classic Chicago snowstorm. When I got to the door, I stood to the side to collect myself.

A noise from the street startled me—Larry's stereo. The bass was incredibly loud, rattling the metal railing of the stairwell. That fuck was going to get me killed. So much for collecting myself, I couldn't think straight with his radio boom-booming through the neighborhood.

I decided to go with the "lost old man" routine. I hated doing it, it made me feel dirty, whorish. But when the game's on the line, you've got to play your ace.

I blew on my hands to keep them nimble and knocked on the door. "Hello?" I called out sheepishly, almost drunklike. "I'm lost and I need help, is anyone there?" I waited.

"Whaddya want?" a hoarse voice seeped through the door.

"I'm lost, sir, please help me?"

"Go ask someone else, I'm busy." The voice was annoyed.

"Sir, please. I have been wandering around here since morning. I'm looking for my sister's house and I have no idea where I am. Please help me."

There was silence; then the voice came through the door, louder, "Go away, old-timer, I don't have the time for this."

"Please, sir," I poured it on thick. "No one else is home here to help me."

I heard something crash and him swear. The door opened and Mole Man was standing before me, still wearing his robe and worn boxers.

"All right, what do you need?" He was shorter than I and his pockmarked cheeks were covered with five-day stubble. I saw a broken bowl on the floor of the doorway and macaroni scattered. A cat was licking at the cheese.

"Sir, thank you." I hammed it up. "I've been looking for my sister's house for—"

"Yeah, yeah, get on with it."

"I have her address right here, but I can't seem to read it. My eyes aren't what they used to be." I reached my hand into my coat; my fingers close around the handle of my gun briefly. I grabbed the papers and pulled them out. "It's right here. What does that say?" I slapped the papers on his chest a little too hard for my persona.

"What th—"

Then came the line I had relished saying time and again in years past. That day, the passion was gone and I uttered them for the final time. "Consider yourself served."

He took a step backwards and squinted to read what he

held. "That fucking cunt! I swear to God I'm going to fucking kill her!"

I was already on the stairs. My footprints were nearly covered now, the snow coming down fast and with a passion not seen in years.

"You motherfucker! I hope you rot in hell!"

I cleared the last stair and walked towards Larry's car. Serving papers was not what I had always done with my life, but when I retired from the Chicago Police Department I needed something to keep me active. Serving seemed a natural progression.

I was nearly behind Larry's car before I realized that it was moving. I was going to have to get my eyes checked too. The Impala's shocks squeaked loudly; Larry and his girl were in the backseat. Music pounded through the enclosed car and pulsed off my eardrums. I didn't look long, but Moony was watching the action from the front seat.

"Billy Blain?"

I turned around. A tall, thin man wearing a black sweatshirt and blue sweatpants was standing in front of me. I recognized him as a man I served papers to two years ago. I remembered him because he cried like a whiny little girl afterwards. It takes balls to break down like that in front of another man and I envied him for it.

In fact, a lot of them cried. Some got angry, and that was what the gun was for, but most of them just cried like little babies. The sawed-off shotgun in this guy's hands told me he wasn't a baby anymore.

"You ruined my life, motherfucker."

I didn't know what to say. My insides screamed to pull out my gun, but his barrel persuaded me not to.

"I've been waiting for this for a long time."

I wanted to say I'm sorry. I wanted to plead for my life. But I saw it in his eyes. I was a dead man.

He fired.

I felt the searing heat explode in my gut and I fell backwards. The pain was close behind and I nearly passed out. I looked up; I could clearly see Moony in the front seat. If he looked a millimeter to his left, he would see me and my killer. His eyes never left Larry's bitch.

I screamed, but spurts of hot blood were all that left my lips. It streaked down my cheeks and crept over my ear. I could see the circle of crimson grow around me. I heard him reload; the spent casing bounced around my left ear. I felt warm metal slip between my lips. He was standing over me now, his face accentuated by falling snow. There was a white haze creeping into my field of vision, making him glow like some askew angel.

He twisted the shotgun in my mouth back and forth nervously. He regained his composure and stiffened. "Consider yourself served."

A loud thunderclap resonated down on the empty street. It was swallowed quickly by the blizzard.

Buddha Behind Bars

Daniel Hatadi

The room wasn't what Banjo expected. He was thinking fancy rugs, a lot of red and orange, candles and incense, hippy shit. But the walls were bare except for a black-and-white poster of a staircase. It was just another cell.

Banjo shrugged, nodded to the other inmates, stood in the back corner. Laid out in a grid on the floor were about a dozen blue cushions. Nothing fancy; plain.

The door opened. A huge bald man walked in, wearing a gray track suit with a picture of a poodle on it. Every part of him was big, almost like he'd never stopped growing. He nodded, looked around the room, eyes twinkling. "We'll wait a couple more minutes." He busied himself by rearranging cushions.

The others filed in, took a cushion each, crossed their legs, and sat. Banjo stayed put.

"Okay," the bald man said, "Remember the Stairway To Heaven?"

A couple of the inmates laughed. One piped up. "How's that go, Sam?"

"You forgot? Don't know about you." Sam chuckled. "It's easy. Just think of the song. Imagine all the people you ever knew are up in heaven, and there's a stairway leading up to them, like the one on the poster. At the top, it's all white light. Imagine taking a step at a time, one with each breath." He clapped his hands and closed his eyes.

"All right, I'll bite. Why won't you take a cushion?"

Banjo took a moment to figure out who Sam was speaking to. " 'Cause this is a load of shit."

Sam laughed in a gentle way that washed over Banjo like rain. "Maybe. But what I told the boys last week was this: you can handle most situations in two ways—one bad, one good."

Banjo said, "Pile it on."

"Your legs might get sore, maybe your back too. There's nothing stopping you sitting on a cushion and taking it easy." Sam opened his eyes. "See? Two ways."

Banjo noticed an empty spot in front of Sam. He picked up a cushion and took it over, sat down, stared at Sam for a few seconds, then nodded.

"That'll do," Sam said. "Now we'll try another exercise, one we haven't done before. To make it easier, get in whatever position you like."

Everyone shifted. Banjo kept his legs crossed, matching Sam.

"Up till now, I've told you all exactly what to do. This time, I want you to get creative. Close your eyes and breathe slow. While you're doing that, keep your mind on something else. That something else is up to you. A beach at sunset, a big old tree on top of a hill . . ." He looked around. "Just don't make it tits and arse."

They all laughed.

"The point is to remind you of a time when your life was at peace. Five minutes, no talking, just breathing. I'll tell you when it's over. Has everyone thought of something?"

There were a few grunts around the room.

"Okay, start."

Everyone except Banjo closed their eyes. Some of them looked like they'd swallowed a lemon. Others were smiling.

"This is bullshit." Banjo stood up, walked to the wall by the door.

Sam said, "It's open."

Banjo reached out and tried the door handle. It worked. He went out, let himself fall back against the wall.

Outside in the corridor, there were three inmates on cleaning duty. One of them was a burly Maori that everyone called Kong.

"Big man Banjo's gone to see the sky pilot," Kong said.

The inmates on cleaning laughed like a pack of wild animals.

One with a bandana tied too tight around his skull let his mop go. The mop fell against the wall of the bucket, sloshing the dirty water around. He stepped forward, laughing at Banjo.

Banjo stared until the inmate backed away, knocked into the mop, and tipped the bucket over, spilling dirty brown suds all over the floor. The water came up to Banjo's feet. Kong wasn't so lucky.

Kong glared at Banjo. "Now look what you done, robe fucker, you messed up my boots."

Banjo had had enough.

He leapt at Kong with a speed that startled the others, who scurried back to the wall, staying out of the way of the fight.

Kong was taller than Banjo and built strong, but Banjo grabbed Kong's dark, curly hair, letting all of his weight rest on it. The speed of the attack and the pain of having his hair ripped brought Kong to the floor.

It was on.

Banjo didn't waste any time. He balled up his right fist and held Kong's head down on the concrete with the other hand. Banjo's fist came down hard. Once, twice, again. He pummeled Kong's face, cheek, nose. The third strike drew blood, but by then, Kong had twisted his larger frame around, kicking Banjo in the back.

A dozen shoes came pounding down the corridor. The screws had their nightsticks raised, brought them down on the two fighters. Outnumbered and further bloodied, Kong and Banjo backed down.

On the way back to his cell, Banjo thought about the class. That thing about the stairway to heaven might have worked, might have given him some peace—if he knew what peace was. But Banjo couldn't see himself setting even a foot on that stairway. No fucking way.

He was stuck in hell.

Banjo stared at the wall, his back to the bars. This whole place was already behind him. He would stay strong, keep it together. Kong was nothing, tough because of his size, not his will. He'd keep.

After a few days, Banjo started thinking about something that Sam had said. It ran around his brain, knocking against the sides of his skull, like rattling the bars.

A time in your life when everything was at peace.

At first, Banjo laughed at the idea. Of course he'd never had peace; his dad had brought him and his brothers up on his own. Mum left before he could remember her. Banjo's older brothers all remembered something, even if it was little. The smell of her hair, her yelling in the morning, the green dress with Hawaiian flowers—these were only things he'd heard about, never remembered them for himself.

Banjo's father had it hard, working in the mines, picking oranges, whatever it took. They moved around all the time, piled up in the back of Dad's truck, bouncing on dirt roads, fighting with each other.

Sometimes they'd eat rice for a week, boiled from a huge

ten-kilo bag. Dad would beat them up if they stole one of the other brothers' bowls, but that was fair enough. You had to eat.

Banjo nodded to himself, started thinking about his brother Darren.

Dazza.

Poor bastard. A smackhead, died the same way all smackheads did. Overdose. They'd lay off the stuff for a while, then they thought one more hit couldn't hurt, just for old times' sake. But the tolerance wasn't what it used to be. Didn't take much.

Banjo clicked his fingers. It echoed off the walls.

One of the inmates here reminded him of his brother. Kev.

Kev wasn't tough, couldn't look after himself. Tall and lanky, with that spotty skin that smackheads get, that blank look in the eyes. Someone had to look after him. Banjo wanted to, but he knew that it couldn't look that way. Kev would have to learn to survive on his own.

Maybe he could be taught.

Banjo held his head in his hands, crossed his legs, tried to relax.

Peace. Who needed it? Peace didn't make you strong, didn't help you out there in the real world. Or in this one.

When they let Banjo out for lunch, Kev was on the other side of the room, as far away from the door as he could sit. There was something different about him, something missing. That nervous, twitchy energy he always had. That was it. It was gone.

Banjo walked straight over to Kev. The conversation in the lunchroom stayed the same, but everyone listened, watched, waited.

Kev in his seat was almost the same height as Banjo standing behind him. The inmates at Kev's table stopped eating and the seat next to Kev was made empty. Banjo stared at Kev.

Kev chewed. "Hey, Banjo. Aren't you eating?"

Banjo stared some more until Kev swallowed.

"What did I tell you?"

Kev looked down, fiddled with his lunch tray. "I dunno."

"I told you something."

"Nothin'. You told me nothin'."

Banjo leaned over, slammed his hand on the table. The trays clanged and rattled.

Conversation stopped. The screws around the lunchroom pretended to look the other way.

Kev kept his hands on the tray. He had the shakes.

"I told you to quit."

"I did, I quit. I told you I never do that stuff. Not again, no more."

Banjo looked at Kev's skin. It was parched. Cracked. Red. It hung on Kev like it would melt right off. Eyes like a bug. His hair wasn't combed and it fell over his head like he'd just woken up. But Banjo couldn't be seen to show sympathy. Not here, not for this.

"Who gave you the needle?"

"You know, I just get 'em where I can."

Banjo backhanded Kev.

Kev spat out gravy, but kept looking forward. He was breathing heavily through his nostrils. "Fuck! What for?"

Banjo leaned closer.

"I told you about survival, didn't I?"

Kev nodded, his breathing slowed.

"To survive you have to be strong, you have to be clear. You can't be getting messed up on smack. Who gave it to you?"

Kev turned his head enough to whisper, "Kong." He turned back and spoke louder. "Okay! I won't do it no more. You can count on me, honest." He nodded fast, as if that made his words true. "No worries, Banjo."

Banjo straightened and patted Kev on the head.

He picked up the tray and smacked it on Kev's face, hard. Meat and potatoes spilled onto Kev, the table, the floor. Again, harder. Banjo hit Kev with the tray until Kev fell off the chair.

Kev was on the floor under the table, whimpering. "No worries, no more. No more."

Banjo used the tray to flip a piece of potato off his uniform. Brown stains on the front of his shirt mixed with spots of blood. He put the tray back on the table and walked over to the counter, grabbed another tray that was already filled with food. Plonked the tray down with a clang on a table nearby and set to eating.

The screws were still looking the other way.

When Banjo walked into the meditation class this time, everyone was already cross-legged on their cushions, eyes shut.

Banjo snorted and walked to the front of the class, looked around, didn't find an empty spot. A few cushions were leaning against the wall behind Sam, but Banjo wasn't in the mood for squeezing past. He grabbed a young inmate by the scruff of his uniform. The inmate took in a sharp breath.

Some of the others opened their eyes, but Sam kept his shut. The inmate looked up. Banjo tilted his head, pointed it at the back of the class. The inmate understood, walked over without a word, and sat on the cold concrete.

Sam breathed out. "That's five minutes, everyone." He looked around the class, skimming over it, looking at Banjo as if he'd been there the whole time. "Did anyone get further? Who held the image for the whole five minutes?"

Troy, a young Italian, his voice pitched high with excitement. "I did it, boss. Held her in my mind for the five. Fully sick. She had all this light around and I felt, like, this energy all through me. Tingly."

"Who did you hold on to this time, Troy? Megan Gale?"

The inmates laughed, a little too loudly, Banjo thought.

Troy didn't say anything, his face flushed red.

Sam looked at him with that twinkle in his eye. "Seriously, Troy, what was the image you came up with?"

Troy waited for the chuckles to die down. "Well, I know you're Buddhist and all, but I was brought up Catholic, so I thought, who's the most holiest person I could think of? She came to me, straight up, the Virgin Mary. Don't get no bigger virgin than her, Sam."

Even Banjo couldn't help letting out a snigger.

Sam said, "Troy, there's nothing wrong with using the Virgin Mary, or any other religious icon. It doesn't have to be Buddha, that's not how this class works. The image that is the best for you is all that counts." Sam paused for a moment. "What image would you pick, Banjo? Who makes you the happiest, or brings love to you?"

Banjo had been waiting for Sam to say something to him, but not this. He expected Sam to complain about taking the cushion from the other inmate, the inmate now sitting at the back of the class, not saying a word.

"No one brought us love, we didn't have to be happy, just had to survive." It was more than Banjo had planned on saying. How did Sam get him like that?

Sam uncrossed his legs. "You say 'us,' and 'we.' Who's that? Your brothers and sisters? Is that it? Maybe something happy—"

"That's none of your fuckin' business."

There wasn't a breath to be heard in the room, not a single movement.

"Your life can't have all been this, Banjo. I can see that in you, see the way you take care of the others."

"Fuck this. And fuck you." Banjo stood, picked up the cushion, clenched it tight. "You like spending time in prison, do you? You got no fuckin' idea. What is it? You like boys in uniform?" He looked around the room, everyone watching him, Troy's face red again. Sam didn't move, but the twinkle had left his eye.

Troy said, "Hey, Banjo, don't get pissed off at Sam, it's his job. He doesn't . . ." Troy trailed off into silence.

Banjo looked back at Sam. "Looks like you've got them all on your side, Sky Pilot. Fuck me if I'm gonna join them." He spun around and walked straight out, throwing the cushion in the corner of the room. It bounced off Troy's shoulder, but Banjo didn't look back, and no one said anything as he left, not even Sam.

After another week in the dry cell for refusing to do the class ever again, the screws let Banjo out to lunch. A group at one of the tables chattered. They were excited about something. Banjo watched them as he fiddled with his food.

Kong carried his lunch tray past Banjo's table, stopped, then backtracked a few steps. He looked down at Banjo, tipping his head in the direction of the talkers. "Looks like your boys are all robe fuckers now."

The guards were at the other end of the lunchroom, laughing and talking. Banjo didn't look at Kong. "Keep moving."

Kong looked behind him. The guards stopped talking. Kong moved on.

Banjo picked up his tray and took it over to the group of talkers. He didn't like being out of the loop. "Troy, Kev. What's all the excitement?"

Kev said, "Hey, Banjo. It's all good. I been clean. Nothin' to worry 'bout."

Banjo smiled and patted Kev on the back. "That's good to hear." It was as if nothing had happened the other day. He looked at them all. "What I want to know is what's got you boys covering your mouths, like no one can tell you're talking."

Troy said, "Nothing much, boss. Just that class, with the

monk guy, all in robes and shit." Troy looked around, the others laughing. "Maybe not, but it feels like he's got robes on. Fuckin' weird. But good."

Banjo stopped smiling. "Didn't seem like a big deal to me."

Kev, all nervous and twitchy, said, "Hey, Banjo, we can't take the dries as good as you. I'd go nuts in there. Make me wanna . . . you know, that thing I can't do, 'cause I'm all cleaned up."

Banjo's face tensed for a moment, then relaxed. "Fair enough, Kev."

While the inmates were talking, a couple of screws walked over, stood behind Banjo. One of them tapped Banjo on the shoulder, bent down to speak in his ear. "Warden says you'll do the class, or Kev'll be spending a few nights on his own."

Banjo stared at his tray, silent.

Kev moved back in his chair, eyes darting between everyone at the table. He sputtered and coughed.

The guard stood up. "Tomorrow. Eleven a.m."

Banjo was early to the class, taking the front cushion for his own again. If he couldn't avoid doing the class, he would make it his own. He wouldn't let it beat him.

The inmates filed in, sitting a respectful distance from Banjo. A minute before 11:00 a.m., Sam walked through the door.

He wore maroon and yellow, the fabrics draped around him like a robe. His head was shaved clean. He walked straight over to Banjo and sat next to him, facing the front of the room.

"Hey there, Banjo," Sam said.

Banjo grunted a reply.

"Look, mate, I don't want you to do this class if you're not into it, but the warden makes the rules. I'm happy for you to sit in a corner and do whatever you please, as long as you don't disturb the class." He paused for breath, adjusted his robes. "Some of the boys are really getting somewhere with this, and if that can make their time in here easier, then I've done my job."

Banjo looked at him, and up this close he could see that Sam meant every word. Had to respect him for being straight up. And the warden knew that the boys would follow Banjo. Maybe Sam was right, maybe Banjo had to give the guy a break.

"What's with the robes?"

Sam laughed, that twinkle back again. "This getup?" He looked it over as if it was the first time he'd seen it, shrugged. "Politics. We've got a visitor coming from overseas. I'm heading there straight after this."

Banjo nodded. "Fair enough."

The room had filled out while they spoke, so Sam got up and took position at the front.

He clapped his hands together. "Okay, boys, we'll start off with a quick five minutes on the Stairway to Heaven. You all know the drill."

The class went quiet, except for their breathing, which slowed down to long and deep. Banjo kept his eyes open, staring at the poster on the wall. A white staircase wound its way up to a faceless robed figure lit by a halo. In the distance, the land joined billowing clouds in the sky. Banjo tried closing his eyes and he could get the poster in his mind, but it didn't give him any sense of peace or happiness. It was just a poster.

"Having trouble, Banjo?"

Banjo opened his eyes to see Sam staring at him, looking relaxed. It was hard to get angry at the guy.

"How'd you guess?"

"You're the only one not taking deep breaths." Sam flung his hand in a dismissive gesture. "But that doesn't really matter. The point is to find something that works for you. Meditation is always personal." He looked at Banjo for a second. "Stick with the staircase, but forget about the idea of heaven. I want you to try imagining someone standing at the top of the staircase, holding their hand out as if they're going to help you up. Pick someone you trust."

Banjo narrowed his eyes, pulled in his lower lip, chewed on it some. He thought about all the people he'd ever known, images of them flashing in his mind. Kev, his brother, a couple of buddies from the outside, even his father. None of them were exactly trustworthy.

Sam said, "They don't have to be perfect."

The sentence unlocked something in Banjo's mind. He closed his eyes and saw the staircase again, but it wasn't in black and white. It was wooden and crumbling, leading up to a loft. A place he lived in at about the age of six, a time when his dad had the cushiest job of his life, mowing lawns in a decent neighbourhood. Dad appeared at the top of the staircase, holding his hand out, just like Sam said, but it wasn't just an image. He was moving, and Banjo was moving too, up the staircase, taking his dad's hand and stepping past a hole in the stairs. The staircase creaked and buckled, but never broke. When they reached the top, the room faded away, Banjo's dad faded away, and so did Banjo.

White light flooded everything, but it wasn't bright, and it felt warm. For what seemed like only a second, Banjo felt like he wasn't there, he wasn't anywhere, he simply wasn't.

When he came out of it and opened his eyes, he saw Sam's twinkle staring back, and when Banjo looked around the class, everyone was staring and smiling.

Banjo turned back to Sam. "What happened, what's everyone—?"

"We finished the five minutes, Banjo, but I told the class to keep quiet. You were out for another five."

"What? It was a second. There was that white light, but it was only a second."

Sam nodded, a warm smile spreading across his face.

And that's when it hit Banjo: his dad didn't have to be perfect, no one had to.

And if that was true, it didn't make sense for Banjo to stay angry.

* * *

The exercise yard was filled with small groups in green huddled in corners, lone walkers pacing their way around the confines of the fence. A few of the inmates played cricket with a garbage bin as a makeshift set of wickets.

Banjo walked around the yard, nodding and smiling at everyone. Most of them didn't know how to take it, few smiled back, but Banjo didn't mind. He understood. His head was clear for what felt like the first time in his life. He felt alert, all his nerves on fire, but relaxed at the same time; almost as if he were falling asleep.

Kev and Troy were lazing around at the corner of the fence, leaning back against it, throwing pebbles at a rock on the ground in front of them. Laughing, seeing who could get the closest. When Banjo was near, they stopped laughing, looked up at him. Not scared, but unsure.

"Hey, boys, good class today."

Kev looked at Troy, didn't say anything. Troy wasn't as self-conscious.

"Sure, boss. Good shit. I almost *flew* outta there." Troy's eyes lit up, not a hint of sarcasm in his voice.

Banjo liked Troy. The kid had heart, seemed like he didn't care much what people thought of him. Kev had heart too, but it was all messed up. Banjo wanted to say something to Kev, make Kev see things as clearly as Banjo could. But nothing came to him. So he just stood and laughed with them as they played.

He hadn't noticed it, but while the boys were playing, Kong had made his way across the yard with a handful of his gang in tow. They were all Maoris, built like brick shithouses, and rough as guts. There's something about tribal tattoos on a Maori that can put the fear in, but it didn't bother Banjo one bit.

Kong walked up to Banjo. Their faces were only centimeters apart. He said, "Now you're bum chums with the sky pilot, eh?"

Banjo's head was still clear. He could see how Kong was trying to move up in ranks, become the biggest gorilla in the jungle. So Banjo was the one he had to fight first.

"There's two ways of handling this: one good, one bad. Which one today, King Kong?"

Using that name might have come across as loaded, but there was something in Banjo's voice that surprised everyone. It should have started a fight, but it didn't. Kong creased his forehead, not sure what to do.

Troy came forward, big smile on his face. "Hey boys, what's the deal here? What's the score, what have we got?" Troy really put it on, swaggering and gesturing like a Mafia henchman in a cheap movie. One of the Maoris in the gang let out a chuckle. Kong silenced him with a glare.

The group went quiet. Banjo and Kong hadn't moved. They stared at each other.

Two ways of dealing with this, Banjo thought. One bad, one good.

Kong moved his head to the right, just a touch. Two of the Maori boys stomped over to Kev, grabbed him on either side. A third came with something in his hand. Banjo caught a glint off it. Something shiny, sharp. The Maori stuck it into Kev's neck.

Before Banjo could move, Kev shouted out a quickly muffled scream. The Maori moved away and threw the needle over the fence, holding it with his sleeve pulled over his hand so he wouldn't touch it. Kev crumpled to the ground, eyes glazed, saliva sliding down his chin.

Banjo turned to Kong, jumped, flexed his whole body, and threw a fist at Kong's face, connecting with a wet crunch. Kong's head snapped back and his body lurched, staggering, but he held his ground.

Kong flew at Banjo and they fell, Kong on top, hammering away at Banjo underneath. A jab to the ribs, a full fist in the temple. Banjo shifted his weight and sent Kong over his head. They were standing again before the dust settled.

Banjo shook his head. "No, not doing this." He had a huge melon of a bruise puffing his right eye up, leaking blood, but he didn't move to wipe it away. He just shook his head again. "Not doing it, Kong."

Kong's face was twisted up in a way that made him look a demon from Maori mythology, the tribal tattoos running down the side of his neck seeming to glow with anger. He shook his head like a hellhound, shaking the anger off, relaxed a little, then stepped towards Banjo.

He came right up to Banjo's face and said, "Got to be strong to survive." With the last word, Kong moved his fist in a flash to Banjo's gut. When he pulled away and let his fist open, there was a knife in his hand, blood on the point.

As Banjo crumpled to the ground, Kong stepped forward and threw the knife over the fence. "Being strong means being first."

Banjo smiled, holding his side as blood oozed around his dirt-caked fingers.

Too right, Banjo thought.

Strong.

Strong enough to take that first step.

The first step up the stairway to heaven.

The Days When You Were Anything Else

Marcus Sakey

She calls sometimes. Late at night, drunk or worse. She calls to say she hates me.

One time she said a guy offered her money to blow him in a bar bathroom. Then, defiant, told me she'd done it. Fifty dollars, she said. That's what she's worth.

My Jessica. My baby girl.

The last call, three months ago, all she did was cry. Not heaves and jags. Gentle sobs like rain that falls all day. She never even said who it was. I held the phone and whispered, over and over, that it would be okay. That she should come home. That I loved her and would take of her.

When she finally spoke, just before she hung up, she said that it was all my fault.

She's right.

After I got out of Dixon, I didn't want to be part of the game anymore. It wasn't a moral decision. I wasn't trying to prove anything. It's just that hustling is like Vegas. Play long enough, you always lose. And I'd lost enough.

So I talked to some people, and I landed a job working the stick at Liar's, a dive under the Blue Line. I'd hung around there often enough anyway. It was the kind of bar where workingmen go to find someone to kick them ten percent for leaving the back door to a warehouse open. I'm not talking criminals. I'm talking honest guys with more bills and children than a nine-to-five coupled with a six-to-midnight could cover.

The criminals were the guys they talked to, guys like I used to be before I trusted the wrong person, before a job that should have set us up for six months instead sent me up for five years.

Tending is no way to get rich, especially at a dump like Liar's, but my life is pretty simple. I have a studio in Little Puerto Rico and a phone number I make damn sure stays listed. At work, I keep a Louisville Slugger behind the bar, but rarely pull it out. I know these men, even the ones I've never met. After a year or two, I struck up a few friendships, guys that hang around after I flip off the neons. We talk and drink and smoke the place blue, and if Lester White is feeling magnanimous, do a couple of bumps. It isn't quite a family, but it's what I have, and it's okay.

Sometimes, I even get to feeling good. Last week Lester was talking on his cell, chewing out the guy who runs a house he deals crank out of. He's nice enough, Lester, until he isn't. Then he's, well, not nice at all. I've heard stories about him and pit bulls, and I don't ever want to know if they're true.

When Lester hung up, I asked if everything was okay.

"Fucking kids," he said. "I don't know how many times I've told him to get a fucking security cage put on the back door. Kid thinks because they've got one on the front, they're safe, but these days . . ." He shook his head.

He didn't finish, and I didn't ask him to. I just topped off his Glenlivet. The rest of the guys I only spot Beam. Lester nodded at me, smiled, said, "Frank, when are you going to quit this bartending shit and come work for me? Kids these days, they aren't worth a goddamn."

Like I said, sometimes I get to feeling good. Silly, maybe, but there it is. I have a job and friends and a daughter who calls every couple of months, even if only to say she hates me. And as long as she keeps calling, there's hope.

Hope is a dangerous thing.

He comes in around three, when the bar is all but empty. A thin kid in his twenties, sporting that cocaine skeeze: long, limp hair, a complicated goatee, a mean twitchiness to the eyes. A pack of Parliaments in his left pocket. A plastic-gripped pistol barely hidden by a half-buttoned work shirt. I know his type. I've been his type.

The locket dangles from his closed fist, rocking like a hypnotist's crystal. "You know this, old man?"

Do I know it?

Till the day I die.

A lot of the stuff I gave Lucy over the years was pinched, and she was generally understanding. From the beginning, my wife knew how I made our money. But I spotted the locket in a display window one day I happened to be flush. When she saw that it came in a box, with a ribbon and everything, she hit me with that smile of hers, the one that lit me up inside. *I know just what to put in it*, she'd said. I'd asked, *What?* as I hung it on her. *Us*, she'd said, and shivered when I kissed the back of her neck.

That was a long time ago. I haven't seen the locket since the last time she visited me at Dixon. "That's my wife's."

"Not anymore." His lips curl into a shape nothing like a smile. "You know who was wearing it last?"

And all of a sudden I know where this is going. "Yes."

"Say it."

I force the syllables. "Jessica."

"Who?"

"My daughter."

"So, then, Frank." He curls his lips again. "I guess you better do exactly what I say. Right?"

I don't have many pictures. Three, to be precise.

We used to have tons, albums full. I once joked Lucy that she must've been born with a Nikon attached to her head, all the pictures she took. And once Jessica came along, forget it. Our daughter was the most documented kid on the North Side.

But you can't take that shit inside. They'll let you, but you don't want to. It kills you slowly to have proof of the way time passes, all those frozen instants that used to be yours. So you keep a couple of shots, two or three, and you stare at them until they don't mean anything anymore, and at the same time, they mean everything.

After I got out, I tried to find out what happened to the rest of our pictures. But after Lucy died, shit fell apart. What little we had that was worth anything was sold for bills, and the rest probably ended up in a dump. I like to think that maybe a collector got the photos, one of those guys who sell random snaps in boxes down at the Maxwell Street Market. I check it some Sundays, flipping through other people's lives, but I never find mine.

Three.

One of Lucy, dressed as a sort of slutty angel for Halloween a million years ago. It's faded and blurry, but she looks the way I remember when I close my eyes.

One of the room in Cook County Hospital, Luce red-eyed but smiling, Jessica bundled like a burrito in her arms.

One of Jess from Nag's Head, the summer before I went in. Eleven years old, just beginning to fill out the bikini Lucy and I fought about her having. I'm dragging her into the surf, and she's fighting me, legs scrabbling at the sand, face framed into the kind of mock fear you only have around someone you trust. You can almost hear her shrieking, almost hear her laughing.

I can, anyway.

I reach out, and he lets the locket slip from his fist, the thin chain coiling in my palm. The filigree is worn, the hinges dark with age. I stare at it, and then I look up at the kid and think about taking that pistol away from him. Cracking his fucking skull with it. Then I say, "I don't have it."

"You think I don't know who you are? What you do?"

"I'm a bartender."

"Bull-*shit.* I know all about you. The jobs you've pulled. Lucky I'm not asking for twenty."

"Those jobs were a long time ago." I gesture down the bar. "You think I had any kind of money, I'd be working here?"

He looks it over, taking in the two geezers staring at their beer, the Cubs sign in the dingy window, the bowls of pretzels the regulars know better than to eat. For a second, his confidence seems to slip. But then he shakes his head, fingers his shirt to make extra sure I get a view of the cheap Chinese pistol. "Ten grand," he says. "By Friday. Or she fucking dies."

My fingers go to fists. "Don't," I say.

"Don't what?" His mask is back in place, all insolence and swagger.

"Don't threaten my daughter."

He curls his lips again. "Friday," he says. Then he turns and struts out.

I open my hand to look at the locket. I know it's warm from

being in his pocket, but it's hard not to pretend that it's because she had it around her neck.

Ten years ago—Jesus, a decade—one of the neighborhood kids came to get me.

It was eleven in the morning, and I had been up all night doing a thing. When I heard the doorbell, I wanted more than anything to bury my head under my pillow. But Lucy was at work, so I staggered out of bed.

The kid was named Jimmy-something, a scraggly little brat that had lately been sniffing around Jessica. She was nine and he was maybe eleven, but things happen earlier these days. I didn't open the screen door, just glowered down at him. "Yeah?"

And Jimmy-something, he said the scariest words a father can hear. "It's Jess. She's hurt."

I didn't even change out of my pajama bottoms.

Growing up in the city, it's a blessing and a curse. Kids are wired to run around shrieking like carefree morons, and that's exactly the way it should be. But between drug dealers and speeding buses and evil fuckers in raincoats, it's tough to just let them go. So Lucy and I had set up boundaries; Jess could go to the school playground but not to the city park. She could walk on Augusta but not on Division.

So of course this Jimmy idiot led me straight down Division to the city park.

The first thing I saw was a ring of ten or so kids clustered around someone on the ground, and my heart kicked up to a hundred beats a minute, sweat running down my sides like it never did on a job, ever—not even the time Leo-fucking-Banks shot the security guard because he thought he was reaching for a piece—and I tore ass across the street, shoved through the kids, and there's my Jess on the ground, clutching at her ankle, which is bent way too far to one side, and her face is squinched up in pain, tears cutting tracks down her cheeks, and then she spots me.

Ever seen your baby girl look at you with relief and terror at the same time? It'll rip your fucking heart out.

I dropped to my knees beside her. She looked at me and then at one of the other kids, and said, "I fell." I glanced up at the kid she'd eyeballed. A boy, maybe twelve and already got that scraggly not-quite mustache, pale and shaking and looking like he was about to take off running. It was obvious there was more to the story, but I didn't really give a damn. I just wanted to take care of her. So I scooped her up and walked out of the park.

Warm and trembling, scrawny little arm clinging to my neck, smelling of dirt and sunshine, she looked at me, and she said, "I'm sorry, Daddy," and my heart broke all over again.

Everyone talks about how a kid changes you. How there's this whole sense of wonder, like, I don't know, like you woke up and could see colors that hadn't been there yesterday. Everything is still the way it was, but it all looks different.

So you change too. Become a different person. Self-preservation goes out the window. All of a sudden you'd do anything, *anything* for this helpless little creature. That's what everyone says, and they're right.

Especially if it's a girl.

I drive an '86 LeBaron. My furniture comes from the Brown Elephant resale shop. Towards the middle of every second week, I have to downgrade from Marlboros to Basics.

Ten grand. May as well ask for a ticket to the moon.

After my shift, I go home to pace my shitbox apartment and smoke and think.

I think about going to the police. Telling them there's a cokehead who says he's kidnapped the daughter I haven't seen in seven years, and how I have two days to get him what I make in four months. I think how they will listen to me very intently at first, making notes with silver pens while they wait for my file. I think how when it comes, they will see arrests for assault, bad checks, unlawful entry, plus the conviction, five long years.

The note taking will stop. The pens will vanish.

Truth is, I don't blame them. I really don't. First rule is that everybody lies. Why would they bust their ass running around to check out a story like mine?

After all, they don't know Jess.

I think of the last time she called, when all she did was cry. How each sob was like a spike through me, because I knew every single one was a wound done her. Done to my baby girl, who had once loved and trusted me, and then found me gone when she needed me most. Whose mother had died while I was inside, and who never knew what that did to me, how it emptied me out to lose my wife. My baby girl, who ran away before I was released.

Who had to do the things a sixteen-year-old runaway has to do.

I figure that if I sell my car and my records and empty my joke of a bank account, I can probably scrape up two, three grand.

So I put on a clean shirt and I go to work. I spend the longest afternoon of my life pulling Buds for losers. I greet the dusk rush eagerly, glad for the distraction. I pour shots and light cigarettes and forget orders and knock things over, and a couple of the regulars make jokes about it until they see my eyes, and then they wander away from the bar to the siderail on the back wall.

Finally, at eleven, Lester White comes in.

The place reacts the way it always does, shifting to acknowledge him, like sweeping a magnet above iron filings. Men who work for him nod and raise glasses. Hard kids vie for his attention. Suckers who owe him money stare at their beers and hope to Christ he won't pick them to make an example of. I pour his Glenlivet rocks as he steps to a suddenly open space at the bar.

"Frank," he says.

"Lester."

He turns to lean an elbow, picks up the highball glass, and sips at it. "Heard on the radio, they're saying snow tonight."

"Yeah?" I can't imagine anything I could care less about, what with the words *my daughter, my daughter, my daughter* going round and round in my head, but I can't rush into this. Lester is the only option I have. How else am I going to get the money by tomorrow? Rob twenty liquor stores?

"Winter again." He shakes his head. "This fucking town."

"I hear you," I say, and run a towel over a glass that's already dry.

He nods, starts to step away.

"Hey Lester, you got a second?" I try not to sound anxious, but I can tell it creeps into my voice by the way he narrows his eyes. He turns back, rests his forearms on the bar. He knows something is coming. You don't get where Lester is without an eye for desperation.

I set the towel down, take a breath. "I was wondering if I could talk to you about a loan."

He raises an eyebrow.

"There's a . . ." I sigh. "My daughter."

"She okay?"

I think about telling him everything, the cokehead, the locket, everything, but I know it's the wrong move. Lester may hang around after hours, but that doesn't make us friends. He's a big man, a player, a very dangerous guy. If I tell him the situation, it's the same as asking him to help directly. A bad play for a couple of reasons. First, he wouldn't do it. Second, I couldn't afford it if he did. Third, and most important, Jess. If something went wrong . . .

So I just hold my hands open and look him in the eye. He finally bobs his head. "How much?"

I force myself to say it. He stares at me. Sizing me up. Wondering if I'm for real.

I stare back. *My daughter, my daughter, my daughter*. The bar noise goes away.

After a minute, Lester scrunches up his mouth. "Frank, you know I like you. But ten grand?"

"I'm good for it."

"Say I give you a friend rate, call it seven and a half. Almost a grand a week, and that's just the juice. You stop eating, stop smoking, give me your whole paycheck, it's what, five? So you owe a full grand the week after. One and a half after that. Just in juice, you understand, I'm not talking principal." Lester shakes his head. "Sooner or later, I'd have to send someone to put your fingers in a car door. Can't do it. I like you too much."

I pick up the rag, start wiping the bar. Truth is, I knew what Lester was going to say. But I had to ask. Now there's only one option. The one thing I said I'd never do again.

My daughter, my daughter, my daughter.

I rub the same circle over and over. "What if I worked it off?"

"Doing what?"

I shrug. "Whatever you need." I look up.

Lester meets my gaze, starts to smile like I've told a joke. Then something creeps into his eyes, but I can't tell what it is. He breaks the stare and looks away. "Come on, Frank."

"I'm serious. You're always saying you need good people."

He turns back, and I realize what I saw on his face.

Embarrassment. Lester White is embarrassed for me.

"When I say that, I'm just, you know. Blowing smoke, playing around." He shrugs. "You were a serious man back in the day, but now . . ." He waves his hand, and doesn't finish the sentence, which was probably meant as a kindness. Except that I can fill in the blank: *Now you're a fifty-one-year-old bartender. That's* all *you are. The days when you were anything else—an earner, a husband, a father—those days are gone.*

There's a lead numbness in my stomach that I've only felt a couple of times. When the judge stole five years of my life away. When Lucy told me the doctors had found a tumor in her head. When my little girl called me to weep into the phone and I couldn't do a goddamn thing about it.

Lester is clearly uncomfortable. He breaks the spell by downing the rest of his scotch, then pulling his roll from his pocket. "Look, don't think I'm a bad guy, though," he says. "Let me help you." He flattens a wad of money a half-inch thick, and snaps off three crisp hundreds. As an afterthought, pulls off two more. "Here you go, pal." He smiles at me. Then he sets his empty glass on the bar and gives the tiniest nod towards it.

And, sick to my stomach, I reach for the bottle and do what a bartender is supposed to.

Usually a couple of guys would stay after I lock the doors, but tomorrow is Friday, so tonight I kick everybody out. Then I pour myself four inches of Jim Beam, light a smoke, and sit on one of the stools in the dark. Through the front window I can see the snow falling. When the El clatters overhead, orange sparks spray out to shimmer amidst whirling flakes of white.

I'm short ten thousand dollars, and I have until tomorrow morning to get it.

I get off the stool and walk behind the bar, punch open the register. Maybe two dozen twenties, twice as many tens and fives, and a thick stack of singles. Call it a thousand dollars. If

I'm lucky. Taking it means losing my job, but that doesn't matter a damn.

But it doesn't matter, because a thousand dollars isn't ten.

I crush my square and light another. Suck hard, picture the smoke twisting and curling into my lungs. I tap my lighter against the bar and I take a belt of the bourbon and I think about the way my feet feel like someone is scraping barbed wire across my heels and I watch the sparks and snow mingle and none of it helps relieve the thought that I'm about to let my baby girl down again, maybe for the last time.

And before I can think too much about it, I lean down, grab a couple of paper clips from the junk cup beside the register, take the bat from beneath the counter, and head for the front door.

Three in the morning, snow whirling from a sky stained pink with reflected light. The city sleeps.

I try not to think about what I'm doing. If I think about it, I might back out, and if I back out, I lose everything. So I just focus on Jess and the road.

It takes half an hour to find the right block. The house is somber against the sky. A thin layer of snow drapes the porch. I'd like to circle back to take another look, but I can't be sure that someone isn't watching. So I keep my speed steady, go two more blocks, then swing into the alley and kill the engine.

There is no silence like the middle of the night in the midst of a Chicago snowstorm when you are about to do something truly stupid.

I take a breath.

I take my Louisville Slugger.

I get out of the car.

I rifle through the trunk for the ski mask I wear to shovel the car out. Putting it on does nothing to muffle the sick-sweet odor of trash. I stick to the side and move carefully. The air is sharp. Snow crunches under my boots. My fingers are cold, the skin waxy and thin. After two blocks, I'm right behind the house. And sure enough, Lester was right.

Kids these days aren't worth a goddamn, because there's still no security cage on the back of his stash house.

Taking delicate steps now, careful not to disturb the broken bottles and chunks of concrete that line the sides of the alley, I move to the building. There's no screen, just a solid-core door with a metal kick plate. The cold of the wood is startling when I press my ear against it, but I can hear music. Someone is awake. Figures. Twenty-four-seven, people want what Lester sells.

The door is locked, of course. But you don't go down for a robbery beef without knowing a thing or two about locks. I bend one paper clip into an awkward tension wrench and the other into a scooped pick. My tools are clumsy, and it's hard to work with numb fingers, so it takes almost ten minutes. But finally the cylinder of the deadbolt gives, spinning counterclockwise.

My heart is hammering my chest hard enough I'm afraid my ribs might crack. There's no way to know what's on the opposite side of this door. I could be walking right into the barrel of a shotgun. Even if I'm not, there will definitely be two or three guys in the house, definitely armed and probably jacked up. Tweakers aren't known for trigger discipline.

Trying to remember the words for a Hail Mary, I turn the knob, pull the door a scant inch, and press my eye to the crack.

It's dark, but looks like a back room or a pantry. I can make out metal racks sagging under the weight of shadows. There's an archway screened by a bedsheet, and beyond it, yellow light. The music is clearer now.

Gripping the bat so hard my hands shake, I step inside and

close the door behind me, and just like that, I'm back where I started. The last time I broke in where I wasn't supposed to be, it cost me five years, my wife, and my daughter. And now here I am again, and just like last time, I'm doing it for Jess, even if she'll never understand.

The kitchen is on the other side of the curtain. It's been converted to a lab, every surface covered with burners and flasks and tubing and jars. An efficient little operation: cook meth in the back and sell it out the front. No muss, no fuss. Of course, when the cops get wise to it, everybody inside will face federal time. But what does that matter to Lester? There'll be nothing connecting him, and there's always another stupid kid ready to step up for a spin of the wheel.

I can hear voices now. The music swells, and I realize it's a television. Perfect. If they're caught up in something, maybe I can sneak right by, find the stash, and get the hell out without anyone the wiser.

Adrenaline sings in my blood as I step through the kitchen towards the stairs.

One night in a past life, Lucy rolled on her side and looked at me. Leno was on mute, and the light flickered across her features. "I think Jess is starting to figure out what you do."

"She say something?"

My wife shook her head. "Not exactly. But she roots for the bad guys on TV."

"What, I'm a bad guy?"

Lucy touched my cheek. "No, baby. But you're not a model citizen either."

I snorted and rolled over on my back, stared at the ceiling. "I don't know. Maybe it's time I quit."

"Maybe it is."

I looked over. "A little fucking judgmental, are we?"

Lucy smiled, that slow sweet thing. She turned to take the locket from the bedside table. Dangled it from her right hand and used her left to open it. Inside were two pieces of tan paper, cut to ovals and glued in place. Us. On the left, her thumbprint; on the right, mine. Whorls and spirals marked in black ink, two one-of-a-kind things brought together. Facing each other.

I waited for her to say something. But after a minute, I realized she had.

I can hear my pulse. Not just feel it—hear it.

The house is a small bungalow, with two bedrooms and a filthy bath opening immediately off the top of the stairs. Which means that before I've even reached the second floor, I can see straight into the opposite room, where a man lies on a bed with his hands laced behind his head and a shiny automatic beside him.

I freeze three steps from the top, one foot stopping in midair. I'm a stranger wearing a ski mask and carrying a baseball bat. If he looks over, I'm going to die. A warm fist spins greasy in my belly. I realize I'm holding my breath. I was scared before, but now panic hits, and it's all I can do not to turn and run. I can be out the back door and heading home in minutes. No one ever needs to know I was here.

Then I see the money.

It's in a paper grocery bag on the floor, which seems strange until I realize that it's not like addicts pay in crisp C-notes. There are hundreds of dirty bills piled loose in the bag. More than I need.

The man doesn't stir. His eyes are closed.

I stare at the money, and then at the man, and then at the gun, and then at the money again, my eyes flicking in a circle as my mind races, but the truth is, I've already made up my mind, I'm just working on my nerve.

Gently, very gently, I lift one foot and put it down on the next step. Again. Again.

A board squeaks and I freeze like I've been turned to stone. Wait a long moment. Nothing happens.

I step onto the landing. The bat is a comfort, and I grip it tight enough to leave marks. Force myself to breathe, and take another delicate step, and another. The bag will be awkward, and I'll have to lift it carefully so as not to make a—

The man's eyes open.

We stare at each other for what's probably less than a second but seems longer. He looks to be in his twenties. Black hair, soap opera scruff, blue eyes. I've seen him before. He's been in the bar. A vodka tonic man, I recall, absurdly.

And then he's lunging for the pistol, his right hand flying, moving so fast I can almost see a blur behind it. He must not have been napping, only lounging, he's too alert, and before I can move he's got his fingers on the pistol and is starting to bring it up and I don't think, just step forward and crack the bat into his head like I'm swinging for the fences.

The sound is nothing like hitting a baseball.

Everything stops. I stand and stare at what I've done. And for no reason I can understand, I think of that day Jess broke her ankle, the way she said, *I'm sorry, Daddy*, and how all I wanted was to hold her and keep her safe from every bad thing.

Then I reach down and pick up the bag and tiptoe back down the stairs and through the kitchen and out the back door, a grocery bag full of cash in one hand and a bloody baseball bat in the other.

A whirl of soft white erases me.

The shirt is different. Everything else is the same: the sneer, the cokehead twitchiness, the pistol tucked where I can't help but see it. Standing across the bar from me, he says, "You have what I want?"

I take a moment to study him. Not a bad-looking kid if you could convince him to take a shower, get a haircut. He's young, and too cocky. I could yank the bat and sock him in the head, and the way he's got it tucked under his shirt that gun would do him no good at all.

Instead, I open the cupboard and hand him the duffel bag. There was almost fourteen thousand in the grocery bag. I was up till dawn counting and bundling.

He unzips it, glances inside, and I can see triumph flow through him. I remember what it feels like, that raw and animal joy from taking something you could never earn.

"Smart move, old man." He straightens. "So here's how this works. I'm going to walk out of here. You follow me, or I get any hint the cops are following me, and your daughter dies."

And I laugh. Was I ever that young?

He's not ready for that, and it throws him. "You think I'm fucking kidding?"

"Come on, kid." I shake my head. "You got your money. No need to keep pretending you really kidnapped her."

He goes tense. His eyes dart right to left and back again. "How—"

"Only a person that believes I have money would bother to run an angle on a guy like me. And the only person who'd believe I have money is Jess." I shrug. "She always believed in the bad guys on television. Why she ended up with you, I guess. You two are together, right?"

The kid nods, looking like he's trying to do math problems in his head.

"Was this your idea or hers?"

He finally finds his voice. "She was always going on about

how her dad was this big criminal, been to prison and everything. So I figured, you know . . ." He shakes his head. "Wait a second. If you knew from the beginning, why—"

"Do you have a daughter?"

"Naw, man." He says it almost boastfully, like the idea is ridiculous.

I sip my beer and shake my head. "Then you wouldn't understand."

He stares for another few seconds, finally blinks, shrugs. "Whatever." He backs towards the door, keeping an eye on me, like I might lunge for the bag.

"Hey."

The kid pauses, nervous.

"Give this back to her, will you?" I hold out my hand. The locket dangles.

His features war with themselves, the sneer faltering. He's young, doesn't know how to handle his emotions yet. It's easy to see that he doesn't understand why I'm letting him walk out with that money. It just doesn't compute to him.

Not yet, at least.

For a long moment he just stares at the locket swinging back and forth. Finally, he steps forward, and I let the chain unspool from my fingers.

After he leaves, I think of following, letting him lead me to Jess. The daughter I haven't seen in seven years, who calls every couple of months to say she hates me. My baby. Instead, I pull a pint of Bud and drink it slow. I top off a regular's beer. I wash some glasses in preparation for the evening rush. Then I lean on the bar and light a cigarette and watch the snow fall.

I think about the guy I hit with the bat, and whether or not I killed him. I wonder how long it will be until Lester White runs down the list of people that knew about the back door of his stash house, until he puts that together with me asking for a loan. I wonder if it's true what they say about his pit bulls, and I think it probably is.

I wonder if, maybe, just maybe, my phone will ring one more time before I find out.

Cramp

Anthony Neil Smith

I got the E. coli really bad the morning of the heist from hot dogs earlier in the week, but I didn't see the other three sweating and cramping and squeezing back their bowels like me, suffering in the backseat of Winona's Saturn coupe. It was me, Winona driving, Lewis back with me trying to keep his distance, and Abe riding shotgun. Abe and Winona had a thing. I'd wanted her first. He'd acted first. I don't know, maybe I still had a chance. We really had good talks. I hated listening to them fuck at night.

Only two more hours south, the Indiana/Michigan state line. Our first destination, State Line Steve's Adult RelaXXXation Den.

My roommate Abe thought up the heist on the way home from his aunt's funeral in Ohio. He noticed the state line porn shops and imagined they'd be loaded with cash since pervs wouldn't want the shit on their credit cards. Not a bad idea. I'd never robbed anything before, but my options sucked after I was kicked out of school on a "sexual assault" charge. One of

Winona's friends—she said the charges were nothing personal, but the bitch got a sweet settlement from the school. All I'd done was try to show her that a back massage from me would melt her tension like butter. Instead she kneed me and called security.

Winona was still my friend, though. She trusted me, probably because touching her would result in Abe touching me badly. I didn't want that, remembered two purple fingers and a makeshift cast. One still won't bend right.

Lewis was melting into the door, telling them to turn on the air.

"No," I said. "Freezing."

"It's fucking May."

"But he's sick," Winona said. "Chills. Come on. Poor guy."

Lewis said, "If he's got food poisoning, aren't we gonna get it too?"

"Could've been a bad frank. Just one that didn't get cooked enough. Or maybe it'll take longer for one of you to get sick. You're more muscular."

"What if it's the flu? Or worse?"

Abe turned his head. "Would you shut up? It's a fucking stomachache, that's all."

"Actually, it's bacteria," Winona said. "Most things that make us sick are bacteria."

Lewis glanced at me like I had plague. "You sure? How do you know that?"

Her eyes rear viewed him, rolled. "*Duh*, I was taking classes, remember? To be a med lab tech?"

"You get far enough to know a cure?" I said. Every word strained, couldn't risk releasing.

She shrugged. "That would've been the next semester. It was just too hard for me."

I didn't buy it. I knew how smart she was. Her problem was,

she'd rather drown herself in lemon drops and Jell-O shooters than study Immunology. Her new major at Grand Rapids Community College was Social Work, her fourth in two years.

"I need a restroom," I said.

Abe turned farther, couldn't get his face around that far. "Really?"

"Urgently."

Lately, things had been "make do." I was C student from a farm family, got booted from school and had to mop floors at Taco Bell to pay rent. Abe wasn't sympathetic. He still expected me to pitch in a hundred more than him because, "Hey, I'm not here as much as you." So I made do. I made do with a half-assed relationship with Winona when she was waiting for Abe to either show up or wake up. I liked our mornings, coffee and Pop-Tarts watching music videos—her, bare-legged, wearing one of Abe's giant Gap rugby shirts. The guy was a hulk, I'll give him that. Some mornings she'd stagger towards the table and say, "Sometimes I wish he'd ease up. I don't need bruises every night."

Oh, sweet Winnie, I'd be gentler. I'd listen to you. Just let me give you a back massage.

No, I didn't say that. I said, "Yeah, that's pretty tough."

I made do with a crap job, couldn't dare tell my folks about the assault charges. It didn't get as far as a trial. I didn't want to fight it. Figured it was easier to let everything cool out and then start over later, my record clean of anything official as long as I kept away from trying to make something of myself—although that dream of being a vet had pushed me out onto the road and just kept on without me. I supposed I could work in pet stores eventually. Wanted to give Abe's way a try first.

Made do with a nasty gas station bathroom too. I three-plied toilet paper as a seat protector because of the brown stripes that wouldn't wipe away. The light kept flicking off. It smelled like week-old stew. And then I released.

Whispered, "*Yeeeeeeeeeeessss.*"

Moaned.

Took in another breath, like week-old stew and bad pork.

Read black marker graffiti:

Had me a long dick here, 4/25/04.
Jesus Saves
He sure does—saves the best weed for himself.
Galatians 1:20

Lewis pounded on the door. "You can't set up house in there!"

I reached for toilet paper, pulled. The last five squares fell off. I tried for the backup roll. There wasn't one.

"Son of a bitch."

No paper towels for your hands. Just an air dryer.

Lewis shouted, "We can't risk being seen, asshole. Come on." Then to Abe, "I'm trying. He won't fucking answer!"

"Five minutes, all right? Can you wait five more fucking minutes?"

I tried my best. I made do with five squares to deal with my slimy ass, the bacteria turning everything to a syrupy pond scum. I worked it off, sometimes getting a little on my fingers and palm. Shit, shit, shit. The aches were coming back and I had to start clenching. My friends were bound to take off without me if I stayed any longer. The best I did with five squares was about eighty percent clean. Fuck it. I had a long day ahead.

A bigger surprise when I tried to wipe the shit smears off my hands. The water didn't work. Tried cold. Tried hot. Tried spinning them as far as I could. Nothing.

Fine, then. Okay. Just make do. Maybe the air dryer would evaporate them, kill the little microbes, anything. So I hit the button and held open palms beneath. No air, no heat, no nothing.

I wanted to cry.

Twenty miles later, the nausea moved in.

I'd asked Winona the night before why she wanted to come along. I was surprised to learn Abe had told her. She said, "Don't know."

"You could get hurt. You could go to jail."

"It's not like we're killing someone. People rob all the time."

"But they go to jail for it."

"A little." An index finger and thumb almost touching.

I'd figured her out then. She didn't like Abe because she saw the gentleman underneath the scars. She just liked the scars. Same with anything else in life.

We waited until the parking lot was nearly empty at State Line Steve's. I was nearly paralyzed by then, any motion set to make me spew. I had another growing cramp bubbling inside too. Abe and Lewis would have to handle the whole thing themselves. I planned on heading for the men's room.

The plan: walk to the shop, do the job, then walk out. Winona would come to get us only when we were on our way to the road. I didn't know if I could even walk.

Abe took a look at me. "Why don't we let him drive? Winona can come in."

"That wasn't the plan." She sounded pissed, but also a little scared. She was in this for vicarious thrills—a part of the gang, but just driving. "I'm not going in."

"Fuck." Abe stared at her a moment too long before turning to me. "You gonna make it, champ?"

"No." I meant it. "I'd tell you if I could."

Abe snorted. He choked. He recovered and said, "If you don't . . . I'll kill you."

I think Lewis and Winona stood up for me, came to my rescue and all. Told him we should call it off, go home, get some pizza. It was a stupid idea. Come on, man, let's bail.

I knew what it meant to him, though. He'd told me Internet poker had him out five grand. He'd stolen it from his dad, bit by bit, but the old man finally caught on. Abe was sure he'd win. Just one fucking flush. One fucking full house. Even when he hit them, they weren't enough to make him stop. One more fucking straight. One more fucking four of a kind. Without a few scores, Abe was sunk. His dad had already threatened to take the tuition, take the car, take the AmEx card.

Abe looked back at me again. He'd never cry, but the look was close enough to it for anyone's money. "Champ?"

What sort of friend was he to me, then? That didn't matter. We could settle that later. The bigger question was, what sort of friend was I?

I told him, "I'll power through for you."

There was no Steve at State Line Steve's that night. We got a skinny wild-haired guy named Damien, who looked as if he just worked here to support himself until "the band hit it big."

Abe and Lewis handled shaking him down—their guns cheap pawnshop .38s that were still frightening enough shoved up against your face. I didn't have a gun, just pretended. My job was to control the patrons. But there weren't any. Perfect timing. So I fingered over the magazines on the mismatched racks that looked like they'd been collected over the last forty years, some plastic, some wood, some wire. The teens and model-hot chicks were all closest to the register. I was still trying to rub off shit, even though I'd wiped most off on my jeans. Still felt dirty. Kept sniffing at my fingertips. Down the row. Hairy girls. Mature women. Lesbians. Got a little hard off a Mature Woman/Younger Chick cover, but that didn't help my condition.

Quickly back up front as Damien shoved money into the bag Abe held for him.

"Abe."

He glared at me. *"Names!"*

"I need a break."

"No fucking break. We don't have time."

Acid bubbling. I burped. Felt bile rise. "Can't . . . can't wait."

He gritted his teeth. Damien had stopped filling the sack.

"Wait, that's it?"

The clerk nodded. "The rest is credit card slips."

"You can't have more credit card slips than cash."

"Oh yeah. It just rings up as a gas store purchase, you know. We're discreet." Even though he was scared of the guns, you could tell he'd probably said the same thing to ten other robbers before.

I said, "Abe, I need the bathroom."

He put his finger to his lips, pained look on his face. I didn't mean to ruin the job. I couldn't help it. Desperate. My body doing its own thing now.

I looked at Damien. "Bathroom."

He said, "It's in the back. You'll need the key. Let me get it."

The clerk reached under the counter, none of us really having time to think that wasn't such a great idea. I just wanted the key. A key, a bowl, a sink.

Damien's hand popped up with an automatic pistol. His face was already twisting, at the ready, when Abe caught Damien's wrist, slammed it hard on the counter. Kept gripping, struggling. Abe forced the clerk's wrist to the side, the gun pointing at none of us. Like arm wrestling, the strain showing in both their necks. Lewis pointed his revolver at Damien yelling things like, "I'm not joking! Let it go! You wanna die?" Damien ignored him, deep into his battle of wills with Abe. Jaws clenched now. Heavy breaths through their noses.

Then I threw up on them. Heaved hot dog and cola and acid all over the counter, slicking up Abe and Damien's arm battle. Damien tried to pull away harder, a high-pitched wail coming out of him. He started gagging. The wetness gained him some wiggle room.

"Get the gun!" Abe said.

He said it to me. I leaned over them, still not able to get any air past the thickness in my throat. Heaving, trying to control it. But then there was another round of the hot reddish mess spewing from me. Abe's grip on Damien slipped even more.

"The gun!"

Lewis kept his distance, still shouting. He wasn't going to shoot anybody. Couldn't depend on him.

I grabbed the top of the pistol, tugged. It wasn't going to be so hard. Tugged some more. Definitely slipping. Damien's finger was still in the trigger guard. Abe and I both caught that. Abe growled, louder and louder, then jumped up, slammed his forehead into Damien's. The clerk was dropping, all muscles slacking. His hand released the gun and it went flying down an aisle of dildos and vibrators. I followed, scrabbling for it, tripping, falling, landing hard. Then it was mine, and I felt a little bit better than before I had puked.

Abe leaned over me, the wet bag of cash dripping myself back on me. "We've got to go."

Only Lewis talked in the car. Pissed at first, then laughing, then satisfied when the fear dissipated the farther we drove.

"Fucking *pukes* on the guy, can you believe that? Makes it too slippery for him to hold the fucking gun. Righteous, man. Let me see that gun."

He reached for the piece sticking out of my waistband. I grabbed his wrist, twisted. "It's mine."

"I just want to see. Let go."

My fingernails bit into his skin. He tried to kick me, couldn't get his foot free from between the seat. "Hey, cut that out! I'll kick your ass."

I released and he pulled back, his arm now dirtied up. Winona was the only one still clean. I wondered how long before Abe and Lewis came down with what I had. Winona had said it wasn't contagious by air, but by contact with fecal matter and vomit. No one was saying it, though. Everyone pretended we each had our own force fields.

Lewis finally said, "Jesus, the *smell.*"

We found a cheap hotel that night out in the cornfields of southern Illinois, used Winona's ID info since we were pretty sure she'd kept out of sight during the job. The desk crew didn't see the condition we were in, stained and broken. I poured sweat. More bubbles expanded in my guts, my ass clenched as tight as humanly possible until we pulled up in front of the room. I wanted to beeline for the toilet, but by then I was too weak. I released as soon as I climbed from the car, the liquid shit trailing down my leg, dripping on the pavement. A trail of splats followed me inside. I didn't get past the first bed in the room. Fell across it and shivered.

"Oh my God." Abe. Maybe an ounce of feeling. If I hadn't been cramped, chilled, and covered in my own filth, I would've been touched. "Is he going to make it?"

Winona said, "Should pass in a few days. But we need to worry about you guys."

Like he hadn't heard, "A few *days*? We don't have a few days. Hell, staying here one night is dangerous enough. We need to hit again before the cops get a bead on us."

"In a couple of days, we'll all be like him anyway, so maybe we should cut our losses and go home."

Nobody answered. All three standing there staring at me. Winona finally sighed, came over to the bed, and carefully removed my shoes. She said, "One of you get me a washcloth. Soak it in warm water."

Lewis nodded, went to take care of it.

To Abe, she said, "Help me get his pants off."

"Oh, I don't think so."

She glanced up at him, withered him. She worked my zipper, and I let her. Felt a little throb in my cock in spite of the embarrassment. Sometimes you're so sick, embarrassment can't reach you. I wasn't quite there yet, but close. Winona and Abe slid my jeans off. I held tight to the gun I'd taken at the store, the only thing propping up my strength—you always feel bigger with a gun.

Then Winona peeled away my soiled jockeys, sat by my side, and gently wiped my ass clean with the warm cloth. Such a peaceful look on her face too. Maybe she liked living on the edge, but I sensed an angel in there who would help me until the end.

"Thank you," I said.

A Mona Lisa grin. "Feels good?"

Actually, it hurt. My ass was raw and the cloth was rough. "Like heaven."

While she took care of me, wheels spun in Abe's mind. Pacing, pacing. Lewis brushed by him on his way to the sink, set his gun down, and then tore open the soap wrapper.

"It's too late. Washing might've helped a few hours ago, but not now."

Lewis kept on. "It can't hurt. I'd rather be clean and sick than not clean and sick."

Pretty soon you won't have a choice, I thought. It made me laugh. The gun I had taken was pressed against my stomach, cold and cutting. Hurt when I laughed. I pulled it away from my skin. Soon as it was free, another convulsion. Up my throat, out my ass, at the same time. Every muscle tightened. Including the finger around the trigger.

The mirror over the sink shattered. The bullet had gone right over Winona's shoulder, right through Lewis.

"Ohgodohgodohgod, no, no, no." He held soapy hands over the giant hole in his chest while Abe and Winona went ape shit grabbing towels, pressing it against the wound. Lewis growing quieter, his wild eyes drifting like he was high, man. I tried to watch but was puking all over the bed, using all my leftover willpower to hold myself up.

The blood saturated the towels. Winona kept pressing. Her arms were bloody to her elbows. Lewis sank to the bed, then onto his back, a low whine his only sound. Then it stopped.

Abe shoved the gun at me. "*What*. The. *Fuck*?"

I couldn't speak well. Too much heaving. "Accident . . . sorry . . . accident!"

He leaned closer with the gun, looked determined, then fell away and paced, ran his hand through his hair. Then came back at me with the gun. "He's gone, man. Oh, we're so screwed. So fucking screwed. Fuck. Ing . . . ssssss. *Damn it!*"

Winona was sitting on Lewis's feet at bedside, bloody towels in her lap as she stared into space. Nothing there.

Abe said, "Come on, Winona, we've got to go."

"What?"

"Let's get out of here. No way no one heard that shot. Hurry."

She lifted her chin at me. "What about him?"

"Same as before, just a little sooner is all. We don't have time."

I saw where this was going. He'd wanted it this way the whole time. I wondered if Lewis and I would even have gotten a cut. When I finally glimpsed his eyes, I knew the next shot was for me. He shook his head.

I rolled onto my back, double-gripped the pistol, and trained it on him. Wavering, little circles. Three feet away and I doubted I could hit him. But I would damn sure try.

"Take me," I said.

"Fuck, buddy, *look* at you."

"We weren't a part of your plan anyway, were we? Just some warm bodies to help pull off the jobs, and then you and Winona would sneak out in the middle of the night, leaving us stranded or dead."

The guy took it hard, looked hurt. "Aw, dude. I wouldn't have killed you. If you had tried to turn me in, you'd have been in about as much trouble. How about you take it like a man, see? At least you'll get a free trip to the hospital tonight. You'll feel better."

I kept aiming. I had to admit that his friendship wasn't a complete disaster. He *did* keep us in pizza and video games, beer and cable TV. He was always there to urge me on, tell me I should try harder than I did. Even said he'd have been a character witness at my hearing on the sexual assault, as long as it wasn't before ten in the morning. But to bring me in on something like this, something I never would've *imagined* committing in my wildest dreams unless it was on an Xbox, then double-cross me? Fuck that noise.

My body answered for me in the end. Arms throbbed, chest ached, and the bubbles were growing faster. More sickness on its way up.

"You son of a bitch," I said as the gun fell beside me on the bed. Winona got to her knees and reached for it, cradled it, before climbing to her feet.

Then Abe was aiming again, not so confused this time. Determined. Drawing down on me. What could I do anymore? Lying in a puddle of my own mess, exhausted, a newly initiated killer. Abe said, "If it were only the money, I'd trust you could keep your mouth shut. But with all this, well . . . that changes the deal. I can't risk it."

"You said so yourself. You can trust me." Fighting to stay up on my elbows.

"I don't know what to think anymore, man. I've never been in so deep before. For fuck's sake, why'd you have to go and get sick?"

"You can't blame me for getting sick."

"It doesn't matter." Steel nerves. Brass balls. He had what it took to shoot me.

When it came, it was Winona doing the shooting. Right into Abe's neck. A gusher. He strangled on a *K* as he fell, cupping his palms around his throat, trying to hold in the life that was leaking out too fast and warm and slippery to control. I looked at Winona, gun loose in her fingers, one bloody hand over her mouth. When she pulled it away, she looked like a horror movie zombie, a red print across her mouth and cheek.

She peered down at Abe until he stopped croaking. Then she cleared her throat, turned her face to me. I reached for her hand.

"It's okay," I said. "You did the right thing."

"I know," she said. Weak, though. As if it hadn't mattered either way. "I couldn't let him kill you."

It warmed me to hear her say it. A reason to fight, a reason to live. She *did* care after all. All those late evenings, early mornings, confessions, "true friend" talk, had been building to this.

"You made the right choice, sweetie. Please, hand me my jeans and let's go."

She snapped to attention, started looking around. "What?"

"I can wash up at the next stop. I'm feeling better."

She kept looking around, grew frantic, then found what she was looking for. She knelt at the foot of the bed so I couldn't see her. I sat up, the stomach growing restless again, to find her yanking the bag of money from beneath Abe's body. He'd died with his eyes shocked open.

"Baby? Winona?" I scooted towards her. "We're going to be all right."

Winona must've sensed me moving. She leapt up with a sharp intake of breath and bug-eyed me, holding the pistol and the money to her chest. We were like that a good minute or two. I reached for her again. This time she reeled backwards towards the door. Soon as she was flush against it, someone started banging on the outside. Freaked her out, looked like a scared ferret.

"Everything all right in there? Were those gunshots? Are you okay?"

"Winona? We can do this," I said.

She shook her head. Not a word. Not even the courtesy of one word. She reached for the doorknob, opened the door, and pushed past the manager who had been banging.

He said something to her but she kept going. Then he looked in the room—Abe, me, then Lewis, then the cracked mirror, then me again. I grinned at him.

Two dead guys and some loon naked from the waist down, covered in shit and vomit. I said, "A little food poisoning, that's all."

I heard a car engine turn over; then the room was bathed in headlight glare. The manager turned to the parking lot. I didn't have to see for myself to know it was Winona's car.

"Hey! Get back here! Hey!" The manager took off after her,

leaving me alone. It was a safe bet. Even my sense of survival was sick at that point. I fell back into my puddle with a loud *plop*, thinking that maybe after they let me out of prison, I could be a massage therapist. I'm telling you, if the girls would just let me rub their backs, they'd never want anyone else.

Private Craps Shooter at Dawn

Steven M. Messner

The rising sun tries to lift the heavy blanket of smog off the sleeping city, but it is only partially successful. Nothing too beautiful can ever fully come out in a place like this.

I look down from where the sun should be and inhale on my cigarette. "Would you roll the damn dice?"

"You're holding them," Billy Strap says.

I look in my hand and I'll be damned if they aren't in my palm right next to the knife scar. "Right," I say, and hand him the dice.

Some nose-to-the-ceiling dame with curves like a violin tramps right through the middle of our game. She's expensive looking: tailored business suit, leather briefcase, and one of those classy Dutch boy haircuts.

"Hot, hot, hot," Billy Strap says. "I'd like her in my stable."

She doesn't look back. Her kind never looks back. Looking back would be admitting someone like me exists. In a world like hers I don't exist until something goes wrong.

Billy's dog, Cordoba, starts to bark and pull against its choker.

This breed is something designed in the deepest pits of hell by demons with too much time on their hands.

"Shut that beast up and roll the dice."

Billy studies the dice, rolls them back and forth in his palm, talks to them, cajoles them, and all but fucks them until I'm pretty sure I'm going to strangle the little bastard.

"Roll!"

He rolls the dice. They bounce off the brick wall and land on an oily piece of cardboard in the alley.

Billy jumps up. "Eleven!"

The one die seemed to me to roll real funny, as if it were somehow off center, as if Billy Strap were a dirty low-down cheater. I hate cheaters.

"What the hell is going on with that die?"

Billy tucks his Afro under his purple fedora. "There ain't nothin' wrong with that die."

I look for a weapon and spy a loose brick. I pick it up over my head and come down hard.

"Oh, no you didn't," Billy says.

"If didn't means did, then yes, I didn't. You low-down cheater."

I lift the brick. We look. There's nothing there but pieces of broken-up dice.

"It looks like you owe me some motherfuckin' dice," Billy says.

I toss him a balled-up ten spot. "Here, take it. Buy yourself some real dice and not the fuzzy kind either. The fleas on that leopard-print coat of yours would send all their young ones into a pair like that, and then when you'd roll them they'd dance around all funnylike. Wait, your regular dice do that already."

"You're crazy, Ludlow."

"Yeah, well, at least I know it. I don't go around pretending to be something I'm not."

I stand and my knees creak like the doors of a rusted-out Impala. My body isn't so much a temple as it is a lean-to. Hard living, I suppose.

Billy Strap stands using his gold cane for support. "If I were a younger man I'd whup your ass, Ludlow."

We stare each other down until a fruit fly from the Dumpster hits my left eye and I'm forced to blink. Billy smiles triumphantly as if he's just won something and struts off down the sidewalk holding his gold cane in the air like some sort of deranged high school bandleader. Cordoba follows reluctantly glancing back at me every few steps. He wants a piece of me.

It's noon and I'm eating a sandwich at Ritz's Diner. Billy Strap rushes up to my booth. "Burma, Burma, someone stole Cordoba."

"Stole? I don't think so. He's probably off eating a pack of Cub Scouts."

"I had him tied up outside the bank. When I looked outside I saw some guy jam a needle in his neck and then throw him in a van and take off."

"Did you get a look at the guy?"

"Not really . . . yes, wait, he was wearing a Yankees baseball cap."

"Well, let me get right on that. I'll check every man, woman, and child in the city who wears a Yankees hat. That should only take about forty years."

Billy grabs my arm and I spill coffee all over my lap. "I read about this in the paper. They've been kidnapping dogs and putting them in fights. They're gonna kill Cordoba. Come on, you have to go find them."

"Can I at least eat my breakfast?"

Billy scoops my eggs up with my toast and makes a sandwich. "Here, you can eat this on the way." He slaps down a sawbuck on the table and pulls me out the door.

"I don't have time for this. I have a case I need to work on."

This of course is a complete lie. I haven't had work in weeks.

Billy pulls a thick wad of cash from his pocket and hands it to me. I have a soft spot for dogs, kids, sexy women, and money. That bastard knows all my weaknesses. I've been too candid with him.

"So, you'll do it?"

"Sure, sure, I'll do it. I'll find your damn dog."

As a kid I had a dog, a Chihuahua named Tank. At my command he'd latch on to the ankles of my enemies and rip with his little needle teeth. I loved that goddamn dog. His life ended one night in our driveway when my stepfather, weaving his way home on a drunken bender, squashed him underneath the wheels of his Pinto. Funny thing, the Pinto disappeared that night. If I were a betting man I'd bet it was at the bottom of Lansing's Quarry collecting silt.

The sign reads HARRISBURG CITY DOG POUND. What a fucking dump. It wouldn't surprise me one damn bit if a tumbleweed suddenly rolled by. The building itself looks like an old car dealership: big plate-glass windows, a huge broken-up parking lot, and four garages.

I go inside the building and make for the front desk. The dogs are stacked in cages against the big windows. I avert my eyes. The last thing I need is to see some abandoned Chihuahua that reminds me of Tank and end up taking the mutt home with me.

There's a guy behind the counter reading a *Dog Fancy* magazine. He looks like he might be Howdy Doody's twin brother, only he's fat and doesn't wear the cowboy getup.

I figure small talk is the way to go. "Is that any good?"

"You've never read it?"

"I don't read anything with 'Fancy' in the title."

"What?"

"We need to talk."

He sets his magazine down. "Okay."

"First of all wipe that smirk off your face."

He touches his lip. "I'm not smirking. I had a harelip. It was surgically repaired when I was an infant. It's a scar."

"That's what they all say."

"They do?"

"No, not really but I won't hold that against you. Now, tell me what you're doing selling these dogs."

The color drains out of him. I gambled and laid it all on the line because that's the only way I know how to do things and I got damned lucky. First stop and I'm on to something.

He sits down on a stool. "What are you talking about?"

"Don't 'what are you talking about' to me, Howdy Doody. The word's out you've been selling dogs to lowlifes for fighting. We have you on video making several of these transactions."

"Are you a cop or something?"

"Or something is right, now spit up the details or I'll have to rough you up."

"I want to speak to my attorney."

"Sure, why don't you speak to your attorney, and while you're busy planning a legal strategy I'll go spreading the word around town that you gave up the dog fighters."

He puts his head in his hands. "You don't understand. These people will kill me if I tell you."

"There's an upside to the scenario that you're not looking at. If you don't tell me I'll kill you."

"That's an upside?"

"Shut your piehole. I'm not done laying it out. Now, if you tell me, I let you live and then maybe, just maybe, you'll have enough to get out of town before they come looking for you."

"Shit, all right."

"Good. Now, I'm curious, why do they snatch dogs off the

street if they can come here and pick up a stray pit bull or firedog?"

"Ha-ha, firedog? You mean a Dalmatian?"

I grab the dog treat bowl on the counter and smash his right hand with it. There's crunching and blood.

He holds his injured hand and hops around. "Ouch! *Fuck*, my hand. You didn't have to go ballistic on me."

"Ballistic is what I do best. Now answer my question."

"They go through a lot of dogs. Ouch, my hand . . . sometimes we don't have the types of dogs they want. Hell, they've even fought stray Chihuahuas if they're desperate for dogs."

"Those sick bastards. I had a Chihuahua named Tank."

He snickers. It's involuntary but so is my reaction. I slam his face into the *Dog Fancy* magazine and the counter.

"Ow, fuck, why did you do that?"

"I'm the one asking the questions here, Carrot Top. You think it's funny to hurt a Chihuahua?"

"No, no, it's not funny."

"That's right, it's not funny. Now tell me, where do they hold these fights?"

He hesitates and I don't blame him. Anyone who would fight Chihuahuas is a sick bastard and capable of any atrocity. "They fight the dogs in Still's Billiards Hall over on Amity Road, every Tuesday night."

"Tonight is Tuesday night. You have to get me into these fights."

"I can't, the invite list is very strict."

"Then I'll have to find my own way into those fights."

"How?"

"I have my ways, fancy pants."

The parking lot of the Penn National Racecourse is packed with cars and I have one hell of a time finding a spot. Oftentimes driving a boat like the Monte Carlo necessitates creative maneuvering like parking on a bush or pushing a compact car out of the way. After driving around for ten minutes I end up parking in a flower bed and hanging a T-shirt out of the driver's-side window so it looks like my car broke down.

Inside the building it's five minutes until race time and the gambling junkies are flitting around like hornets after someone's blasted their nest open with a shotgun.

I place my bets and search for a busy area and find a nice one right next to a concession stand. Let the show begin.

I scan the crowd. "This is nothing like the dog fights in Tijuana. Now, that's some real sport."

No one pays me the slightest bit of attention. So I move to another area down closer to the track and repeat my little speech.

"This is nothing like the dog fights in Tijuana. Now, that's some real sport."

Still nothing. I head over to the bar and repeat, "This is nothing like the dog fights in Tijuana. Now, that's some real sport."

I look around the place and I notice some dame noticing me. It sure as hell isn't for my looks. My face looks like a bus full of kids was playing hopscotch on it. I press on. "I wish they had dog fights like that around here."

She turns away, attacking a tall glass of giggle juice. I saddle up to her at the bar, purposely rubbing up against her hip. It's important to make physical contact . . . okay, maybe not important, but it's damn nice.

She smiles like a dame ought to smile, and I'm transported to that golden place in my head—the place like Vegas with gaudy lights and sin and smut, where a man can roll naked in a bathtub of whatever it is that flips his switch and all the while a high-class call girl sucks his toes. . . . Maybe I've said too much.

I make my move. "They call me Stern, uh, Howard Stern."

Damn, that was a bad fake name.

She sets her glass down. "Like the radio shock jock?"

"The name sounds the same, but if you saw it spelled out, well, you'd realize that it looks nothing like the other name sounds."

"Huh?"

"Right."

I try to take her mitt, introduce myself properlike, but she pulls back as if I've just tried to hand her a used handkerchief.

"You're not my type."

"This whole metrosexual thing has put a dent in the business of being a man. If you wring one of those bastards out like a washcloth you won't get an ounce of testosterone. They wear those funny black-rimmed glasses, tight pants, and shiny shirts. I'd never wear a shiny shirt."

"You wouldn't look good in a shiny shirt."

"Who are you trying to fool? I don't look good in or out of any shirt. This face has been intimate with a fair share of closed fists and my body, well, I've been told by my doctor not to bother to leave it to science."

"You've got a lot going for you."

"Yes, I don't. Fortunately there are a lot of dames that like a guy just for his money."

"You're rich?"

"Thanks, you're not bad yourself."

She frowns and there's silence between us for a moment and not the sexy kind either. We're watching the end of the race. Everyone around is consumed with either complete disgust or utter joy. That's the life of a gambler, there's no more than two ways about it. Win or lose.

My horse finishes dead last. If they paid out for picking losers I'd be a millionaire.

I pull out the wad of lettuce Billy Strap gave me and make

sure the she sees it. "Horse racing is for the birds. In Tijuana they have dog fights—real sport—but then a dame like you probably wouldn't go for dog fights."

She looks over at me. "A dame like me?"

"Yeah, you'd probably faint at the sight of blood."

"Maybe some dames would, but I'm not just some dame."

"That's what they all say. When I lived in Mexico I had a girlfriend who would go to the fights with me when I was fighting my dogs. Every time a little blood would be spilled she'd faint."

"You fought dogs?"

"Not personally but I had dogs that would fight other dogs."

"That's what I meant."

"I bet you did."

She looks over each shoulder and then back to me. "What if I told you I had a ticket for the only dog fights in town?"

"I might say you're a liar."

"You'd be wrong. So what do you say? Are you up for some real action?"

"I'll get the rubber sheets and baby oil."

"Not that kind of action."

"Oh, right. You mean dog fights." I try not to think of Tank, but his bristly little mug keeps popping up in my head. "What's your name?"

"You can call me Natasha."

"Sure, Natasha, I'm up for some dog fights."

She takes a pen and piece of paper out of her purse and starts writing directions. "Do you still raise dogs for fighting?"

"I raise them but I don't have anywhere to fight them right now."

"Well, maybe we can change that."

"Yeah, maybe we can."

* * *

The Monte Carlo makes such a racket I have to park it at a fast food joint a quarter mile down the road and hoof it to Still's Billiard Hall. Goddamn heap. It's been coughing up terminal black smoke lately, pinging and panging like it's on its last wheel. I can't take a chance of anyone seeing me pull up in the Monte. The illusion of me being a high roller would be all but destroyed. I can't have that, my life depends on it.

I go around back and whisper the secret password to some guy in a bad black suit. He ushers me in. I don't like what I see. This is a dark place, a place where sick bastards with twisted inner secrets come to get off. This isn't strictly about gambling. It's about power, control, and a blatant disregard for Lassie. That's right, I said it. Something happened to these sick bastards as children. Maybe it was as simple as not having enough love or maybe they just didn't like how a dog like Lassie was better than them at making friends and they've held a grudge against canines ever since. Whatever is broken with them, whatever it is all those psychologists couldn't figure out, whatever makes these sick fucks tick, I'll cure tonight.

In the center of the room everyone is gathered around a deep pit. Immediately I spot Cordoba chained to the wall. That I never liked the bastard doesn't seem to matter now. He doesn't deserve this, no beast deserves this. He looks up at me and I can see in his eyes that he knows who I am. Good dog. He doesn't give me away. It's not lost on the mutt that something bad is about to go down.

"Hello there, stranger."

I turn and standing there like a Polaroid of my wettest dream is Natasha. She's got the "come hither" thing down pat: tight red latex, black straps, fishnets, and heels a mile high. And then it hits me, and it hits me hard. She's wearing a blond wig. She was the dame with the Dutch boy haircut who cut through our craps game this morning. She was scouting out dogs to snatch. I've never been surer of anything in my life.

"Howard, I'm glad you could make it."

I look over my shoulder, thinking she's talking to someone else, but then I remember I told her my name was Howard Stern. "Uh, yeah, it's damn nice to be here. Who decorated this place? Martha Stewart's evil clone?"

"Very funny, I don't think anyone actually decorated this place."

"I think you're right."

She does some sort of little hop and her tits jiggle underneath her red latex dress. It's all I can do not to unfold like some sort of card table. There's something bothering me, though. She just seems too goddamn nice to be mixed up in this dog fighting stuff. Or maybe it's me projecting on to her, maybe I just don't want to believe someone so beautiful on the outside could be so rotten on the inside.

She grasps my arm. "Ooh, there is Tan Blancard. I want you to meet him. This is his setup."

I know this guy from somewhere. I hope he doesn't make me.

"Who is this?" Tan asks. "And what happened to his face?"

He rubs a wispy little porno star mustache with his thumb and forefinger. I hate porno star mustaches. I can tell by the way he carries himself that he considers himself a tough guy.

"This is Howard Stern," Natasha says.

"Howard Stern, like the disc jockey?" he asks.

"Yeah, but it's spelled differently."

I can tell by the tone of his voice that he doesn't buy my name. He grabs me by my collar. "This isn't Howard Stern. This is Burma Ludlow. He was my wife's private investigator. This fucker helped to screw me over in the divorce. He even slept with her."

"Actually there was very little sleeping going on," I say.

"Private who?" Natasha asks.

"He's right, I'm a private detective. I've come to take back my friend's dog."

Chances are I'm not going to make it out of this place alive. I'm okay with that, I have to be. Every day you go in search of the truth you know that odds are you won't live to see another day. I can't let these dogs die, though. They didn't do anything to anyone. Me, I probably have it coming. At least I tell myself that because it will make the end that much easier.

I'm surrounded and I didn't even get a chance to blink. A dozen goons dressed in black, a dozen goons with chains, guns, and pipes, a dozen goons wanting to sing me a sweet lullaby.

Be tough, I tell myself, *you're not going out like this. You were destined for a much more grandiose exit, something preceded by a lobster dinner, call girls, and a big explosion.*

They start closing in and my fists lock around Mom's brass knuckles. "Who's first?" I say, and uncork my fists. It's a glorious bloodbath. Mom's brass knuckles behind my powerful fists are breaking jaws and crushing noses. I'm a human wrecking machine, but there are too many of them. Someone hits me in the back of the head with what feels like a magnum of champagne and I go down.

My body rises off the ground and I'm tossed into the dog pit. I land and the dogs chained to either side of the pit start barking.

I rise up onto all fours and spit blood. "There'll be no dogs dying here tonight."

Everyone from every direction is still laughing, having themselves one hell of a time.

"Release the dogs," Tan Blancard says.

The dog handlers obey. The only things I can see are flashes of teeth and yellow eyes. I won't hurt the dogs.

This is a damn hard pledge to keep, though, as the first pit bull rips into my arm and the second bites into my calf. "Good dogs. Nice puppies."

I try to keep a picture of Tank and Lassie in my head. I picture them in a meadow sharing a couple of Whoppers. It helps the pain from completely reaching my brain.

"Stop, damn it! *Stop*," I yell.

I see angels or something damn close to them fluttering around my head and I have to admit that this just might be the end. It's been a damn good run—maybe too good for a no good bastard like myself.

Snap! Snap!

The dogs fall limp next to me. It's Natasha. She's shot the dogs with a tranquilizer gun. I know what was bothering me about her now. She's a cop. Okay, maybe I was wrong about her snatching the dogs, but what I'm not wrong about is that she's in trouble.

Tan Blancard comes up from behind her and beans her with a club. She goes down hard. I reach into my trench coat and pull out my roscoe. "This is for you, Tank."

All those that came to watch the dog fights are scrambling for the exits. There's smoke and flames. One of the bullets must have hit something flammable.

I pull myself out of the pit and see one of the goons mounting a giant stereo speaker. He lets loose with an Uzi, spraying lead all over the joint. It's ugly. The rich guys dive behind their escorts. A bullet skims my scalp and blood runs down my face. I grab one of the dead dogs from an earlier fight by the collar and use it as a shield as I move toward the shooter.

The corpse takes shots and I can feel warm dog blood running down my forearm. I reach around the dead dog and fire one shot after another, hitting the guy on top of the speaker, blowing his arm off at the elbow. He's in too much pain to come after me now, but I shoot him through the head anyway.

It's a damn shame all this dying, but I figure that every time one of these bastards gets snuffed the positive balance of the universe is righted. I'll make sure hell fills up real quick.

I reload and reload again, shooting up every bad guy in the joint. Soon everyone else is dead or gone except for Tan Blancard. I give him the bum's rush as he unloads his pistol into the dog corpse and then I chuck it in his face, knocking him down.

Tan Blancard says something like, "Fuck you." But at this point it doesn't matter what he says. He's going to die.

I jump on top of him, pinning his arms down with my knees. He's got more teeth in his mug than a pack of werewolves and they're glaring at me all yellowlike. I swing with my brass knuckles and half of them are lying on the ground in bits. I pick several pieces out of my fingers and then, as if my fists have minds of their own, they start pounding his face in. With each strike of my brass knuckles I feel power surge through my body. "You'll . . . never . . . kill . . . another . . . dog." It's a goddamn beautiful thing. I see Tank, Lassie, and my mom smiling down on me from heaven.

"Ouch, my head."

It's Natasha or whatever her real name is. My fists are still working, grinding Blancard's face into pulp. I have to make a conscious effort to make them stop.

I get up, tossing my brass knuckles to the ground. The smoke is getting bad now.

"What's going on?" she asks.

"We're getting out of here," I say.

I drag Natasha and Cordoba up and out of this hellish place—through the blood and gore and the smoke—and as I reach the top of the steps I can see the cops are already here.

"Freeze, drop your weapon."

I drop my roscoe. Everything looks hazy. Out of the corner of my eye I see something move. "Tank, is that you?"

A cop with his own roscoe pointed straight at my mug shuffles toward me. "Who the hell is Tank?"

"He was my best friend."

I turn and start walking back into the burning building.

"Freeze," the cops yell.

"There are two dogs still in there. I'm going back."

The cops are yelling at me to stop, but none of them is willing to chase me into a burning building. I know it's not romantic to die for a couple of dogs, but there's no way I'm going to let them fry in that hellhole. I can't have that weight on my conscience.

I sit in an interrogation room with cops yelling and working me over. I'm sure their punches hurt, but I'm in the golden place in my head where I see Tank and Lassie tussling over a bucket of KFC.

One of the cops answers the phone. He hangs up and they all leave. I'm given a box of donut holes, a pack of smokes, and a large cup of coffee and left alone. An hour passes very slowly. The door opens.

"Natasha?"

She extends her hand. "My name is Detective Uma Pocket."

I push the box of donut holes towards her. "Private Investigator Burma Ludlow."

"I've been working undercover for nearly a year trying to bust Tan Blancard."

"Well, look at the bright side—now you won't have to go through all that messy legal stuff."

She looks through the box and picks out a chocolate one. She looks at it but doesn't eat. "What you did was reckless, irresponsible, and downright dangerous. I should have you locked up for the rest of your natural born life."

I stick my hands out so she can cuff me. "What are you waiting for?"

"Unfortunately what you did was also unfathomably brave. You did all that to save a dog?"

"I did all that because it was the right thing to do. Don't go placing me on a damn pedestal. A piece of scum like Tan Blancard deserved what he got. If I have to go down to get rid of one of his kind, then so be it."

Her eyes soften and meet mine. I'm pretty sure we could get a game of ring toss going if she unzipped my fly.

"You're not going down. I made sure of that," she says.

"Well, maybe you could go down . . . on me."

"What?"

"Uh, nothing."

She lays my charred brass knuckles and my roscoe on the table.

"I suppose I owe you big," I say.

"You don't owe me anything. I wish there were more men like you out there, Burma Ludlow. What passes for a man these days is nothing short of pathetic."

She walks up to me and holds my head in her hands. Our lips meet and I'm transported to that golden place in my head.

They release me at dawn and I pick up Cordoba from the pound. The dog rests with its head on my lap as we drive back to my hotel.

Outside the hotel Billy Strap is playing craps as I pull up. He jumps to his feet when he sees me.

"Did you find Cordoba?"

I point down to my lap.

"Cordoba!" Billy cries.

I step out of the Monte Carlo, light up a cigarette, and watch the sun disappear behind a cloud. Billy hugs and kisses Cordoba. It would almost be touching if Billy wasn't so sleazy.

"Thanks, Burma, I owe you big time."

"Nah, you paid me. We're square."

"Well, that's what I wanted to talk to you about. I need to borrow back that four grand I gave you. I'll pay it back next week."

I take the wad out of my pocket and hand it to Billy. This case actually cost me money. I'll never see that stack of lettuce again, but at least I saved those dogs. At least that's something.

"All right, now, how about a game of private craps?" Billy asks.

"I don't have any mazula," I say.

Billy takes the wad out of his pocket. "I'll lend you some. How much do you need?"

The Trouble with Trolls

Patricia Abbott

Heading for the driveway on a Sunday morning, Denny noticed that the eight or ten cars outside his neighbor's house the night before still lined the street. Did grown men routinely host sleepovers or should he risk embarrassment and check things out? He settled on removing Matt and Ralph's Sunday *Times* from the yew where the direct hit of the irrigation system had already saturated it. Denny liked to be regarded well as long as the cost was low. The house was preternaturally quiet for nearly noon, the stillness broken only by the sprinkler's hum.

He managed to beat Dad to the store by a full fifteen minutes and sat nervously eyeing the display of garden sculptures. More than once lately, he had stumbled over an emancipated troll idling near the rear exit or guarding the bins of screws and nuts. They had taken on the dusty, glazed look of objects that had sat too long in stockrooms. For some reason, Dad found them comical and never failed to chuckle when he came on one unexpectedly. Once or twice, Denny had smuggled one home, burying it in the backyard since he wasn't sure of its recycling requirements. Thankfully, the decline in the store's troll population had so far gone unnoticed.

His father arrived with the usual query, tossing his sweat-stained hat on the counter. "Have you heard from your brother? How's the new project going?" This was strictly a rhetorical question since, as Patrick's backer, Dad knew everything about his business. "Listen, Den," Dad continued, not even waiting for an answer, "I have a small errand for you boys."

Denny fixed his eyes on the dark computer screen. A small errand could mean anything from a trip to the bank to deposit funds to strong-arming one of Dad's recalcitrant clients for payment. Besides the hardware store, a flower shop, a small restaurant in Allen Park, and the financial backing of his son's aquarium business, Dad was an attorney with a practice in a section of the city populated by Eastern European, Latin American, and Arab émigrés. More than once, Denny and Patrick had been dispatched to collect fees from a Turk or Serbian immigrant who wanted his child support burden lowered. Or, on one rather frightening occasion, to calm a Colombian drug czar, requesting that his ex-wife be deported or disposed of ("Whatever," Quatro Velasquez told them obligingly, fingering the square-cut sapphire on his pinky). There had been other errands too, of course—tasks Denny would prefer to forget. "All part of the show," Dad had said to his sons more than once. "Get used to adult life."

Michael Patterson had built an empire of sorts in just one generation, coming from a family of auto workers who never thought to do more than side their house in vinyl, drink a beer on Saturday night, and camp in July in the UP. Consequently, complaints from clients regarding his prices drew little sympathy. "You should see the fucking rates I pay in personal insurance," he told anyone who questioned his prices or practices.

"You want me to take risks, you gotta pay for it." Despite his ever-decreasing height and the flabby girth that eating at his own restaurant had added, Dad remained formidable. He had a strong and jutting chin, a persuasive left hook, and the mental acuity to back both up.

While Denny considered the possible nature of the small errand, Dad walked over to the wall and raised the setting on the thermostat. "You don't need to cool the whole fucking place when you're in here alone, Den. Turn on a fan, for Christ's sake. Open a door." His father grabbed a stool from under the counter where the wallpaper sample books rested and sat down. "I'm talking about Tuesday night. She arrives at six forty-five p.m. Air Beirut."

"Who arrives?"

Dad cleared his throat. "Some woman, what else? From the old country."

"What old country?" Dad had been born and raised in Detroit.

"I met her at a wedding. Remember that client of mine—Mr. Shalaby—the one who bumped into his wife a couple years ago?"

Denny remembered. The bump had been with Shalaby's Caddy, and following an altercation that broke two of the woman's teeth, a cheekbone, and blackened both eyes. She was in Henry Ford Hospital for weeks. "I got him community service when he pled and he invited me to his nephew's wedding," Dad continued. "We got to talking—this lady and me—and anyway she lands at Metro Tuesday night. She could use a little help."

"Language problems?"

"Sure. Sure. Language problems. That—and other things. Just get her. You and Patrick. You know what I mean, Denny. Remember how you helped me with Olga—what's her name?

This one's even more . . ." His father jabbed the air in front of him and Denny, involuntarily, stepped back. "What? What? You think I'd hit you, Den?" His father seemed pleased by this thought and jabbed the air a few more times. "When did I ever hit you?"

"Does Patrick have to come along?"

"You're in this together. He's like an ox from carting those tanks up and down the stairs. Never can tell when muscle could come in handy."

Denny nodded. "So where do we take her?"

"The Apollo Hotel in Greektown. Make sure those nitwits give her a nice room. Order some flowers maybe—to throw her off. Put it on the store card." The old man grabbed his Tigers cap from the counter and headed for the door. "Anyway, take care of her just like you did with Olga. You guys did great with Olga."

"You didn't give me her name?"

"Right. Her name's Nahla Khalil. She's on Lufthansa, I think." Michael Patterson turned back from the door. "Oh, and get her some orchids. Nahla likes orchids. She says they look like a tunnel of love." Stepping forward a bit, he almost whispered. "When I used that line on your mother once, she said, 'Stop talking dirty.' Does it sound dirty to you?"

Denny shrugged. "Hey, I thought you told me Air Beirut?" But his father was gone, the heavy metal door to the back alley slamming on Denny's last words. The troll by the door seemed to blink in the light.

It had been a long time since either Denny or his brother harbored any illusions about their parents' marriage, but participating in the demise of women who became inconvenient to their father was unsettling. How many women must die before the old man let his prescription for Viagra lapse? Of course, Dad didn't knock most of them off. There had just been that

Olga until now. But one day soon, Michael Patterson would go too far with something and it would be time for Denny to take over—ending the pretense that his father was still the big cheese. And he would never allow a mere sexual conquest to compromise his position.

When Denny got home, a fleet of emergency vehicles were backed clear out onto Mack Avenue. Monica was glued to the window. She wore a white dress with a halter top that looked as skimpy as a handkerchief and was holding a festive glass of white wine in her hand.

"What's going on?" he asked, easing in beside her. "It's Matt and Ralph's house, right?" He remembered the line of cars he'd ignored earlier.

"The EMS guys carted three bodies out," she said breathlessly. "Now, don't jump on me, Denny, but I wonder if we should invite the Blakes over?"

"Why would you want to invite them over now?"

"We have the better view. And we still owe them from their Halloween party. A little wine, a little brie—"

"Oh, look," he said, interrupting her intentionally. "They're bringing someone out through the side door."

When it was over, two bodies and half a dozen, semiasphyxiated men had been evacuated, the survivors attached to oxygen. "It must have been some sort of poisonous gas," Denny surmised.

Monica, now on the phone with a neighbor, shouted, "Somebody turned on the air without turning off the furnace. Every time the air came on and cooled the house, the heat came on to warm it up. And vice versa."

"Our unit wouldn't do that."

"Yeah, but that house has probably never been updated. Remember Matt's dad?"

Denny did indeed, an old policeman who lived in the house

when the area was still known as Cops' Corner. He'd been a racist and the reigning neighborhood skinflint who turned out his light on Halloween and didn't belong to any of the neighborhood associations. When he had died three years ago, some assumed his son's sexual preference contributed to his demise.

"Anyway," Monica continued, "the vent outside was shut and the negative pressure caused carbon monoxide fumes to back-draft into the utility closet. The detector was disabled, who knows why, and over the course of the party, they were asphyxiated."

"What about Ralph and Matt?"

"Oh, I forgot to ask!" She stood up, her breasts straining mightily against the fabric of her blouse.

"Dad's got a little job for me on Tuesday night. That's why he called this morning." He stood right in front of her, so she would have to look at him. "Years ago, he'd have handled it himself but recently he's begun to depend on me. I'll be taking over in a matter of months. Oh, sure, Patrick might have to be dealt with in some fashion, but he's got that fish business. It'll be my empire and I'm already planning on a few changes. Those trolls in the store for instance—"

She looked at him with what seemed like great understanding, then said, "There's some cold chicken in the fridge. I promised Mother I'd be over by two."

Patrick climbed into the car on Tuesday evening wearing the damp look Denny associated with him since he'd begun tending tropical fish. Low on IQ but high on muscle, Patrick roamed from dental to doctors' offices, from library to restaurant, maintaining both the fish and their habitat, toting unexpectedly intricate equipment in a chrome handcart, which cost more than Denny's Civic. Luckily, Patrick was a large man.

Surprisingly, the business *was* taking off, though an emerging decline in the fish population in metropolitan Detroit threatened its success. Arriving at his appointments hungover or high, Patrick routinely sucked priceless fish into his hose. Or forgot to remove valuable specimens before applying lethal chemicals. Or spent too much time flirting with the receptionist. Or got into ridiculous disputes. Or failed to show up at all. Patrick had inadvertently hit upon an unmet need in the community but lacked the disposition to exploit it.

His face looked bloated and blotchy, his eyes red-rimmed. Was it too many showers, too many drugs, or did he dive into some of the larger tanks to do his work? A trace of white powder dotted his upper lip.

"Jeez, Patrick! Couldn't you wait?"

His brother rubbed a finger across his upper lip and put it to his mouth. "You wouldn't believe how physically demanding fish can be sitting in front of the computer screen all day like you do." He sighed, opened his mouth, and threw a Rolo in. "Lately, I've had to drag that damned cart with me everywhere. I can't leave it in the car because I let the policy lapse. Dad'll skin me if someone takes off with it." He laughed lightly, and then harder as he looked at his finger. "You know what this shit is, Denny? It's goddamned tank cleaner. I hope it wasn't what I put up my nose half an hour ago." He unpeeled another Rolo, then offered the roll to Denny.

"Probably no worse than a dozen other things you've ingested." They drove along in a companionable silence, munching their candy.

"So, why can't this lathy take a tathi into town?" The caramel was affecting his speech.

"He gave me a lot of crap about making sure her room's okay. Getting her flowers." Denny nodded at the slim bouquet of carnations in the backseat. "I ordered the orchids for her hotel room from Dad's shop, of course."

"Who thc hell is this chick anyway?" Patrick interrupted. "I don't remember the old man doing anything like this before. Flying his girlfriend in, putting her up in a fancy, schmancy hotel. Wooing her."

"Wooing?" Denny repeated, immediately attracted to the word. "Does Dad woo?"

"We all woo. I've never been convinced that screwing is that wonderful for women. Wooing makes it seem better. Puts a spiffy gloss on a messy business."

"Anyway, he's not wooing Nahla. He's giving her the Olga treatment."

Patrick blinked twice. "So that's how it is. When were you planning to tell me?"

Denny shrugged. "I thought it might not pan out."

"Oh, how thoughtful. Are you sparing me or cutting me out, Den?"

Denny pulled into a short-term parking lot, and the brothers hurried over the bridge to the terminal. "Dad's probably a pretty fair wooer—growing up like he did after the war. Was there anything too corny for them?"

"That's what they should call them. The corniest generation."

"Even the word *corny* is corny," Denny offered.

"Exactly."

Trying to keep pace with his taller brother, Denny quickly grew winded. "Dad should have taught us his wooing techniques instead of how to field ground balls."

"No one bothered to tell us we'd grow up to prefer women to line drives."

"I have a theory," Denny said. "Actually it's Monica's. She claims Dad didn't teach us anything useful on purpose. That way, he can keep us under his thumb. Don't you find it odd that he never let us change a tire, mow the grass, or balance a checkbook when we were kids?"

Patrick had lost interest. "What's her name?"

"Who? Oh, Nahla." At that moment, Denny caught sight of a woman in a wheelchair being pushed in their direction. If this was Nahla, she'd already run into some trouble. One of her legs was missing.

"Oh, Christ," Patrick said, watching the wheelchair approach them. "Did Dad mention that little detail?"

Denny shook his head. "Not a word." Both men grinned simultaneously as the chair approached them, the uniformed airline attendant smiling with relief as the handoff was made. "Miss Khalil?" Denny said, half kneeling in front of her. "Nahla? Do you speak English?"

She looked around and removed her shades. "Where's Michael? He promised he'd meet my plane." Her tone had the familiar mix of petulance and imperiousness used by all Patterson-related women. Clearly, she spoke English.

Denny didn't answer immediately. He was wondering why Nahla didn't wear an artificial leg. If it was a matter of money, why hadn't Dad stepped in? He glanced over at Patrick, who was apparently struck dumb. "Dad's stuck in Dearborn with a client," Denny finally said.

"Unavoidably detained," Patrick added, coming out of his trance.

"Then let's shake a leg," she said, without a glimmer of a smile. Patrick looked at Denny from under his thick eyebrows; Denny tightened his mouth. Was she a kook? Both men looked at her missing leg without meaning to. Or at where the leg would be if it hadn't been missing.

"Yes, I'm here for a new *leg*," she said easily. "Odd as it seems, Detroit is where I had it made originally, so they have the precise measurements." Looking at their glassy stares, she added, "I lost it at sea."

The original or the artificial one? Denny wondered. Images

of a black-stockinged wooden leg floating like jetsam filled his head. He wondered if she dressed it separately before strapping it on. "Christ, how did *that* happen?" he finally managed to get out.

"The porter carried it off with my cases and by the time I realized his error, it had disappeared. I find it easier going through security without it," she explained. "So I always remove it. You'd think Homeland Security would make allowances, but a one-legged woman only seems to increase their interest. I get strip-searched all the time." The brothers tried not to look at each other or her missing leg.

"Who would have taken it?" Denny asked, aghast.

"You'd be surprised," she said without elaboration.

"Do you insure something like that?" Patrick asked.

"Certainly you insure it! It's the most valuable thing I own. Every inch has to conform to the rest of me." She held out the other leg for their inspection. If the missing one had been a perfect match, she had lost something pretty spectacular, Denny thought. Twice.

"Well, the car's just across the bridge," he said weakly, moving her chair in that direction.

After a few fumbling moments loading the chair into the trunk, they were back on the freeway. "Nothing ever changes," she said tiredly, looking around. "Fists, tires, potholes, rust, gunshots, cacophony." She directed them to the hotel, obviously familiar with the route. The check-in went smoothly although she changed her penthouse suite to a room on the first floor. "You get worried about fire," she told the clerk.

The corridor to Nahla's room was mirrored, the carpet plush enough to give Denny's arms a good workout. This was where Patrick might have come in handy, but instead he cavorted ahead of them, chattering in that desperate way he had at the end of a hit of coke. He fit the key in the lock with some difficulty and finally stepped aside, allowing the chair to pass. Inside, they found a young man wearing only patent leather shoes and black socks held up by garters making love to a pantyless woman in a violet bridesmaid's dress in a king-sized bed. With the frilly, hooped skirt framing them, the couple looked like a midpicture sequence from an old Busby Berkeley movie.

"How entertaining!" Nahla said, and proceeded to address the pair in a series of languages until she hit on the correct one. "Spanish!" she finally announced. "They're friends of one of one of the maids. Apparently, Conchita told them they could use this room for an hour." Nahla looked at both Pattersons. "Could you see about getting my room switched again, Dennis? I've lost my appetite for sleeping here." She nodded toward the jumble of bedclothes, the tangle of limbs, and the distinctive tang of fresh sex.

Denny tramped back to the reception desk, where a clerk informed him there were no vacancies, and, in fact, the room Nahla had rejected minutes earlier had been given to a new arrival. "Not even the wedding suite?" Denny asked, certain his father would spring for it. The clerk shook his head.

Denny opened and closed his mouth several times, trying uselessly to come up with the proper threat or bit of reasoning to bring it home. But if the hotel had no more rooms, what could be done? Glumly, Denny returned to the room and told Nahla the news, wondering how Monica would feel about an overnight guest. Between them, they could carry Nahla up to the second floor using that fireman's hold they'd learned in middle school. They could settle her in and if he heard her rise in the night on her one good leg, he could rush in and . . . But he doubted Monica would approve of bringing her with them. Or condone, for that matter, the execution of a one-legged woman in her own home.

"Call Michael," Nahla demanded immediately. "He'll deal with it."

"No need for that. I'm sure I can . . ." Denny started to say before realizing he had no idea at all about how to handle it. Money, threats, tears. Why hadn't Dad taught them such things? It was their business too, wasn't it? "Your turn," he said weakly, passing Patrick the cell phone.

"I thought I was only here to provide muscle," Patrick complained as he dialed the number.

It took Dad less than five minutes to sort things out, although they never learned what means he used. If he was annoyed at the interruption in his evening, he didn't say so. If he was angry with his sons, he kept it to himself. Patrick slipped the phone into his pocket and they waited in silence for the inevitable call from the front desk.

Nahla's room was a newly available suite on the first floor. She offered them a drink, which they both declined, recognizing the lack of enthusiasm in her invitation. Denny stopped at the desk on the way out to see about redirecting the flower delivery.

"I wish I had ordered more than two dozen," he told his brother in the car. "She deserves the entire shop after that debacle. The cart's refrigerated so they won't lose their freshness."

"Yes, I well remember that cart. You know, Denny, you hardly notice her missing leg after a minute."

"In some ways, it makes her even more attractive," Denny agreed as he swung onto 1-94. "I wonder how . . ." His voice trailed off.

"You mean how did Dad find a girl like that?" Patrick asked. "Or how she lost her leg?"

"I mean— I wonder what it would be like to make love to her." *Someone who couldn't get away,* Denny was thinking.

Patrick nodded. "The delivery guys shouldn't have much

trouble with Nahla. She has a certain amount of spunk, but how far will that get her with a couple of gorillas?"

"Handy she's not wearing the artificial leg. I wonder if Dad had something to do with that." The brothers paused to contemplate this. "Remember the trouble they had with Olga? Dad goes for the big girls, doesn't he? He likes the big bottoms."

"Did we ever find out why Dad got rid of Olga? What did she do?"

Denny shook his head. "Dad's not very forthcoming."

"I wonder how Mom's survived all these years," Patrick said, popping another Rolo into his mouth.

"She's long past fitting into a florist's cart," Denny finally said. "And he must know we'd draw the line there." He said it firmly, hoping to convince himself.

Monica was curled up in the farthest corner of the king-sized bed when Denny crept into their room. She might as well have worn a Do Not Disturb sign across her chest. The phone rang just as he was headed for the bathroom. He picked it up and took it with him. "Denny?" an unfamiliar voice said.

"Yes?"

"Denny, this is Ralph. You know, from across the street?"

He looked out the bathroom window and saw lights. "Ralph! I didn't recognize . . . Home again? Great! Anything I can do? I've thought about—"

"Actually, there is. I was wondering if your father was taking on new clients. We have some legal problems. Well, not problems exactly. Questions. We have some questions."

"You want my father?" Had he even mentioned Dad to Ralph?

"I—or, that is, we—we heard he was a . . . a crackerjack attorney. Good for a special sort of . . ." He cleared his throat.

"Anyway, the name sounded familiar and then Matt put it together." He cleared his throat again. "He's not retired, is he?"

"Not completely. You know, I'm an attorney myself, Matt."

"No kidding. Do you have a practice?"

"Well, no, but the majority of attorneys don't actually have practices."

"Would he have a problem with my calling him this late? Your father, that is," Ralph interrupted, adding softly, "We need someone experienced in litigation." He sighed quietly. "Funny how your closest friends can turn on you. Just because we both got out alive is no reason . . ."

"No, he's used to late calls." He hung up a minute later and his thoughts returned to Nahla. The missing leg was certainly a lucky break. He tried to picture her as she had looked earlier at the airport, but the image of how she must look stuffed into the florist's cart kept pushing it away.

Denny slunk into an almost empty theater showing the movie *Girls Girls Girls XXX* the next day. It was the only spot in town cognizant of the fact that a small but select group of patrons couldn't watch certain types of DVDs at home. As he made his way down the dark, center aisle, he managed to trip over some obstruction in his path, breaking his fall in the last seconds by grabbing a nearby seat back. What the hell? Had the usher left a trash can? Was it a patron's wheelchair or oxygen? Someone's bike or shopping cart? A passed-out moviegoer?

Running his hands up and down the impediment, he discovered it was a hose of some sort. Some kind of mammoth vacuum cleaner perhaps? On his knees, the smells of popcorn, rug cleaner, vomit, and licorice nearly overwhelming him, he followed the hose it to its source—a tank, then a carrier, and finally, Patrick, gawking at the screen. Denny wasn't sure whether

Patrick could see him, but that afternoon both boys pretended the dark was absolute, impenetrable. There was not another soul in the theater, so Denny had his choice of seats.

Across the city, as always, Michael Patterson conducted business.

Eulogy for a Player

Richard J. Martin Jr.

They say that prostitution is the world's oldest profession. Pimping, then, is the second oldest. You are a pimp. I know that because you said you were a pimp and being a pimp is just like being an actor—once you say you are one, you are. You've made your choice and now you want the knowledge that will make you an elevated pimp, the kind that makes money.

In order to pimp hard and pimp right you have to understand that you are part of something larger than yourself—something that has gone on long before you and will continue long after. You also have to learn a little about the theory and concepts behind pimping. Most of the would-be players out there are long on practice but short on theory. You must understand that like the prostitute, the pimp provides a service. Today, I'm going to tell you how you can provide that service, but you have to keep this to yourself until it's time to pass it on to the right person. That's part of showing respect for the game.

One of the country's most famous pimps, Fillmore Slim, once said, "You pimp with your mind and not with your hands." He said this because people often confuse pimping with extortion and strong-arm robbery. Beating women and robbing them of their money is not pimping. If you want to make it by being an intimidator, then go ahead on. It's easy. You just find somebody weaker than you and rob them. Just remember to victimize people that are outside the protection of the law. Don't just focus on prostitutes. Beat on weak drug dealers, dishonest store owners or dope fiends or anyone else that the police won't protect.

But being a pimp is harder—it requires a different mind-set and a different skill set. If you pimp right, you won't ever have to raise your hand to a woman and you'll always let her know that she is free to leave at any time. You will start to provide a service instead of standing around saying that you're a pimp, waiting to get paid—and things will go better for you. That's why we're here today.

I know you have a working knowledge of pimping practice; you've got game and Mack-ability, that's why you're here. You've got your pimp clothes, your pimp rap, and you're working on a pimp car but you don't really need that until after you get started. You're familiar with terms like "turnout," "catch," and "knock," which describe the ways you might break into the game. You've looked at yourself in the mirror for a long time and you know that you can do this. You've practiced standing the right way, talking the right way, and feigning disinterest. That's good. You'll need all that stuff, and you'll need that kind of confidence to make it once you get your first working girl. Those things are essential to the practice of pimping.

Now let's talk about theory.

What most young players don't know is that the quickest way to make money as a pimp is to fall in love with a prostitute.

You think I'm crazy, but remember . . . the pimp provides a service. His service is to meet the needs of the prostitute. In return, the prostitute provides the pimp with all her money. This is the pimp equation.

To really be successful pimping you have to understand

Maslow's Hierarchy of Human Need—players call it The Pyramid.

See, the pyramid is a triangle; you know what a triangle is, right? To categorize human need you divide the triangle into five different parts, each of which represents a basic need that all human beings have, including prostitutes. The largest area of the pyramid—the part at the bottom—shows the most pressing of human needs: food, air, and water, called "physiological needs."

Everyone needs these things to survive and everybody that is alive is getting them. You probably won't be able to find a prostitute that is not getting her needs met in this respect, at least not in America. However, at every other level of the pyramid, there exists an opportunity for you to be a pimp. Because the pimp assesses prostitute need and then finds a way for the prostitute to get her needs met.

At the second level of the pyramid is the need for safety and security. You might be able to find a way in here. The prostitute may not feel safe. She plays a dangerous game. She is unsafe from crazy tricks, from unscrupulous police, and from intimidators masquerading as "pimps" (not like you), who might beat her or smear her makeup. To get in at this level you will say something along the lines of "I want to protect you," but that is usually not enough. You need to combine this need with a need from one of the other levels of the pyramid.

At the third level of the pyramid are the human needs for Love and Belongingness, such as the love of family and friends. Usually, the prostitute is not getting these needs met. That's why the easiest way to get started pimping is to fall in love with a woman who is turning tricks. She probably has a need for love that is not getting met. The average guy on the street does not see her as a logical prospect for a love relationship and her family doesn't love her—they probably sexually abused her when she was a little girl and then lied about it. Her only friends are other prostitutes, who by and large are dishonest, confused, and needy themselves.

This is where a good pimp can make a living—if he's got the right stuff to be a pimp. All of these women need love. A lot of them are good-looking, resourceful, and funny. If you can find a way to "have feelings" for them you will be rewarded financially. The problem is, once you fall in love, you have to watch the woman you love go out and have sex with different men each night and that is not easy. This is what separates elevated pimps from wannabes. It takes a man's man, a true player, a Mack, a pimp, to really love a woman who is having sex with other men every night.

If you think you can do this, you are ready to become an elevated pimp. If you could never love a working girl, then you're better off calling yourself a pimp and looking for a puddle of water inside Walgreens so you can fall down, injure yourself, and then mount a lawsuit.

Of course, if you have good theatrical skills and knowledge of the Pyramid, you might be able to provide an illusion of love—that is, to make her think that you love her. But these women, through their work, become astute judges of human nature and they can spot a lie from down the street. They've heard pimp lines before, and although they may appreciate the attention, in the end they are going to support the man-pimp who they believe is in their corner.

As you get near the top of the pyramid, the area of need is less, but it still exists and may provide a way for you to be a pimp. At the fourth level, right underneath the top, is the need for "ego-self-esteem." Everybody wants to feel good about themselves and that is a hard thing for prostitutes to do. They need to feel respected—it's not as pressing a need as the need for food and water, warmth, or love, but it is the kind of thing that can ruin a person's life if they don't get it. That is why so many working girls are addicted to drugs. They feel bad about themselves, so they shoot heroin every day to forget about it. A lot of them were abused as children, most of them, in fact, and they have been feeling bad for a long time. You, as a pimp, will understand the pathway that brought her to be a prostitute and you'll show some understanding and sympathy. You'll respect her and show her that she should respect herself.

At the top of the Pyramid is the need for self-actualization—the need to *be all that you can be*. It's hard to find a way in at this level, but it is possible if you provide a dream for the future—a way out. You explain that what she is doing now represents something temporary; that you know she is better than this so she is just doing it until you "get your insurance settlement," inherit some money, or make it as a rapper or a rock star.

If you meet the prostitute's needs at different levels of the Pyramid, simultaneously, you will make money. You've got to meet needs at the third and second levels while you are trying to find a way in at the fifth level. Then you will have a devoted woman pulling for you. You will call her your "baby girl" or "hope-to-die woman." Once you have that, you will enjoy the benefits of being an elevated pimp and know that it is time to expand your empire. Your hope-to-die-woman will help you to recruit new women. She will think she is your business partner.

The only other way to become a pimp fast is to provide a business opportunity for a prostitute—to show her she can make more money in an easier way than what she is doing right now. See, it's all about relationships. If you have a relationship with someone who sets up dates for girls, a massage parlor, acupuncture studio, or the tricks themselves, you can go up to a girl who already has a pimp and offer her something better. A bigger cut of the money, a safer work environment, or maybe even a fun group of people to hang out with between dates. If you can connect with a pimp who is running a business—a house of prostitution or an out-call service—and then see what their needs are, you might be able to be a liaison between working prostitutes who might take advantage of good business opportunities and the people offering those opportunities.

It's important to behave like a businessman. Go to a massage parlor and ask if they need help. Make it clear that you have a "girlfriend" who is looking for work and that she does the kind of work that this business offers. Be friendly and ask them if there is some kind of bonus that you might receive if you bring them good earners. In these arrangements the house gets half and the girl gets half plus tips. It doesn't leave much for you.

You make these choices and then you have to live with them. The time will come when you want security and the Life will not have as much appeal for you as it does now. After you've learned that pimping is a job, you'll want a vacation. You can't put yourself on Front Street after you reach a certain point in your career.

You won't want to be "high-siding." Showing your car and your women around the track won't have any appeal because you will realize that the people out there are really crumbbums and the only thing that separates you from them is your respect for the game. By that time you will want to move in different circles and get respect from a different kind of person. You will have become accustomed to a certain quality of life and may be unwilling to compromise that lifestyle. Your business may flounder and you will start to run Murphy schemes or blackmail or you may look at opportunities outside of pimping, like selling dope or doing robberies. Then you will make mistakes, you'll take chances you wouldn't otherwise take, and you may wind up in the penitentiary. When you get out it's harder to come up. Maybe your hope-to-die lady will send you some money for the prison commissary at first, but in time, she'll find someone new. You may end up walking around the

Tenderloin asking people for beer money and eating at St. Anthony's like so many retired pimps do. But you will have your memories. These are the choices we make.

So, that's what you need to know. You've got all the Mackability now. You are the real thing, baby. Remember your responsibility to all the players that came before you. Work on having a name that people will remember. Pair-a-dice is already taken. So is Iceberg Slim. Don't put yourself on Front Street and always show respect for the game that puts food in your mouth, gas in your engine, and respect into the eyes of the young players looking to come up. Skip the light fandango for me, Fast Ricky. You are my piece of the rock.

Politoburg

Jedidiah Ayres

Maria is upset. Her chubby fingers, trembling, can't cover her mouth sufficiently to smother the sobs. Wakes you up. Judging by the light coming through the gaps in the tin roof, it's near nine. The atmosphere is like an amniotic sac.

"What is it, for fuck's sake?"

Her reply is lost on you. She sounds like a Pentecostal Rosie Perez, frothing and speaking a hundred miles an hour. Four months here and you haven't grasped the language. Haven't even tried. You aren't planning on sticking around.

"English. Speak English *por favor.*"

Hysterical shrieks.

"No, forget I said anything. I need a smoke." You fish through your clothes beside the bed mat, till you see the cigarettes on her table. Clothed only in sweat, you stand and strike a match. She still sounds like a maniac, running in circles around the room. You grab her by the shoulders to slow her down, and speak very deliberately.

"What . . . is . . . your . . . problem?"

She slaps you hard across the face and chest and you slap her back. She grabs your clothes, tosses them outside the hut, and pushes you after them. Fine with you. You haven't paid yet.

The dust clings to your damp parts. In this heat, that's pretty much an entire outfit. You collect your clothes and carry them under your arm as you start toward the cantina.

You've been to Mexico once before, but this time had fuck-all to do with Sammy Hagar and margaritas. This was all dust and rocks and heat stroke, skin turning to leather and sunshine so intense, your balls disappear when you squint. The Sierra Madres hemming you in sounds good for a movie, but actually makes you feel like a fish in a bowl.

You make your way barefoot towards the only road around, trying like hell to extract some nutrients from your cigarette. The dog carcass from the day before has disappeared from the roadside and you make a mental note not to chance Ramon's stew today.

A debris cloud still hangs in the air, which means an automobile instead of a mule cart has come by recently. That could mean a couple of things: extra shipment this week or trouble in paradise.

A half dozen tin shacks like Maria's pock the desert in no particular pattern. Thrown up without a thought to symmetry or community. A crowd gathers outside the farthest, next to the cantina. The cloud settles behind a black Cadillac, which means the answer is in fact B. Polito sent some of his muscle to settle something.

The crowd is comprised entirely of women, the whores who live here at the whim of Harlan Polito—who is decreeing judgment from on high back in the States. Also here by his will is a small group of gringos: roughnecks, punks, and psychos who do dirty deeds for money and pleasure. You belong to this group. You stay here till the man sends for you to return to the bosom of society and contribute again.

No one seems to notice your nakedness as you approach, not even Metcalf, who comes out to meet you.

"Dude." Metcalf, the near retard you're reduced to socializing with these days, is trying to relay gravity with his tone.

"S'up?" you offer in his native tongue.

"Dude."

"Yeah, I got that part, what's—"

"No, dude. Dick . . ."

Dirty Dick, the oldest, most senior of the gringos. A stone-cold killer. You all look up to him. He's a legend back home. Killed five men, bad motherfuckers all, in one hit. Disappeared after that one, years ago. No one knew if he was dead or relocated. No one but you. Nearly plotzed when you'd met him here. Retired. Kicking back in old Mexico, getting stoned, getting pussy, getting fat.

"Where's Dick?"

As you speak, the crowd parts and two beefy guys in black suits—the uniform of a Polito dipshit henchman—haul a dead man by his arms, his heels dragging in the dust, from the cantina to the back of the car. As they drop him into the trunk, you recognize the corpse as Conrad, one of the other gringos living here. His front is blackened with blood. His own, judging by the color of his face and the gash in his throat.

"Fuck me," you whisper.

"Dude," agrees Metcalf.

"Where's Dick?" you repeat. Metcalf is rooted there; breathing through his open mouth, glad to have another civilized white man to stand next to. He doesn't answer.

You start to pull your pants on. The sight of your dead friend, scumbag that he was, seems to require a gesture of dignity, even one as feeble as this. The two men had disappeared back inside the cantina and reappear now dragging another body, this one female and local. It's a Maria, one of the prostitutes. All the women here are prostitutes the gringos call Maria, but this is Dick's Maria, plain as day.

Dick is the third body hauled out. Though beaten and bloody, he's definitely breathing as they drop him on top of the other two and slam the trunk. The henchmen get in either side of the Cadillac's front seat.

Ramon, the barkeep, catches your eye as the car backs up and drives away. The crowd turns to watch it go, but you study Ramon grinning after the hearse. It's always bad news when Ramon is happy. He wipes his face with his right hand and you notice his knuckles. Broken. Swollen. Bloody.

No wonder he's smiling.

You get good and drunk. Pass out late in the afternoon. In the meantime, you gather a loose narrative from Metcalf: Dick and Maria had a spat about the new Maria he'd been spending time with (the Marias outnumber the gringos about five to one). She'd taken Conrad back to her place to piss Dick off.

Got his attention.

Got them all killed.

Ramon is replacing the lock on his door, which looks kicked in. The safe he keeps behind the bar is compromised. There's no reason for more security. The only times anyone steals or kills here, there are immediate and permanent repercussions. You guess that after slicing their throats, Dick's idea was to grab the money and run over the mountains.

A hasty, ill-conceived plan fueled by jealousy, tequila, and boredom. Simple in concept, the killing and theft was no big thing. He'd murdered them as they slept, and Ramon's safe could be violated with a can opener, but escape?

Escape is a bitch. A man alone and on foot would have to be crazy to try.

Apparently, he was.

* * *

You wake up an hour or so past dusk. In a heap. In the gutter. Smelling like piss. You just hope it's your own. Ramon's little ghetto blaster is on eleven, in the back of your consciousness, broadcasting some station that plays mariachi music. All those greaser tunes sound the same, so it's hard to know how long you lie there drifting in and out. But you wake up long after midnight, naked once again, while Maria washes you with a sponge.

You are in her hut, but you have no idea how you got there or why she's taken you in again. Just her nature, you suppose.

She stares at you with those spooky, mongoloid eyes of hers. She is stripped to the waist, cradling your head between her breasts, which brush against your cheeks as she wrings water out, wiping away your guilty stains.

She speaks softly to you. All is forgiven, it seems. You feel an unfamiliar sensation in your gut. Shame. Shame about the way you'd treated her that morning. She'd lost a friend too—not the first—to this place.

You fall into your usual pattern, carrying on two mutually exclusive conversations. Each language a bastion of solitude and anonymity. You have no idea how her conversation went, but yours tend to go like this:

YOU. What was he thinking, killing Conrad like that? And over what? Some passed-around piece of beaner trim.

HER. It makes perfect sense. Stupid. But flawless logic.

YOU. How'd you get that scar on your thigh? Looks like someone used a knife.

HER. Somebody did.

YOU. Why?

HER. Only reason to. It made sense.

YOU. Who?

HER. Son of a bitch with a knife.

YOU. Why are you here?

HER. Paying for my sins, just like you.
YOU. Actually this is payment for my sins.
HER. What's the difference?
YOU. One's reward. One's punishment. One you earn. One you owe.
HER. How very middle class of you. It's all just price in the end.
YOU. Prize?
HER. That too.

She soaks the sponge and wets you both with giant drips that roll between her generous bosoms into your eyes and ears. As you drift off to sleep again, you think you hear her say: "It falls on the just and the unjust alike."

It's called Politoburg, this ramshackle camp in the middle of the desert. It's so remote and desolate, it may as well be on the moon. There's no agriculture or natural resource other than dust and lizard shit. The economy consists entirely of the goods sold from Ramon's cantina and the services of the Marias. Ramon's is stocked in weekly truckloads, and Ramon sends the contents of his safe back with the drivers.

Sweet fuckin' setup. Harlan Polito hires you for something. A job he needs a little distance from, doesn't wanna use his regular guys. Says, "You'll need to lie low awhile. Get outta town. I've got a place in Mexico. You like Mexico? You'll love it. Get laid. Get a tan." And he pays well. There's a reason everybody wants to work for him.

So you do your job. You've already been paid half and thinking about the rest of it is driving you crazy. A truck meets you at the rendezvous and the driver tosses you a fat envelope that hefts like the first. As you get in, he says you should sleep 'cause it's going to be a long ride.

For a week or so, you actually enjoy yourself. You've never had a proper vacation before. Maybe you'll grow a beard.

Maybe you'll stay in Mexico; you kinda dig the vibe. Ramon's got every kind of substance you've ever tried and a couple you're curious about, and the Marias don't care about your car or your education or whether you're hung like a mule or a ferret. It's all sunshine and beans and rice.

You get bored pretty quick.

You begin to think about it, a bad idea. You realize you're just shoving Polito's money back at him as fast as you can eat it, fuck it, or shoot it away. Starts to get to you. Don't think about it. It'll ruin your buzz.

But of course you do. Worse, you get yourself a little plowed one day and say something to this effect to Ramon and wonder further, just when will you be going back to civilization, air-conditioning, and escort services?

Ramon smiles, grabs that short bat he keeps behind the bar, and smashes your teeth in. He pats your kidneys while you grab your face and when you've stopped crying, he really puts you in your place.

"The fuck you think you are, *pendejo?* Huh? The fuck you think this is? A vacation?" Then he laughs. A cruel and practiced laugh. He's made this same speech dozens of times. It's the part of his job that he enjoys.

It begins to sink in, the horror, when you realize that you're not a tourist. You're a local. You belong here. You're fucked.

The idea has kicked around in your head since Ramon had gone all Hank Aaron on you, but it takes Conrad getting his throat slashed for you to decide. Problem is, it will take two. And now your only choice is to use Metcalf, the only gringo left.

At least he shouldn't be hard to convince. Dick had been a stabilizing presence for him. Metcalf was going downhill fast.

"So, how 'bout it, man?"

Bleary and sullen, he makes you wait.

"Hey!" You slap him to get his attention. "Are you in? I need to know that I can count on you."

He rubs his cheek and his eyes clear a little. "Yeah, I'm in. Fuck this place, dude."

Maria sits behind you on top of the table. She plays with the hair on the back of your neck. It's beginning to curl. She's singing softly under her breath. The tune is familiar, but the words you can't follow.

The three of you sit at the picnic table outside the cantina, which closed an hour ago. The wind is fierce tonight. Metcalf's long stringy hair is whipped into impossible knots, but Maria wears hers in a loose braid. The desert is cold and you lean back into her for warmth.

"Is she coming?" asks Metcalf.

"No. She'd just slow us down. We'll have to keep moving. Polito's got reach."

Maria senses you're talking about her. She stops singing and rests her chin on your shoulder, waiting for you to repeat what you said.

Metcalf smiles dopily and says, "Yeah, but she speaks Spanish. . . ."

Shit. He has a point.

She's no prize. Fat and dumb and can't be a day over nineteen. She's seen some heavy shit in her time. How, you wonder, in her young stupid life had she arrived in this shit hole? How long could she survive here? She was tough, you had to give her that, and maybe that explained your reluctant affection for her.

Fuck it, she's coming.

You watch her mending a blanket with an animal grace, which you'd catch every once in a while if you paid attention. When she was immersed in a task, cleaning or cooking or fucking, she was possessed of this. But it disappeared in anything less intimate than your company. She was awkward and slow in society and that translated through any language, but she was comfortable for some reason around you.

"How did you wind up here?"

She looks up from her work, her features spread across her broad face like craters on the moon. Not beautiful. Not to you. Not to a blind man.

"*Como?*" The hoods of her eyes blink slowly as she waits for you to repeat the question.

"Where is your family?"

She squints, leaning in as if proximity and not language were the problem. You take her hands to hold her attention. "Do . . . you"—pointing—"want to leave"—your fingers walking—"with me?"—pointing again.

You repeat the whole thing a couple of times, faster.

Still no response.

"Never mind." You let go of her hands and lie down. A few moments later she lies down beside you. Her fingers reach around from behind you and find yours. You give them a squeeze.

Metcalf is worrying you. He seems determined to kill himself. Before the heist, he's spending all his money. His reasoning is he's going to steal it all back in a few days anyway.

Tequila, coke, and blow jobs all day, all night, all week. He's out of control. Twice, Ramon's had to throw him out of the cantina and beat his ass. He's in no kind of shape, but what're you going to do?

You know what you're going to do. It's clear you have to. Doesn't mean you like it. Doesn't mean you won't hate yourself awhile. Doesn't mean you'll hesitate. At his best, he's a liability. Now he's completely unhinged. What choice, really?

You can't sleep tonight. You're up before sunrise. You leave Maria packing a few things. If it goes bad, you don't want her implicated. That, and you want to spare her what happens to Metcalf. You find Metcalf passed out in the ditch beside the cantina. Let him have a little more sleep.

When the dust cloud appears you wake him up. Takes some slapping, but he's surprisingly sober and right-headed in less than a minute. You're the one who feels sickly and when he smiles and claps your shoulder in anticipation, you vomit. His smile turns to alarm.

"You okay, dude?"

"Yeah. Just nerves. I'm fine."

The truck starts honking its horn a quarter mile out and Ramon is fumbling with the locks and shaking his head clear as it comes to a stop. Ramon and the driver begin bringing in the delivery, their arms full of boxes. Canned goods, sacks of flour, rice, and potatoes, hygiene products, pornography, and scandal rags, a few clothing items, and a first aid kit for a laugh. The bulk of the shipment is liquor. You wait till they're behind the truck together, lifting a crate; then you slip into the cantina and take positions at the door.

Ramon's short bat for you and a bottle of Jack for Metcalf. Ramon comes through the door first, backing up. In the split second it takes for him to register surprise, Metcalf has broken his jaw with a wicked two-handed swing. Following suit, you take out the driver, stepping into the doorway. The crate of liquor crashes to the floor, just missing your feet.

Metcalf falls upon Ramon, straddling his chest and concussing him well beyond the point of necessity. You've never seen him alive like this, having his pathetic revenge. A wave of nausea washes over you and you wipe your palms on your shirt and get a good grip on the bat.

Metcalf slows down, panting and happy. Still on top of his victim, he wipes his bloody hands on Ramon's shirt, then runs them over his face and through his hair.

He lets out a whoop. "Yeeeaaahhh! How you like me now?"

Laughing, he turns his face up to look at you. You lay the bat across the bridge of his nose. It smashes like a ripe plum. He's dead before he falls.

You stop in front of her hut and she scampers aboard like an excited puppy. That changes when she sees you. The hard look of violence still on your face, blood on your clothes, and no Metcalf. The truck lurches forward and she's thrown back against the seat. In the rearview, you spot a couple of Marias running after you and others out staring, not understanding what's happened. You mutter, "Kiss my ass, Politoburg."

The cab of the truck is awash in emotions. Maria stares at you, waiting for an account of the blood and missing Metcalf. You smile at her, annoyed that you have to remind her to be glad to be gone. Timidly, she smiles too, but the question doesn't leave her eyes.

You feel a conversation coming on.

YOU. Look . . . he's not coming. . . . We've got to take care of each other now.
HER. What happened?
YOU. It was bloody. I told you it would be bloody. That's why I made you wait for me in the hut.
HER. What did you do?
YOU. What I had to. What I'd do again.
HER. Do you love me?
YOU. Are you serious? Let's not have this conversation. Ever.

She sits there watching you have this conversation, all by yourself this time. She senses its conclusion and sets her eyes on the horizon, where they belong.

You abandon the truck a couple miles outside the city and hike through the hills surrounding, looking for a spot to sleep. It's a few hours before midnight and the lights look delicious.

It's hard not to go down and find a drink and a meal and spend some of your cash on a hotel, but you've got to play this smart.

Maria sleeps with her head in your lap. The night is cold, but the exhilaration of freedom warms you, though you don't join her in slumber. Tonight, you confess your sins to her. All of them.

When lights begin coming on again, you wake her up and the two of you make your way down the hill, towards the harbor. Maria understands what you want when you put cash in her hand.

You watch her work out passage for the two of you on a fishing boat for South America. She looks over her shoulder and smiles when she catches you staring, her tongue goes to the gap between her front teeth, and you call the feeling in your gut devotion. You know it's just a by-product of circumstance, two souls shrugging the weight of a common oppressor, but it's there.

All day you sit on the deck, watching the sea.

That night you rock to sleep in your cramped cabin that feels like a five-star hotel. The ocean smell sears the dust from your lungs. Maria hums a lullaby and your dreams are filled with the future instead of the past for the first time in years.

It's past midnight when they come for you. You wake up a second before they burst into the room, suddenly aware that you're alone and it's about to go bad. Four sailors haul you from your bed naked and kicking up to the deck.

You scream her name every second, but you can't locate Maria.

On the deck the captain is waiting. She is at his side.

"If you touch her I will fucking kill every last one of you!" you yell as they drag you to the rail. The stars provide the only illumination, but it's bright enough to cause the blade to glint an instant before the pink mist and the hot rivulets rush down your chest.

The world tilts and you hit the water with a smack you can't even hear. The salt water fills your gasping mouth and when you break the surface you struggle to see the deck, wondering if she's to join you in your grave.

As your strength fails and your vision dims, she appears at boat's edge, looking for you. She's alone and unmolested. She's wrapped in a blanket against the chill. She's not screaming. She's calm and she's free for the first time in her life. She waves to you once and watches serenely and without malice as you go under for the last time.

Good for you, honey.

Haermund Hardaxe Was Here

Allan Guthrie

The following story is inspired by graffiti inscribed on the walls of the prehistoric chambered cairn in Orkney, Scotland, known as Maeshowe or Orkahaugr. The inscriptions, circa 1150, are thought to have been written by Viking crusaders. More info here: http://www.orkneyjar.com/history/maeshowe/maeshrunes.htm

Hours had passed since we crawled into the gut of this Orcadian burial tomb. The tunnel opened into a high-ceilinged central chamber where Tholfir Kolbeinsson, Einar Orkisson, and Ofram Sigurdsson now lay sleeping. In the lightflicker, Arnfithr Steinsson carved letters in the stone.

Inside the mound of Orkahaugr, we sheltered, warm inside its flint-raked walls. While outside, snow fell thick as flour shaken from a thousand sacks.

I listened to the scratch of Arnfithr's words until sleep stole my soul.

The wind moaned. It howled.

Flames swathed my thigh. Fiery droplets skittered down my calf. Neck-split, Erlingr lay death-still where he fell. The Damascene arose, a hole punched in his chest, and kissed my bleeding lips.

I cried aloud and woke, shivering. Cold sweat pooled above my buttocks.

I stretched my leg. The lazy clink of sword and axe, the scrape of hide on bald clay, stirred no one. Piecemeal, the snuffle and snort of my band of sleeping Jerusalem-farers soothed the dream-lashed weals of my mind.

My tongue flicked over ever-foul lips.

Arnfithr still wrote. He glanced my way yet did not speak.

"Are you telling of our deeds?" I asked.

His smooth-skinned arm dropped to his side. "I am the man most skilled in runes in the Western Ocean. Yet I have no stomach for those tidings."

"What are you writing?"

"My name. That I was here."

"Carve something for me."

"What shall I say, Hardaxe?"

I thought for a moment, my fingers probing the hollow chambers of my axe. Sockets pocked the shaft where once gleamed jewels. I gripped the handle and squeezed. I smiled. "Say: Ingigerth is the most beautiful of all women."

Arnfithr roared. His laughter brought Tholfir scrambling to his feet.

Nervous Tholfir. A good soldier. He hid his fear.

I spoke to him now as I spoke to him in the dusty heat when our skins burned and blistered and burned again. "It's okay," I told him. In some ways, despite his thirteen years, he was still a child.

He lay down, nestled against me, and was asleep again before Arnfithr had stilled his shaking shoulders.

"Be serious, my friend," Arnfithr said. "These ancient walls want to know what Haermund Hardaxe has to say."

We trudged over ridges of drifted sand. Waded though this great ocean of ill-tinted sea. A coating of finest sand layered our tongues. We plodded footsore and back-weary towards the distant mountains.

At length, the terrain hardened. Beneath our feet, the earth had baked.

In Iberia promises of plunder had girded our loins. After our failure in Damascus, the glow of adventure had dimmed. And now, riven from the fleeing Franks, our mercenary band of five staggered and weaved in the hostile sun with thoughts only of staying alive.

"We should find shelter," I said, squinting in the sun's glare. "It is too hot. We will travel under the stars."

"Might we steer our path back to the City of Blood?" Arnfithr's eyebrows rose.

"You jest." Damascus. The very name means "dripping with blood." But I too thought of the orchards of fruit trees and my mouth watered. Trees wreathed the city. Mud-walled orchards lined the stream hugging the eastern wall, enclosed the western wall, and stretched five miles to the north towards Lebanon. Within the walls, narrow paths snaked through ample trees of violet damson.

When our army marched forth, the Damascenes, hidden in the thickets, repelled us with ease. Inside the orchards were many walls, behind which lingered spearmen who thrust their weapons through thin slots as we passed and stabbed without fear of harm at our crowded number. From tall houses arrows rained on our heads.

Shouts and screams pulsed all around us.

I clutched the helve of my axe and trampled over a fallen body.

Erlingr turned and faced me, an arrow cleaving a path through his neck. A rattle in his throat. On his knees, he swayed.

By my side, Tholfir paled. "My stomach," he said. "I think, I think . . ." He bent over and heaved.

I seethed and raged at our blindness and the blindness of those who had ordered us forward. I could bear no more of this folly. "Get the fuck out of here," I yelled at my men.

I bent, scooped up Erlingr, hoisted him over my shoulder. I barged through the crunch of surging bodies. Some turned and joined me. Others shouted curses in a tongue I barely grasped.

For the briefest moment, the world was still.

A silence shrouded us.

And then, all around, men dropped their weapons and began to dance. Faces gnarled, strangled voices singing, they batted urgent rhythms with arms winglike, flightless birds in this Muspell, this World of Fire. Above our heads, bronze tubes that lanced the peepholes of a tall building hurled jets of liquid flames into our midst.

Greek Fire. A noxious brew of sulfur, naphtha, and quicklime. It grabbed my leg and clung with burning fingers. I stumbled and fell. Erlingr lay still, his blond beard stained dark red, blood no longer spurting from his slack mouth.

Arnfithr hauled me to my feet.

"Erlingr," I said.

"Leave him."

I wiped the sweat from my brow. Ahead, at the top of a slight incline, a shelf of crumbling rock promised shade. "A good place to rest," I said.

We laid our weapons on the ground and curled up beside them. Helmets covered our faces, shielding our eyes from the rising sun. Arnfithr lay next to me. I listened to his restless breathing. After a while he brushed my arm. I turned, uncovering my face, and nodded.

We rolled up our blankets while our sleeping colleagues whistled into their helmets. We wandered towards a distant row of juniper bushes. A screen.

We unrolled our bedding and stripped. The fire in my loins burned as hot as the fire in my leg.

I fucked Arnfithr.

Then he fucked me, whispering the name of Ingigerth, his betrothed, in my ear.

Afterwards, I slept soundly.

I awoke with a start. A hand was clamped over my mouth. The high sun blinded me. Slowly, my eyes adjusted to the light and I saw Arnfithr crouched over me. "Quiet," he whispered. He stabbed his finger at the camp two hundred paces away.

Nine. I counted them. Nine jeering Damascene soldiers grouped around our startled brothers. Drunk with discovery, the band of infidels prodded and poked our rudely awakened men. An anger swelled in my belly. Arnfithr grasped my wrist. Fiercely calm, he said, "Hardaxe, we have no weapons."

I was sickened. Like fools we had left our weapons at the camp. We could do nothing but watch.

Rousing cries spewed from the Damascenes' mouths. They frolicked like children with new toys. Living toys. Was this the best Nour Ed-Din had to offer? Had the new ruler of Damascus sent this rabble to hunt for stragglers from the retreating armies?

More likely they were scavengers.

I tried to spot their leader.

The one with his hair scraped back? The one strutting around Einar? The ox about to strike Tholfir in the face? How could I tell?

Tholfir staggered backwards, fell. After a moment he turned where he lay and began to scramble across the cracked ground on hands and knees. The Damascenes laughed, pointed, circled him, kicked him, spat on him.

Ofram broke free of his captors, bolted towards Tholfir. A tall Damascene stepped in his path. Raised an axe. Ofram stopped. He cried, "Hardaxe," and folded to his knees. He looked towards us for an instant. He may have smiled. Huddled behind our needle-leafed shield of juniper, his expression was hard to read. He yielded to the tall Damascene, wrists held out for binding. The Damascene lowered his axe. The handle glinted.

Him. He was the leader. The axe in his hand was mine.

We watched and waited. No one was gravely hurt. The Damascene soldiers rounded up our ragged threesome and tied them up. After they'd tired of kicking and spitting and slapping and punching, they dragged our men down the slope and out of sight.

I turned to Arnfithr and swore. Arnfithr moved like the earth was burning the soles of his feet. I grabbed our blankets and hastened after him. My leg stung. The wet cloth swathed around it to keep it cool had dried out as we'd slept. Not for the first time, I brooded on the moment the fire had burned my skin. A sickness buckled my legs. I picked myself up, slung the blankets once more over my shoulder, and scurried towards the camp.

Arnfithr lay on his belly, staring into the distance.

I cast the blankets aside and crept towards him. I lay down. Although the ground warmed my stomach, my heart grew cold as I watched our band of rope-threaded Jerusalem-farers being led away like beasts of the field. The Damascenes were heading into the desert. Away from Lebanon. Away from Damascus.

I said, "What shall we do?"

"I am at a loss," Arnfithr said. "We cannot fight them. Unarmed. Two against nine." He turned his head slightly. "How is your leg?"

"Of no matter." I gazed into the distance. "We will shadow them," I said. "And strike at nightfall."

"You have a plan?" He reached out and touched my shoulder. I clamped my hand over his.

They traveled on foot, upright. We were not so lucky.

We kept low to the ground, often crawling on our stomachs over the rocky terrain, always keeping our enemies in sight. Two toothless predators stalking fat prey. Their smells drifted towards us, stirring our nostrils, sweetening our mouths.

They had slept. We had little time to do so. Full of anger and outrage, our minds were alert but our muscles ached with the strain of hugging the ground. The heat beat down on our heads, on our necks.

I had told Arnfithr I had a plan. I had lied. Could I outwit our foe? Could we play a shrewd trick to disarm them, conquer them, rescue Einar, Tholfir, and Ofram?

Weaponless, we would be slaughtered. We had to win back our weapons. Or steal those of the Damascenes.

Slithering over a dry scum of sand, I set my mind to the task of finding a way to free our men and escape.

Easier to free myself from the mouth of a serpent, I thought. But then an idea came to me and I thanked God.

The Damascenes stopped for the night at a village of no more than a dozen dwellings. The villagers chattered angrily at the soldiers' arrival. We understood not a word they said. Perhaps they did not want these city soldiers eating their meager food stocks. Perhaps they did not want the soldiers near their women. Perhaps they did not want those pale-skinned captives in their village. They'd heard that Norsemen were crazy. They fought like demons, ripped their enemies apart, and ate their souls.

Whatever the villagers' pleas, the soldiers ignored them. An old man fumed. A soldier batted him aside and knocked him over. Another villager strode forward, shouting. He pointed to where the old man scrabbled in the dust, then folded his arms and barred the entrance to his pitiful house. Without warning, the Damascene leader struck him a heavy blow with his new axe. I hoped he was pleased with the result. The man clutched his stomach, surprise in his widening eyes. He fell forward, hands never moving from his belly, and bled furiously.

The Damascene yelled something at the villagers. They grabbed what they could and fled. After a while the man on the ground stopped jerking and the soldiers dragged his body away.

Arnfithr and I lay still and waited for dark. When it fell, it was as if nature had thrown a dark, wet sheet over us.

My body was chilled. Only my leg had heat in it.

We waited, the darkness pressing in on us.

They had lit a fire. Two guards sat by it, warming their hands, jabbering. Behind them, our brothers lay roped together. Silent.

I unfolded my plan to Arnfithr.

He switched his gaze to my leg. "There can be no doubt as to who will play which part."

I nodded, then took a gasping breath to fetter my unsettled mind. "Twice," I said.

The first punch knocked me on my arse. I shook my head but stayed dazed. I put my hand to my nose. Blood dripped from the left nostril.

Arnfithr held out his hands, meekly.

"It's necessary," I said, rising to my feet. "Another," I said. I closed my eyes. The second blow knocked me down again. I lay where I fell.

Arnfithr bent over me and began tearing my clothes.

I powdered my cheeks and lips with dust. I hoped I looked the part—bleeding, dirt-masked, limping on my scalded leg. As I lurched towards the village, I croaked: "Help." No break in the Damascene guards' prattle. A little louder. "Help."

One of them looked up. He stood, one hand seeking his sword, the other lighting a torch from the fire.

I staggered forward a few more steps.

The guard spoke to his companion. After a moment he crept towards me, sword drawn.

I crumpled, fell at his feet.

He kicked my ankle. I groaned. He kicked me in the ribs. I groaned again. "Piss-drinker," I said, knowing my tongue was a thick muddle to his ears.

His dark eyebrows arched.

I placed my hands palms up in front of me to show I was unarmed. I pointed to my face. Blood still seeped from my nose. I showed him my leg, where I'd earlier shed the cloth to bare the blistered skin beneath.

I opened my mouth. Made drinking signs with my hand. "Understand, you son of a dark-haired whore?"

He steered the torch closer, bending over to study the beaten and burned Viking, peering closely to sift the truth from what he saw: this curious savage, isolated from the rest of his men, had walked into the hands of his enemy rather than die of thirst.

At least that's what I hoped he was thinking.

Abruptly, he stepped aside and backed off to the campfire. The plan had been to kill him swiftly and silently while Arnfithr rid us of the other guard. But the moment had passed. I dragged myself to my knees and scanned the village.

Arnfithr was nowhere in sight. Our men were awake. They knew we would come for them, of course. And they knew not to make a sound.

Out of sight, I stood up and bolted, my feet thudding like gentle heartbeats on the softer ground. Fifty paces away, I stopped and watched the guard lead his companion to where I had lain. As they neared the place, I saw Anrfithr flit behind our brothers.

I prayed for his success.

My target was the hut where the Damascene leader slept. In the dim moonlight, a dark trail snaked from the doorway where the corpse had been dragged away.

A cloth draped the entrance. I pulled it aside. Bright lights flashed as my eyes tried to pierce the darkness. Silence pounded in my ears. I stood still and listened.

Snoring from my right. Gentle, swinelike grunts. Like a woman's snores. I shuffled towards the sound. Closer. Still closer.

My foot touched something solid. I stopped. My skin prickled. My mouth dried. My stomach filled with heavy stones. I crouched. He had not awoken. The Damascene leader's snores still rattled in his throat where he lay on the floor. My hand slowly moved towards the sound. I touched hair that felt like silk. At once, my left hand darted towards his neck and my fingers clenched around his throat.

The snoring stopped.

My right hand joined its fellow and I squeezed.

Awake now, the Damascene grabbed my wrists. My fingers tightened around his throat, and I pressed down from my shoulders.

By the time I heard the sound behind me it was too late to react. The blow struck me across the cheek. A second blow struck my nose. I fell off the Damascene and rolled across the floor. I was on my feet, my nose bleeding again. It was too painful to dab the gore away. I thought I might choke. I shook my head vigorously and spat.

My stupidity shamed me. How had I not reckoned there might be a brace of them in the room? I saw only the leader entering the abode, but a companion, a bodyguard, a lover perhaps, had sneaked in unobserved.

I didn't know which one I had tried to strangle. But he was still alive. The sound of his coughing now filled the room.

The moment the other spoke, his words intended for his fallen companion, I sprang forward. I knew I risked death. He would be armed. But better to risk death than face the fate that awaited me should I linger in an unwarriorlike fog of doubt.

The heel of my hand struck bone. A second blow shunted him to the side, clearing a path ahead of me.

I plunged through the doorway and looked up.

The moonlit glints of the laughing Damascenes' weapons were silver flashes of lightning.

They hair-dragged me towards my brothers. I readied myself for the bleak sag of Arnfithr's jowls, the wretched faces of my three other men. All knew they were about to die in this godforsaken land. I ground my teeth against the Damascene's kicks of encouragement.

But maybe Arnfithr had succeeded. Maybe at least that side of the plan had worked. Yes, he had freed our companions and they had escaped into the darkness! And now they awaited their chance to free me! Hope clung to me like rotting flesh on a skeleton.

Not for long.

Arnfithr had managed to loosen the ropes around the wrists of Tholfir and Ofram. Einar remained tied. Arnfithr was unbound, his head bowed, closely guarded by three Damascenes.

The Damascene leader stood in front of me. His dark eyes

sparkled in the firelight. I spat blood in his face. His eyes narrowed. He wiped the red-frothed spit off his cheek and showed me his axe. My axe. He'd plucked out the jewels. Was he offering it to me? I thought not. I looked at him again and he struck me on the shoulder with the helve of the axe. And again. As if he was knocking a stake into the ground. I fell to my knees. The third time I was ready for him.

I caught the axe handle as it swung down and ripped it out of his grasp. Before he had time to tumble to my intent, I planted the blade in his skull. I tugged it out and sent it crashing down again.

Around me, the Damascenes looked at each other. Leaderless, they didn't know what to do. Surprise turned to outrage. Outrage battled with fear. Fear yielded to stupor. They stood as still as trees.

Not so Arnfithr. Two of his guards lay on the ground. The third gargled, a knife hilt-sunk in his throat. Tholfir, silent despite the tears in his eyes, untied Einar's bonds. Ofram picked up a sword that had belonged to one of Arnfithr's victims and stood beside me.

Arnfithr started to yell. He roared like a berserker. I joined him. Ofram took up the call. Einar joined us. Then Tholfir. Together, the noise we made caused the ground beneath our feet to tremble.

Still yelling, I plunged my axe into the Damascene leader's chest. The blade tore into his body. I chopped at him as if I were splitting a log.

The remaining Damascenes backed off.

My men kept up their crazy noise.

The Damascenes kept their distance.

Their leader's chest was spoiled red, the mess a pack of dogs would wreak. I stuck my hand inside and grabbed his heart. I ripped it out and held it high.

Our chorus was the roar of an angry God. I placed the bleeding flesh to my lips and bit into it. My mouth filled with warm blood. I passed the heart to Ofram.

Suddenly there was silence. A single Damascene soldier had stepped forward, his right hand shaking as he held out his sword.

"Brave man," Arnfithr said.

Ofram dropped the leader's heart and wiped his hand on the ground. He darted towards the advancing Damascene and slew him with a single blow to the neck. "Dead man," he said. He picked up the fallen man's sword and gave it to Tholfir.

Tholfir looked at me.

"It's okay," I told him.

"What now?" Einar asked.

"Let's get the fuck out of here," I said.

We bunched together and backed away from the Damascenes. When we could no longer see them, we turned and ran, heading for the safety of the Lebanese Mountains.

Had the Damascenes chased us, they might have beaten us down and crushed us before long. They had food and water. We were hungry and thirsty. But they chose to let us go. Now and again Tholfir let out a cry and pointed at a glimmer in the distance. But each time, it was only his fear-fevered fancy.

When we reached the mountains, we prayed, quietly, each asking his own favor of the Lord. On my knees, salt tang still on my lips, I whispered, "Give me strength to forget."

And God answered, "What is past is dead."

Outside the flint-carved walls of Orkahaugr the wind still howled. Tholfir stirred, legs kicking like a dreaming dog where he lay curled at my feet.

Arnfithr finished his latest scratchings on the wall. "You

must say something, Hardaxe," he told me. "For those who are yet to come to this place."

I gazed at him. "Write only this," I said. "Haermund Hardaxe was here."

I closed my eyes and tried to sleep.

We All Come from Splattertown

Hugh Lessig

I am surfing the edge of a Friday night drunk as Angelo arrives. He comes to the end of the bar, hooks the rail with a steeled toe.

He whispers, "You want to play some paintball tomorrow?"

"That sounds good to me."

My stare slides away. You never look directly at Angelo because he'll take it the wrong way, even with me.

He gets a beer, takes a swig. When he says nothing else, I add the rest of it.

"You want to bring Benny too? He'll get pissed if we don't call him."

A smile crawls up one side of Angelo's face. The cobra tattoo on his neck uncoils in rhythm.

"We can call him, if you insist. He loves his paintball. But he's not you. You taught me everything I know, brother."

We tap fists. Angelo takes a backseat to few men, but he defers to me on paintball issues. It's funny how that works. I am not big or strong. I don't shave my head or have angry tattoos scrolling across my back that speak of white power. I don't wear black boots with red laces. But I can move through the woods and pick my targets. I am a calm shot with a paintball gun. I can plan strategy. I see things happening ahead of me.

Angelo thinks this makes me some kind of warrior. He thinks I'll come out and shoot jigaboos with him when the United States breaks out in a race war. Except I don't call them jigaboos, I don't hang out with his comrades, and I don't give a flying fuck about his race war. I just like nailing people sometimes. Yeah, I pretend it's killing, and I talk about it when the beers start going down—about how I could really kill people. But it's just talk. Angelo and I became friends in grade school and we've woofed on shit since then. The thread of our friendship has stretched thin through these strange and empty years.

He asks, "What is it you study again?"

"I've told you a hundred times. You don't need to bust me about it."

"I'm not busting you. Do you like it?"

"It's interesting."

Angelo laughs. "It could some in handy sometime, that's all I'm saying."

"Handy how?"

He claps me on the shoulder, throws down a five. "You call Benny, and then call me. We all go up together."

He leaves without another word. The conversation rewinds in my head. Something sinks in my gut and leaves a terrible hole.

Two months ago, I enrolled in Carbon County Community College to study mortuary science.

I want to be a funeral director.

Why would that come in handy?

Benny wants to drive, so the three of us pile into his Jeep and head up to Splattertown, which is on a mountain five miles outside town. The coal was played out there years ago, and this guy from Jersey bought the land for a song and dance. He put up some pallets and plywood towers, and he configured battlefields with names like Maze City and Killer's Kanyon. It costs thirty bucks to play half a day.

Benny is hard-wired today. He is a skinny kid with a caved-in chest who barely comes up to my nipples, but he acts like he's ten feet tall, thanks mostly to the video games he plays.

"You guys are in for trouble. I'm playing point this time."

He swings the wheel as he talks. The Jeep veers onto the shoulder, and then returns to the road. The three of us went to high school together, and for a moment we are invincible and the road is clear and no one lurks in the mirrors.

"Whatever you want," I say.

I'm in the backseat and Angelo rides shotgun. He stares at nothing in particular, or at something the rest of us can't see.

There isn't much to paintball, really. You get a gun with a CO_2 cartridge that shoots little plastic balls filled with fluorescent paint. You rent the guns, the ammo, helmets, goggles, and gloves, pretty much everything you need. I have my own gear, but Benny and Angelo still get theirs by the hour.

You play in a group, and the three of us are teamed with a bunch of high school kids from Aliquippa. They have rental gear from top to bottom. We board a couple of Hummers for the drive into the woods. The high school kids are giggling like six-year-olds, and I'm thinking I'll have to lead this group.

The first game is Capture the Flag—eleven on twelve, the three of us playing together—and we win easily. Most people try to skirt around the edge of the battlefield and get caught in bad angles. I lead a group up the middle and get the flag, which is just a piece of red cloth attached to a barrier.

The last game we play is Run and Chase. We pick one kid from the group to take off through the woods, and the rest of us go after him. The Aliquippa kids had someone singled out—

some little dude who played football and could run like the wind—and we spend a good thirty minutes chasing him through the trees. Then the referee blows his whistle, a signal that everyone should stop. I figure the game is over, that someone finally nailed the kid. Instead, we find the referee frantically punching numbers into his cell phone and standing over Benny, who is face-down on the ground with the hilt of a knife protruding from the back of his head.

The state police separate us for questioning, and I pretty much tell the truth.

I was involved in the game. Everyone ran around trying to find this one kid. I didn't see Benny. The helmets cover everyone's face and the rental gear all looks the same. Benny is your basic skinny kid. He could have been next to me and I might not have known it.

The cops get my contact information and Social Security number. They drive me back to town. I catch a glimpse of Angelo in the parking lot. He's sitting down and the cops are dusting the soles of his shoes.

Benny's murder makes the front page of the Sunday newspaper. According to the story, the police have no "immediate suspects" but are working on "a couple of leads." It says Benny went to play paintball with "a few friends," but the story mentions no one by name.

There isn't much to say about Benny himself. His dad moved away when he was young and his mom died in a wreck several years ago. The story says he is survived by a sister and an aunt who raised him.

Monday passes and nothing happens. On Tuesday, I go to my 9:00 a.m. class. Afterwards, someone yells my name as I walk to the parking lot.

I turn around as a girl runs towards me, her breasts bouncing in rhythm. She has dark hair, dark eyes, and olive skin. There is something familiar about her. She sticks out her hand.

"Hi, I'm Beth."

"Hey. Harold."

"I know. We were in advanced bio together."

I look around the parking lot. "I'm not taking advanced bio here."

"No, no. Senior year at Trolley Tech."

Trolley Tech is what we call my high school because it's in Trolley Township. Now I seem to remember someone who looked like Beth. She sat behind me. She might have been my lab partner, but her hair was different and she sure as hell didn't have those knockers.

I ask, "Eighth period? You were in Mr. Bower's class?"

She gives me a wide smile. "You remembered. You helped me out so much back then. I hoped you might be able to talk about what happened."

Oh, shit.

Beth Weiss. Beth is Benny's sister, the smart one who skipped a grade and caught up to the rest of us.

"You look different, Beth. Your hair is longer."

Her hand touches her forehead. "I let it grow out. Listen, could we go for coffee somewhere? I'm all strung out over this weekend."

The student union building has a cafeteria. We get big coffees and grab a corner table near the window. Our knees touch as we sit down.

Beth wants to be an accountant, but she doesn't have enough money to attend a four-year school, so she's getting her associate's degree first. She lives with her aunt—a different one than Benny lived with—and she's basically on her own.

"You were always so smart," I say, "always with your head in a book."

Her laugh sounds like tinkling music. "I took advanced bio against my better judgment. I got a B, but it took a lot of work. I decided being a doctor wasn't for me."

"That's not for everyone," I agree.

Beth stares into the swirls of her coffee. "Benny was into gambling. I assume you knew that much."

"Can't say that I did."

"Well, he was. He always liked sports, but he let it get the best of him. He liked to gamble on football mostly."

My breath comes in short spurts. I bite down on my back teeth to keep calm. "He liked gambling on football?"

She sips her coffee, gazes out the window. "He owed a lot of money. He wouldn't tell me how much, but it was four figures. He came to me two weeks ago, wanting to borrow some. I blew him off. I said it would serve him right if he got beat up, because we're poor and gambling is stupid."

I'm trying to think. Angelo runs a sports book. Sometimes he even carries his tip sheets into the bar. Fuck me. I should have seen it coming.

"Is something wrong, Harold?"

"This person Benny owed money to—did he say who it was?"

A hand goes over her face. The tendons and cords stick out and the knuckles go white and the tears bleed through.

"You know damn well who it was," she says.

"I do now."

"I don't even want to say his name."

"That's probably a good idea."

Beth and I spend the next couple of days together. We eat lunch on campus and go out for dinner and beers. She drinks just enough to redden her cheeks and get her thinking out loud.

"I told the police about Angelo," she says. "They already suspect him. Do you think they'll arrest him?"

"For the one hundredth time, I don't know. It may take a little time. They always want to be sure."

Her hand slides over mine. We're at this coffee shop just off Market Square, trying to avoid the bars where we might see friends. Angelo knows half the people in town, and the fact that Beth and I are hanging out makes me hinky, but I can't help it. Her eyes go straight through me and it feels so good.

She squeezes my hand and talks in a small voice. "I'm scared. I can't go on like this. This town is too small. At some point, I'm going to see him. What will I do then? How will I act?"

She asks very good questions. The fact is, people can rehearse stuff like that, pretend they'll behave a certain way, but they are clueless until the moment comes.

Beth agreed to babysit on Saturday night, so I head to the bar and find my regular seat. I don't care if anyone shows up or if I get hammered. I just want to think about Beth and how I can inch closer to her.

Angelo arrives around midnight. He finds an empty seat at the other end of the bar and starts dropping whiskey shots into his beers. He smiles at no one in particular, acting like he has no worries in the world.

I pay my tab and walk over to him. "Hey, Angelo."

"Hey."

"Long time no see. Hear anything more about Benny?"

He fiddles with an empty shot glass. "It was muddy around where they found the body. They took prints of my shoes, the cops did. I been in twice for questioning. Got me a lawyer from Pittsburgh."

Angelo is lubed up. His eyes twitch from something other than beer.

"There was another game in the general vicinity," he continues. "Some other paintball dudes. One of those kids could have migrated over to our field. That's what the cops said—'migrated.' Two of those kids from Aliquippa have juvenile assault records. Fucking niggers. Maybe Benny pissed them off. He can get like that—trash talking and whatnot. But they took my shoe prints and I got a lawyer from Pittsburgh."

"You said."

He orders another shot and beer. His hand slides towards the empty mug. "So, you been up to much? Haven't seen you around."

"I figured you were busy."

He slowly shakes his head. "Harold, Harold, Harold. How is she, man? I mean, really? How is she?"

"How is who?"

"The Jewess."

"Who do you mean?"

"You been down to the coffee shop with her, holding hands and shit. She's crying on your shoulder. Making goo-goo eyes. You slamming her yet?"

I jam both fists into my pockets. "She goes to community college. We have a class together."

"But are you slamming her? Are you having hot Jew princess sex? Is she spreading her—"

"She's upset, Angelo. It was her brother. Wouldn't you be upset if it was your brother? You've got that much of a heart, I assume."

He catches the hint of a challenge. He brings the empty mug to my chin and holds it there, ever so softly. "You're not with her tonight. How come?"

"She's babysitting."

"Are you sure?"

Tap-tap-tap goes the mug against my jaw.

I get out of there as fast as I can.

Beth doesn't answer her cell phone, doesn't return a text. Of the two hospitals within driving distance, St. Gabe's is the closest to her apartment. I call the main number and ask if someone has been admitted under the name of Beth Weiss.

The phone clicks and there is the sound of breathing.

"Hello?"

"Beth. It's Harold."

"I was going to call you. It's okay, really. . . ."

I slam the phone and get down there.

Two guys with hockey masks dragged her into the alley behind her apartment building as she left for her babysitter's job. They pulled down her pants and finger-blasted her, smacked her hard enough to raise a welt below the right eye, and broke a finger on general principle.

The ER was going crazy that night because of a three-car wreck on Interstate 80. When Beth said she fell down the stairs, the doctor took her at her word. She tells me the real story as I hold her hand in the room.

"You need to call the cops. This was a sexual assault. They can put those guys away for years."

"Thank you. I'm aware of what happened." Her eyes turn dark and empty. "They know that I blabbed about Benny's gambling debts. They have a friend on the police force, some white power guy. They said I should keep my mouth shut or they'll come back and do worse. They said the same goes for my boyfriend." She smiles weakly. "I guess that means I officially have a boyfriend."

"Congratulations. See what it's gotten you?"

We share a long, quiet moment. Beth gives me the look of someone who has an unspoken question.

"We can't trust the police," I say.

"What will we do?"

"I'll take care of it."

* * *

The planning takes a week or two. We talk over the phone and text each other, but we never meet face-to-face. Towards the end, we drive separately into Pittsburgh and hang out in a bar and stay in a Motel 6, going over the details. We fall asleep on the cheap bed, and in the morning I want her so bad that it hurts. But I know what those guys did, so I just kiss the top of her nose and tell her everything will be okay.

I imagine the old light in her eyes has returned. It belongs to the type of woman whose future holds babies and big dogs, who scours the bushes for lost toys and smiles because the happiness is so wide that it hurts. It is a pure, clean look, and I need to look towards it every chance I get.

Two weeks from the day that Benny died, we walk into the mountains, to the spot where Angelo always drinks beer late at night. Like everything else outside town, his drinking spot is old coal lands. I have seen it during the day, so I feel comfortable leading Beth up here at night. It is nothing but a small clearing with a shaft that runs into the ground. It was apparently dug years ago by bootleg miners who wanted to steal coal from the mining company. I say "apparently" because you never know how these stories get started. Anyway, it's a good place to drink because you can toss an empty bottle into that shaft and never see it again. I've done it myself.

Beth and I step on the flat rocks so we don't make noise, but it doesn't matter because Angelo's headbanger music drowns out everything as we get closer.

I have studied Angelo's nightly drinking routine, sneaking up here after saying goodnight to Beth. I know when he arrives, when he leaves, how much he drinks. I didn't tell Beth because she would have worried about me coming up here alone, but I figure this is on-the-job training. The best funerals are preplanned.

My heart hammers a beat to the angry music as we move through the fingers of white birch trees.

The moon is high and full, the sky cloudless.

Angelo's shaven head is visible through a stand of mountain laurel. He sits cross-legged next to a cooler of beer, near the mine shaft. The boom box is next to him. CDs are spread among the sharp rocks.

I have my paintball rifle and Beth has a can of pepper spray.

Angelo nods his head to the music. The cobra on his neck twitches. Next to him Fat Norman, one of his skinhead friends, yells about mud-colored bitches and swarthy immigrants. He likes to get up and stretch, which he does right now.

"Here we go," I whisper. "Are you ready?"

Beth holds the pepper spray like a time bomb. "I'm scared, Harold."

"We discussed this. Go, Beth!"

"God forgive me."

She moves into the light. She wears tight track pants and a sports bra and her running shoes.

She waves her hand like I told her. Norman eventually sees her standing backlit against the moon with those breasts and that ass curving into the night like nobody's business.

By now, Norman is so drunk that he can't even speak. He tries to say something and it comes out sideways.

Beth backs away and starts to disappear down the hill. Fat Norman lumbers after her, just like we planned. Beth ran track in high school and there's no way Norman will ever catch her. She will lead him down the mountain and lose him. The pepper spray is just in case something goes wrong.

Angelo says nothing as Norman disappears. That's how it is when you're drunk. You see things and simply accept them for what they are.

I break cover and walk straight towards him. He takes a second to recognize me.

"Harold," he says. "What gives? Good to see you."

I move the barrel to his face and pull the trigger. I don't even think about it. That's what you do in paintball. You decide when to move and you just go.

Angelo screams. It is a terrible, high-pitched noise, and he rolls on the ground, clutching his right eye. Rule number one in paintball is to always wear goggles.

The next step requires me to push him into the mine shaft, but he rolls towards it and falls in on his own. He screams for a second or two; then comes a whoosh of breath and the tinkle of glass as he lands on a generation's worth of broken bottles.

I drop the boom box and the cooler down on top of him, and sprinkle the collection of CDs into the hole.

Later, halfway down the slope, I come across the body of Fat Norman. His misshapen head rests against the hard ground. It's as if his face has begun to melt into the earth. Part of it looks caved in. His arms are all twisted underneath him.

Beth holds the pepper spray and a flat rock. Her eyes stare at nothing in particular. Her breath comes in spurts of excitement. "He hasn't moved. He hasn't moved. It's fucking over."

"Beth . . ."

"He's chasing me, right? Then I stop and hide behind a tree. When he comes up, I'm out there with the pepper spray. It blinds him. He screams like a little kid. I can't believe you didn't hear it, Harold."

"I was dealing with my own screams."

"I let him roll around, let the pain sink in. He ended up on his back, hands over his eyes. I brought the rock down on his nose. He had talked about my nose, about how big it was, and I wanted to pound it back into his skull."

"He talked about your nose? When?"

I knew the answer as soon as I said it. Fat Norman was one of the guys who dragged her behind the Dumpster.

She is not listening. The string is finally unwinding and it's got to come out.

"I felt the cartilage break. It was like in advanced bio when we dissected that fetal pig. This guy has a pig nose too."

She goes on and on, but I'm not listening. I'm thinking about how to get Fat Norman up that slope and into that mine shaft, how to hide the drag marks, if there is blood on the ground. I'm thinking of the satisfaction of knowing that he will never be found.

It's true what morticians say: funerals are not for the dead. They are for the living.

"You hit more than his nose, Beth. Are there, um, pieces of him elsewhere?"

"I dunno. I dunno. All I know is this. When you hit someone and break a bone? That's a totally different sound than when you get hit on the playground. It's like cracking ice in a tray."

The police will assume Angelo skipped town to avoid arrest. It's safe to say there won't be any AMBER Alert for Fat Norman. And me? I'll get rid of my paintball gear just in case. Angelo's body has fluorescent paint from where I shot him, and if the police question me, I'll just say Benny's death left a bad taste in my mouth and I didn't want to play anymore.

I reach out for Beth, my anchor of light in the falling darkness, but she is among the bushes now. Chattering about this and that, she scours the ground for lost pieces of the monster that we must try to bury forever.

The Switch

Lyman Feero

I wake up behind a desk. Some banal article about some equally inane fact is splashed across the monitor of the latest Intel-enhanced box wedged beneath my desk. Coffee rings make java Olympic symbols on the blotter. It's one of those green leather-trimmed calendar blotters that all mahogany slabs have. Each day lined up like soldiers. Their blocks crammed with thin green lines so I can write down all the mundane crap that I have to do during the week. By the looks of things, I have my share, as there is more ink than blotter. The funny thing is—I'm really not quite sure this is my desk. I'm assuming it is since I'm sitting behind it.

The desk is mahogany, sultry swirled mahogany, like the eyes of a lovely South Sea islander whose mother slept with one too many Frenchmen. The chair, however, is vinyl; the same stick-to-my-thighs vinyl that covered the chairs of my mother's small, dingy, eat-in kitchen; the kind of vinyl that groans like flatulence if you move to stand up. Mom's name was Betty, like Betty Crocker. Obviously, I'm midmanagement, as the seat is not leather. Nor is it some form of poly-blend stretched over the plastic frames that adorn the offices of the invisible mean-nothings. Flatulent chairs are reserved for the higher-paid peons. Leather is only attainable by those who do the pissing.

I look at my watch and see that it's ten o'clock. A woman by a long row of filing cabinets sits there staring blankly at me. Before I know why, I flip her the bird and she smiles back and blows me a kiss. I think I hate her, though I don't know why. I don't know much of anything at this moment. I feel hungry. Then someone throws the switch.

I wake up and again and I'm behind a desk, or is it a table? It doesn't matter because my wrists are cuffed and my ass squeaks on vinyl. I get the strange sensation of home. Some sweating greasy little prick tries to tower over me. His coffee cup leaves hidden marks in the workaday jungle of stains. I think that maybe he is compensating for his stature. He flips open a folder, shoves it at me. A horror show spills out across the table and an auburn-haired woman whom I didn't even notice makes a retching sound beside me. Her cherry-red lips kiss the back of her hand. I touch the photos. The traitor between my legs twitches and I start to speak about Betty. She grabs my arm and advises me to stop talking. The silk of her blouse bulges right where it should, straining the middle button. I pray for a wardrobe failure. I close my mouth and think of her tits. She says something about a plea. Death penalty off the table. Waiting for that fucking button to pop may as well be waiting for death. Greasy Prick lobs a yellow legal pad at me with its blue confessional lines, little priests lined up down the page. A pen slides up to greet it. Button slides it toward my hand. Betty Button. I push the pen away and blow her a kiss and give Greasy the finger. I start planning my last meal. Then someone throws the switch.

I'm at a restaurant. I think lunch is a good idea, but I have no way of knowing how or why I know it's lunchtime. I check for a clock, then look for a watch. I find one on my wrist and it reads 12:10 p.m.—just a dime after lunch. A waitress scurries across the room, hopping from table to table like a hummingbird, her green T-shirt clinging too tight to her firm, supple body. I order some potato skins and a hamburger. I thank her and call her Hummingbird. She smiles a gap-toothed grin that reminds me of Madonna and I'm reluctant to smile back, fearing I look like Jay Leno, though I have no reason to believe I do. I don't really remember what I look like.

I grab a spoon off the table and spit-shine it while I'm waiting for my potato skins and hamburger. I squint at my reflection and only see a bug-eyed freak in the streaked and scratched stainless steel of ordinary mealdom. I flip it over and try the inside, but my reflection is squashed and distorted. But at least I don't have bugeyes. The waitress returns with my meal and I call her Hummingbird again. She seems less enthused this time.

Across from me in a booth is a woman in a tight dress with brilliant red lips and flowing auburn hair. She raises a glass of orange juice. FRESHLY SQUEEZED, the sign on the door says. Somehow I think it's the same watered-down orange juice of every diner. She looks directly at me and blows me a kiss. A potato skin hangs from my mouth. I give her the finger, then draw a .38 from my sports coat. Some piece-of-shit Saturday night special that will most likely explode if I fire, but I do anyway. As my finger squeezes the trigger, I think I'm indifferent. Flip the switch.

I'm sweating like a pig in a beat-up Chevy Malibu headed down a highway in what I can only assume is the desert Southwest. The heat leaps off the pavement frantically, distorting everything. I feel distorted as well. Where the hell am I going? All I know is that I need to get away from whatever is behind me and I have to get away now!

There's a .45 Smith & Wesson on the seat beside me, bullets

spilled out of a half-empty carton of hollow-points. A bottle of Smirnoff sloshes on the floor. The dashboard has a gaping hole in it that is vomiting out its cheap foam filling. The bench seat is maroon vinyl, the slick ass-varnished vinyl of a high-mileage car. This one's tallied up well over two hundred thousand. The back window has three holes in it, which I'm assuming are bullet holes and which I'm assuming explain the ragged puking hole in the dash.

A moan comes from the backseat and I almost lose control of the car. It's her, dressed in a white T-shirt loosely tucked into her too-tight jeans. I can see she isn't wearing a bra, because of the way the blood from the gaping wound in her chest makes the cloth of the tee stick to her nipples and form to her breasts. For a second, I think, *This must be how a vampire wet T-shirt night must go and she'd win*. I just know it.

With her mouth bloodied and her eyes wild, she looks at me. I think she's dying; I blow her a kiss. She coughs and blows blood across the back of the seat and the side of my face. I think I love her. The switch.

I'm in excruciating pain. Oh, Christ. Nothing has hurt like this in my life. Pit-of-your-stomach sick pain. And it's dark—very dark—ink-black dark like a woman's mascara, black like a windowless basement. I can't tell what hurts anymore. It feels like my body is in pieces. I can't move.

Four lights overhead flip on. A woman in army-green nurse's garb leans over me, her auburn hair tucked into her surgical cap. I think there must be red lips beneath the mask. Searing pain from the shrapnel wounds in my gut, my ass, and my legs because of a Bouncing Betty. I wonder if her name is Betty, but now she's the doctor and the scalpel gleams like the spit-shined silverware in my mother's dining room. Utensils untouched by the stained enamel of relatives and the potbellied belching coworkers Pop used to bring home.

She slices into me and her soft crepe shoes make a farting sound on the tile that reminds me of sweaty thighs on vinyl. I gurgle blood out onto my shirt. I must look like a vampire buffet. She gives me the finger, then drives it deep into my gut, digging for the shrapnel buried in my bowels. I gasp for air like a freshly caught mackerel and she thinks I'm blowing her a kiss. She puts a bloodied hand to her mask and mimes a kiss back. My mind wanders, wondering if she's a Bouncing Betty. Maybe a Bobbing Betty. Did I say that out loud? A stabbing pain rockets to my brain. Switch.

I'm on a table. I'm strapped down, unable to move, with some sort of rubber chuck driven into my mouth. It has a hole so I can breathe. I feel vinyl beneath my hands and beneath my ass where the hospital gown doesn't quite close. I also notice that the braces that hold my head still are also coated in unnaturally green vinyl. I try to twist free, but the vinyl clings to my cheek like a kitchen table chair on a naked ass. I wonder why art deco was ever so popular. It was the art of chrome and strange squared angles, repeating, repeating, repeating, and forcing you to like it.

I'm sweating and I can feel it plastering the material of the hospital gown to my chest. I think it's a shame I don't have breasts, as I'm sure the thin material would show the darkness of my nipples and the doctor would get a hard-on. I hear her crying from the corner. I can see her in my mind's eye. Her lips red and her eyes just as red, crying what I am sure are crocodile tears. Her mascara running down her cheeks like some cheap imitation of Tammy Faye moved by the spirit of Jesus. I once thought I was Jesus. Hallelujah, I was wrong. The doctor, as if speaking through a mouthful of crackers, says, "Only one more," and I grasp the vinyl. I hear my fingers squawk across it as my teeth clamp down reflexively. For some reason I think of baked fish. He throws the switch.

* * *

The room is too bright. Even under the hood that is supposed to obscure my vision, I can tell the room is way too bright. I hear the deep voice of the warden swearing in the background. Jon Doe Executioner's voice counters. Something about the juice. Weak juice. I wonder if the sign on the door read FRESH SQUEEZED. The warden cries, "For Christ's sake get it right this time." I hear women crying and a man say this is seven. My hands hurt from the leather straps that hold them down. Something smells burnt, fishy . . . and I know it's me. So here I am in the death knell. I somehow thought it was grander, like waiting for a button to pop, or maybe a cherry, cherry red. I can smell the remnants of my last meal, fishy fish, the most fragrant of fish, baked mackerel with potatoes and peas. A special tribute to all my bouncing and bobbing Betties. I can feel the leather of the seat and back of the chair. I'm finally important enough for leather.

I think of her with her auburn hair and her lips so cherry red. She swished and swayed in her tight T-shirt, braless and unashamed. Her ass poured into her too tight jeans. Her thumb was cocked up in the air like some pagan phallic symbol and I stopped to give her a ride. And that I did. She offered me a blow job if I took her to Houston. I balked. She offered me vodka. I shot her with the .44 magnum I had under the seat. She squeak, squeak, squeaked against the seat of my station wagon, occasionally making the vague sound of flatulence as her skin caught on the vinyl. The blood from the single shot to her chest stuck me to her with each thrust. It plastered my T-shirt to her breasts. I held her dead hands above her head and when I was done, one fell to her mouth and bounced away almost like she blew me a kiss. I gave her the finger and pulled out my .44 and shot her again just to be sure. I held her and kissed her forehead and called her Momma even though she said her name was

Christa and I knew I'd left Momma for dead long ago. I buried her in the desert.

I hear the click before the jolt hits me. I hear the leather squawk as my shoulders strain against the backrest. Funny how I was wrong about flatulent chairs. Even leather sticks to searing flesh, fart, fart, farting as each jolt of electricity flows through me.

I wake up. I'm bound to a kitchen chair. Red vinyl on chrome. Mom's kitchen. It's Wednesday. Market-fresh mackerel cooks in the oven. The scent of orange juice heavy on my lips, its sticky sweetness running down my cheek. She touches me as my naked ass slides and groans back and forth. Sweaty vinyl, farting out my shame. The juice-hidden Stoli is a hot coal in my stomach even though it was ice cold from the freezer. I think of the weight of her tits on my thighs, her lips, her frantic and perverse suck, suck, sucking. I beg her to stop. Mom, please don't. She stops, then slaps me hard. She won't look me in the eye. She takes a drag off her cigarette and a haul off the bottle. Her breasts loll in her threadbare blouse, nipples like dark half-dollars peeking out. She grins and blows me a kiss. She reminds me sweetly to call her Betty and that she loves me. I'd give her the finger if my hands weren't bound. Then her auburn hair bobs away again. Vodka-driven pressure builds, then bursts, shooting. Shooting. Shooting into Betty, betrayed by my own gun. I love her even though I hate her. I close my eyes and succumb to the darkness, dark, like Betty's mascara. Whore black like my soul. Maybe someday I'll find a way to shut off the pain. Flip it off, you know, like a switch.

Big Load of Trouble

Greg Bardsley

I came through the front door and found Cujo and Angel snuggled in the kiddie pool. Nude and hairy. Tattooed legs intertwined. His beard flowing over her head like a kinky black wig, her arms around him, water beading atop his body fur. The television flashing raw footage of a white toy poodle trying to mount a morbidly obese opossum.

"Hey, dude, check it out. Animal Kingdom Humpathon, Volume Eight. Some little poodle's getting it on."

I stood over them. "Cujo, you promised."

He laughed at the screen, sighed happily, and glanced up at me. "So?"

"And so you're here."

Cujo lidded his eyes and grinned. "I am."

"You promised."

He cocked his head and gazed at the water, raising an eyebrow. "I did."

I tried to be stern. "I'm really disappointed, Cujo."

He looked at me for a moment, bit his lip, and broke into a prolonged cackle.

* * *

An hour later, I returned to the front room and tried again. The television was flashing shaky footage of two gerbils squeaking as they made fast and frantic love. Angel watched open-mouthed and laughed. "Duuuuu-uuuuu-uuuuude."

I stood over them again. "I'm surprised you're not bored."

Cujo kept his eyes on the screen. "Yeah?"

"I mean, I just figured you'd be more of a get-out-and-explore guy."

"Nah, it's better here." A gerbil squeaked extra loud, and Cujo giggled. "We love it here, bro."

They did look comfortable. They lay in the pool, happily soaking in a mealy mixture of dirty water and black body hair, all of which had reduced my roommate's kiddie-pool cleaner to a thrashing, moaning tangle of plastic. Drowning insects rolled around in the floating hair as others struggled to climb back onto Cujo. Empty cans of Coors Light and Colt 45 encircled the pool.

"Cujo, this isn't home." I paused. "You agreed."

Eyes still glued to the screen. "Hey, dude, have you heard? I'm an artist now."

What do you do?

What do you do when you have a six-foot-five, 295-pound Raiders fan in your house? A paroled Raiders fan you barely know. A friend of a friend; an acquaintance of an acquaintance, really. A large furry mass of delinquency and physical aggression. A big load of trouble soaking in your indoor kiddie pool, groping his new lover with this triumphant look on his face, like he's saying, *Look at what I can squeeze, bro.* A guy who doesn't like to work, a guy who'd rather get high in your kiddie pool, fuck in your kiddie pool, and doze off in your kiddie pool. A guy who has the goods on you, a guy who knows you can't call the cops and make him leave, on account of the illegal activities and substances that could be found in, and around, your rental house. A guy who knows that if you're gonna call the cops on him, you're gonna have to be okay with going to prison.

What do you do?

What you do is, you go to the fridge, pull out a Pale Ale, and take a long pull. And you lean against the counter and watch as he laughs and points at the television, the screen showing a couple of bush babies getting it on, their eyes extra large as they squeak and chitter and shiver.

And you stew, thinking of what he said.

Now he's an artist.

"Me and Angel got a gig tonight, dude."

I was still leaning against the counter, still nursing my beer. I had no idea what the hell he was talking about. "Gig?"

"Yeah, dude. Some artist chick saw me and Angel dancing around out front. Had my Black Hole clothes on." He let his eyes cross for a second. "She says we're artists."

Black Hole clothes. That would be the spiked dog collar, the black shoulder pads with spikes, the black cape fastened underneath, the little rubber horns attached to his frontal lobe, and the ass-kicker boots. Cujo liked to wear his Black Hole clothes when he was feeling frisky.

"Artist chick," I said, more to myself.

"Angel and I are grinding out there, and this hippie-looking piece of ass comes walking up and starts yammering about how much she likes the way I express myself. Next thing I know, she's writing directions to some fancy coffee place where they're doing some kind of performance-art thing all night. Café Popana or something. I guess we got the eight-thirty slot."

And then he broke into another prolonged cackle.

* * *

I lay on my bed in the back room and stared at the ceiling, reviewing my options one last time.

My out-of-town roommate, David, had a crop of cannabis skunk growing in the backyard. Big fat fuckers with huge buds. Probably worth ten thousand, he was saying. Everything had been going okay until Cujo and Angel paid us an unexpected visit, noticed the crop out back, and decided to use that knowledge to extort free lodging out of us until they had someplace better to go—which probably would be the game in Oakland this Sunday. If I called the cops, David and I could be spending the next year or two in orange jumpsuits. But if I let them hang out a few more days, the chances were they'd be gone by Saturday night, headed for the Black Hole, and that would be that. Only problem was, someone could get hurt by then.

After all, it was only Tuesday.

David was three hours away, visiting his dad in the hospital. I didn't want to bother him, but I was starting to think it was necessary. I sat up, grabbed the phone, and rolled the receiver from hand to hand, thinking about it one more time—at which point Cujo and Angel pushed through my door, dripped naked across the room, and slipped out my back window.

Cujo popped his head back in. "You got a pig out front, dude. We're not here."

The cop looked like a rookie—soft skin, rosy cheeks, a full head of blond hair. Even so, the sight of him there on my porch—in uniform, his radio buzzing every few seconds, the badge almost glowing—rushed blood to my face and shot convulsions to my stomach.

Harboring a parole violator. Growing pot. Fuck, I don't want to go to jail.

His eyes locked onto mine. "We have a problem in the neighborhood."

I stared back, feeling like a fucking idiot, my heart pounding, my eyelids fluttering, saliva welling up, my lower lip feeling like it was drooping past my chin.

"Have you seen a large bald man, long black beard, approximately six foot five, three hundred pounds, heavily tattooed?"

I feigned confusion. "What's happened?"

The cop smirked. "Well, let's see." He flipped open a tiny notebook. "I've got home invasion, theft, robbery, vandalism, assault."

"Home invasion?" I blurted.

"Got a house a few doors down saying they were watching TV when a bald bearded suspect entered their house, unplugged the television, and walked out with it."

I crinkled my brow and looked away. "No resistance?"

"No resistance." The cop referred to his notes. "Got another house where this guy walks through the front door, makes a beeline for the fridge, removes a twelve-pack and a pizza box, turns around, and exits the premises."

I mumbled to myself, "Raiding fridges."

The cop was staring at me now. "And he's cleaned out the entire block of car batteries."

My heart was pounding so hard I could feel it in my arms, but I knew what I had to do. I had to lie. "Wish I could help you."

The cop looked at the kiddie pool, then at my walls. "Who did this?"

"What do you mean?"

He laughed. "Are you kidding? The holes in your walls, the giant erection drawn over the sofa there."

"Oh, that." I looked down and scratched my head. "We just had a party that got too big, too rowdy"—I glanced up at him—"too quickly."

Studying my face. "Right."

* * *

I found them in my backyard shed, still naked, and sweating heavily. The odor in there was atrocious, a mix of warm rotting milk and body cavities, but Cujo didn't seem to mind. He was sitting on the unfinished plywood floor with Angel spread out beside him, belly up, snoring loudly. Stacked neatly to their left were the car batteries and the stolen TV set.

"You know what I do to Willards that don't knock?"

"We need to talk," I said.

"What I do is, I take their little heads and stick them between these two hairy beasts"—Cujo nodded to his tree-trunk legs—"and I give them the scissors."

"We need to establish some ground rules here."

He laughed. "The pig scare you?"

"Cujo, I don't want you stealing from my neighbors."

He gave me the serious eyes. "This ain't stealing. It's just a matter of survival of the fittest, and no one gets that." He nodded to his loot and puffed out his chest. "I take what I want because I'm the fittest."

"I don't care who's the fittest. It's not yours."

"No." His eyebrows turned in, and he pointed at me. "In the beginning, it wasn't mine. Now it's mine. It's right there."

I pulled my hair back and closed my eyes. "You're going to get me arrested."

"Chill, dude. We'll be gone soon enough. We got a gig tonight. Remember?"

And then that cackle.

When I reached the front doors of Café Popona that night, the show had already begun. Angel had just hog-tied a young man and was now dragging him behind the counter, drawing a loud round of applause from an audience of espresso-sipping patrons.

Fuck.

"Pardon." An older man slid past me and proceeded to the counter, at which point, Angel came from behind and whacked him on the head with a coffeehouse thermos. He crumpled to the floor, and a collective gasp came from the audience, followed by murmuring. A woman whispered, "Was that real? That looked real."

Angel sat on the floor, lodged the ball of her foot into his armpit, and yanked on his wedding band, gritting as she worked on the ring.

I came up and kicked Angel lightly in the boots. "Okay, fun's over."

Angel looked up and squinted. "You?" She stood up, grabbed a spool of twine off the counter, and began to hog-tie her victim. "This is art, dickwad. Take a look. You see anyone freaking out?" She finished with the twine, and the audience applauded.

I pointed at her. "You *will* give everything back."

"Like hell." Angel fingered through the man's wallet, stuffed three twenties down her front pocket, and threw the billfold at the audience, nailing a frail, goateed man in the face. "They love me."

A pretty woman with long brown hair and a purple peasant skirt glided towards me, her hands out like she was trying to prevent a stampede. "Stop right there," she snapped. "We don't need you."

"Believe me," I said, "you don't want this."

She still had her hands up. "If you can't comprehend what we're doing, don't intervene."

I was flabbergasted. "You really don't want Angel here," I said. "Seriously."

Her eyes narrowed. "Either you stop it with the censorship bullshit, or get out."

"No," I pleaded. "You don't understa—"

"No, *you* don't understand. This woman here is an arrrrtist." She leaned in for emphasis. "That's a person who creates with style and expression." She motioned to a lean, well-kept man exchanging observations with a young couple at a nearby table. "Ever since Tom and I moved up here from the city, this café has become an important venue for developing artists." Then she glanced at my old high-tops. "You people need to have your little rural-suburban worlds shaken up."

Angel stuffed a wad of napkins into her victim's mouth, sparking applause.

"Cujo and Angel aren't artists," I said. "They're—"

"Listen, John Boy." Her eyes popped and her face reddened. "If you can't handle art that is out of the box, if you think art is the Kmart oil painting in your daddy's farmhouse, this isn't the place for you. Just go back to your 'basic cable' and let the rest of us enjoy the performance."

Basic cable? I stared down at her for a long second. *Suit yourself, honey.*

Leaning against the side brick wall of the café, I started to rethink everything.

Shit, maybe it was possible. Maybe it was possible that Cujo and Angel had been expressing their artistic sides all their lives. Maybe, instead of embracing clay or watercolors or scrap metal, they'd simply chosen the timeless media of aggravated assault, armed robbery, forced entry, and so forth. Maybe they liked to make crime beautiful, or ugly, or something beyond mundane, something *not* banal. What the fuck did I know?

A large athletic guy walked through the doors, approached the counter, and was blindsided by Angel. Elbow hitting the jaw, making an awful noise. Audience clapping. Guy looking completely dumbfounded as he lost balance and crashed backwards into a tangle of chairs. People booing and hissing as he fought her off, made a run for the doors, and darted into the dark. A man fingering a cappuccino, snarling, "White trash."

A patron in a goatee and black-rimmed glasses looked up at me, his blue eyes giant behind the lenses. "This is marvelous."

He looked away and threw a hand into the air. "It's aggressive, it's delinquent, it's full of mischief." He turned back to me. "I think what we're witnessing here is the birth of something so primal, so base, and yet so graceful and compelling that the only term coming to mind right now is Criminal Performance Art."

Someone in the audience yelled, "A second artist, a second artist," and all eyes turned to a large, dark figure dance-walking at the back of the café, near the milk steamers. Decked out in his Black Hole clothes, Cujo stretched a furry arm over the granite countertop and bulldozed the poppy seed cake wedges, lemon bars, glass platters, and tea packets—all of it crashing to the cement floor in a deafening spectacle.

The crowd gasped. The café owners winced.

Most of the patrons suddenly got it and began to scatter. Some made a mad dash for the front door as Cujo tripped a horrified man, bent over, and relieved him of his wallet. "All right, ladies," he roared. "It's time to quit your bitching. You pencil necks wanted performance art, you got it. Who's first?"

Someone shrieked.

I took a step forward and scratched my head.

Angel began to empty the cash register.

Purple Peasant Skirt squeaked from under a table, "I trust this is art."

Cujo turned, squatted, and peeked under the table. "You call something art, I call it making money." He took her hand, yanked hard, and rolled her into a headlock right there on the floor, making it look effortless. She squirmed and clawed at his arms as Tom stood ten feet away, in shock, frozen. "I can take a dump on you right now, and if some pinner says it's art, that's what it is. If no one's moaning about art, it's just a matter of me pinching a loaf on your back. The word *art* don't mean shit, do it?"

Finally, the distant echo of sirens.

Cujo tightened his lock on Peasant Skirt. "When the pigs ask, what are you gonna tell 'em?"

She gurgled and gasped.

The hairy arms tightened. "You're gonna tell 'em this was art."

She gasped. Tom touched his chin and took a step closer.

Sirens getting louder.

"Aren't ya?"

She moaned yes.

"Because that's what it is, sweetie—crazy-ass art. Art that fucks you up."

She tugged at his arms.

"And when they ask about tonight, you're gonna say it was all a big misunderstanding. You're gonna say some people just didn't 'get it,' just didn't understand what we were doing here, what kind of performance art we were creating here tonight."

Sirens closer.

Angel threw a Glad bag of loot over her shoulder. "It's getting late, honey." She tugged at Cujo. "We should thank our hosts and say goodnight."

Cujo released Peasant Skirt, who scampered on all fours to the front of the café. Tom chased after her with an open mouth and outstretched hands.

Sirens approaching.

Cujo looked around the ravaged café. "The party poopers are almost here," he said, and followed Angel to the back door, "which means it's time to make haste."

I stood there a moment, then ran after them. There was no way I was going to be the one answering all the cops' questions tonight. I just wanted to go home and forget the whole thing. I just wanted to sit on the couch, nurse a beer, and enjoy the silence with the comfortable knowledge that Cujo and Angel were speeding out of town, away from here, away from the cops, away from my home, away from me.

Cujo was waiting in the alley.

He looked down and smiled, his lids heavy. "Go fetch old Cujo a bucket of KFC and bring it back to your place." He glanced at Angel with a hungry moan, and she leered back. "We'll take it in the kiddie pool."

Violated

Mike Sheeter

Bill Gurevich's first parolee of the day was a tier-one mope named Sheldon. Sheldon was fifty-seven, a weepy ex–middle school band teacher and statutory rapist.

Gurevich was forty-nine, a retired Los Angeles County Sheriff's deputy. He ran the sex offender detail at the California Board of Pardon and Parole's Van Nuys office, where he presided over eighty or ninety of these court-mandated interviews every week.

The ex-felons he supervised had been locked down for offenses ranging in severity from weenie wagging in the park to tossing a ten-month-old infant out of the window of a municipal bus.

Gurevich checked Sheldon's pay stubs to make sure he was showing up regularly for his new job at the car wash.

Sheldon was afraid of the other parolees, so Gurevich walked him out through a waiting room full of fidgeting ex-cons, and down the hall to the elevators.

On the way back, he stopped at the check-in counter and

rapped his knuckles on the bulletproof partition. Tasha the receptionist looked up from her magazine.

"I've got a citizen coming to see me today, a Mrs. Sheila Halpert," Gurevich said. "Be extra nice to her and call me the second she gets here, okay?"

Tasha shrugged, disengaging the electronic security door. Gurevich returned to his cubicle, got his electric razor out of his desk, and gave himself a quick once-over. He wasn't looking forward to sitting across a desk from Sheila Halpert. One of his new parolees had abducted and raped her daughter.

Gurevich accessed the Department of Corrections database, calling up Richard Lencheski's prison records and psychiatric reports.

Lencheski was a tier-two offender, released after doing a dime, first at Camarillo, then at San Luis Obispo.

He was six weeks out of the halfway house, still under full electronic surveillance. A vocational training course behind the walls had earned Lencheski his current, real world job as a baker's helper. The parolee had been fully compliant since his release date, at least on paper.

Ten years ago, Lencheski had accosted the Halpert girl at a Panorama City playground, feeding her a crushed ice drink laced with codeine cough syrup before he abducted her in his camper truck. Several hours later, when he dropped her off at a bus stop, his nine-year-old victim was catatonic, with deep fingernail scratches and bite marks.

Gurevich looked at Lencheski's prison ID photo. The guy was one of the rare sex offenders who looked the part, with fish-belly white jailhouse skin and scraggly, untrimmed eyebrows that reminded Gurevich of ticking oozing out of a flophouse mattress.

Gurevich glanced up from his computer monitor, startled, as the security lock buzzed someone through.

Thanks a bunch for the heads-up, Tasha, he thought.

He slipped on his jacket and stepped out into the corridor. Sheila Halpert strode towards him, hand extended.

Her pleasant expression caught him off guard.

Mrs. Halpert had been a fixture on the evening news since Lencheski's release. When she agitated to abolish the parole system on the state house steps, or picketed Lencheski's home with her supporters, all four local news stations ran with it.

On the tube she wore a boonie hat covered with campaign buttons and a trademark T-shirt—a yellow one—with an iron-on picture of her daughter on the front. Today, though, she was going low-key and professional in a designer suit.

Lauren Halpert would be a young adult by now. As Gurevich shook hands with her mother, he wondered how Lauren was getting along these days. He decided not to ask.

He ushered Mrs. Halpert into his cubicle. She sidestepped the stacks of file folders surrounding his desk and took a seat, checking out the wanted fliers for parole absconders covering his walls.

Gurevich offered coffee and she shook her head.

He said, "You look different in person."

"That's because I'm wearing my work clothes," she said. "If you want any media coverage in this town you have to turn yourself into a cartoon character. When the camera crews show up, I pop into a phone booth and change into in my Vigilante Mom outfit."

Gurevich was still trying to think of a tactful way to say what he needed to when she beat him to the punch.

"I know why you asked me to come in," she said.

"You do?"

"Sure," she said, "you want me to lay off Lencheski. That's not going to happen."

Well, there it was.

Gurevich made his voice flat and official.

"Mrs. Halpert, let me caution you. If you and your supporters get somebody worked up enough to take Lencheski off the count, you'll be subject to prosecution."

"Call me Sheila," she said. "I'm a paralegal, Mr. Gurevich. If I need any legal advice I'll ask one of the lawyers I work with."

"How about meeting me halfway?"

"What did you have in mind?"

"You want to raise public awareness or campaign for new legislation? Great, I'll sign your petition. But stop surrounding the man's house. And call off those shock-jock buddies of yours."

"Shortstack and Poppa Pete?" Sheila said, looking amused. "I don't control those wild men."

"C'mon, Sheila. They're practically offering a bounty on Lencheski's scalp. Somebody's liable to take them seriously and kill him."

"What a tragic loss to humanity that would be, huh?"

Gurevich shook his head. "I'm a parent too. I don't condone or excuse anything Lencheski has done," he said. "But the man's under the protection and supervision of this office. So I'm asking you . . . I'm begging you, disband the lynch mob before everything spins out of control."

"The system's out of control, not me," she said.

She picked up the framed photograph of Gurevich's wife and daughter on his desk and examined it.

He had taken the photograph last spring, in the front yard of his heavily mortgaged ranch house in Mar Vista.

It showed Kay and Annie, his two redheads, side by side in golden late afternoon light, planting a rosebush. They wore matching straw sun hats. Annie, his little girl, looked like a solemn porcelain miniature of her mom.

"Precious," Sheila said. "How old is she?"

"She just turned nine."

"And you keep her picture right out here on your desk, where your parolees can see it?"

"It hasn't been a problem," Gurevich said.

He was lying. During Lencheski's first visit to the office Gurevich had noticed the parolee's gaze keep returning to his wife and daughter's image. It had taken every scrap of his professionalism not to bat Lencheski out of the chair with a telephone book.

"Tell me something. God forbid, but what would you do if it was your little girl that animal assaulted?"

"I'm not going to answer that," Gurevich said.

Richard Lencheski lived in the Hollywood wastelands near Yucca and Wilcox, in one of the last bungalow courts from the '30s. The bungalows were crisscrossed with earthquake cracks and patched with battleship-gray driveway sealant. The eight-unit court stood on a cul-de-sac lined with smog-blackened royal palms and twenty-year-old cars.

Lencheski began his day kneeling in the box of gravel at the side of his bed, petitioning the Holy Ghost to turn away the wrath of his enemies.

Sheila Halpert was outside with her electric bullhorn, exhorting her followers against him.

His windows rattled in time with the vibrations of her voice. Their hateful call-and-response chants were the first sounds Richard heard every morning. They had been for three weeks now. He wondered if she had any TV trucks out there with her today. Or maybe a gun.

Before he stepped into the shower, he wound plastic cling wrap around his electronic ankle bracelet. He stood under the pinpoint spray, scrubbing his genitals with a loofah until they were raw. After five minutes under the icy water his teeth started chattering. He toweled off and went into his bedroom to dress for work.

He swallowed a couple of Excedrin with his coffee, lingering over it until he couldn't ignore the blinking clock on his microwave any longer.

Crowd or no crowd, he needed to be at work soon. Janet, his boss, had a thing about punctuality. Janet was an ex-con too, had hung some bad paper back in the day. She knew about his registered sex offender status, but she never mentioned it.

All he did at work was clean up, watch the timers, and measure out ingredients from recipe cards. The bakery was his refuge. But first he had to get there in one piece. He went into his living room, leaned the detached front wheel of his ten-speed bike against the sofa, and peered through the venetian blinds at the demonstrators waiting for him to come outside.

One of them saw him looking and shied an egg at him. Lencheski jumped back as it smashed against the pane. The protesters jeered and whistled.

There must have been thirty people milling around on the narrow strip of grass between his place and the street. Most of them carried homemade picket signs. There were even some children out there.

He thought, *Jesus, why aren't those kids in school? What are they supposed to be anyway, bait?*

He dug out his parole officer's card and dialed.

"Sexual offender detail, Bill Gurevich."

Lencheski said, "Mr. Gurevich, they're demonstrating in front of my house again. I need help getting to work."

"I can't be holding your hand every day," Gurevich said. "You wanted out, you got out. Now deal with it."

"But they're all charged up. Sheila Halpert was on the news again last night, accusing me of all kinds of vile crap I never did."

"I called her in here and warned her," Gurevich said. "If she's slandering you, call your lawyer."

Lencheski said, "I can't lose my job, Mr. Gurevich. It's all I've got going for me."

"If I drop by there unannounced, am I going to find any contraband?"

"No, sir, you won't."

Gurevich sighed heavily and said, "You been to the clinic this week?"

"I got my Depo-Provera shot yesterday."

"Okay, but this is the last time, Richard, you hear me? From now on, if you're being threatened, call the cops. I'll honk when I'm out front."

Call the cops? Lencheski thought as he hung up.

Me? Yeah, right.

Lencheski stuffed magazines inside his waistband to protect his belly, liver, and kidneys and put on his bicycle helmet, pulling the chinstrap snug.

The raised scars on his torso reminded him of the day he got shanked. They made him wait for it in prison too.

It happened midway through his sixth week in general pop. At first he thought he had been sucker punched.

Then came a scalding sensation as blood welled out of his shirt, pints of it saturating the cloth, speckling his running shoes and the grass at his feet.

Some Chicano dude, an Aztec Warrior from C block, had rolled up on his blind side in the exercise yard, punching a cement-sharpened shard of Plexiglas into his belly. His attacker waggled the jailhouse dagger like a stick shift as the two of them went down in a tangle, the Cholo on top, running the gears inside him.

Richard felt like he was freezing to death in July. He blacked out from shock and blood loss. On the gurney, he regained consciousness just long enough to ask a CO why he'd waited for so long to pull the guy off him.

The screw said, "Because I have kids too, scumbag."

Don't ever let them get you on the ground, he told himself. They do, and you won't be getting up again.

"This neighborhood's a zero-tolerance zone for sex perverts!" Sheila's electrified voice boomed.

Twenty-five minutes later, he heard Gurevich's car horn. Lencheski took a series of rapid breaths, hoisted his bicycle wheel high, using it as a shield, and bolted out the front door.

Walking fast, eyes down, Lencheski shouldered his way through the mob and unchained his bike from the telephone pole out front. Gurevich stood at the curb by his state-issue sedan, the trunk open, watching him approach.

The crowd was surging closer now, starting to throw stuff, more eggs and a few soda cans.

Lencheski tossed his bike into Gurevich's Chevy and scrambled into the shotgun seat.

As they pulled away from the curb, Sheila yelled through her bullhorn, "You believe what you're seeing? Child molesters get limo service! Our tax dollars in action, right?"

Lencheski and Gurevich rode past the Cyrillic- and Hebrew-lettered storefronts of the Fairfax District without speaking to each other.

The Chevy turned west onto Pico Boulevard and pulled to the curb in front of Dharma Buns just as the neon sign over the doorway flickered on.

The pink and yellow bakery's logo featured a blissed-out Buddha sitting on a cupcake in the lotus position.

Gurevich spotted Janet behind the counter and said, "Go punch in, Richard. I need to talk to your boss."

Lencheski took his bike around back and chained it up. He let himself in the delivery door, went to his locker, and changed into his baker's whites.

Out front, Gurevich walked up and down and peered into the display cases while Janet ignored him.

She was using an icing sleeve, edging a big sheet cake with a wavy pink border. Gurevich inspected the cake. There was a photo-realistic portrait imprinted on the frosting, a good likeness of a beaming black lady in her sixties. Probably for her retirement party, Gurevich decided.

"How's our boy been getting along?"

"Real good."

Janet put the cake into a pink Dharma Buns box and wiped her hands on her apron, giving him her Frontera Women's Prison deadpan.

Gurevich said, "Richard has enemies, you know? Somebody might come in here looking to harm him."

She said, "You want me to fire him?"

"No," Gurevich said, "but for his safety and yours, keep an eye on any customers you haven't seen before."

"Richard stays in the back. He never deals with customers."

"And he never has any contact with kids in here either, is that right?"

Janet shook her head. "No way," she said. "He's scared to death of kids, and just about everybody else."

Gurevich said, "What about that computer? Does he ever use it to go online?"

Janet shook her head. "I doubt he even knows how to turn it on. It's just for special orders, like picture cakes."

"I was wondering how you did those," Gurevich said. "The pictures on top are pretty realistic."

"Nothing to it," Janet said. "Watch."

She brought the monitor to life and clicked on a desktop icon. The same black lady's face Gurevich had noticed before appeared on the screen.

In seconds, the printer disgorged a semitransparent sheet imprinted with the woman's picture. It resembled amber cellophane. Janet broke off a corner and offered it to Gurevich. It tasted gummy, like a fruit roll-up.

"A customer sends a digital image or brings me a photo and I scan it," Janet said. "The transfer medium is made of spun sugar and shortening. The image prints out as an overlay and bonds to the frosting after a few minutes in the oven. It's the same technique scam artists use to get the Virgin Mary onto a tortilla."

"Thanks for showing me," Gurevich said.

He took one of his cards out of his wallet and put it down on the counter in front of her.

She looked at it, but made no move to take it.

He said, "If anybody hassles you, call 911 and give the officers my card as soon as they get here, okay?"

After a few seconds, Janet picked the card up, slipping it into the pocket of her apron.

Gurevich pointed to a tray of crullers in the display case and said, "These look good. What d'you call them?"

"Dharma Doughnuts," she said. "You want one?"

"Sure, that'd be nice," Gurevich said.

Janet picked up a donut with a pair of tongs, wrapped it in wax paper, and said, "Eighty-five cents."

Annie was carrying the conversational load tonight, chattering away about fourth grade politics. Kay's strained silence during dinner told Gurevich something was worrying her.

She sat with her eyes down, picking at her food. Gurevich couldn't tell if she was fretting about finances or fuming about something he'd done. Marital telepathy warned him that whatever it was, Kay didn't want him to mention it in front of Annie.

Annie finished eating and went into the living room to watch TV. Gurevich helped Kay clear the table.

When they were alone in the kitchen, Kay took a letter out of her purse and handed it to him. He went over to the island and read it under the overhead light. It was a parental alert on the letterhead of the Los Angeles Unified School District's School Police.

A man with a telephoto-lens camera had been spotted taking pictures of kids on the playground at Annie's school. School police officers had attempted to detain and question the guy, but he escaped on a ten-speed bike.

The unknown suspect was late middle-aged, Caucasian, medium height and weight with bushy eyebrows, wearing white pants and a dark blue sweatshirt.

Gurevich's throat tightened up.

He pictured Lencheski gliding up to his daughter on his bike as she walked home, gaining her trust, offering her one of his doped-up fountain drinks.

Still darker images from his days as a sheriff's deputy came back to him, memories of cadaver dogs and methane probes, of explorer scouts and police academy cadets grid-searching a brushy hillside, one of the dog handlers calling out as he spotted a backpack under some leaves—Jesus—and then the first heart-stopping glimpse of those little white legs . . .

Kay said, "I hoped you'd know who to call about this."

Gurevich refolded the letter and stuffed it back into its envelope. He stepped over to the refrigerator and poured himself some milk.

He felt her eyes on his back and took a few seconds before he answered her.

He sipped some milk and said mildly, "Don't worry about it, babe. I'll take care of it tomorrow after work."

Kay said, "Oh, Bill, that'll be great."

Lencheski stood at the foot of the cul-de-sac on his ten-speed, scanning the shadows for potential ambushers.

The demonstrators were gone.

He glided down the street as quietly as he could. He dismounted the bike and stood on the sidewalk in front of the bungalow court with the rubber-coated security chain in his hands, watching and listening.

There was no foot traffic, no one lurking in a parked car. He detached the front wheel and padlocked the ten-speed's frame to a light pole.

He started to relax as he approached his bungalow, the bike's front wheel on his shoulder.

His front door opened from the inside and the light over the stoop flicked on. Lencheski braced for an attack.

"Getting in a little late, aren't you, Richard?" Gurevich said. "What have you been up to this evening?"

"Racking up some overtime," Lencheski said, relieved. "We had a rush order on a wedding cake."

Gurevich stepped aside. Lencheski entered the bungalow. The place had been tossed, furniture overturned, all his stuff strewn around.

"Did somebody break in here?" Lencheski said.

"Yeah, me," Gurevich said. "These crappy locks of yours, all I needed was a credit card. Probably don't see many of those in this neighborhood, though. Don't you have anything worth stealing here, Richard?"

"Just my bike and my TV is all."

"What about a camera? Maybe with a telephoto lens?"

"What's this about, Mr. Gurevich? What are you looking for?"

"We'll talk after I finish my inspection."

Gurevich walked into the bedroom.

Lencheski followed him and watched him yank the dresser drawers out, dumping their contents on the floor.

Gurevich kicked apart the jumble of T-shirts, socks, and shorts with his shoe. He turned his attention to the closet, rattling wire hangers as he pulled pants and coat pockets inside out.

Lencheski said, "Like I said before, I don't keep any contraband here, Mr. Gurevich."

"Keep your mouth shut until I tell you different," Gurevich said. *The camera is probably in his locker at the bakery*, he thought. *If I find it, he's going back inside on the next bus.*

He looked at the bowl-shaped piece of frosted glass that shielded the overhead lightbulbs. There was a dark rectangular shadow behind it.

Gurevich dragged a chair over and stood on it, retrieving the hidden object. A moment later he stepped back down, staring at the bottle of terpin hydrate and codeine elixir in his hand.

"I never saw that before," Lencheski said.

Gurevich slipped the codeine into his pocket. He grabbed Lencheski by the collar and punched him under the heart. Lencheski cawed in distress and jackknifed forward.

Gurevich took hold of Lencheski's greasy hair, yanked him upright, and said, "What'd I tell you about talking?"

Lencheski struggled to reinflate his lungs, his eyes and nose streaming. Gurevich shoved him into the nearest corner and resumed his search.

He flipped Lencheski's stained mattress off its metal frame.

There was a pink pastry box from Dharma Buns under the bed. Gurevich opened the box and looked inside.

It was a cake with white butter frosting, its top bearing a photo-realistic image of a little redheaded girl on a playground swing set. Her denim skirt was billowing high on her thighs, her legs akimbo.

Her feet and ankles had been partially eaten away. The tines of a fork had scored deep gouges into her abdomen.

It was a likeness of nine-year-old Annie Gurevich, a candid shot taken during recess at her school.

Gurevich came into the office a half hour late the next day and told Tasha to reschedule all his interviews.

He closed the door to his cubicle and booted up his computer. When the California Department of Justice site came up, he launched the appropriate application and typed in Richard Lencheski's parole number and the code number of his electronic surveillance anklet.

Seconds later a map of Hollywood and West Los Angeles appeared on his monitor. The map showed a series of yellow dots superimposed on a grid of city streets, along with a time code. Annie's school was at the terminus of the dots.

Gurevich was still staring at the electronic map overlay five minutes later when Tasha transferred a call from the West L.A. Sheriff's homicide dicks.

Gurevich took the call, listened for a moment, and said, "Yeah, he's one of mine, all right."

He checked out a Chevy and drove to Lencheski's bungalow. When he arrived at the cul-de-sac, Sheila Halpert and her supporters were nowhere to be seen.

Today's crowd consisted of two sheriff's radio cars, an SUV from the Scientific Investigations Unit, and a white panel van from the medical examiner's office.

Gurevich showed his credentials to the scene control officer and signed the log. He ducked under the yellow police line tape, and went into Lencheski's bungalow.

He followed the sound of voices into the bedroom. Two sheriff's detectives were standing over Lencheski's corpse.

The older of the two men was a friend.

Joe Coyne had been one of Gurevich's training officers when he started with the sheriff's. Joe was beefier now, but still looked like the UCLA wrestler he had once been. The other detective was Bert Engelman, a twenty-something ex-marine, Coyne's latest detective trainee.

He shook hands with both men as Joe introduced Gurevich to his partner. "I knew Bill when he used to work for a living," Coyne said.

Gurevich avoided looking at Lencheski's body and said,

"What can I tell you? I got too old to chase 'em. Now all I do is check their ear tags."

"Somebody tagged this homeboy real good," Engelman said. "Beat the crap out of him, then crammed cake and frosting down his gullet until he suffocated."

"Sweets to the sweet, huh?" Gurevich said.

The medical examiner yanked a probe out of the dead man's liver and made a note.

Lencheski's face was smeared with cake and frosting, his eyes open, his dislocated jaw agape. What remained of the cake was still in its box at Lencheski's side, smashed, the picture on its top obliterated.

"Anybody you like for this?" Joe Coyne said.

Gurevich said, "You know about the Halpert woman, right?"

"She was the first one I thought of too," Coyne said, "but we can place her with her husband last night. He's LAPD, a lieutenant at Newton Division. They were in Palm Springs when this went down, attending the D.A.R.E. To Keep Kids Off Drugs Golf Tournament."

"Hell of an alibi," Gurevich said.

"Partner, give us a minute, okay?" Coyne said.

Engelman stepped out of the room. Coyne took Gurevich's arm and led him a few steps away, out of the ME's hearing.

"I hear what you're saying," Coyne said. "Maybe it's too good. Maybe the husband leveraged a snitch or another ex-con into whacking Lencheski for him. Or hell, maybe it was one of the wife's supporters."

Gurevich said, "Yeah, any of that's plausible."

"Between you and me, though, this diaper-sniper son of a bitch got what he deserved," Coyne said. "He molested a cop's kid. So screw him, I'm writing this one up as a bottom-of-the-pile residential burglary gone wrong."

"I've got no problem with that," Gurevich said.

"Glad you feel that way, Bill," Coyne said. "LAPD or sheriff's or corrections, none of that interagency turf war crap matters now. This one's still in the family. And we take care of our own, right?"

Gurevich watched the ME's men wrap Lencheski's body in a sheet and lift it onto their gurney.

"If we don't, who will?" he said.

Black Sun

Gary Carson

I

Duke pulled into Colfax after a brutal deadhead—two days through Colorado and Nevada, a blur of truck stops, crank, and short blackouts in the cab.

Nobody gave him a second look. He dropped the rig at the lot, grabbed some food, then crashed for ten hours at a Super 8 on the highway. The radio alarm blasted him awake: Art Bell talking UFOs and gray aliens on Coast-To-Coast A.M. It was four in the morning—the Day Of Revenge. He got some coffee, then walked over to pick up his load.

Moths swarmed an arc light over the lot gate. The warehouse used to be a transload facility for animal feed, but now it was the staging ground for the end of the world. Duke shivered and rang the bell. A bolt lock clicked. The old man opened the door, his shadow fanning across the dock in a frame of yellow light.

"Ever'thing's ready." Gramps passed over keys and papers, his hand knotted with tendons, a Black Sun tattoo on his wrist—the symbol of infinite light and the secret philosophy. "They finished loadin' an hour ago. Cleaned up good. I put the switch under the radio." He squinted, his eyes cloudy. "Red knob on a black box. Turn it all the way to the right . . . that's all she wrote." He lit a Pall Mall, the match flaring in his cataracts. "Ten thousand pounds of ammonium nitrate and fuel oil primed with TNT. It's stable enough, but you flip that switch in the middle of the span and they'll never know what hit them."

Duke didn't say anything. He stared at the blacktop, watching a beetle crawl over a broken bottle.

"We won't forget." The old man shook his hand. "Ain't nobody gone forget what you done."

Duke's rig was a Mack, six axles, with twin exhausts and a forty-foot trailer. He pulled himself into the cab, strapped in, and turned it over. The diesel caught and rumbled, pipes muttering, and he could feel the vibrations down the levels of his spine. He backed out with a clash of gears, braked in a wheeze of hydraulics. The old man stood in the headlights, giving him the Roman salute.

Duke worked the transmission, put it in low, then clattered out of the lot, banging over potholes on the way to I-80. A quarter moon drifted through clouds over the Sierra, watching him like an ancient eye.

Next stop: rush hour on the Bay Bridge.

II

The feds had him under surveillance the whole time. Duke spotted one of their tail cars, but it fell back on the highway and he never saw it again.

Hunched over the wheel, he rolled through New England Mills, Weimar, and Heater Glenn, heading towards Sacramento and the Central Valley. Taillights floated through the dark and the wind fluttered in the vents. He turned on the radio as the sun cracked the mountains, glinting on Lake Combie west of the Placer Hills.

The radio spewed trash and propaganda. Punching buttons, he skipped over the news: a Viagra commercial, some hip-hop, and a spot for the latest diet pill. A shock jock asked a stripper her cup size, then cut to a break.

The pawn in the White House ranted about militias and right-wing extremists.

Duke turned it off. He ran nasty flashbacks.

Two months ago, his son died in Iraq, his wife divorced him, and he volunteered to blow himself up to kick-start the Revolution. When he came to his senses, it was too late to change his mind. You're our driver, his cell leader told him. Die for the Race or we'll blow your head off.

A meth bust had saved his life.

The BATF knocked down his door a couple weeks later and popped him with five pounds of crystal, sixty grand in cash, a sawed-off Mossberg, and a copy of the *Turner Diaries*. He flipped after a six-hour talk with the feds downtown. Thirty years or rat off The Order—that was the deal. ZOG needed a high-profile bust to justify the War on Terror.

Duke caved. He turned informer.

Call it a sweet relief.

III

The feds were waiting for him at a rest stop a couple miles from Clipper Gap. Duke pulled in and parked the rig by the johns; then he climbed down from the cab and walked over to a white van and a panel truck parked by the exit. Dawn bled over the dark hills. Bugs clouded the lights by the picnic shelter and the air smelled like crap and damp grass.

"Give me the keys." Special Agent Johnson of the Internal

Security Division stood by the van in his trench coat, smoking a cigarette. The van door opened and a couple of goons stepped out, carrying tool kits and wearing body armor under vests marked BOMB DISPOSAL. Duke gave Johnson the keys and he passed them to one of the goons. "Take your time, okay? We don't want any accidents."

"They rigged the primer to a switch," Duke said. "Black box with a red knob under the radio."

"That's what they told you anyway."

Voices babbled on a scanner in the van. Five suits wearing headset mikes got out of the panel truck and walked over to the rig, circling the trailer, checking the cab while the bomb guys unpacked their gear on the blacktop.

"You had a tail." Johnson blew a smoke ring. He looked like an insurance salesman, but he had the eyes of a robot. "The CHP pulled them over a couple miles back."

"I ain't surprised."

"Two skinheads in a black Ford," Johnson said. "They were there to make sure you didn't back out."

Duke didn't say anything.

"We'll disarm the bomb." Johnson checked his watch. "Don't worry about that."

"Why not stop it here?" Duke asked. "You got the truck. You can round them up any time."

Johnson shook his head. "We need you to follow the original plan all the way to the end." He crushed out his cigarette and shoved his hands in his pockets, watching the disposal team open the trailer doors and climb inside Duke's truck. "Drive into the city and stop on the bridge per instructions. We'll have three teams on you the whole way and we'll stage the bust in the middle of the commute—right in the middle of rush-hour traffic." He smiled to himself. "The Director wants maximum exposure before the budget hearings next month, so just stick to the program."

"What happens then?"

"We'll have a Nazi roundup on Prime-Time Live." Johnson shrugged. "You go into Witness Protection."

IV

The show hit the road.

Johnson and his team followed Duke through Sacramento as a red and bloated sun came up over the Central Valley. Clouds piled over dairy farms and orchards on the horizon. Dust devils whirled through grubby towns full of wetbacks and bikers.

Duke listened to CB chatter, watching the traffic in the rearview. He spotted the white van a couple times, hanging back in the cruise lane, but he knew there were a dozen cars around him—feds watching his every move, tracking the beeper they had planted in his cab. A helicopter dogged him for a while, then circled to the west and vanished.

The miles ticked by at sixty-five. Dixon. Vacaville. He spaced on the highway, bugs spattering the windshield, the rig bouncing over ruts in the road. He wasn't worried about setting off the bomb; the disposal team had pulled the primers and clipped the leads on the switch—he could see the wires lying on the floor. The load was inert, Johnson had told him when he handed back the keys. Duke was hauling a trailer full of fertilizer and oil: ten thousand pounds of rolling dud.

Fairfield. Suisun City.

The traffic got worse, the rig struggling on the hills in American Canyon. He checked the radio and caught a news report: fifty dead in Baghdad, a car bomb at a mosque, mortar fire on the Green Zone. He flashed on his son—dead at twenty in a war based on lies. He saw his wife split with her luggage, burned out on hate and fear, the meth deals and bikers, the Aryans plotting revolution, and the downfall of ZOG. It's all over, she had said. It don't matter anymore.

"The Director of the new Internal Security Division denied reports that he plans to step down," the radio jabbered. "Faced with growing criticism in Congress, he said that budget cuts and opposition to his new guidelines for domestic surveillance threaten the security of the country. In a statement released today, the director accused his critics of downplaying the threat of domestic terrorism, calling them appeasers playing politics with the lives of American citizens. It may already be too late, he said, to stop the next attack."

Duke turned it off. He wiped his hands on his jeans.

He made Vallejo, passing Mare Island, then stalled in gridlock on the Carquinez Bridge. The bay glittered below, rippled by gusts, sails cluttering the water off Novato. He saw the helicopter again, circling the bridge like a dragonfly, its rotors flashing when they caught the light. When he checked the rearview, he spotted the white van two cars back, stuck behind a Beemer in the slow lane. He thought about ditching the truck, but he couldn't do it. Johnson had threatened to charge his wife as an accomplice if he crapped out on their deal.

The traffic started moving again.

He drove through Richmond and El Cerrito, rolling past Golden Gate Fields and Eastshore State Park. The Berkeley Hills spread to the east and San Francisco rose on the peninsula on the other side of the bay, the skyscrapers in the Financial District a jumble of glass and steel in the haze of the Pacific. He had made it on schedule: 8:15 a.m., the height of the morning commute. Eight lanes of traffic crawled along the water, thousands of cars and trucks heading to work in all directions.

He was sweating, his heart thumping, his hands damp on the wheel.

The Bay Bridge loomed ahead, eight miles long, the east span running from Oakland to the tunnel on Yerba Buena Island, the west span with its double decks and suspension towers connecting the island to San Francisco. The feeder highways had backed up for miles and the westbound commute flickered on the upper deck of the bridge, five lanes of traffic crawling bumper-to-bumper, windshields flashing two hundred feet above the water. A quarter of a million cars, trucks, and buses crossed the bridge every day.

The Order had picked its target well.

Duke followed the Eastshore Freeway and merged with the traffic backed up at the toll plaza. Metering lights flashed in a haze of exhaust. Horns blared. Cars maneuvered for position at the gates. Twenty minutes later, he paid the six-axle toll and started up the bridge, checking both his mirrors as fifteen lanes converged into five on the truss causeway. Rising on the east span, he could see Alcatraz, Angel Island, Tiburon, and the San Rafael Bridge miles to the north. Dark clouds piled over the Pacific.

He entered the Yerba Buena Tunnel, an echo chamber full of exhaust, brake lights, and glossy windshields. The pulse ticked in his throat. He licked his lips, squeezing the wheel and checking the rearview. The white van had vanished in the flood of traffic. He hadn't seen it for miles.

The commute had bogged down somewhere ahead and it took ten minutes to reach the end of the tunnel. When he came out on the west span, the traffic stopped completely, moved forward, then stopped again. He took a breath, then put the rig in neutral and turned off the engine, settling back in his seat to wait for Johnson and his goons to stage their big arrest.

The white van was behind him somewhere and he knew there were feds all around him, tracking his beeper, talking back and forth on their radios. They would have to get out and run through the stalled cars, block off the traffic, shut down the bridge in the middle of the commute. It was going to be a mess. The traffic would back up for miles, engines overheating, cars running out of gas. Johnson was going to get his publicity.

When the traffic started moving again, he just sat there,

waiting to get arrested. The drivers trapped in his lane pounded on their horns, but they couldn't get around the truck and the noise got louder and louder. Duke closed his eyes, thinking about his wife. He had trials ahead, years of testifying against The Order, but when he finally got clear, maybe he could save his marriage, try to put it together again with a fake name in the Witness Protection Program.

Someone pounded on his door and he opened his eyes, expecting to see Johnson or one of his goons holding a badge up to the window, but it was some angry commuter yelling at him to move the rig or get on his radio for a tow. Duke flipped him off and closed his eyes again. For the first time in months, he felt kind of relaxed. It was over. He had delivered his load.

Then the cell phone hidden under his seat started to ring and the wireless pulse triggered the primer.

A black sun opened in his head.

Infinite light.

Darkness.

Nothing.

V

The explosion vaporized the truck and destroyed five lanes of traffic, cars and buses flying apart as the fireball flashed across the span and the shock wave punched a hole in the deck, smashing windshields a hundred yards away, scattering axles and tires and engine blocks as the blast echoed through the city. Cars tumbled over cars. Cables snapped. A wall of burning oil surged through the tunnel, clouds of black smoke boiling over Yerba Buena; then the upper deck collapsed, spilling tons of concrete and steel onto the lower deck, which buckled and split, dropping the eastbound traffic into the bay.

Agent Johnson could hear the screams from Point Emery two miles to the north. He put away his cell phone and walked back to the white van, where two of his men stood by the open door, watching the smoke drift over the burning bridge.

"Call the units," he said. "Tell them to start the raids immediately. Secure the warehouse in Colfax and call in the forensic team." He lit a cigarette. "Remind them that evidence in this case is classified as Sensitive Compartmented Information requiring Special Access Clearance and media access will be restricted to Senior Command by orders of the Director."

Sirens wailed in the city. Johnson watched the agency helicopter circle the island, filming the carnage for early release.

They needed maximum exposure.

Customer Service

Matthew Baldwin

The telephone rings as I'm loading my gun. I jam the clip home, slap the pistol into my shoulder holster, take two short steps to the faux-mahogany end table, and glower down at the ancient, rotary phone.

There's no reason for this thing to be ringing. For starters, it's quarter to two on a Tuesday morning, well outside the acceptable hours for calling anyone. Furthermore, the phone's number is known only to the Client, and he's been instructed to never contact me again. I'll do the job, he'll learn of it later today, and our business will be concluded.

That's the plan anyway.

I arrived by plane yesterday morning, encumbered only by a change of clothes, some toiletries, and a paperback biography of Alexander Hamilton. My first stop was at the home of an associate, who gave me the Smith & Wesson he'd procured on my behalf. Then I drove to Seattle and checked into a small and shabby motel, just within the city limits. The clerk—a truant middle-school student, surely—assigned me to this first-floor room on the front of the building. With shag carpeting, a fraying floral comforter, a television that predates the remote control, and a single faded seascape painting adorning the otherwise barren walls, it's as if I've taken up lodgings at a thrift store. Still, they accept cash and it suits my modest needs, so what do I care?

I could have completed the job hours ago, but felt no sense of urgency. Drive to the Target's home, fulfill the contract, arrange things to look like a burglary—by my reckoning, the entire operation would take little more than an hour. So I frittered away the evening, first reading my book, then alternating between the television's two stations. Procrastination is a bad habit of mine, and one of the many reasons I am self-employed.

Finally, five minutes ago, I decided to get on with it. I slipped on my shoes and jacket, started preparing the weapon. It looked to be a straightforward assignment, and I anticipated no difficulty.

But now the phone is ringing, and that *can't* be good.

I settle on the edge of the bed and study the telephone warily. It rings a fifth time, and a sixth. If someone has dialed a wrong number, they are in it for the long haul.

That, of course, is the likely explanation: a drunk in a bar, somewhere out there in the city, has accidentally punched a 7 instead of a 6 while calling a cab, and is too soused to even consider hanging up. But I know otherwise. Professionals in my field can sense impending complications like sailors smell rain.

I sigh on the eighth ring and pick up on the ninth.

"What?" I say without inflection.

At first I hear nothing but an intermittent hiss, the hallmark of a cell phone. Then a voice I immediately recognize as the Client's. "Is . . . is this the, the person . . . ?" He trails off, bewildered.

It's strange, though not unpleasant, to hear him at a loss for words. Whenever I've seen the Client on television—and when I briefly met him in person yesterday afternoon—he's been self-confident to the point of arrogance. Understandably, I guess, as one of the few dot-com billionaires to survive the crash in the late '90s. His Web site, Opulence Online, sells luxury items to the obscenely wealthy—art, yachts, jewelry, even low-orbit space flights—and he currently presides over the company as CEO. While not the richest man in the country, he is rumored to be in the top twenty.

So I let a couple seconds tick by before answering. Let him sweat, for once in his life.

"This is Xerxes," I say at last. "Did you forget our arrangement? No more contact, ever. Those were the terms to which you agreed."

"The . . . ? Ah yes! That's why I am calling!" He instantly reverts to his typical, businesslike manner. "It's off. I'm canceling the job."

I shrug. "Okay, fine. It's off."

"Excellent." The Client's voice is fraught with relief. "I'm glad I caught you in time."

"Just. I was walking out the door."

"My lucky day."

He hesitates, waiting for me to ask something. I don't take the bait. "I suppose you want some sort of explanation," he prompts.

"Not especially," I reply. But I know he's going to provide one. They always do.

It's the same when they hire me: clients seem compelled to account for themselves. I tell them up front that I don't give a damn, but they tell me all the same.

When I first started in this line of work, I thought they felt guilty, or didn't want me to think them a bad person. But you become a pretty astute observer of human nature after a few years of doing this, and I eventually tumbled to the truth.

See, here's the thing. To get to the point of killing someone, the typical person has to invest considerable time and energy into justifying the decision. They don't call it "premeditated murder" for nothing. By the time they contact me, clients usually have a nicely polished rationale all queued up and ready to go. A real labor of love. Something to be proud of.

And they want to show it off. Convincing yourself that murder is acceptable takes as much skill and dedication as building a ship in a bottle. My clients don't want to set their completed project on a shelf somewhere; they want someone to admire their handiwork.

So I pretend to listen, assure them that, were I in their shoes, I'd be doing the same thing. They beam like they've won a blue ribbon at the fair.

I don't often get to hear the other end of the story, where they explain why they no longer want a target dead. Only three of my assignments have gone uncompleted—four, if you count the guy who keeled over from E. coli the day before I got to him. Even in the cases where a client calls it off, it's never because of misgivings. It's always for reasons as self-serving as the first.

This client's tale is no different. The Target is a business rival who'd been blocking a key acquisition. Suddenly, the situation has changed. They'd been up all night negotiating a new arrangement, one in which the Target is now essential to the transaction's success. Or something. I'm only half listening, honestly, though I dutifully hold the receiver to my ear for the entire story.

He reaches the culmination of his narrative, and I utter some stock phrases to imply I've paid attention. My goal is to wrap this up as quickly as possible.

"Anyway," the Client concludes, "our meeting just finished, and I'm on my way to your motel. I should be there in ten minutes."

"Why are you coming here?" I ask. "Our business is complete."

"Well, yes. Except for the refund."

Huh. That's a first.

I should simply hang up, but can't resist a riposte. "Ah yes, I see what the problem is: you appear to have confused me with a Radio Shack. I do not give refunds. Under any circumstances."

"You never said that."

"You never raised the possibility that the contract might be terminated," I counter. "If you had, I would have made the policy explicit."

"Your oversight," says the Client, "not mine."

At this point it occurs to me that he might be joking. It happens. Some clients, having hired a hitman, come to fancy themselves "hard-boiled," start thinking they can treat me like a drinking buddy. They pull out all the stock phrases they've heard on *The Sopranos*, asking what kind of "heat I'm packing," wondering when I'm going to "whack the guy." I had one client—a woman, even—who managed to cough out the phrase "twenty-five large" with a straight face. You can see why I strive to keep my contact with these idiots to a minimum.

I have a hunch that the Client is serious, though. A refund is the sort of thing he would expect.

The customer service provided by Opulence Online is legendary. Small items are hand-delivered to the buyer within hours of purchase, occasionally by the Client himself; ownership of larger items is transferred with lightning speed. You can buy an island in the morning and be sitting on its beach in time for sunset. It's often said that the company will bend over backwards for all their customers, and bend over forward for an elite few. And they never—*never*—refuse a refund.

But I have a different business model, a fact I reiterate.

He barrels ahead, undeterred. "Look, I know you had to fly out here and everything. And I'm sure you had other expenses, meals and your motel. I don't expect you to pay for that stuff out-of-pocket. But there's no way I'm going to let you keep forty grand for nothing. That's outrageous."

The Client pauses, as if considering. Then: "Let's say you keep five thousand and return the rest? I think that's more than fair."

"How about I keep it all and you shove off?"

I appear to have touched a nerve. He abruptly shifts into Intimidation Mode, bellowing, "Do you know who I am?"

The question is certainly rhetorical, a line used to bully his way into restaurants and out of speeding tickets. But I decide to answer anyway. "As a matter of fact I do, Mr. O'Sullivan."

I like to foster, in my patrons, the illusion of anonymity. I tell them not to reveal their names or any information that might enable me to identify them. It's a charade, of course. As soon as my intermediary tells me that someone is interested in my services, I conduct a thorough background check on the potential client. The goal is to weed out the nutcases. Mr. Sullivan is proof that it doesn't always work.

The legwork was unnecessary in this case, as the Client had delivered the money to my motel room himself. I told him to send it via courier. But when I opened my motel door yesterday afternoon, there he was, Steffen O'Sullivan, with his ridiculous hair and trademark bomber's jacket, a duffel bag of money in hand. Behind him, in the parking lot, I could see his brand-new Lexus wedged between a run-down pickup truck and a Datsun with a garbage bag taped over a missing window.

He was restless and giddy—nervous, I assumed. That was to be expected, meeting a guy like me in a neighborhood like this, with no visible form of protection. Then I realized he was exhibiting excitement, not fear. He cheerfully handed over the cash and attempted to make small talk; I cut him off and closed the door in his crestfallen face. Afterwards, I wondered if his primary interest in doing business with me was novelty, the thrill of purchasing one of those rare things he'd never bought before.

I'd given no indication during our meeting that I knew who he was. Maybe he thought I wouldn't recognize him, as unlikely as that sounds. Maybe he just didn't care.

Still, I expected him to drop the matter when I actually spoke his name.

Instead he sounds pleased.

"Excellent," he says. "And do you know how I got to be where I am today?" This time he doesn't wait for a response, answering the question himself. "Six simple words: 'Give the customer what he wants.' I've built an empire on that motto, and it's a good rule for any business. Even yours."

"Now," he continues, "I'll make this . . . hang on."

I hear honking horns and screeching tires, though no sounds of collision, alas. The Client swears colorfully at another driver, but I'll wager he was the cause of whatever happened. People who talk on cell phones while driving are a goddamned menace.

"I'll make this as clear as I can," the Client resumes when the crisis has passed. "I am your customer. And I am asking for my money back. What do you say?"

"What I've been saying all along. I don't give refunds."

The Client remains silent. I listen to the petulant hum of my room's decrepit alarm clock. Someone, a few rooms down, is watching late night television, and I can hear every line of dialogue through the paper-thin walls. I close my eyes and pinch the bridge of my nose, hoping we are done.

"Fine," says the Client, but I can tell he has some new subterfuge in mind. "However, most businesses that don't offer refunds at least allow exchanges. A substitution would be acceptable."

"A substitution for what?"

"The Target, as you call him."

"You want to switch the contract to someone else?"

"I don't *want* to," he says, "but will settle for that, in lieu of the refund you so stubbornly refuse to provide."

"Who?"

"I don't care. Anyone will do."

By now I've decided that the Client never jokes, even when jest seems the only explanation for a statement. "You think it's that simple?" I ask. "Do you have any idea how much effort I put into planning an operation?"

"I'm not asking you to plan," he says magnanimously. "Just shoot the next person you see. Take his driver's license and mail it to me afterward. I'll have someone verify that he was killed, and we're square. You keep the cash, I get my money's worth, everyone's happy."

"That's ridiculous."

"Take it or leave it."

"Listen," I say. "I read the papers. I know how much you're worth. If forty grand fell out of your pocket it wouldn't be worth your time to pick it up. We made a contract, and you broke it. Write the money off. Why drag an innocent person into this mess?"

He barks out a theatrical guffaw. "Yes, heaven forbid an 'innocent person' gets involved. Everyone you've murdered in the past had it coming, no doubt."

Well, he's got me there.

I mull over his proposal. Targeting a stranger has some advantages, actually. For one thing, there will be no way to trace the victim back to me. With a hired hit, there's always a chance that someone will blab, or the death will prove so convenient for a client that the authorities start poking around.

But I am hesitant to select the target myself, even at random. I wonder why. Maybe because doing so would run afoul of *my* nicely honed rationale: that I am just a gun to be pointed by others. Just doing my job, just following orders. Ultimately not to blame.

The Client remains quiet, patiently awaiting a reply. I curse myself for even considering the idea—my delay in responding implies that the "no refunds" policy is negotiable.

I am about to say something, but sensing indecision, he pounces.

"I'm about a minute from your motel, so let's cut the crap. I want my money back. Or I want another killing in exchange. If you don't have the guts to do the latter, then I'm taking the cash. If you don't do either, I'll drop a dime on you."

Drop a dime. Christ, I hate these people.

"And what?" I say. "You think I'd just neglect to mention your name?"

He laughs, and it sounds genuine. "Say whatever you want; I'll take my chances. In the unlikely event that anyone takes you seriously, I have the best legal team in the nation on speed dial. You don't want to scrap with me, boy. You'll come out the loser ten times out of ten."

That's the problem with these rich guys: they think they are above the law.

No, I take it back. The problem with these rich guys is that, by and large, they *are* above the law. He's absolutely right about the odds. If it comes down to a legal pissing match between me and the Client, I'll wind up in jail and he'll come through unscathed. If anything, the rumors of dirty dealings will probably bolster his reputation as a hardball negotiator. I know it, and he knows I know it.

The blinds on the front window glow briefly as headlights rake across them. A moment later, through the phone, I hear the sound of a pulled emergency brake. The purring of the car's engine, which had served as a backdrop to our conversation, ceases.

"So," he says lazily, "how about that refund?"

I consider my options one last time, but he has me over a barrel. I have no choice but to comply with his demand.

"All right," I growl, "we'll do it your way."

"Excellent." He speaks briskly, closing the deal. I hear him open the car door; when it slams shut a moment later, the sound comes to me in stereo: a sharp report from the receiver, a distant bang from the parking lot outside. "I knew you'd come around."

A crescendo of footsteps, expensive shoes on asphalt, ceases outside my door.

"Knock, knock," says the Client into his phone before ending the call.

I cradle the receiver and yell, "It's open."

The Client, clad in the same clothes he'd worn yesterday, lets himself in. He takes two steps into the room, pivots, and closes the door. He is grinning when he turns back around, his face awash with triumph.

We lock eyes for a second. Then he breaks contact, glancing around the room in search of the duffel bag. "Is the money still here?"

"I think I've made my policy clear," I say, rising to my feet. "No refunds."

He continues to smirk, but his eyebrows knit in puzzlement. "I thought we were doing it my way."

"Oh, we are," I reassure him. "I believe your exact words were 'Shoot the next person you see.' "

His smile falters as I draw the gun.

"Give the customer what he wants," I say. "That's my motto."

High Limit

Scott Wolven

Stripers swam up the Hudson earlier than usual that spring, and right away the fishermen were talking. I was working near Woodstock, hauling shale and aggregate for my cousin, and every day the other drivers would bring back stories about who caught what. Describing the good fishing spots on the river in detail, or lying about them—to keep the good fishing to themselves. The truth depended on who you were talking to. Baseball scores came first, then the fish stories. As far north on the river as the Athens lighthouse and as far south as you felt like sailing, although most of the guys didn't go below Poughkeepsie. My cousin's materials outfit was acting as a subcontractor on a state job, so we weren't hauling weekends. Saturday and Sunday were good days to be on the river. I was simply glad to be out in the world and earning money at the time. I got involved with the wrong side of things up in Canada—moving meth on the northwestern border of Maine—and had just come back after four years away. It was my first stretch and I wanted to put it behind me. Listening to the guys talk about fishing made me want to get out there and put a line in the water. They were catching some big ones.

I was living on an old run-down farm—thirty acres—between Saugerties and Catskill that had been in my family for years. My great-grandfather's brother George had owned the property. Nobody remembered what George had done for work, but he must have enjoyed his privacy. The farm was set way back off the road—the dusty dirt trail that led to it was close to a mile and the mailbox on the road never had a name on it—with the two-story main house on a slight hill. The main house was white and blue, with a wraparound wood porch overlooking the pond. A couple large sturdy red barns and two buildings about ready to fall over. The property had three little gray cabins on it, facing the mountains. Someone, years ago, put the cabins up and tried to get people to stay there. It hadn't worked. The cabins each were equipped with a sink and a stand-up shower in addition to a flush toilet, which was probably illegal given the size of the property. The cabins had black phones in them, hanging on the wall, and when you picked them up, they rang to a single phone in the main house. For the guests, I imagined. There was still a gas pump and buried tank next to the one barn. I suppose if I went through the trouble of having someone come out and inspect the pump, I could have had my own gas on-site. It was an empire of dirt, but it was paradise to me.

I pulled the truck up the road that Friday and my father's silver truck was parked in front of the house. He was sitting on the front porch in a lawn chair with his ball cap on, drinking a soda. He'd retired two years before from a local lumberyard.

"Hey there," he said.

"How's it going?" I said. "How's retired life?"

"Can't complain," he said. "What are you doing tomorrow?"

"Nothing," I said.

"You're going fishing with me and Rich, okay? Be the best thing for you."

"Sounds good," I said.

He was getting in his truck. "See you at six a.m. Catskill dock."

"See you tomorrow. Say hello to Mom for me."

"Will do," he said. "She's going to visit her aunt."

"Wish her a good flight," I said.

He waved as he pulled away from the house.

Rich had a new boat he kept at the Catskill dock. It wasn't brand-new, but it was new to him and he kept it shining. He was retired too, from a state conservation job. He made extra money running fishing charters out of Catskill and did pretty well for himself. Rich knew where the fish were. The other guy in Catskill who knew where the fish were was Tom, the man who owned the bait shop. Tom was a big, tall guy, an old basketball player. He had owned the bait shop in Catskill for years, and it was the best bait and tackle shop on the Hudson. All the fishermen along the river knew to stop at Tom's before they went fishing, to get the latest report on conditions and fish. And to buy bait and everything else—reels, rods, the latest lures. Maps and charts. Tom could wind your reel with new line while you stood there and have you back out on the river in half an hour. Listening to Tom could keep you from getting shut out. No fish was no fun. When I passed Tom's on my way to the dock, I saw my father's truck in the parking lot. He pulled into the dock parking lot behind me and we headed out onto the Hudson River with Rich driving the boat.

"Tom says go north," my father said to Rich.

"We'll try it," Rich said.

My father turned to me. "I asked you here for a reason," he said.

"Go ahead," I said.

"Do you remember Bob?" he said. "Bob Threepersons?"

"Sure," I said. "Still lives in Florida?" Bob had been in the army with my father and Rich. They hadn't been in the same units, but met back here in the States when their tour of duty ended. Bob had been a tunnel rat. He was originally from Idaho. His whole family lived on a reservation out there. He still had a sister who lived on the reservation. He came and visited, almost twenty years ago. He stayed in one of the little cabins on the old farm. I remember Bob kept an owl for a pet.

My father nodded. "He's having a heck of a time."

"What type of problems?" I said. We were moving north through the water. The great Rip Van Winkle Bridge was overhead, with its huge stone pilings diving deep into the water around us. Rich stayed in a channel and we passed underneath. Rogers Island was on our right and the train tracks ran along the bank.

"Money," my father said. "Drugs. Booze."

"Is he ready to clean up?" I said.

"He says he is," my father said.

"Does he need money?" I said.

"No." My father shook his head. "Having extra money is part of his problem right now."

"Are these the type of money problems that are likely to follow him up here?" I said.

"There's a chance of that," he said. "Anything can happen."

We let the conversation sit, because he'd hooked a fish. Rich and I watched him bring it to the boat, as the pole he was using bent around. Rich got the net and we wrestled a good-sized striper to the deck. The fish had bright-colored scales and a white belly. After we removed the hook, my father tossed the fish back into the Hudson.

"You want him to stay in one of the little houses?" I said.

"Yeah," my father said. "That's a good plan. He kicked heroin there one summer, so he knows he can get clean there."

"I never knew that," I said. "I just thought he was visiting us."

"He was," my father said. "But he was having some problems at that time too."

"Why do you guys keep helping him?" I said.

My father sipped his coffee. Rich shrugged.

"You can't turn your back on people when you know what they've seen," Rich said.

My father nodded. "War loves young men," he said. "Those aren't my words, somebody else said them first, but I don't remember who. Anyway, Vietnam got hold of Bob and hasn't let him go yet. We're lucky"—he motioned at Rich and himself—"that we don't have the problems Bob does." He drank another mouthful of coffee. "I can't watch TV anymore except baseball. The war coverage makes me think about those men and women overseas and how, even if they make it back and with all their limbs, it could still ruin their lives. I can't stand people—ordinary, average, everyday people—suffering the consequences of politicians. Bob is like that. He's nobody special, he's just special to us." My father finished his coffee and Rich nodded as he watched the water.

"And this time," my father said, "Bob's problems seem a little tougher and different."

"These new problems," I said. "Gun-type problems?"

"Yes," my father said. "He might need some help watching his back."

"I've got a brand-new shotgun," Rich said.

"I've already got a shotgun," I said.

"I meant for Bob," Rich said. "Do you have a dog?"

"No," I said. "I work too much to take care of one."

"I used to have a good German shepard named Shane, but he's long gone. I can't help you with a dog," Rich said.

"Okay," I said. "When should I expect Bob?"

"Soon," my father said. "Tonight."

We caught another striper north of Hudson—Tom had been right—and headed back to the Catskill dock. After we moored the boat, Rich brought a gun case out of the backseat of his truck, along with three boxes of shells. I put the stuff on the backseat of my truck and shook hands with both of them before driving off.

I stopped and picked up some groceries on the way home. At the farm, I got things ready to have a guest. I cleaned out the cabin and put some food and a jug of water out there. I put a bar of soap and shampoo in the shower, a razor, shaving cream, toothbrush, and toothpaste on the sink. I put the gun case Rich had given me and the boxes of shells on the bed. Next to the gun I put a case of cigarettes, two plastic lighters, four bars of chocolate, and a couple candy bars. I started a fire with the coals and after it died down and the coals went white hot, I put some burgers on. I loaded my own shotgun, checked the safety, and leaned it inside the screen door. I sat on the porch and ate.

The sun had gone down when Bob pulled up. He was driving an old beat-up station wagon with fake wood paneling and Florida plates. The passenger's-side front tire looked low. When I got close to the car I could see a long jagged crack in the windshield.

"Hey," he said. We shook hands. He wore his long hair in a ponytail with gray in it. He looked tired and thin. He was wearing a long-sleeve shirt that he'd sweated through. "Well, hell, John," he managed. He was carrying an old tan suitcase and a blue gym bag. He set the bags on the ground.

"Good to see you," I said. "Do you want a hamburger?" I pointed at the grill, still glowing in the twilight.

"That sounds great," he said. "No beer."

"Yeah," I said. "My dad told me. No problem."

"I just need to relax a little," he said. He shook a cigarette out of the pack and lit it. "We need to hide this car."

I walked over to the big barn and swung the door open. "Pull it right in here."

He guided the station wagon into the empty space between an old Jeep under a tarp and a pickup truck. He shut the engine off and took out a big screwdriver.

"Got to get these plates off," he explained.

"Sure," I said. He was sweating. "Can I help you?"

"Work on that back plate," he said.

I lay on the rough concrete floor and sweated, using an oversized screwdriver to get the screws out of the license plate. I skinned my knuckles. We finished and put the plates on the front seat. I made Bob a burger with a roll and gave it to him.

"This is your cabin right here," I said. I pointed at the middle cabin. "Hasn't changed much since your last visit." I carried his two bags up to the small porch.

"I really appreciate your help," he said. He had taken a couple bites out of the burger.

"If you need anything, lift that phone next to your bed. It calls me in the house."

"Okay," he said.

"See you in the morning," I said.

"Thanks," he said.

I gave my father a call when I got back in the house.

"Bob's here," I said. "He ate and went to bed."

"Good," my father said. "Let's try some fishing again tomorrow. Bring him with you."

"Sure," I said. "See you tomorrow."

I shut the lights out and sat in a chair looking out the window. I could see the end of the driveway and the road and I watched for an hour. Cars passed in the dark, but nobody slowed down or stopped. I slept with my shotgun on the floor next to my bed. I didn't know how big Bob's trouble was and I wanted to be ready.

I drove Bob to the Catskill dock the next day. He didn't look well—he was wearing a light blue jacket despite the heat—when he got in the truck, but we stopped at a gas station and I bought him a coffee. It was good to watch him drink something.

"That's good coffee," he said.

"Nice," I said. "How're you doing?"

"I've been better," he said. "I've been much worse. This will pass."

"Sure," I said.

It smelled like gas and oil and fish at the dock. My father and Rich were already on the boat. Bob and I got on. Rich gave us all rods, all rigged up. My father and Rich shook hands with Bob and they both gave him a hug. Rich piloted the boat into the Hudson and nobody said anything. We were busy fishing. We were headed slightly south today. One of the large Hudson mansions sat on a hill on the east bank and we all looked at as we passed. Rich hooked a nice striper, brought it up into the boat, and released it.

"I remember the last time I visited," Bob said. "We fished then too."

"I remember we caught a couple good ones," my father said.

"We ate those fish, didn't we?" Bob said.

"We did," my father said. "Things have changed in the river."

"That's too bad," Bob said. Less than a minute after that, he hooked one and fought it to the boat. After he released it, a large hawk took off from a dead tree close to shore. The hawk gained altitude and floated high in the blue and the clouds.

"The sky is part of the color of that bird," Bob said. "In a blue sky, the bird looks a certain way and in a gray sky, the bird looks another way. The bird doesn't pick the color of the sky, he just lives in it. He doesn't try to change it. I remember my grandfather telling me that." He was crying now. My father and Rich sat close to him and I watched the boat. I couldn't hear what they were saying. Rich stood up and took over, heading back to the dock. My father stayed close to Bob until we were getting off the boat.

"It's hard to be off drugs," Bob said. We were headed towards my truck.

"Everything's hard," my father said. "You can do it."

"Good luck," Rich said.

Bob and I drove back to the farm and when I came out of the house, he was sitting on the porch, looking at the sky. I fixed us some dinner and we both went to bed. I got up at 2:00 a.m. to take a look around. To be safe. The house phone rang and I picked it up.

"Hey," Bob said. "Are you awake? I thought I saw a light."

"Yes," I said. "Checking things out."

"I'm going back to sleep," he said.

"See you late tomorrow," I said. "I've got to work."

"Sure," Bob said. "I'll fix dinner."

"Sounds good," I said.

We went fishing as much as we could that summer. We went out on the river with my father and Rich. One time, Bob's pole bent so much, we all thought he'd hooked a sturgeon. It would have been a once-in-a-lifetime catch. Whatever it was spat the hook before he could land it. The next weekend, we were out on the river again.

"What did you do?" I said. Bob had been staying on the farm for five weeks and we were sitting on the porch, eating sandwiches.

"I counted cards at the high-limit table," he said. He finished his sandwich. "More than once. At more than one casino, all along the Gulf Coast." He scratched his head. "I learned I could count cards when I was in the Army," he said. "Wish I never had."

"How much did you get away with?" I said.

"Not enough to be worth this," he said. He inhaled his cigarette. "That's for sure." He took another drag and then went on. "It used to be like I couldn't tell if I was awake or dreaming. I had this big pile of chips and I'd cash out and the money would pile up."

I nodded. The sky was night-dark except for the stars and on the edge of the mountains, we could see the static charges of heat lightning, flashing.

Bob seemed like he was talking to himself. "I had that money and off I'd go, on a bender. I shot dope again. I drank all the time. I did everything I could get my hands on. Until it was like I wasn't real anymore. I came home to my house at one point and thought people had broken in, that's what a wreck it was."

"That sounds bad," I said.

"Then the pit boss at the one casino, he must have seen me doing something because the next time I went to play, they wouldn't let me sit at the table. So I went down the street and counted cards there and took them for all they could handle." He shook his head. "Men followed me out of the casino and tried to beat me up, but I got away. I realized they must have put a price on my head. That's when I decided to come up here."

"What would they gain by killing you?" I said.

"Nothing," he said. "Probably a couple thousand dollars from the casino management firm."

"Can you pay them back?" I said.

"I don't even know how many times I won off them, or what casinos I won it from. I took a couple loans from bookies to cover myself. It's an ugly mess."

"That sounds bad," I said.

"I came home one night late and turned on the TV and I think I fell asleep. I woke up and there was a cowboy and Indian movie on and I started to lose my mind. I thought, that's all they show, is us being killed." He pointed at his head. "My own mind is my worst enemy." He looked over at me. "What did you do?"

"Got into a scrape up in Maine," I said.

He nodded. "Did your father ever tell you about the scrape I got into in the late seventies?"

"No," I said. "He didn't." The lights from planes moved slowly through the night sky, among the stillness of the stars.

Bob put his cigarette out. "I tried to make some money as a big game scout. Signed on with a guy out of Florida named Mackenzie, who arranged hunting trips to Africa for wealthy clients."

"What did you take them hunting for?" I said.

"When they signed up, supposedly it was for antelope. Large game deer, mostly. But we were really going over to shoot rhinos," Bob said. "Everybody knew that." He pointed through the darkness to the little cabins. "Imagine an animal the size of one of those cabins, faster than your truck and basically plated with armor."

"I've seen them on TV," I said.

"Well, I saw it in real life," he said. "That last afternoon, a rhino came out of the grass after the truck and we all started shooting. Five men. I had one of those newer Mauser rifles, but it was still bolt action, and I'm slamming that thing home and firing and the rhino hit the truck like a fully stacked freight train, *wham*." He made a flattening motion with his hands, then lifted them into the air. "Up I went and down I came."

"What happened?" I said.

"I couldn't fire anymore, because I was out of shells. The

rhino stomped and gored everyone but me. Put a hole in Mackenzie that I could see through. The ground was so soaked with blood that the natives who rescued me were afraid the smell of death would bring other animals to the spot. The natives took me to a ranger station."

"Jesus," I said.

"Sometimes," Bob said, "I used to stay awake for days at a time, so I wouldn't have to dream about that stuff and what I'd seen in Vietnam. Drugs helped me keep the past quiet, in the short term. Till it got the best of me." He paused. "Did you ever try to wash someone else's blood off you?"

"No," I said.

"For some reason," Bob said, "it's hard to get it off. Almost as if blood holds onto your skin, because it knows your skin is still alive."

We picked up the plates and put them in the kitchen sink. I saw him smoke another cigarette on his small cabin porch before going inside.

It was about 4:00 a.m. when I heard the car door slam in the yard. I flipped the lights on downstairs and outside and opened my bedroom window. I put the barrel of the shotgun out first and racked the slide.

"What do you want?" I said.

The two men blinked against the light. "We're looking for somebody," the one man said.

"This is private property," I said. "I'm calling the cops."

"We'll be gone before they get here," the man said. He had a pistol holstered on his right side.

"Get back in that car or you'll need an ambulance," I said. "Last warning."

I hoped that Bob was awake at that point, ready to back me up if shooting started. They weren't sure where he was, so he could get off a couple rounds from the middle cabin before they knew what hit them.

Both men walked back to their car, turned it around, and spit gravel going back down the road.

In the morning, I walked to the middle cabin and opened the door. There was nothing there. It looked as though no one had ever slept there at all. I went around to the back barn and found what I was looking for. Under the tarp that used to protect the old Jeep was Bob's station wagon. A set of New York plates was missing too. Bob was on the road again. I called my father and told him.

I came home from work in the middle of the week and found everything torn apart. Whoever those men were, they must have come back while I was gone. The beds were out of the cabins, stuff spread across the lawn by the pond. The big barn door was open, exposing the cars. The tarp was off the station wagon and the doors were open. The door to the main house had been jimmied open and sat on bent hinges. But there was nothing to find.

The first letter I got wasn't really a letter at all. It was an envelope with an Idaho postmark and two photographs. The first picture was of a huge fish—what appeared to be a white sturgeon—half in the water, ready to be released back in. The second was a similar picture of the fish from a different angle and the photographer had allowed his shadow to fall out over the water and into the shot, along with the tip of his right boot. The boot looked like Bob's, and the shadow looked like it had a ponytail.

Two months later, a postcard showed up in my mailbox. It bore a Vancouver postmark. "Still OK still sober" was all it said on it.

* * *

One night I was sitting there during a terrible lightning storm. The cabin phone rang. Scared the hell out of me. I answered it and in the darkness, it sounded like someone was there.

"Bob?" I said. "Bob?"

There was no answer. The lightning must have made it ring. I was alone.

The stripers were hitting in the Hudson in April and May this year. I caught my share on the weekends, with my father and Rich. I fished from shore some weekends during the summer and got a pass to one of the reservoirs. I saw some eagles early one morning and the fireworks got rained out on the Fourth of July, so they shot them off the following weekend. I watched them from the porch of the farm, what I could see of the lights above the trees. The shale business kept on and I drove every day and got dusty and dumped and hauled all the loads my cousin gave me. I was grateful for the work.

I pulled up the dusty driveway one Friday in late August and my father's truck was close to the house. He was sitting on the porch with his ball cap off. I got out of my rig and walked to the house and he didn't say anything. He was holding something and when I got closer, it looked like an envelope.

"Hi," I said. "What's going on?"

He just handed me the envelope. It had an Idaho postmark and my father's address handwritten on the outside. Inside was a newspaper clipping from a week earlier, from a newspaper in Spokane, Washington. I read it.

A man the Idaho State Police had identified as Robert Threepersons had died from gunshot wounds in a parking lot outside a truck stop casino near the Idaho-Washington border. The police were investigating the shooting, although there were no clues at this time.

"I should have told him to stay here," my father said. He indicated the clipping. "His sister must have sent this from the reservation."

I didn't know what to say.

"Between the war and the drugs and the gambling, the poor guy must have been afraid of his own thoughts," my father said.

"He probably was," I agreed.

"And people coming after him," he said. "It was too much."

"Yeah," I said.

"I can't draw a straight line from the war to Bob's problems for you to see, but I know it's there," he said.

We sat on the porch till it started to get dark. My father headed home to his house and my mother. And I looked over at the middle cabin, to the place where Bob had been sober for a little while. To where my fishing buddy had lived for a summer.

What if it wasn't him that died in that parking lot? What if somebody got the drop on him but he shot them and put his identification on them, to throw the cops off? Or what if he were finally dreamlessly asleep and peaceful, delivered by violence into someplace else. Off this earth, with the beautiful blue sky coloring him forever.

About the Authors

Patricia Abbott writes literary and crime fiction from Detroit. Stories have appeared recently in *Pulp Pusher*, *The Thrilling Detective*, *Demolition*, *Spinetingler*, *Hardluck Stories*, *Bayou Review*, and *Storyglossia*. She has just completed a novel set in Detroit.

Jedidiah Ayres lives in St. Louis, Missouri.

Matthew Baldwin spent the late '90s as a customer service rep for an online store, right at the height of the dot-com bubble. He is now a programmer by day, freelance writer by evening, and sound sleeper at night. He maintains the Web log Defective Yeti and lives in Seattle with his wife, son, and a handful of good-for-nothing cats.

Greg Bardsley is a former newspaper reporter who covered everything from politics to deranged, homicidal psychos. Since then he has worked as an editor, ghostwriter, speechwriter, and video producer. In addition to *Thuglit*, his pulp fiction has appeared in *Demolition* and *Pulp Pusher*.

Gary Carson is a former feature writer for the *Kansas City Times* and the *Westport Trucker*. His fiction and essays have appeared in *Hardluck Stories*, *Thuglit*, and *Noir Originals*. A California refugee, he currently lives in Rolla, Missouri.

Lyman Feero graduated in 2006 from the University of Southern Maine Stonecoast MFA program in creative writing. He is also a published alternative fiction author with works in several genres including crime, horror, and science fiction. Most recently he participated in the Blog Project #3 and L.A. Noir's Mugshot Challenge. He is currently working on his first novel.

Allan Guthrie is an award-winning Scottish crime novelist.

Jordan Harper, born and raised in Missouri, is a frequent contributor to *Thuglit*. He has been nominated for the Derringer Award and has had two stories selected by the Million Writers Award as notable short stories of the year, including "Like Riding a Moped." He is currently working on a novel and is turning "Like Riding a Moped" into a screenplay. He currently lives in Los Angeles. Contact him at author@jordanharper.com.

Daniel Hatadi wasted lots of valuable time as a musician, a petrol station attendant, and a programmer in the shady world of gambling before turning his attention to crime fiction. The Sydney-based writer has published several short stories and articles and is currently working on a novel. He is also the founder of the Internet crime fiction community, Crimespace. Visit Daniel online at crimespace.ning.com or at his Web site, www.danielhatadi.com.

D. T. Kelly grew up on the mean streets of Chicago. After years of dodging firebombs, two-bit hoodlums, and drive-by shootings, he now resides in upstate New York, having traded in his bulletproof vest for hiking boots. He can be found online at www.dtkelly.net.

Jónas Knútsson committed arson at five. When Jónas was ten someone not unlike Viddi Golbranson tried to throw Jónas into a duck pond. Jónas enjoys the distinction of being the only person to be expelled from a prestigious German film school before commencing his studies.

Patrick J. Lambe lives in New Jersey, the cradle of civilization. He's had short stories in various Web sites and magazines, as well as short stories in the *Plots with Guns* anthology, *Dublin Noir*, with more coming out soon. His short story "Union Card" was listed as a distinguished mystery story in *The Best American Mystery Stories of 2005*. He's currently working on several novels while working as a telephone technician. Please visit his Web site at http://patlambe.com

Joe. R. Lansdale is the author of thirty novels and many short works. One of his novellas, *Bubba Hotep*, was filmed to considerable acclaim, and his short story "Incident On and Off a Mountain Road" was part of the *Masters of Horror* series on Showtime. His works have received The Grinzani Prize for Literature, the Edgar, seven Bram Stokers, the Herodotus, and numerous other awards. *A Fine Dark Line* is scheduled to be filmed next year.

Hugh Lessig is a career newspaperman who has worked in his native Pennsylvania and Virginia. He now lives in Richmond, Virginia, where he reports on state politics, a beat that provides occasional inspiration for things nefarious and noir. Besides *Thuglit*, his short stories have appeared in *Plots with Guns* and *Thrilling Detective*.

Richard J. Martin Jr. was born in 1956 in Bossier City, Louisiana, and came to the San Francisco Bay Area in 1962 at age six. He is a graduate of San Francisco State University's Creative Writing Program and works as a grant writer for nonprofit human service agencies. His stories, poems, and articles have appeared in the *San Francisco Herald*, *Seattle Weekly*, *Thuglit*, *Working Magazine*, *Bay Area Reporter*, *In the Fray*, the *Noe Valley Voice*, *Tea Party*, the *Red Hills Review*, and *Frisko Magazine*, as well as trade publications like the *Walden House Journal* and *Successful Fundraising*. He's a member of San Francisco Musicians Union Local 6, and currently divides his time between San Francisco and Lakeport, California.

Steven M. Messner lives in Harrisburg, Pennsylvania, where he is employed as a legal assistant and personal trainer. He received his bachelor's degree in English from West Virginia University in 1994. In 2002 he graduated from Johns Hopkins University, where he received his master's degree in fiction writing. He has recently finished his first book, *The Barbecue Wire Boy*, and is currently working on a book based on his Burma Ludlow character.

Justin Porter was born and raised in New York. He's crass, uneducated, obnoxious, and has lain down with dogs so many times that he's on a first-name basis with three generations of fleas. He's been published a few places online for his fiction and for journalism in the *New York Times*. He's been a teacher, a skateboarder, an amateur fighter, a Rollerblade salesman, and a number of other ridiculous things. He's eagerly awaiting the next round of absurdity. And he thanks everybody who does, for reading.

Marcus Sakey spent ten years in advertising, which gave him the perfect background to write about criminals and killers. His debut novel, *The Blade Itself*, was a *New York Times* Editor's Pick, featured on *CBS Sunday Morning*, and named one of *Es-*

quire magazine's 5 Best Reads of 2007. It has been translated into numerous languages, and the film rights have been purchased by Ben Affleck for Miramax. His second novel, *At the City's Edge*, was released to similar acclaim, and he is currently working on a four-book contract for Dutton. Marcus has shadowed homicide detectives, toured the morgue, interviewed Special Forces officers, ridden with L.A. gang cops, and learned to pick a deadbolt in sixty seconds. He swears it was all for research.

Mike Sheeter attended Ohio State University. He has worked as a magazine editor, advertising copywriter, and screenwriter.

Anthony Neil Smith was born and raised on the Mississippi Gulf Coast, has lived in Michigan, and currently resides in Minnesota. He is the author of the novels *Psychosomatic*, *The Drummer*, and *Yellow Medicine*, and his short stories have appeared all over the place, including *Thuglit*, obviously. He is also the editor of the *Plots with Guns* Web-zine. Okay? Is that enough? What more do you need to know?

Jason Starr is the Barry and Anthony Award–winning author of eight crime novels, which are published in ten languages. He also writes screenplays, cowrites a series of books with Ken Bruen for *Hard Case Crime*, and is at work on a graphic novel to be published by DC Comics. He lives in New York City.

Albert Tucher began writing about Diana Andrews with the new millennium and is now up to fifteen published stories and five unpublished novels. Why is he obsessed with a hooker? Because prostitution is as hard-boiled and as noir as it gets. Self-deception is at the core of the transaction, and it always runs out.

Scott Wolven is the author of *Controlled Burn* (Scribner). Wolven's stories have appeared six years in a row in the *Best American Mystery Story* series (Houghton Mifflin), including 2007, selected by guest editor Carl Hiaasen and series editor Otto Penzler. Wolven also contributed a story to *Expletive Deleted* (Bleak House) edited by Jennifer Jordan.

Raise Your Glasses . . .

I don't know if any of you out there in Citizens-ville know just how hard it is to pare down a year's worth of blood-and-guts, balls-out stories into this anthology.

It's torturous.

My first edit—my "dream edit"—came in at over 260,000 words. I'm not kidding. More than double the number of words you've got clutched between your hairy palms right now.

SO, in order to avoid a couple of slugs to the back of the skull from the divine Michaela Hamilton over at Kensington, I had to cut some stories that flat-out deserve to be in here.

Listed below are the contributors to our second year of *Thuglit*. Raise your glasses of hooch high, cats and kittens. They've earned my respect, and damn sure deserve yours.

Hana K. Lee—Mark Bowen—Kevin McCarthy—Miles Archer—Ann Androla—Pete Hogenson—Marianne Rogoff—Cristobal Camaras—James Williams—Tim Wohlforth—AT Mango—Dave Zeltserman—Joseph Taverney—Robert Spencer—Karl Koweski—J. D. Smith—David C. Daniel—Alejandro Pena—Max Glaessner—Tony Black—Lloyd Hudson Frye—Keith Gilman—Michael Colangelo—Paul Beckman—Bryon Quertermous—Barry Baldwin—David Rosenstock—Kieran Shea—Ed Lynskey—Geoff Hyatt—Glenn Gray—Ian Nicholas Carleton—Nathan Cain—Hilary Davidson—William Boyle—

Brian Haycock—Tim Murr—Kim Cushman—Brian Murphy—Linda Sharps—Anthony Rainone—Katherine Tomlinson

Thank you all. Without you, there is no *Thuglit*.

Thanks to YOU, Not-So-Gentle Reader, for slinging down your dirty blood money for the book. Next year, buy two, ya chiselin' mugs. . . .

And to Allison, my Bruising Bride of the Beatdown, my Lady Detroit . . . Without you, none of it would be worth spit.